Call the Reavers

From Annie Pearson

Chaos House

RESTORATION RULES SERIES
No One Dies
Reap Justice
Call the Reavers

RAIN CITY INCIDENTS SERIES
The Grrrl of Limberlost
Artemis in the Desert
Nine Volt Heart
The Pirate King

Restoration Rules
Number Three
Call the Reavers
Annie Pearson

Print ISBN: 979-8988286202
Published by Jūgum Press
Seattle, Washington U.S.A.
www.jugumpress.net

Cover design by Jacyn Stewart

For Laurie Cropp, who also wants another story.

Contents

More>>

Part IV: No Whig Majority

Part V: Crooked Passageways

Principal Persons

Ysabel Foxe (Lizzie)

Former lady-in-waiting to Princess Mary, now a watcher for the Crown; fiancée to Rowland Foxe, her second cousin.

Eduard Wijck (Ned)

Painter of growing renown; close companion to Perry Frake and half-brother to Lizzie Foxe.

Rowland Foxe (Rollo)

The honorable Earl of Marborne; formerly an intelligencer, now watcher for the Crown, known for exposing traitors.

Thomas Foxe (Tom)

Barrister practicing in London; twin to Tamsin Fox.

Thomasine Foxe (Tamsin)

Manager of Revelstone House and farms; Tom's twin; close companion to Camilla Candecote.

Peregrine Frake (Perry)

Former intelligencer and sergeant to Lieutenant Rowland Foxe; close companion to Ned Foxe.

—

Historical Persons

James Stuart

King of England, 1685–1688; brother of Charles II.

Mary Stuart

Daughter of James Stuart; wife of William of Orange; after 1688, Mary II of England.

William of Orange

Stadtholder (governor) of the Low Countries; after 1688, William III of England.

Friends of the Foxe Family

Aurora Rôche

Lizzie's housemate and Tom's ladylove; formerly wife of the Marquess of Withersea.

Camilla Candecote

Heiress to a Cambridgeshire baron; survivor of an annulled marriage; close companion to Tamsin Foxe since childhood.

Duke of Bagsham

King's advisor; Rowland's mentor.

Felicity Oakes

Actress; owner of Chalgrove House.

Jacob Rôche, Earl of Cloudesley

Tom Foxe's ward; Aurora Rôche's brother.

Michael Oakes (formerly, Michel Chêne)

Rowland's secretary; Felicity's brother.

Poynter, current Earl of Hawksmoor (and Viscount Heydon)

Neighbor and Foxe family friend in Cambridgeshire.

Winwood Oakes

Physician; cousin to Felicity, Michael, Aurora, and Jacob.

—

Not Their Friends (After Foxe Restorations)

Danvers Duncombe

London banker; hanged as a traitor by order of Judge Jeffries.

Earl of Hawksmoor (the elder)

Disgraced neighbor to Marborne; self-exiled to Barbados.

Marquess of Withersea

Traitor and cheat; crimped to South Asia.

Milestones
The Foxes of Marborne Parish

1650: Samuel Foxe leads local royalists in Civil War

Commonwealth & Interregnum, 1649–1660

1655: Samuel Foxe is 15th Earl of Marborne

Oliver Cromwell is Lord Protector

1660: Foxe cousins born, 1659–1661

Restoration; Charles II, 1660–1685

1665: Foxe cousins orphaned

London Plague and Great Fire

1670: Foxe cousins at Revelstone House

Test Act, 1673

1675: Ysabel serves Mary Stuart; Rowland in Paris

Mary Stuart marries William of Orange, 1677

1680: Ysabel and Rowland in Amsterdam

Charles II repeatedly dissolves Parliament

1685: Ysabel at home, February; Rowland at home, August

James II, 1685–1688

Duke of Monmouth invades, June

...

James deposed, 1688

Mary II & William III, 1689–1702

Call the Reavers

PART I

BRISTOL

Mid-October, 1685
West Country

—

Restoration, Defined:

1) The era after the English Civil Wars when the monarchy was restored.

2) The Foxe family actions to achieve justice when English law fails, abiding by the family's Restoration Rules.

—

Restoration Rules:
No one dies.
Reap justice, shun revenge.
Reave when sins are ripe.
Never trick a woman.
Never bilk a neighbor.
Our allies shall be innocent.

—

Doctor Foxe's Rules for Enlightened People:
I keep my promises.
My family obligations are sacred.
I was born to help others.
The world improves from my toil.
I never fool an honest man.

1
In the West Country

—YSABEL FOXE—

MONDAY LATE AFTERNOON

THE ENORMOUS SHAGGY BLACK dog scrambled up and off Lizzie Foxe's feet when Rowland, the Earl of Marborne, opened the carriage door. It jumped over Ned Wijck's long legs, leapt from the carriage step, and bounded away.

"Countess, come!" Rowland stepped gracefully from the carriage and snapped his fingers.

The dog continued scampering toward the wharves.

Lizzie felt grateful that it wasn't raining in Bristol, like it had everywhere else across England. Rather, a clammy October fog hung like a veil, stinking of a tidal stew. Condensation dripped down the stone walls around a chandler's yard. Ferns and moss grew along the roofline of a warehouse across the way, its bare wood walls slimy from the fog.

She came down from the carriage, brushing dog hair off the breeches she'd borrowed from Rowland for travel across England. ("Call yourself Viscount Orlando," her brother Ned had said. "And you must walk the part.") The Bristol fog clung to her face, and her foot slipped on the wet cobbles. She could not get used to wearing Rowland's boots.

"Behold," she said, "the piratical Foxe family has arrived to seize its booty, led by my lord, the Earl of Marborne."

Though no one outside our circle knows to call us either pirates or highwaymen. And all we ever want is justice.

Last August, King James had given Rowland three ships confiscated from the Marquess of Withersea's holdings, a reward for having exposed the marquess as a traitor. In truth, the Foxe cousins had observed all their Restoration Rules while running a gambol that tricked Withersea into exposing himself.

"Please call my dog, Lizzie. She only listens to you," Rowland said. He shook his head in dismay, the braided queue of his chestnut hair popped out of his coat collar, so that for one foggy moment, Rowland in his leather travel clothes resembled an old-time cavalier in a portrait.

Except Rollo is clean-shaven, thank all the gods on Olympus.

Savoring the aesthetics of his narrow form, Lizzie said, "Your clothes look well on you, my lord."

His quizzical brow arched in puzzlement, he glanced at his rumpled travel suit, then took the wrong meaning from her words. "I can't travel for days and look as good as you do in my clothes. And why must you be so provokingly formal?"

She couldn't admit out there on the street that she'd been appreciating the sight of his tall, graceful body, not his clothes. "I say 'my lord,' because I am the only sophisticated and worldly cousin in the Foxe family who knows proper behavior. I seek to remind you that you're no longer plain, broke-pocketed Lieutenant Foxe guarding diplomats in the Low Countries."

"You say it only to tease me."

"You often forget it, my lord." She worried that Rowland was not adjusting well to his new position. She meant to help, not tease, but he took it wrong. Another sign of his discomfort at being the earl.

"Lizzie is right to remind you, Rollo." Ned emerged from the carriage. "You never introduced yourself properly at any inn between London and Bristol."

Ned tugged a second, heavier wool coat over his long, lanky frame. He jammed his wide-brimmed black felt hat over straggling locks still bleached white from last summer's sun. Paint streaked his fingers, though it'd been five days since Ned quit his easel for this journey.

"It doesn't feel right, getting a better bed and supper just because I'm an earl. That was purely an accident." Rowland called his dog again. Countess yipped, pausing to dance in the street and begging to be followed. "Why won't my dog obey me?"

"It's especially a mystery," Lizzie teased now, "since you have more power to command than most men in England. Perhaps she doesn't know you're the new earl of Marborne."

Rollo holds the smallest, poorest earldom in all of England.

Ned said, "Your Countess doesn't listen because she gets your affection and a treat, whatever she does. And I'm talking about your dog, not Lizzie. It's not how to teach a dog, Rollo."

"My dog is learning." Rowland said. "She only met me two weeks ago. Countess, come!"

"Can she please have another name, *mon cœur*? Bouncer? Mopsie?" Lizzie sneezed, a hair tickling her nose. The dog had been shedding its shaggy coat since the Duke of Bagsham sent it to Rowland's house as a gift.

"She came to me with that name. Countess!" Rowland called. The dog skittered on the cobbles but didn't turn back. He lowered his voice, his breath a warm whisper near Lizzie's ear. "She gets a new name the moment you marry me, when I can call Ysabel Foxe my countess. Now I can only call you my Dark Lady, as the Bard would, if he'd ever met you."

Rowland habitually quoted sonnets and lines from plays ("teach me, dear creature, how to think and speak"), and that bad habit worsened once he'd conquered his innate shyness and begged Lizzie to see him as more than a third-generation second cousin.

"Oh, lambkin. You know exactly what will bring us to that moment." Lizzie clapped her hands. "Come, Countess."

Under the darkening Bristol skies, a black form bounded across slick cobbles to stick her muzzle in Lizzie's outstretched hand. "Who's a good girl?"

Ned stretched his long limbs. "Are we going to seize our pirate booty now? I'm ready, though I'm wrecked from days in that blasted carriage. Why couldn't the *Skylark* just sail to London? It'd cause far less bother."

"The Duke of Bagsham warned me that customs agents didn't let the ship land in Portsmouth," Rowland said. "So we came here to protect Marborne property."

"Oh blithe-kin, Ned wasn't asking you to explain," Lizzie said. "It's what our Uncle Absolom would call...What? Aporia? Bathos? Ah, a rhetorical question."

"I know nothing of rhetoric," Ned said. "I came here because the promise of an exotic cargo means more to me than the Puritans' promise of heaven." He pulled on thick leather gloves. Lizzie felt a pang of what must be envy, because she had no gloves. "We'll have tropical woods. Porcelain. Jade. Minerals for paint. Perhaps ivory for carving and inlays." He glanced at Rowland. "Oh, and spices enough to pay Marborne taxes for a decade."

"And I want possession of the ship," Rowland said. "I hope we all find our hearts' desire."

Decidedly envious of Ned's gloves, Lizzie jammed her chilled hands in the pockets of her coat, which smelled of Rowland's shaving soap and rosewater. When she'd won her plea to come on this journey, she'd worn borrowed breeches to travel on horseback. But a day later, Rowland hired a carriage in Reading, as if he'd divined how painful she found riding so far. Then he'd given her his topcoat when it turned cold.

"Rollo, did you check that the king's letter is still in your pocket, to prove you are the ship's owner?" Lizzie prompted, then grimaced, again sounding like a scold although she'd meant a kindness, since he'd shuffled the contents of his pockets when he gave her his heavy topcoat.

Thankfully, Rowland smiled. "Ah, sweeting. Temporarily possessed by the soul of Hamlet's Polonius?" Countess nosed at his hand until he scratched her ears. "I vow to 'neither a borrower nor a lender be.'"

"Unlike me." She tightened her borrowed coat.

He leaned forward to kiss Lizzie, but Countess lunged between them, preventing what appeared to be one man kissing another on the streets of Bristol.

"Good girl, Countess." Lizzie stroked the dog's back and came away with hair sticking to her fog-dampened hands.

"Aye, good girl," Ned said. "That's a poor way for three men from London to introduce themselves in Bristol."

"I shall also vow to be circumspect with my affection." Rowland said. "Now, I'll ask the carriage driver to find us an inn for the night. Then we'll go down to the wharves."

Countess followed Rowland, likely seeking a reward.

"What do you wish for today, Lizzie?" Ned looked like a pure innocent, which left Lizzie feeling protective of him.

"I wish that we find Rollo's booty has arrived."

In the frigid fog, Lizzie also wished for the impossible: Rowland's arm around her. And she wished for the gloves Countess had chewed ragged while they ate a hurried breakfast at Swindon, where the innkeeper mistook Lizzie for a manservant. ("Best send your lordship's dark servant to eat in the kitchen.") When the ruined gloves were found, guarded between Countess's paws, Rowland offered Lizzie his gloves, but she'd been rash.

("You shouldn't be punished for your dog's crimes.") She deserved frozen hands for refusing his kindness.

—

When Lizzie looked up from buttoning her coat, Ned hovered at her elbow. "Lizzie, what did you mean, 'You know exactly what will bring us to that moment'? It'd be a great kindness if you'd say when you'll marry Rollo."

"I don't know when." She answered honestly.

"Why not?" Ned asked a simple question. Yet, Lizzie felt that question as if a provoking finger dug into her ribs.

It's not like Ned to play nosey posey. My brother is the only one in England I can share secrets with. I'd best answer.

She said, "Rollo wants to ask the king's permission to marry, because of an older earl's promise to the first King Charles. But I don't want James in our business. And Rollo won't agree to…"

Ned prodded her boot—Rowland's boot—with his toe. "What, Lizzie? What wild idea won't he agree to?"

"You know I've longed to return to Princess Mary's court in the Low Countries?"

"Aye, since she sent you home to find a titled husband, so you could keep being a lady in waiting. If you would finally marry Rollo, *voilà*, you're a countess."

"Yes. I want to live in Mary's court half the year. But Rollo wants to stay in England. To take care of Marborne business."

"You could visit Holland on your own." He offered the same solution Rowland had, but without sad eyes. "Why not? You always do what you want. I admire that."

"Because I'd feel lonely the whole time." She'd been surprised to discover that feeling and was surprised now to be telling Ned. "Besides, Rollo's afraid—"

"Of not much," Ned said. "Perry tells hair-raising stories from when he and Rollo served as king's intelligencers in the Low Countries. What can Rollo fear now?"

"That my service to Mary might dangerously complicate the service he owes the King of England, since James fears betrayal all around him."

"Truly?" Ned's eyes flicked to the side, piercing her with an innocent glance. "Perry thinks you're in love with Mary. Or in love with serving a princess. I insisted that he's wrong, either way. Am I right, or are you in love?"

"Perry should mind his own business."

Mary was my only close friend (besides my family) until I met Aurora. But that's too pathetic to confess to Ned.

Ned buttoned his overcoat. "So, you won't marry Rollo for now, but you came on this journey with him. Why?"

"I came to avoid a…a difficult situation in London."

Ned will never understand. It's not a world he knows.

"Is it one of your chores as a watcher for the king?"

"Ah, Perry told you about that? He should keep secrets, and Rollo shouldn't know what I'm asked to do for the king. No good can come of either Perry or Rollo knowing."

"Zooterkins! What are you doing?" His expression changed from innocence to consternation in a single breath.

"I attend fêtes and parties with courtiers and lords. The kind Rollo hates and avoids. I'm sent to play coquette, solely to judge men's worth and loyalty, because our King James fears Protestants might be plotting against him. I came on this journey to escape a new invitation."

I have done such for Mary too, and I loathe it. I can do more. And much better.

"Rollo isn't allowed to know you are compelled by the king to be beautiful and popular at fêtes?" Ned was laughing at her, like only a brother can.

She should accept that, as just the way she and Ned tease each other. But indignation rose from her belly. "Rollo is compelled to serve, too. Uncle Absolom raised all the Foxe cousins to serve England."

"Not me," Ned said. "My Dutch father taught me to be a *godverdomme* painter."

"And he taught you more Dutch expletives than even Perry knows. You know I cannot escape the call to serve?"

"Serve England, yes. But I don't give a Christmas fig for royalty. England should have rid itself of all of them decades ago."

Ned has never spoken such political heresy!

"Oliver Cromwell was a tyrant," she said, offering the kind of inconsequential argument that their late uncle Absolom the philosopher would never tolerate.

Ned was laughing at her again. "James is a tyrant who forces you to tease lords at fêtes."

She coughed. It must be the cold wet air. He patted her back.

"I understand your resentment, Ned. I ate regularly while I lived in Mary's court while the rest of you—and all the Marborne villagers—were starving."

"I never resented that." He blinked, as if bewildered. "What are you talking about?"

"I don't understand why you are harassing me to marry Rollo right now."

"Harassing?" He'd tipped his head, as if studying a figure while painting. "I intend to paint a commemoration of your nuptials, so I wanted to know when that will be."

"A commemoration?" Her cold lips felt numb. She'd entirely misunderstood his initial question.

"Aye. I can see it in my mind's eye, so I need the proper minerals and compounds for the color palette I've planned. Please promise to wear a golden gown. You are always radiant in gold silk. Else, a bright Merry Widow yellow if you wait until spring to marry."

"I promise to sew a golden gown, when the time comes."

"Zooterkins," Ned said. "You have a good heart, but why was it so hard for you to answer a simple question?"

Rowland was suddenly at her side, asking if she needed water or wine before they ventured down to the wharf.

"No, thank you," she said. "Let's go to the wharf in search of Ned's booty."

> *I need to regain possession of myself. Ned only asked when we'd marry, not why I blame King James for the delay. I confessed far too much.*

—

The day's light was smothered, as if a wool blanket had been thrown over the sky. Rusty leaves lay in sodden messes under dark, bare trees. Here in Bristol, the cold sucked heat from one's bones, stung lips, and chilled bare fingers.

They followed Rowland along the waterfront, seeking the harbormaster's quarters. Rowland and Ned continued their usual banter, but Lizzie didn't care to open her mouth and breathe the chill salt air. Her scarf? She'd left it along with her hat on the cushioned seat in the carriage.

Where I must have also left my natural wits.

"Can you read that ship's name?" Ned asked.

Rowland said, "I could if we hadn't arrived so late in the day. If it hadn't rained for the last fortnight, we might have made better time."

Ned said, "And if Lizzie hadn't insisted on coming along, we'd have been on horseback and—"

"Don't blame Lizzie." Rowland said. "Faugh! The stench!"

The chill air of the Bristol Channel carried a wretched stink from the nearby ship. It was so thick, she choked on it.

"Tell them who you are, Rollo." Lizzie pointed to the guards. "It's too cold to hang about being modest."

Usually reluctant to claim his privileges as an earl, Rowland went directly to the two red-coated men who were stamping to stay warm, their hands under the pits of their arms, their muskets clamped in their crooked elbows. One as tall as Ned, the other not as tall as Lizzie. The two men stirred to stand at attention.

"Good evening. If I might present myself, I'm Rowland Foxe, the Earl of Marborne. Is this the *Skylark*?"

"Aye, 'tis, my lord." The smaller man answered in an accent Lizzie associated with Somerset.

"For what black sins are you poor fellows condemned to stand in the cold, guarding it?"

Rowland's way of speaking always put men at ease and avoided conflict. Lizzie once more wished for a portion of his talents. No one ever said of her, *What a fine fellow! So jolly!* Likely they whispered, *What a haughty gilflurt. Wanting to be a countess, but can't yet bring her fine self to marry her earl.*

She tucked her hands under the pits of her arms like the militiamen did.

"No sins," the tall one answered. "Just the rota. Our good luck, in truth."

Both voices echoed sounds of Somerset, hence they'd been recruited locally. Rowland and his former sergeant, Peregrine Frake, never agreed with such local placements, insisting the Romans never did so.

"Aye. We only stand freezing our gingamobs," said the other. "Better, though, than having to move the cargo."

"Move the cargo?" Rowland asked. Lizzie heard the hollow, anxious tone in his voice if no one else did.

"My exotic woods and ivory?" Ned murmured.

"That job's done," the first guard said. "Now we'uns stand here to keep any town rowdies from burning the ship."

Hearing Rowland's sharp intake of breath, Lizzie spoke. "Because of the stench?"

"Aye. It's rare such a filthy slaver dares to dock. When they come to Bristol, they've already cleaned their holds in Barbados. It's rare for any captain to go off his head, thinking the king won't seize a slaver's cargo in England."

"A slaver?" Lizzie repeated the words, stunned.

"Cargo's been taken to the customs house," the second redcoat said. "Our colonel wants us to guard the ship 'til the king's customs man comes to see it for himself."

"Better to let the town burn it," the first guard said. "It's what the people want." Both guards nodded at this wisdom.

"Where's the crew?" Rowland asked.

"Ran off soon as our men came to the quay."

"We got our hands on one," the tall one said. "Our colonel will learn who owns this ship at least, if that sailor has enough wit to speak."

In the dim afternoon light, Lizzie could see Rowland's lips move, though he said nothing aloud. With a tip of his head, he motioned them away from the guards.

"Mayhap just as well the king has them," Ned said. "We want nothing to do with slavers."

"Think so?" Rowland sounded disgusted. "I wager we'll see some of them next season in powdered wigs and royal livery, serving the bad green wine that the king calls champagne."

Lizzie's stomach turned on the stench, now knowing what it was. She wanted to scream, damning the king and all the men in Withersea's secret syndicate. They called themselves Hawkins' Heirs, after the slave-runner captain from Queen Bess's time.

We own a filthy slaver!

2
Sanctuary

— LIZZIE —

MONDAY LATE AFTERNOON

COUNTESS HOWLED. LIZZIE WANTED to howl, too. She put her hand on the dog's head to offer comfort, though she felt desolate. The dog squirmed, whined. Lizzie whined inside.

The King of England is a demon slavemonger.

Metal clashed on metal along the ship's side, a familiar harbor noise. It clanged again, louder. Close by. Frightened at the sound, the dog yowled, leapt, and darted away.

"Countess, come!" Rowland called.

Lizzie ran after the dog, more to get away from the vile stench than hoping to stop the big black beast. The dog would come back. It always did. It couldn't bear being out of sight of the master it never obeyed.

"Countess!" she called as she ran, pounding around a corner, hoping for enough light to see the dog or its shadow. More than once she slipped on a cobble, stumbled, had to reach out to steady herself on a wall. A slimy wooden wall, wet with fog. She slipped again.

Arms wrapped around her.

Rollo! Dear heart!

"Steady, my boy." Breath and flesh stinking as bad as that infernal ship. A voice thick with rum. Arms crushed around her ribs. "We got us another runaway."

"Stash him with the rest. Mayhap we'll earn more than a farthing from that cargo after all."

Alarmed, she kicked to get free. Stomped on a foot with Rowland's heeled boots. Kicked again to smash a knee.

Yelps. A ruder grasp around her arms and ribs. Then her feet were kicked out from under her. She crumpled, her knees bashing hard on the cobbles, fear rushing over her like water in a raging flood.

"Here now, my black puppy. Obey your earthly masters, like the Lord's book says."

"A feisty one, eh?" The other rogue growled. "We'll get ten times what any squawking black brat might be worth."

"Put him with the others. I'm hungry enough, my belly is gnawing my ribs."

"And I want a kip."

Shoved hard, she fell on the floor as the door shut behind her. The slam of an iron bolt rang over her head. The room proved too dark to see where she'd been thrust. She felt instead her bruises, breathing deep to quiet the jagged fear that had jolted through her when that rogue grabbed her.

No need for fear. Rollo and Ned will come.

Countess will lead them to me.

She hadn't traveled far from where she'd left them. Cold salt air gusted up through the wet boards, slick with algae. Tidal waves washed below. It must be a warehouse on a wharf. Then she heard she wasn't alone. Children's voices pealed around her.

"O nosso anjo! Tia Angelina!"

"Ela encontrou-nos!"

"Como prometeu."

More hails. Still stunned from falling into the room, Lizzie struggled to hear what tongue the voices spoke. Portuguese. Like the Amsterdam goldsmith who tended Princess Mary's jewelry.

"Our angel…Our aunt…Found us…As she promised."

Small hands tried to help Lizzie rise.

"Não a tia Angelina."

The mournful sadness in the children's repeated words would break any heart. *"Not Aunt Angelina."*

"O meu nome é Ysabel."

Whenever Lizzie spoke with Mary's goldsmith in his own tongue, his lips contracted into a smile at her poor accent and limited words. After naming herself in Portuguese to those girls, she tried French.

"Je m'appelle Ysabel. Parlez-vous français?"

But no one answered in that tongue. Instead, the small figures in the dark warehouse argued with each other.

"He's one of the white devils sent here to catch us."

"No, the devils snatched him too."

"I saw his face when those devils threw him in here. He's not white, but he's not from the devil boat."

"No. He has good clothes. And shoes."

The goldsmith's tongue came back to her as they spoke, so Lizzie understood most of it.

"I am a woman," she said in her terrible Portuguese. "I'm from this country, not from the boat. Call me Ysabel."

The children repeatedly exclaimed that she was a woman: *"Uma mulher!"*

Meanwhile, Lizzie again checked her own wellbeing.

The bruises, not so bad.

The fright, now mostly gone, leaving a residual tremor.

Rollo and Ned have good sense—and Countess.

With that clarity, she did as she'd been raised to do. She sought to reassure the children.

"My friends will find us. We have only to wait while they search. How did you come here?"

She asked to distract their worries in this dark prison. The answers were disjointed, confusing, until she understood that they spoke in different accents. She next asked, "Where do you come from?"

She might well have asked the befuddled crowds walking away from the Tower of Babel.

A village name that wasn't in Portuguese, ten days walk from the city with the devil boats.

One king battled another and sent defeated villagers on a twenty days' walk to Cidade de Benin.

Ten days floating down a river—it didn't have a name, just "the river"—to a devil's town called Bassa, where the boats were.

A village two days' walk from Lagos, where their chief sold her to the devil-men after her parents died.

There were six girls. "Please tell me your names."

"Jesus nomes, como Tia Angelina disse," one girl warned.

"What are Jesus names?" Lizzie hadn't felt so ignorant since the day she'd first left home and was plunged into the strange new world of Mary's court.

"A devil in a black dress walked through the boat and splashed water on us. Gave us Jesus names," one said. "Tia Angelina said we must not tell devils our real names."

"She's not a devil. She's like us."

It was barely light enough that they could see each other.

"There's black devils too," one girl said.

"And half black devils. I saw one in Benin City."

The little girl said *demónios mulatos,* Portuguese words spit on Lizzie once when she spurned a drunken courtier in Amsterdam. It had been many centuries since her foremothers saw Morocco and a full century since her great-great-grandmother came from Aragon to serve Henry's queen. Lizzie had laughed at the foul fellow, which he took worse than her spurning.

While the girls debated the safety of telling their names, Lizzie saw that not one could be older than six, their hair wild, their faces etched with hunger and fear, all in filthy tatters. They must be freezing.

"What are your Jesus names? I promise I won't let anyone hurt you. My friends will come soon. We'll be safe then."

> *Where are Rollo and Ned? I ran only a hundred steps. Countess never ventures far from Rowland.*

She listened closely as the girls spoke their names. By now, she could see well enough in the dark to unite names and voices with thin, starved faces. The names were not so foreign.

> Fortunata's round face must have been sweet when she'd last had enough to eat.
>
> Gloria never stopped wiggling, the most excitable of them.
>
> Ines had a long, narrow face and the wildest hair.
>
> Marta, the smallest, spoke with authority, always believed by the others.
>
> Rebeca, the tallest, stood with her arms wrapped around her torso, as if comforting herself.
>
> Susana coughed again, wanted to hide behind Rebeca.

"Agora, as minhas meninas," Lizzie said. *Now my girls.* She begged them to tell her about their Tia Angelina. She wanted to keep them talking, to stave off fear while awaiting rescue. "Is Tia Angelina your father's sister? Or your mother's?"

"Ela não é a nossa tia verdadeira. Não somos primos."

Lizzie asked that to be repeated until she got it: *"She's not our real aunt... We aren't cousins... We only met on the devil's boat."*

"Tia Angelina found us on the devil's boat and claimed us as her own."

"Because no one on the devil's boat knew us."

Barco do diabo. That's what these girls called the *Skylark.*

The girls took turns to explain, like singers in a round song. They came on the ship as utter strangers to everyone, walking into a dark, miserable world. Tia Angelina claimed them as hers, which was how they stayed alive. She taught them songs, warned them to avoid bad water.

"And she helped us escape," Susanna said.

"She turned us all into ghosts, so no one saw us run away," Ines said.

"Ghosts?" Lizzie sought another word. *"Invisível?"*

"Sim, exatamente," Ines said.

"Tia Angelina is a witch," Marta said, emphasizing this truth with a shake of her hand.

"But a good witch," Gloria said.

"She escaped from the black devils before," Fortunata said. "That's how she knew the magic to escape the devil boat."

"She hid us in here while she went to find food and water."

"But the white devils found us. They must have her, too."

"But you came, Tia Ysabel," Susana said, the girl who needed the most reassurance. "Are you a witch?"

"Make us invisible so we can run away!" Gloria cried.

"My friends will save us." Lizzie said for the twentieth time. Or was it the thirtieth? Rowland and Ned needed to come soon, because she needed water and, having shaken off the fright, to relieve herself.

"If you have to make water," Ines said, as if she knew Lizzie's thoughts, "there's a hole in the floor. By that wall."

"It falls into the sea," Marta said.

"Be careful not to fall in," Gloria said.

So, Lizzie unbuckled Rowland's belt, dropped his breeches, and exposed her bare bum to the frigid air. The tide had turned. It was rising. What else might leap out to grab her?

—

Impatient with Rowland and Ned, Lizzie brewed a plan.

We cannot wait for rescue.

"There's only two men," she said. "If we make ready, when the door opens, we'll overcome them." She begged the girls' agreement. "Is that what Tia Angelina would suggest?"

The girls looked back and forth, avoiding Lizzie's eyes. She prompted again, and they traded notions, until all agreed.

"*Boas meninas!*" She praised them as being good girls, then encouraged them further. "Let's find sticks to beat those devils when they come."

They scoured the narrow warehouse for whatever could be used to attack their captors. Two pairs of girls pried up a large splinter from the decaying floorboards, but it proved too large for any of the girls to wield, so it was declared to be Lizzie's. Then near the door, they found a pile of willow canes, no bigger than the smallest girl's thumb. These may have been destined to be kindling or wicker for chairs, but the girls each seized one and practiced whipping it to make the air whir. By great good fortune, they didn't strike each other in error.

"When the door opens," Lizzie said, "I will spring on them. Marta will jump from the other side of the door with her big stick. Do you agree?"

They shouted, "*Sim! Sim!*"

A spark of enthusiasm captured each of them.

Marta said, "We'll beat them like my aunts beat the white priest's pig when it gets in the garden."

"Then we must swarm through the door. Go that way," Lizzie pointed toward what she thought was the heart of the town, "and run, my good girls."

They practiced what they'd do when the door opened. The sound of the slamming bolt stopped them. Lizzie sprang for the door, hoping with all her being that it'd be Rowland, come at last. But the guttural voices were those of their attackers.

As the door opened, she swung her too-large board, its splinters grinding into her frozen bare hands, a painful jolt running up her arm as she connected with a sailor's skull.

The man fell, dropping a torch that rolled across the floor.

"Hoy!" the other shouted in surprise. But then Marta was on him, beating him like the priest's pig.

The sailor tried to grab Marta's big stick, but Lizzie bashed the back of his knees before he got a good hold. He fell, screaming in pain. Marta swatted madly at his shoulders and head.

"Vamos, agora! Corre, corre!" Lizzie shouted to the others. She kicked the door open further, and the girls ran past her, each pausing to strike at least two times at their fallen captors.

"Corre, corre!" Lizzie cried again. She stopped to be sure each girl had departed. Then she too ran, whooping with joy, but still coping with Rowland's too-large boots.

Success! Freedom!

She glanced back. Those two rogues weren't yet rising up to follow. But her new friends were running toward the wharf, not into town. Lizzie turned to follow. Did they think to find their Tia Angelina there?

The militiamen!

That jolt of fear returned. She cried out, warning the girls not to go back to the ship. She didn't have the right words in Portuguese. Alarmed that they might be captured, she ceased calling to them when she came near the ship.

On the wharf, two girls shouted for the attention of the guards, getting the men to turn their backs away from the ship to look for hidden voices. The other four girls scrambled up the narrow gangway onto the hated ship, struggling for balance while carrying the torches seized from their captors.

"Tia Ysabel!" The two wharf-side girls cried, then skipped away to scramble onto the ship with the others, apparently invisible, because the guards didn't turn to look.

Lizzie approached the militiamen. "Good evening. I was here earlier with the Earl of Marborne. Do you know where he has gone?"

The two guards examined Lizzie suspiciously. Surely, she no longer looked like a member of an earl's entourage. The shorter man said, "They've gone with the harbormaster. They asked you to wait here when you came. Where's your dog?"

The tall militiaman strained to see past Lizzie, where voices shouted, "Fire!"

"'Ware the watch!"

"All men to hand!"

The girls must have used a captured torch on their prison before running back to the ship.

The two guards looked at each other, deciding whether they were among "all men" or still at their assigned watch. While they decided, the six girls swarmed back down the narrow, swaying gangway. Sans torches. One girl gestured for Lizzie, who said to the guards, "Thank you, gentlemen," and ran after her friends.

She didn't know the town and had only one good idea left.

"My young girls!" She called to them in Portuguese. "See that spire? Run for it. Get inside the door and you'll be safe."

> *That was right, wasn't it? That churches offered sanctuary? Or did old King Henry stop that? Or did the Puritans knock that notion aside when they smashed the carvings of the saints?*

—

Lizzie ran, disregarding the pain in her twisted ankle and the frustrating awkwardness of ill-fitting boots. Splinters burned in her chilled hands.

Did I break my elbow? Did I kill him?

She cried out at that thought. Then Countess was at her side, just as she ran with the girls into the bone-chilling interior of a startlingly narrow church. The dog leapt at Lizzie, its tongue lolling in greeting.

"Good dog!"

The only other creature she'd be happier to see just then? Rowland. Who must now be nearby.

By the baptismal font, a surprised rector shouted, "This is a House of God!"

They raced past the man. Lizzie looked back. Outside the church door, dark plumes of smoke rose as if from the rector's head. The *Skylark* and the warehouse must both be aflame.

The rector batted at Countess to shoo the dog away. Instead of cowering, Countess chomped on the hem of the man's clothing and tugged him away from Lizzie.

The rector raised his arms, shouting, "Don't bite!" Which only caused Countess to lunge at him again and tug firmly at his surplice, which tore away, baring his black cassock.

"Homem do diabo!" the excitable Gloria cried.

The others joined. "Devil man! Devil man!"

Lizzie waved her hands to shush them, shaking her head.

"Be quiet," she called in Portuguese, and then in English, "Come, Countess!"

"What is this havoc?" The hard lines and bushy brows of the rector's face must have frightened every child in his parish.

"Homem do diabo!"

"Bless you, sir." Lizzie, still panting, stood by the rector. Countess stuffed her muzzle into Lizzie's freezing hand. She spread Rowland's topcoat wide, and the girls flocked to her for shelter. "These are God's children. We seek sanctuary."

3
The Skylark

—EDUARD WIJCK—
MONDAY LATE AFTERNOON

NED WATCHED DOWN THE alley where Lizzie had chased after Countess, waiting for them to reappear. Meanwhile, Rowland played his pleasant and mild self, working to tease information out of the two guards on the wharf.

But sister and dog were gone too long.

"Rollo." Ned pleaded for attention twice, then shouted, "Lord Marborne! She's gone."

He tugged Rowland's sleeve, dragging him toward the narrow alley where Lizzie had disappeared. But a double file of militiamen emerged from another street to quickly surround them. A small man in a big woolen coat appeared.

"Gentlemen." The fellow bent his head in greeting. "I'm William Keckilpenny, the harbormaster. The customs people insist all men who show interest in the *Skylark* come answer questions at the customs house."

"We're missing a member of our party," Rowland said. "We need to find—"

"In the king's name," Keckilpenny said, "you will come now. You can find your friend later."

"Aye." Rowland agreed, but showed as much shock as Ned felt, hemmed in by the militiamen. They both glanced back often while being marched to the customs house.

"Countess will come," Ned said. "She can never bear to be far from you, Rollo. Lizzie will be with her."

But no Countess. No Lizzie.

Rowland rolled that gold angel coin over his knuckles, which Lizzie called his one bad habit.

Ned folded and unfolded his hands, though he hadn't been taught to pray in the face of bored adversity.

They sat for half an hour in the freezing customs house, no fire lit in the grate, the customs officer never appearing. Rowland repeatedly waved his letter, which proved he owned the *Skylark* by the king's grace. Ned repeatedly begged to search for their friend, missing from the earl's coterie. The harbormaster opened his hands to show it was all beyond him to resolve without the customs man appearing.

The customs official never came.

Cold, sharp dread gnawed a ragged hole in Ned's belly. Rowland's lips were pressed tight, white at the edges. Which meant that fury made up a part of what Rowland was feeling.

At last, Mr. Keckilpenny let them go, since it seemed that the customs officer wasn't coming. He said, "We sent the people from the ship to the baron's great barn east of the city, since there wasn't room for so many here. The king's customs officer must be caught up in business there."

Keckilpenny made Rowland promise to return early the next morning, leaving them to follow their noses back to the wharf while checking every alley they passed and calling out, "Countess, come!" repeatedly, though twice Ned shouted, "Lizzie!"

They found no sign of her.

At the wharf, the *Skylark* lit up the sodden sky, in flames.

A fire brigade stood in rough lines, chattering and laughing. A thin rain fell. Rather, the fog dripped in what Perry called a smizzle.

"Why aren't you fighting the fire?" Rowland asked a man on the brigade line. He sounded remarkably calm, given that a Marborne fortune was in flames. "Who's in charge here?"

"That be George," the man said in a thick West Country tongue. "'Ee be gone for a firkin of cider down to The Siren, since it be lippen." He held out his hand, indicating the drizzle.

"But the fire!" Ned grasped his ears, distressed.

"No danger to the other ships," another man said. "That be our proper job to watch out for."

"Aught all t'be done for the slaver," said the first man.

"Hark at he," said the other man. "Best some bodies in town thought to torch it."

"Have you seen our dog?" Ned asked. Surely if they found Countess, they'd find Lizzie. "A big black dog?"

Word passed among the men gathered to celebrate the burning of the *Skylark*, for that seemed to be what those men were doing there. At last, one man pushed through the brigade that didn't care to fight a fire.

"Thou be'st after a lush black dog? He chased a dark fellow and some babbas down to St John's on the Wall."

"When?" Rowland sounded just as desperate as Ned felt.

"Just as the fire bell be a'ringing."

With Rowland on his heels, Ned darted down the wharf where the man pointed. Their boots slipped and squeaked on the wet wharf and did no better when they reached cobbles. Just as they spied a church spire above a gate into the city, Countess charged Rowland, leaping on him to lick his face.

The dog must have been out in the drizzle most of this time. Its fur was matted and wet.

"Good girl! Down! Damnation, get down." Rowland held the excited dog by the scruff, making noises to calm it, then asking, "Where's Lizzie?"

The dog jumped up on Rowland again when shouts rang from the church.

Lizzie stood arguing inside the open door of the narrow church. She was a head taller than the rector, who shook a finger at her. A woman two heads shorter than Lizzie argued, shaking her finger at Lizzie.

Ned and Rowland approached.

The woman spoke with a heavy West Country accent. "Thou be'st sure, there be naught place in Bristol so safe as the almshouse. Thy wee'uns will have food and dry beds."

"They require sanctuary." Lizzie stood with her hands on her hips, which Ned knew meant she could not be moved from her argument. "They require protection from the king's men."

That's when Ned saw the children crowded behind Lizzie, peeking past her trousers. Frightened.

Then Countess ran past Lizzie to stand with them. The children cried what might be "good dog" while embracing the big black creature.

"God blind me," Rowland murmured, which seemed a mild oath in the circumstance.

One quick flash of Lizzie's eyes meant that she'd seen him, but she returned to quarreling with the other woman, who remained adamant that the children must go to the almshouse. Rowland folded his arms as if prepared to wait.

Ned had learned this past year that close confidantes have unique ways to help each other. His dear friend Perry had, unbidden, pulled Ned out of at least three brawls that Ned wasn't fit for. Here outside the church, Rowland could step up, say he was the Earl of Marborne, and resolve the contretemps. Yet, when Lizzie glanced their way again, Rowland stepped behind

Ned, folded his hands behind his back, and waited, seeming to abide by an agreement not to interfere.

Then the tiny woman spoke softly, the last words of which were, "And there be no Bristol inn what will have them."

Lizzie dropped her hands to her side while agreeing. "Aye then. As you say, mistress. But only until morning."

She turned to the children and spoke words that Ned didn't know. He had some Dutch, Cambridgeshire English, and a smattering of French. It wasn't any of those tongues.

An agreement, and new action!

The girls lined up in pairs behind Lizzie. By the time they stepped out of the church, Ned had counted six children, perhaps all girls, though too young to tell for certain.

But then the rector, whose church raiment was torn and stained, stepped forward and took Lizzie's arm at the elbow. He began to say, "I'll show the way—"

The children screamed, "Diablo! Diablo!" and ran back into the church. Countess barked furiously.

Whatever tongue they spoke, the little ones believed the rector was the devil. Lizzie followed them back into the church and gathered them around her, speaking low. Ned couldn't recall ever seeing Lizzie with children. Yet she calmed them, got them in line again, and then called to Rowland and Ned.

"Please ask the rector how to find the almshouse. The girls fear his black robe." She tipped her head to speak to the girls. "And, Rollo, give the rector recompense for his ruined surplice. Countess tore it when the man first frightened the girls."

By rare good luck that day, the almshouse lay just two streets away. The journey was quick, once the girls accepted Lizzie's assurance that Ned and Rowland were her friends, though the men were consigned to bringing up the rear. Two lines of girls clung to Countess as they followed Lizzie through the streets.

The next ruckus with the girls came at the door to the almshouse, because Countess had to remain outside with Ned and Rowland. The dog didn't mind, since Rowland was there to ruffle her fur and call her the best girl. But the children had to be coaxed into leaving the dog with Lizzie's solemn promise that they'd see Countess the next morning.

While Lizzie settled business inside, the two men stood under the eaves, keeping out of the persistent drizzle as best they could. A cold wind picked up, blowing a chill over them from the Bristol Channel. A dim light from a single almshouse window helped differentiate their shadows in the wet night.

"Did you see her eyes?" Rowland asked. "Have you ever seen her on fire like that before?"

"Never." Ned shivered.

"'The evil that men do lives after them,'" Rowland murmured. The words likely came from his Bard, where Rowland often took comfort. "We are now on a different journey than we began in London."

—

Ned masked his shock when Lizzie came out of the almshouse, where they'd given her a lantern that chased away a few shadows and lit her face.

He'd never seen her so absolutely done in. She pushed her wild, disheveled hair back, revealing fingers streaked with blood and dirt. The only comfort she accepted was Ned's coat thrown over her shoulders, since she'd left Rowland's coat at the almshouse with the girls. She limped and she shivered, yet didn't complain of anything.

"I'm happy to see you." She slipped an arm under each man's elbow. "What took you so long?"

"Detained by the local militia to wait on the king's customs man," Rowland said. "Where were you?"

"Tossed into a warehouse by two rude and smelly brutes." She laughed with a sharp note that startled Ned. "But I made friends with the other captives."

"The girls are from the *Skylark*?" Ned asked.

"Aye. That's why they need sanctuary."

"Rather an antique notion," Rowland said.

Lizzie said, "The customs man came here for you. I'd be a fool not to guess that the king wants those little girls."

"The customs man never came to meet us," Rowland said. "I don't think they know about your new friends."

"Still, it's only luck we weren't all taken to the customs house." While they walked, Lizzie talked about her adventure, laughing, but not like she did when Countess was clever or when Rowland teased her. "I'd have said I'm the girls' mother, and that they've always lived in England."

"Then I'd be explaining," Rowland said, "that my coterie includes a woman in breeches and boots."

Lizzie laughed, but it still didn't sound like her.

"A mother who dresses her children quite badly." Rowland laughed too.

None of this was at all humorous. Ned grasped her arm, but gently. "You're limping, Lizzie. Want to lean on me?"

"I blistered my foot," she said, "from running in Rollo's boots with a rucked-up stocking. They don't fit well."

Rowland said, "I'll make sure my boots fit you better, next pair I have made."

"Thank you, my lord." She laughed again in that strange way. "I might also confess that I twisted my ankle a bit when I smashed my foot into one rogue's knee."

"Good girl!" Rowland said, welcoming Lizzie's jests, but which led Countess to jump on him, slowing their progress.

"Only a modest effort." Again, odd laughter. "It earned me a sharp push into their prison." A few steps on, she said, "We had success later, when we came with weapons in hand."

"We?" Rowland asked.

Ned was eager for Lizzie's story but abided by Rowland's gentler prodding.

"Fortunata. Gloria. Ines. Marta. Rebeca. Susana. She's the shy one with a bad cough." Lizzie's eyes darted to Rowland. "Are you merely humoring me?"

"Never," he said. "Tell us about your weapons."

"I had a rough board. The girls had sticks. Each took a good poke at the ruffians once we knocked the men down."

"Understandable." Rowland spoke quietly, as if agreeing to keep her telling the story.

"Still." Lizzie bit at her lip. "If either man died, it's down to me. 'Twas only me that swung for that malefactor's skull. After I'd already got his nether parts. Countess! Stop! Come, now!"

She left them to grab Countess by the scruff and shake loose whatever the dog had clamped her fangs around.

Ned whispered to Rowland, "How can she laugh while telling such a strange story?"

"It happens. I've seen it in others," Rowland said. "There's many a man who's laughed off a bad fright."

"Is she all right?"

Lizzie returned before Rowland could answer. Countess ran off immediately.

"Your turn to chase her, Rollo." She pointed to where Countess sniffed the stoop outside a shuttered shop.

While they waited for Rowland to plead with his dog, Lizzie stumbled while standing still. Ned caught her, his hands on her shoulders to steady her. She turned still as a statue.

Rowland rejoined them, his hand down to keep Countess close. Lizzie again slipped her hand into the crook of his elbow.

"I hurt my arm when I hit that rogue. Mayhap, I killed him." If there was more to that thought, she didn't finish.

Ned said, "No one talked to us about finding dead or battered sailors. Not the militia, nor those at the customs house, nor the fire brigade."

"That's right," Rowland said. "So, no murdering for you today, my girl."

"Still." She chewed at her lip again. "Anyone who found those rogues in the warehouse will guess they came from the *Skylark*. They might talk about the girls."

Rowland laughed. "'Constable, those girls hit me.'" He pitched a whining screech. "'They whipped us with sticks.'"

Lizzie laughed, haunting and wild.

Ned stopped dead in the street. Because everyone's arms were interlinked, the others were forced to stop too.

"Zooterkins! Can you both stop with the jests and laughing?" Ned felt Lizzie's false calm to be a torment. "Have you nothing serious to say?"

"No, except I do wonder…" Lizzie looked at Ned, her eyes large in the lantern light. "Where are we staying tonight? I'm famished and…and…and I'd like to refresh my habiliments."

"You were imprisoned by rogues!" Ned cried, anguished. He'd sat bored in the customs office while his sister was in grave danger. "You fought rogue sailors and left them in a burning warehouse. Is there more to tell us, dear sister?"

"Not especially. We were cold and frightened. But then we broke free and ran to the church. I begged sanctuary, so the king cannot seize them, but had to settled for the almshouse." Lizzie's voice still held that too-bright note.

"And that's all?" Ned insisted.

"Yes, that's all," she said. "You've heard all of it."

—

Near the wharf, Ned coughed where the air reeked of burnt wood and acrid smoke. They paused to watch the tide lap at the smoldering timbers of the *Skylark*.

"The fire brigade let it burn, seeing no prospect of salvation." Rowland had one arm around Lizzie, the other hand scratching Countess's ears.

Ned said, "Men at the wharf guessed locals set it afire."

"No," Lizzie said. "The girls torched your ship, Rollo. But only to destroy the devils inside."

"I can see how they might feel that." Rowland sounded philosophical, which added to Ned's bewildered anger over Lizzie's assault. "I didn't need a ship with devils inside."

"Best it's gone," Lizzie said. "We have work to do. We must see to the girls' care beyond tonight. That means—"

Countess leapt up just then, paws on Rowland's shoulders, nuzzling his neck, licking his face. He didn't resist.

"Your dog loves you, Rollo," Lizzie said. "But you don't want her to have such a habit. Hold out your hand like this, so she knows to stand down."

Countess jumped off Rowland, then stuck her muzzle in Lizzie's outstretched hand. "Good girl."

"You were about to say? That we're taking the girls home with us?" Ned didn't know why he bothered to ask.

"There's no other choice," Lizzie said.

"By home," Rowland said, "I hope you mean Revelstone House. I don't think London is a good idea."

Of course. The family home in Marborne parish, just off the fens in Cambridgeshire. Where Ned longed to be. Where Ned had paused work on a half-finished portrait of Perry Frake, his dearest friend, who must be waiting impatiently for Ned's return. This was the longest separation they'd endured since the day they'd met in August.

"Lord Marborne?" The harbormaster appeared then, still in his heavy wool coat, drawing Ned's thoughts away from home.

Rowland held out his hand in greeting. "Mr. Keckilpenny! How are you this evening, sir? Any sign of the customs man?"

Of course, Rowland had the wit to remember the man's name. The master pulled Rowland into a private conference.

In the shadows, Ned stood by Lizzie, feeling her tremble as they gazed out at the smoking hulk. He wanted to put his arm around her, since it felt that something had damaged her, that she needed to be held together.

As if she could hear his thoughts, Lizzie said, "I'm fine, Ned. There's no cause to worry. I'm cold, not broken."

Ned did what he'd never done in this life and clutched her in a hug. She pressed her face into his shoulder. Her body shook.

Then, just as suddenly, she stood upright, shook her head, and stepped back to observe the smoldering slaver ship. "Can you help with some tasks tomorrow morning, Ned? We must outfit the girls for travel. And find nursemaids."

"Aye. Of course."

Rowland came back to them. "Mr. Keckilpenny assures me that no one believes the Earl of Marborne knew what cargo came into the Bristol Channel."

Ned took a breath, knowing Lizzie's worries for those girls. "Then no more trouble with customs?"

"No trouble at all," Rowland said. "I must simply come to the customs house in the morning as I promised. Oh, and I'm compelled to give a crew of dorymen ten pounds to tow the wreckage away to where it can do no harm."

"Ten pounds!" Ned exclaimed.

"Guineas, actually."

—

"We need to find the inn where our driver hired rooms," Ned said, thinking of Lizzie.

However, Lizzie said, "We should go in search of the girls' protector, whom they call Tia Angelina."

"No." Ned said it quickly and perhaps too sharply. He didn't want to give Rowland a chance to agree with her. "It's dark. We don't know Bristol. The only thing we need to look for is the inn."

"Our driver is right there," Rowland said.

Their carriage driver stood on the stoop of a whitewashed inn, smoking a pipe, waving them to him. "Alack, it's the best I could do, your lordship. There's but one decent bedchamber to be found so near the wharf. But the landlord promised you a parlor and a decent supper."

"Was there no room for you?" Rowland asked.

"It's the stable loft for me, my lord. I'll keep your dog with me. I made free to take your baggage upstairs."

After Rowland made sure the driver had enough coin for supper and an evening in Bristol, they said good night.

Inside the inn, a toasty fire burned in the common room. Rowland greeted the landlord and learned where to find their sleeping chamber. "Your man also reserved a private parlor. Would you like a supper served there?"

"It would be a kindness," Rowland said. While he settled the details, Lizzie disappeared up the stairs to the bedchamber. Ned and Rowland stood near the hearth in the tiny, hired parlor, warming themselves while waiting for her.

"Do you think," Ned asked, "Lizzie will stay at Revelstone and play nursemaid to those girls?"

Rowland stared at him for a long moment, then poured more wine for each of them. "We are speaking of Lizzie, your sister. Who doesn't own boots for walking beyond a garden pathway and so has to borrow mine. That Lizzie? Staying in the country?"

Ned laughed for the first time since they came to Bristol. The same day in August that the king acknowledged the Earl of Marborne, Lizzie had abandoned Revelstone for London.

"On the way to the inn, I was sure I could do nothing for her," Rowland said. "Then I saw you doing just what Lizzie needed, which she has never let me do for her."

"How can you say so?"

"She wept in your embrace. She doesn't show me her tears, insists on never being less than brave with me."

"That seems sad, Rollo."

"It is what it is. You know Lizzie is making plans that will require you and Perry to help her in London. Our cousin Tamsin will have to do without her overseer."

Tamsin Foxe, as the official manager of Revelstone and Marborne lands, had asked Perry to be the overseer when Rowland was named earl in August.

Ned could cry out, *Never say so!* He and Perry had plans to build their own cottage, to have their own private world. But Rowland was right. Further, Ned suspected that Perry wasn't truly fit for living in the country and digging in the dirt.

Ned said, "Though Lizzie hasn't shared a single thought yet, you can feel the heat coming off her. You're right. She's making plans for her next action."

Lizzie returned, still limping a bit, but now wearing Rowland's best shirt and waistcoat, her hair covered by a slouch felt hat, its jaunty feather transforming her once more into the foreign beau she'd played on the journey to Bristol. Her energy had been restored sufficiently that she bullied Ned into fetching a salve and bandages from the innkeeper's wife.

"Bashing that rogue with a board gave me splinters."

Ned went to beg medicines from the innkeeper's wife. He was at the door of the little parlor when Rowland said, "Marry me, Lizzie. Now. So that we can comfort each other freely. I'll ask the king's consent when we return to London."

"I despair of your ancestor's promise," she said. "I will not ask James for water if I'm dying."

"We serve the Crown. We made promises a decade ago."

"I serve England. But James has made himself an enemy to what is right and proper for this green earth."

"Your heart is afire today. Your head needs to stay cool."

"He's a slavemonger." Lizzie hissed the word.

"Your friend Mary Stuart," Rowland stroked her uninjured hand, "dresses in gold and silk that James's African monopoly paid for. Will you ask her to deliver a better world?"

Trust Rowland, Ned thought, to offer sobering words when Lizzie was drunk with anger.

"The fire in my heart wants to destroy a world of evil."

He still stroked her hand. "I hope I understand. But let's just fix the parts we can manage."

"My head is stronger than my heart. I shall push forward with caution." She took his hand in hers. "But I cannot marry you until I've set the world right for these girls."

"You aren't warming my heart. However, I shall consider that a promise. Now, hold still while I free this splinter."

Lizzie sucked in a breath as if in pain.

"You can weep, Lizzie. Weep like an infant."

"No." It sounded as if she spoke through gritted teeth. "I am the most sophisticated and worldly of all your cousins, and I can endure this."

Ned joined them, carrying a bundle from his errand. He whistled when he stepped into the small parlor with its homely comforts: a warm fire, cushions on the settle and the chairs, a tallow candle on the table. "Ah, the battlefield-surgeon has taken up his work."

Rowland bent his head over Lizzie's hand, probing it with a thin-bladed knife. The one he kept in his boot. He twice poured aqua vitae over her hand. She hissed at the pain.

"Shall I kiss it to make it better?" Rowland said.

Their supper arrived before Lizzie could answer.

4
The Customs Man

— LIZZIE —

MONDAY EVENING

LIZZIE STILL SHIVERED DEEP inside, hoping it didn't show. She couldn't endure more solicitude from her brother and her fiancé, like Ned rising to poke up the fire and peeking over his shoulder to check on her. Yet, as the fire burned hotter, her inner core warmed with gratitude for his care.

They ate mutton stew and hunks of warm, fresh bread while agreeing on the next day's tasks. Ned was moving the remains of supper to the sideboard when a knock sounded on the parlor door. Lizzie glanced at Rowland, who raised his quizzical brow and shrugged, indicating he had no idea who it might be. Ned opened the door.

The smoke and noise of the common room poured in while heat from their parlor rushed out.

"Lord Marborne? If I might speak with you."

The high, thin voice might have been a woman's but for its scratchy edges. A figure stood in the doorway, but the lone candle lighting their table was insufficient to reveal his face.

"Come in, man." Lizzie made her voice husky and commanding. "Close the door and keep the heat in."

"Yes, please do come in," Rowland said in his mild, welcoming voice.

When Ned released the door, it closed with a bang. The fire whooshed, then settled back to its crackling chatter.

"His grace, Lord Bagsham, felt sure I might find you in Bristol, your lordship. I am Sir Bythorn Chudrakes, serving the king's customs office." Looking about, the man settled on Rowland as the person he wanted to address. So, Lizzie studied the fellow's face in profile.

He's come to take my girls away!

Rowland rose to shake the man's hand, murmuring polite greetings. He poked Lizzie's shoulder in passing, which served to remind her to rise like a man would, rather than giving in to paralytic fear.

"These are my cousins, Sir Bythorn," Rowland said. "Ned Wijck is from our home at Marborne."

Sir Bythorn shook Ned's hand, then turned to Lizzie, his eyes asking questions. His knife-blade nose pointed to his shovel-square jaw and a neckcloth that a Puritan might wear, making a stern impression. With that squealing voice, he must need always to appear stern.

"And this," Rowland said, "is our cousin, the Viscount Orlando, who is visiting from Barcelona."

"*Bon vespre, senyor.*" Lizzie stooped in a Continental bow, speaking one of the few Catalan phrases she knew. "Have you come seeking a bribe, like all the customs men in my country?"

She could feel Rowland's sharp intake of breath.

"A little Catalan jest." She showed her teeth, as if she smiled. "You take no offense, *senyor?*"

Sir Bythorn's mouth twitched into half a smile: he did not appreciate the jest. It took several fumbled attempts before he managed to grip her uninjured left hand in his own bony hand.

He gazed frankly into Lizzie's face, while she stared boldly back, not letting him evoke any more frissons of fear.

"You can imagine, *senyor,* our dismay today." She couldn't help poking at him, all while fearing he'd come for the girls.

The man's narrow, milky-blue eyes left Lizzie thinking she peered into the man's soul. His tawny brows artfully matched his wig, styled in the less modern locks of a wealthy Jacobean, but his narrow, wax-pale face argued for hair that should be grey by now; the man had passed fifty before this year. Dyed brows, then, to match the dyed wig.

He squeaked, "You are the Catalan viscount who helped capture the traitor Danvers Duncombe."

How disconcerting. The involvement in that affair of Viscount Orlando—Rowland's disguise at the time—was not a well-known detail.

"*De nada.* However, it was only by sheer coincidence, since I scarcely met the man." Lizzie waved off the compliment. No Foxe cousin wanted anyone to examine the details of that gambol. "*Senyor* Duncombe was—how do you say—a shopkeeper? A man who dissembles from dawn to past the setting sun."

"A banker." Sir Bythorn sought to look down his blade-thin nose on Lizzie, like London men who disdained foreigners. But she was tall, so he had to tip his head back to achieve the effect of looking down. She was still showing her teeth. They'd both decided they didn't like each other, yet she twisted inside, wanting to know whether he'd come for her girls.

Sir Bythorn turned his attention back to Rowland, holding up his hand as if to offer Rowland a blessing.

"Duncombe's confession was taken under torture in the Tower. Such confessions can be worthless." Sir Bythorn made a chopping motion with his hand, then opened both hands to Rowland as if admiring him. "You, Lord Marborne, provided great service to the Crown, delivering facts instead of hearsay."

Rowland abruptly changed the subject. "We sought the king's customs officer earlier at the waterfront, but heard you weren't available until tomorrow. It's kind of you to come out in this chill night air to find us, Sir Bythorn, though you must be used to the Bristol weather."

"No, I came from London, as did your lordship. I'm from the customs commissioners, not the Bristol customs men." He raised his hands, as if to dramatically affirm his introduction.

Rowland's parted lips betrayed his surprise. With a false accent, Lizzie rushed to cover for him. "*Por favor, senyor,* please sit by the fire. You must be sore from traveling the Bristol Road."

Her voice was as warm as melted butter, not wanting to reveal how this customs man chilled her.

"Most kind of you, your lordship." Sir Bythorn sat on Lizzie's warm chair, placing him in the light of the candle, all the better to see his face. She sat in Ned's chair, which left her brother with the less comfortable wooden settle.

"Your lordship," Sir Bythorn squeaked, "I'd hoped to find you before the *Skylark* made port, to bring the king's message."

King's message?

Lizzie's face turned to stone, then she forced it to soften. King James had lost her loyal royalist heart that day. But Sir Bythorn couldn't be allowed to see that sentiment in her face.

Rowland, however, spoke with a light humor that didn't match his words. "As soon as we reached the wharf, I guessed that the king would be forced to take back his gift to me."

"My understanding," Sir Bythorn drawled, "is that neither the king nor you knew the nature of the cargo when he granted you the traitor Withersea's property."

"We expected ivory and rare woods from Malay forests." Rowland nodded toward Ned "That's what my cousin hoped."

"Customs would be forced to seize such a cargo on behalf of the king, just the same." Sir Bythorn folded his hands like an imploring Puritan. "The Royal African Company holds the monopoly for all trade from that continent, beyond cargo intended for New World plantations."

Lizzie stiffened at the word *cargo.*

Rowland must have noticed, because he held his hand just an inch over her shoulder, as if to stop her from any rash act.

"Not Africa," Rowland said. "The ship's papers describe the *Skylark* as sailing to and from Batavia on the Malay peninsula."

"Just what the *Skylark's* captain claimed," Sir Bythorn said, "when he tried to dock at Portsmouth. Even without customs men boarding, our agent could tell what the cargo was. Our agent refused landing and sent a message to London." He held up his hand, fingers spread, as if declaring a triumph.

"Why did the ship come to England?" Rowland spoke as if pondering the question. "I mean, instead of sailing for the plantations? I'm only curious, Sir Bythorn, because I'd like to hear a good story out of all I've lost today."

Sir Bythorn said, "The captain claims his men salvaged a stranded slaver, its Portuguese crew dying. The *Skylark* crew also took sick, and so were lucky they made it to Bristol."

"*Que horror!*" Lizzie said. All that kept Lizzie seated was Rowland's hand on her shoulder, in a very cousinly manner. She clenched her hands. Pain shot through the injured hand.

The customs man squeaked, "That's what the captain claimed. That he intended to deliver the cargo to the king. But likely he seeks only to save his own hide."

Rowland nodded in time to the folding-and-unfolding gestures the customs man made with his hands. "Tell me, Sir Bythorn, will the king pack these folks off to his plantations?"

"That cargo stock was far too unhealthy to ship across the Atlantic in this season," Sir Bythorn said. "If the local militia had managed to keep them."

"If the militia had kept them?" Rowland spoke the surprise on his cousins' faces.

"The militia moved the cargo to a local baron's barn. When my men arrived, the stock had disappeared into the countryside."

Rowland's hand rested more firmly on her shoulder, yet Lizzie said, "Surely this English weather will make it easy to find them."

"Everything we can trace indicates men came prepared to carry them away in wagons. Like Scottish reavers stealing cattle, if you will."

"Certainly not to be sold in England?" Rowland said, which saved Lizzie from shrieking about calling those people cattle.

"No, men are not sold like cattle in England." Sir Bythorn spoke in disgust, though he'd just compared them to cattle.

"In my country," Lizzie spoke her fears, "bold men bribe customs men into giving them possession of such foreign folk."

"Perhaps the local militiamen can be bribed. My men most definitely were not." Sir Bythorn's face stiffened, white as his pilgrim's starched flat collar. He addressed his answer to Rowland. "If your lordship is ever approached by a customs agent who seeks a bribe for any kind of cargo, it is your duty to report such men to my commission."

"I surely will," Rowland murmured. "No one approached me in that way this afternoon. In fact, we waited for hours, but no customs agent came at all."

"Work delayed me from meeting your lordship. I was occupied in attempting to track down that cargo." Again, with open hands, Sir Bythorn averred the truth.

The thud of her heart must be heard by every man in the room. This was the dreaded moment when this fellow would demand that Lizzie give up her charges.

"We've made considerable effort," the man whined. "Our best guess is that a ship lay in wait, prepared to take that cargo out of Bristol. We will have to report that we were unable to settle those Africans in an appropriate way for the king."

If Lizzie gripped the arms of her chair any harder, she'd pop the knuckles through her skin. She loosened her grip, not wanting to draw attention.

Rowland again changed the subject, this time to the bitter weather, the dismal state of Bristol wharves despite all the trade the town saw, the harsh winds of the Bristol Channel. He had also taken to rolling his gold coin over his knuckles, a habit that lent him an air of boredom, though Lizzie knew he rolled that coin to cover deep agitation.

"It will be nice to return to London," Rowland said. "Yet we're going home with nothing. I'd promised the *Skylark's* treasures to my fiancée as a wedding gift, back when we thought it carried treasures from Malaysia."

"You can claim insurance on the ship." Sir Bythorn's high voice grated on Lizzie's every nerve. "We only intended to seize the cargo, it all being African. The ship remains the king's gift to you. That's the message the king bade me bring you."

"If only," Rowland said, "I didn't have to pay for charred timbers to be towed away from the wharf. But such is life."

"I shall send notice in the morning by the king's courier, to let it be known that you've received the message."

Rowland stood, shaking the man's hand again. "Thank you for coming out on a chilly night to bring the king's message. Don't let me keep you from your supper and a night's rest."

Lizzie opened the parlor door, lest Sir Bythorn prove too thick-witted to see that they wanted him gone.

"*Adéu, senyor.*" She smiled, though it hurt her face. "But I must ask, since I am not familiar with customs in this country." She deepened the way she pronounced *customs*. "Were we expected to know to offer without being asked—ah—what they call a sweetness in my country? Is that—ah—customary?"

"I did not come to solicit a bribe from his lordship." The customs man flushed red. "You cannot say so. You must not."

"Indeed not," Rowland said, while Lizzie had thoroughly enjoyed the customs man's discomfort. "We appreciate your help and advice."

"Just so." Lizzie showed her teeth again. "In my country, no public servant would do so much for strangers." She hissed as she said *servant*. She'd deeply disliked him from first acquaintance. "At least, not without a bribe."

—

Lizzie closed and latched the door of their tiny parlor, happy to see the back of the customs man.

"God blind me!" Rowland huffed just after the door closed.

"Why did you tease him about bribes?" Ned proved to be quite unhappy about that. "How can you dare take any more risks today?"

"He's gone! Thank all the gods on Olympus." Lizzie was too busy with her own worries to take on Ned's. She sank back into her own chair, made disagreeably warm by the customs man. "My heart beat so hard, I was sure he heard it."

"Blast and babble!" Ned exclaimed. "We were perfectly safe. The fellow knows who Rollo is. And we committed no crimes. Whyever did you need to aggravate him?"

"I thought he came for the girls." Lizzie tipped her head back, closing her eyes. "To help the king seize every possible soul from the *Skylark*. And I didn't like him. Did you?"

She tossed the metal button on the table that she'd snipped from the custom man's cuff when they last shook hands. It took a moment to tuck her gilt embroidery scissors back into her cuff. One of the few precious things she had from her mother.

"Lizzie!" Rowland laughed. "You claimed to steal buttons only from men who came too offensively close."

"As Sir Bythorn did."

Ned snatched up the button, which winked in the lamplight. "The last time I saw you do that was when Danvers Duncombe made love to you at our uncle's funeral feast."

"The king," Lizzie said, "was excessively harsh with that traitorous banker. He hanged him. I merely stole a button." She took the button from Ned. It was brass, not gold. She tossed it onto the table. "Bythorn Chudrakes would have asked a bribe if I hadn't put him on his back foot."

"Whatever for?" Ned said.

Lizzie threw up her hands, imitating Sir Bythorn's ostentatious gestures. "To stop him from telling the king that Rollo was complicit with the *Skylark*'s African piracy. Or that it was Rollo who stole them from the baron's barn."

"That's an absurd notion," Rollo said. "You were worried about the girls."

"Yes. I still am. However," Lizzie persisted, "even if Sir Bythorn didn't come for the girls, he isn't a good man. How do we know he's telling the truth about those poor people disappearing into the cold Bristol fog?"

Rowland said, "Cease worrying about the girls. I will declare them to be Viscount Orlando's cousins, come from Portugal. Great-grand-nieces of the same Moorish lady who married Lizzie's great-grandfather."

"I like your notion, lambkin. The girls are, however, rather darker than any Portuguese ladies in England."

"Not even one Englishman in five hundred will know that." Rowland said. "Nay, not one in five thousand."

"That Sir Bythorn," Ned said, "was rather full of himself, bringing such an empty message from the king."

Lizzie said, "He wanted to make sure Rowland knew he'd lost all hope of the king's reward. Which is why Sir Hatchet-face Chudrakes is missing a brass button."

"It feels," Rowland said, "as if we sat through Uncle Absolom's lecture on oratorical gestures." He imitated the customs man's hand movements. "*Supplico,* I entreat. *Affevero,* I affirm. He had triumph and prayer in there, too. In fact, Sir Bythorn had only one original gesture."

"What was that?" Lizzie felt baited into asking.

"That chopping motion. He wishes the king would chop off traitors' heads instead of simply hanging his enemies."

Lizzie said, "He's a worthless, merciless waste of spirit made incarnate. Yet he wants us to regard him as *Sir* Bythorn, a knight. A title he likely got by helping the king of England seize large customs fees off English trade. And he thinks he is superior to you, Rollo, though you are an earl."

"You aren't usually so arrogant," Rowland said.

"It's not arrogance. Our fathers helped Charles escape to France in that disgusting war. Bythorn Chudrakes has no business looking down his long skinny nose at us."

"But he's likely gone from our lives forever," Ned said. "Do you think it's true, Rollo, that the *Skylark* captain intended to turn his cargo over to the king?"

"People." Lizzie emphasized, too tired to threaten her brother over his choice of words.

Rowland said, "No. The Marquess of Withersea called his traitorous investors Hawkins' Heirs. I'd guess there never was a plan to go to the Malay islands. I'll wager that the captain had instructions to meet Withersea upon return to England. And Withersea intended to share those people with his syndicate, as a return on their investment."

"Or send them to the plantations. Who knows who has possession of all those people now." Lizzie strained her voice to imitate Sir Bythorn's squeak. "'To settle them in an appropriate way.' At least I hope they aren't out freezing in the wild."

"Aye," Rowland said. "I'm sure that sooner, not later, they'll all be serving English masters."

"As slaves?" Ned sounded amazed. "I've never heard of such in England."

"No, they'll be indentured as servants," Rowland said. "If they'd gone to James as the customs man had planned, the king would likely send a few as gifts to Louis in France."

Lizzie now knew what it was to be tired to the bone. Her injured hand throbbed. "Likely we'll find Tia Angelina when we discover the others. Do you think they'll be sold in London?"

"Indentured, not sold," Rowland said. "If they remain in England, they'll likely have better lives than on a plantation."

Lizzie sighed. "Even if he didn't seize those people today, your King James is the worst slavemonger in Christendom. Every principle that Uncle Absolom taught demands we seek justice. We shall have to search for those people."

When she said it as "*your* King James," Rowland raised his quizzical brow but said nothing.

Ned said, "What will you do about the king taking back your reward for service, Rollo?"

"Nothing." Rowland raised his hand, as if to still Ned's question. "There's no possible way to complain."

"We must take action," Lizzie said. "The king still owes you recompense for your service. You didn't ask for the *Skylark*. It fell on you. And care for these children fell on me."

Ned said, "Do you think the children have relatives among the people who disappeared from the baron's barn?"

"No, they're orphans," she said. "The woman called Tia Angelina took them under her wing on the ship."

"Can we send them back to their villages?" Ned asked.

Lizzie said, "They know only how many days they were marched in chains to the slaver cities. They don't know where their villages are."

"What must you do for them, Lizzie?" Rowland said. "With all my heart, I will help. Whatever you want."

"Tomorrow, we'll get the girls to safety," she said. "And then we'll find Tia Angelina."

"Oh." Rowland realized he'd promised too much.

Ned said, "Do you also want a cherry with no pit? A chicken with no bones? No, of course you don't, because those are all possible. But we will never find where that cargo disappeared to."

"Not cargo!" Her voice broke at the edges, revealing her burning anger. "People. They are people. I shall be impatient if I have to say it again."

Rowland said, "Maybe it'd have been better if Sir Bythorn had captured those people. He could quickly have them in London and safe. But since those people escaped, we should begin by asking in Bristol about Tia Angelina. What else?"

"We cannot stop the Stuart king's slave mongering, as much as I'd like to end it." Lizzie imitated Sir Bythorn's chopping motion. "If everyone from the *Skylark* is still in England, we must find them. And reap justice for them."

"We should go to bed," Ned said, yawning. "We have to start early tomorrow if our mission is justice."

Rowland said, "First, let me pour more aqua vitae over Lizzie's hurt hand, lest it fester. Ned, where are the bandages and salve from the landlord?"

While Lizzie's hand was being wrapped in a fresh bandage, she sent Ned for ink, paper, quill, and more wine.

"You need to go to bed," Ned said.

"Not yet. I want to write letters to send in the morning."

"Surely that can wait."

"I want my letters to go with the king's courier, if you can arrange that, Rollo. The girls need a doctor, so it would be best if Winwood Oakes were at Revelstone House when we arrive there. And I need to find a teacher who speaks Portuguese, to help the girls learn English."

Rowland said, "I'll sit up with you for company."

"I'm fine alone. You and Ned should get some sleep."

"Good night then." Rowland rubbed her shoulder gently.

Ned lingered another moment. "I wish you'd let us help."

"Dear brother, you have helped me. You are a comfort."

"But what you really want to say is, 'Go to bed and leave me alone.'"

"I don't want to bore you."

Ned left her, so she didn't have to say that she was writing a letter to Princess Mary and sending it by way of a friend who could put the letter in a diplomatic pouch. She needed to be alone to find the best words, to warn her dear friend away from James's infernal trade.

When Lizzie finished and went upstairs, she found Ned and Rowland had taken the larger bed, so she settled, only half undressed, into the small trundle near the window. Though exhausted, when she nodded off, her legs jerked her awake, as if she were again fleeing that rotten prison.

In the dark, listening to Rowland and Ned breathe like sleeping angels, Lizzie tried to assess what she felt most deeply in what other people might call her soul. Their cousin Tamsin claimed to find her deepest feelings in her heart and fingers. Lizzie didn't feel anything beneath her ribs except a thumping pulse. She felt things in her belly and her eyes. She should feel in her fingertips, since she liked to spend every possible hour plying her needle. But instead, her eyes felt it. And they burned now, as if seeing again those frightened children under the dim light of that wretched warehouse prison.

Wind rattled the window's insufficient casement, then it whistled through the chamber, ruffling her hair. It looked to be a long winter ahead.

5
Preparations

— NED —

TUESDAY MORNING

THE FOG WAS GONE in the morning, chased off by a nighttime rain. The clouds drifted, higher in the sky than Ned had seen for days. After Rowland set out to give Lizzie's letters to the courier and to settle all business with the harbormaster, Ned and Lizzie set out with Countess to retrieve the children and execute a host of tasks:

> Hire a wagon with a waxed cover and a driver willing to go into Cambridgeshire.
>
> Hire women from the almshouse to travel as nursemaids.
>
> Find a mercer and hand over most all the coins in his pockets for capacious shawls, flannel shifts, baize smocks, woolen stockings, and decent shoes. For children and nursemaids.
>
> Purchase straw bedding and blankets.
>
> Add knit caps, mittens, two balls, and six soft dolls.
>
> Ask the innkeepers' wife to pack several baskets of food.

"We'll do a proper job with the young'uns," the smaller of the two said in a Somerset accent.

"'Twas us'uns washed and fed 'em last night."

Carrying their own small bundles, the nursemaids formed the girls in two lines, ready to depart. However, at the wagon, the girls cried for Tia Ysabel. Lizzie listened, her hands touching each girl's shoulder, patting their hands. They feared that Tia Angelina would never find them if they left.

"I promise you," Lizzie said, "I will find her."

At last, the girls climbed up into the wagon and settled into their places.

Ned said, "How will you make good on that promise?"

Lizzie shrugged. "I have a slim idea that I'll work on in London. Or perhaps I'll be humiliated by my own pride."

"Young gentlemen!" A man called from outside the inn. It was the harbormaster. "Is Lord Marborne about?"

Ned approached, holding out his hand in greeting. "Good morning, Master. Lord Marborne went down to the harbor in search of you."

"He did? Oh, ah…" The man shifted nervously. His eyes darted as he sought words.

"Aye," Ned said. "His lordship wanted to be sure he'd paid all he owed for the trouble you took on his behalf."

"Trouble? No, it's—oh, your lordship!" The harbormaster stepped past them. Rowland had returned. Countess left Lizzie's side to bound over and jump on his master.

Rowland greeted the nervous man heartily. "Good morning, Mr. Keckilpenny. I wanted to ask how much more of my purse I need to leave with you."

"My lord." Keckilpenny stepped close to Rowland and spoke so low that Ned couldn't hear what panic-inducing business had brought the fellow in search of Rowland.

"What?" Rowland's voice rose. The girls were clamoring for Lizzie, so that Ned never heard more than the harbormaster's farewell after Rowland counted coins into the man's hand.

The girls wanted Countess to ride with them. Fortunately, the dog liked the girls' adoration enough to bear being away from Rowland. Then they were on the road at last. When the carriage left the last Bristol cottages behind, Rowland said, "That must rank among the most expensive journeys ever made to Bristol."

Lizzie asked, "Did Mr. Keckilpenny demand more coin for your ship having burned to ash in his harbor?"

"No, nothing like that." Rowland tucked a blanket over Lizzie's lap. "Sir Bythorn extorted five gold guineas from Keckilpenny in return for not telling the king that the harbormaster allowed the *Skylark* to dock in Bristol harbor. And that the local militia lost the cargo. He didn't ask, but I gave him five guineas from my purse as recompense, since it was my ship and no fault of his."

Ned said, "You were right, Lizzie. Sir Bythorn is a poor sort of fellow."

"Being right," she said, "brings me no joy."

"I fear we haven't seen the last of Sir Bythorn." Rowland was drumming his fingers on the window ledge, looking out at the unremarkable landscape. He stopped drumming, examined his hands. "Do you want my gloves, Lizzie? Don't say no just to be stubborn."

"Ned bought me a new pair when we outfitted the girls."

"Good. What do you next need most, Lizzie?"

"To torch the house of every man who invested in the *Skylark*. To sell their sons to Barbary pirates."

Ned choked with shock, but Rowland remained as cool as ever. "Alas, our restoration rules don't allow revenge. There's too little to be gained by practicing cruelty on others."

She pulled on her new gloves. "What do I want? To prove I'm as good at planning a restoration as you and Tom have been."

"You have the strength and wit." Rowland put his hand over hers. "It will take time to plan."

Lizzie said, "I expect to execute a plan by Twelfth Night. But it's best if you don't participate in this gambol. It'll be safer for Marborne if you aren't involved in any new business related to Africa."

"Fine. I shall have my hands full," Rowland said, "trying to collect insurance on the burned ship."

"I wager," Lizzie said, "you'll be old and grey before you see a farthing."

Ned said, "Rollo, do not take that wager."

"Seriously, love, please share your plan's bare essence."

"We shall inspect each member of Withersea's syndicate that invested in the *Skylark*. Then we'll make them pay for the future of all the people who came to England on that devil ship."

"How?" Ned said.

"They'll beg to invest in a new syndicate that promises to make them wealthy. After they've put up their money to join, the money and its banker will disappear."

"The way that Rollo lured Danvers Duncombe into a foolish and false investment?"

"Grander," Lizzie said. "Watch me."

—

All through the journey from Bristol, as the carriage jolted over roads that needed tending, Ned noticed that the trio in the carriage seldom spoke, each deep in their own thoughts. Rowland read from a book he'd fished from his pocket, likely Shakespeare. Blessedly, he refrained from reading aloud. Lizzie stared out the window. Ned had never known her to sit for more than five moments without embroidering a shirt, or tatting braid, or making lace. Yet she only clutched and unclutched her hands while (most likely) scheming to punish the *Skylark* investors.

Ned considered painting his sister again, this new one with a fire smoldering inside her. Whenever he set about a new portrait, he first had to confront how drastically she and he differed, which came down to their fathers. Lizzie lost her parents when she was two, while Ned had been guided by his father until four years ago. Jan Wijck had given Ned his pale hair and skin, and had taught Ned more Dutch expletives than even Perry knew. Ned had learned to paint from that man, who'd apprenticed to a Dutch master. It was from Jan Wijck that Ned had inherited an all-consuming desire to paint.

But Lizzie went to serve in a princess's court and grew to be enamored with all the royalist claptrap their cousins had inherited from their fathers. He'd painted her a dozen times and knew exactly how to mix a palette that captured the light emanating from her. The base was a common cane color, but Ned added more burnt sienna and iron oxide. His experiments proved that Van Dyck brown was as unreliable as his father claimed. In its place, Ned used finely powdered earth taken from under a walnut tree, the one near where Revelstone laundry was boiled.

He always painted Lizzie in Merry Widow yellow or, when he could afford the minerals, gold. This time, he'd best paint her wearing Bristol red, the color of a firebrand glowing hot enough to steam a bowl of punch. In fact, he'd best forget about painting her for now. After this journey, she wasn't likely to sit still again for even an hour's time. The most cultivated and refined person in their family had become a wild, fire-bred creature.

He set his mind to think on a picture he'd like to paint this autumn: the orphaned girls under oak trees at Revelstone House, as if it were Eden, as if to paint over the dark terrors of Bristol and their journey to England. After arranging a palette in his mind and the direction from which the light would fall, he tried to imagine his dear friend Perry in the composition.

No, it couldn't work. Revelstone would not serve as the girls' Eden, only a safe place that might lessen the nightmares they suffered when they slept.

Besides, Perry was too large. And Ned had no idea what Lizzie might say about depicting the children in a mythic way. His friend Simon Touchstone, who'd been securing portrait commissions for Ned, claimed that mythic compositions were the rage for wealthy men in London. But if Ned wanted to paint even one of the girls, it must be a pastoral. And it could not include a figure who'd be misinterpreted as Goliath.

No matter. Perry only appeared in the imagined painting because what Ned wanted most at this journey's end was to see Perry again.

Would he and Perry even manage time alone to talk? The arrival of Lizzie and her girls at Revelstone would prompt a ricochet of activity. Mrs. Bell, the housekeeper, would declare, "We need only air out linen and wool blankets. You'll all be cozy as can be." Then she'd dash up to the attic to unpack clothes the Foxe cousins had outgrown two decades earlier. Tamsin and her dear friend Camilla would take the girls to see the garden and to meet the animals in the great barn.

In the kitchen, there'd be fresh bread, honey, and butter that tasted of home. He'd eat it and lick his fingers. And Perry would come in, saying, "Welcome home, sweet chucking," with that small, teasing smile that lit Ned's heart afire.

Ned felt pure longing to be home, to share everything with Perry—and to not share a hired room with his sister and his cousin. He craved Perry's company, as if he'd never known loneliness until he'd suffered this many days away from the man's irresistible presence.

He'd tell Perry how Lizzie had gone mad, rescuing six girls like a warrior-saint. How the girls torched Rollo's bedeviled ship. How Rollo's dog chewed up the rector's surplice when Lizzie begged sanctuary in a tiny church. That one moment of the adventure made Ned smile each time he remembered it.

As the carriage jerked along the road into Cambridgeshire, Ned accepted that there'd be no painting of autumnal idyls this year. And no snowy rural landscapes when winter came. All he could paint from Revelstone would be a basket of apples and a jar of honey for a still life. No pastorals with Lizzie's rescued girls.

Lizzie would send him to London. He and Perry would chase down the investors in the *Skylark,* while making sure Lizzie didn't catch on fire while running her gambol.

PART II

A SWASHING OUTSIDE

January, 1686
London

—

CELIA
I'll put myself in poor and mean attire
and with a kind of umber smirch my face;
the like do you. So shall we pass along
and never stir assailants.
ROSALIND
Were it not better,
Because that I am more than common tall,
that I did suit me all points like a man?
A gallant curtal-axe upon my thigh,
a boar-spear in my hand, and in my heart
lie there what hidden woman's fear there will,
we'll have a swashing and a martial outside—
as many other mannish cowards have
that do outface it with their semblances.
CELIA
What shall I call thee when thou art a man?
ROSALIND
I'll have no worse a name than Jove's own page,
and therefore look you call me Ganymede.

— William Shakespeare, *As You Like It*

6
Twelfth Night

— LIZZIE —

MONDAY NIGHT

AT THE DUKE OF BAGSHAM'S Twelfth Night masque, a string quartet played from the gallery, the tones of the sonata as delicate as the champagne and marmalade tarts.

The music did not calm Lizzie's excited state. This was the first public foray, a test for her gambol, which would conclude on Friday. She intended to enjoy the night, though slightly compromised by worry that her false moustache might fail. Plus, a quiet urge nagged her to visit the necessary. How to manage that as Viscount Orlando?

She'd last worn a mask to perform a restoration with Tamsin and Ned as highwaymen. She'd never gone among nobility dressed as someone else. Another unease grew when she discovered her fashion *faux pas*. Though she'd chosen her costume carefully, she'd missed learning that this year's mode called for feathered opera masks. She wore an out-of-vogue gilt-rimmed domino, unsuited to Orlando, who was the sort of fellow who'd always be *au courant*.

She relaxed while she did what she'd come here for: to observe the success of her actors among the guests, and to eavesdrop on guests who'd been the *Skylark's* investors. Those men all proved talkative after many decanters of the duke's delicate wine had been passed by liveried servants. To listen, she loitered alone near the foyer at the edge of the duke's ballroom, where the music didn't muffle voices in the crowd. Also, conveniently, she could check that her moustache remained intact.

A male voice spoke quietly behind her.

"When I greeted the duke, he assured me that he was happy to oblige me and had invited every man on my list. Was it you, Orlando, who made that request for me?"

"Rollo! I thought you were on the duke's errand in Oxford for another week."

"Hence, you felt free to steal my clothes? And to beg our best devil-drawer to forge a message from me to the duke?"

Overjoyed at Rowland's surprise appearance, she at first missed Rowland's censorious tone.

She said, "I forced Ned to write it. We needed to watch the *Skylark's* wealthy investors in society." She resisted the impulse to take Rowland's hand or embrace him, since a well-mannered gentleman wouldn't do that. "I'm happy you're here, so don't scold me for what you wouldn't know if you were in Oxford tonight. As you said you'd be."

"How many investors did I ask the duke to invite? Every name on the Hawkins' Heirs list?"

"No. A few men foolishly over-invested, like gamblers. So, the Withersea affair left them with no funds for our gambol. However, all investors have new pairs of servants who speak little English, as you predicted. Later, we'll perform a restoration to free their indentured servants." She said *indentured* harshly.

"It's a consolation that many of the people from the *Skylark* were placed in pairs," Rowland said, his voice softer now. "Then they're not all alone so far from their homes. But isn't it too cold to send people to Revelstone House?"

"I'm not that rash. And we have not progressed that far with my restoration plans. We're about to—"

"Stop. You insisted that I'm not to know details. For my own protection."

"You'll be safe, my lord."

At a pause in the music, the lofty tones of a London nobleman pierced the crowd noise.

"The Earl of Marborne is celebrating Twelfth Night without his dark senorita."

Sir Didlington huddled between two friends. The gawky, crane-like Mr. Cokayne offered a horse's whinny of a laugh. The young and extremely blond Earl of Gomfrey covered his mouth, pretending to be scandalized, his feathered mask pushed up on his forehead.

Lizzie had been watching that trio by way of a gilt mirror by the foyer. She now watched Rowland in the mirror. He wore a sober blue brocade suit with a mask of slashed black silk (which she'd formerly used for highway restorations). Thrilled to see him after a long, lonely week, Lizzie had a hundred things to say—but then caught her beloved's frown in the mirror.

"At least," he said, "Didlington didn't insult my affianced bride to her face. So, I don't have to defend her."

Rowland was annoyed, but with her, not that insulting trio. She chose to speak only to the insult they'd overheard.

"Sir Didlington also called Ysabel Foxe 'senorita' in Amsterdam, and again last summer at the Marquess of Withersea's dinner party. 'Senorita' is a thin insult."

"In this instance, though, Didlington meant to insult me, not Ysabel Foxe, because I'm here with a Catalan lord who's dressed as a gilded Ganymede. And wearing my best wig."

His smile twitched. Lizzie saw it as a judgment.

"I'm sorry, lambkin. Truly, I'd prefer to come as myself, without bindings and a foppish court suit. But Perry and Tom think it's best for Ysabel Foxe to be gone from London while we run our gambol."

Rowland studied her in the mirror. "Yet if Ysabel Foxe were here, then…"

A matched pair of liveried servants offered tall glasses of pale wine. Rowland took one and offered it to Lizzie.

"No, gracias." Lizzie spoke in Spanish while hoping to pass for a Catalan viscount.

I can't make it through the night if I drink even one drop.

Rowland took a long sip of the wine, too busy judging her to recognize the servants that she'd taken great pains to have hired specially for this fête.

Lizzie addressed the liveried pair in the Italian that all the actors had practiced. *"Grazie, amici.* How goes the night?"

The taller boy said, "Your Italian merchants are quite talkative. And popular. They seem to have mastered the accent."

"Venetian," Lizzie corrected. "Italian is the language. The Republic of Venice is the state."

"Grazie. Yet most men here call those merchants Italian."

Rowland said, "My business agent said the Venetians refused all invitations into English society. The men only wanted to lease my ships and quit England." Then he blinked, at last seeing Perry's brothers, Daniel and Neriah. "Oh, hello. Are you working for—well, who?"

"These foreign merchants," Daniel said, "let their servants have the night off to earn extra English coin."

Neriah said, "The actors that Felicity hired came tonight to practice their accents. *Per favore. Grazie. Posso offrirti più vino?"* He offered Lizzie a glass of wine again.

She declined, while longing to accept.

"We must be off," Daniel said. *"I tuoi amici* have empty glasses." He nodded toward Ned and Perry, who stood near that trio of insulting gentlemen.

Neriah said, *"Mi scusi, signore. Devo andare."*

Rowland grimaced after the pair departed. "God blind me! They're my servants and wearing my clothes. At least Ned and Perry aren't wearing any of my suits."

She grimaced too. "I confess that I did borrow velvet suits for Michael and Felicity." She tipped her chin toward two faux-Venetians merchants who were chatting with the Duke of Bagsham.

Rowland's jaw tightened. "You drafted Michael Oakes into your circus. He's *my* secretary. Is all your crew here tonight?"

"Our Mercutio has a bad cough and couldn't come. Now, what were you saying?" Lizzie prompted. "That if Ysabel Foxe were here, what?"

"I'd be holding her hand instead of balling my fists in my coat pockets."

"You know better," she said. "Your pocketed fists ruin the line of your clothes, which makes extra work for your servants."

"It's a shame Ysabel Foxe isn't here to see how elegantly the lace cuffs she made drape from my wrists when I kiss the hands of other women."

"Did you kiss the Countess of Gomfrey's hand?"

"I did. It's damp even through cotton gloves and it smells of lavender. Meanwhile, Viscount Orlando, you have deceived the duke with your actors and made him invite the men marked for a gambol. And suborned my servants to raid my wardrobe. You couldn't at least hire suits for your actors?"

"No. I gave Tom and Perry all my money for actors and the other arrangements for this Friday's event. I'm forced to borrow money from Ned until Tom disburses our next allowance."

"And then you'll buy indentures for every person from the *Skylark* that you find?"

"Will you be mad if I say yes?"

"No, I expect it. I'm curious about when it will happen."

"We'll act on their indentures after Friday's gambol, which will fund that next part of the restoration."

"It's sad that the impoverished Ysabel Foxe isn't here. She loves fêtes like these. Clever masks, heavenly music. Alas, I'm here with a Ganymede who's hunting prey like a wild cat."

"You are here with the most sophisticated member of the Foxe family." Lizzie shifted to stand the way Perry had coached her. Then she changed the subject, since she couldn't argue persuasively there in the ballroom. "Do you know the man who just joined Sir Didlington?"

"It's Wolfric Molewood, the builder and insurance man." Rowland said. "He's a principal in the syndicate that refuses to pay out on the *Skylark's* insurance."

The broad-shouldered man wore a fire-red brocade suit with the thinnest string of a mask over his hooded eyes. Famous actors padded their costumes to appear that manly, but Lizzie thought a good friend should recommend a tailor so the man's clothes might hang better. He wasn't as tall as Rowland, closer to Lizzie's height. His powdered hair formed a pronounced widow's peak, almost down to his dark, winged eyebrows. A perpetual pout shaped his mouth above a tidy beard that Ned might call a Van Dyck, named for a dead court painter. Two streaks of grey ran down the pointed beard, as if Molewood breathed out twin streams of cigarillo smoke.

"Um diabo," Lizzie said. "He hasn't accepted his invitation to Friday's gambol. He's the wealthiest man on the list. Ned and I are pursuing another way to coax him into investing his fortune in the *Skylark* people's future."

Rowland said, "Your Mr. Molewood is busily telling people that he's just been elected to the House of Commons."

"Yes. Tom says Molewood wanted the office for immunity from all the legal suits brought against him for his deadly building practices. And in hopes of a title."

"How curious. Will you mind, Lord Orlando, if I chat with Molewood while he's in an expansive mood?"

"Go, Rollo, since I cannot flirt with you here. Tell him he needs a better tailor. Then tell me later how a man enjoys being elected to a prorogated parliament."

Rowland went off to satisfy his curiosity about the man.

Lizzie pondered what the king's prorogation of Parliament had done for her. Men she pursued were absorbed in what it meant for the king to disallow Parliament to meet. She was able to work elements of her plan—like getting these investors invited to the duke's fête—while people were overly focused on the king.

When Lizzie passed by Rowland a few moments later, Molewood's voice reached her over the din of the crowd.

"Lord Marborne, are you joining the new syndicate to buy into Venetian shipping? I hear your Spanish cousin is putting in all his money and urging others to join."

Egad! Rollo doesn't know Orlando is the tout for our gambol.

Rowland showed no surprise. "Men around the port say it's a sure thing. Alas, every farthing I have is promised elsewhere right now. And I must say, Viscount Orlando de Flores is my fiancée's cousin, not mine. He dwells in a more extravagant world than do I."

Under the candelabra, Rowland's amber eyes flashed bright when she passed, but he didn't look her way. Mayhap he'd forgiven her trespasses. He performed so well in that impromptu moment with Molewood, she wished they hadn't agreed to keep him out of her restoration scheme.

—

The string quartet was busy with a fast-tempo Italian masque that involved too many notes, and which failed to relieve Lizzie's many anxieties. She worried about the likely failure of her moustache, about needing the gentlemen's necessary, and about possible unmasking of her faux Venetians.

She wandered through the chandeliers' shimmery haze to eavesdrop on the duke where he chatted with one of his Venetian guests. That was Michael Oakes, the riskiest of her actors, since he'd often met the duke as Rowland's secretary. The diminutive and nearsighted duke was bound to get a crick in his neck talking to the Venetian signore. The duke wore a court suit trimmed with gold braid and only a tri-horned jester's hat as his costume. But then, the duke couldn't keep his spectacles in place if he wore a mask.

"I don't know how you do it, signore," the duke was saying. "You've been in England only two months, yet they say you've found investors and leased a pair of English ships. You are a magician, Signore di Bassanio."

The counterfeit signore had dressed as Caesar in gold velvet and spoke English with a thick but penetrable accent. "Our family learns business from the cradle. We've had a monopoly on China silk for generations. But in this modern world, we need English partners to avoid pirates. No one can sail from the Mediterranean into the Atlantic without an English ship's pass."

"Peace with the Barbary pirates proves we Englishmen are great diplomats." The duke beamed, always his most jovial self when he hosted a crowd.

His Venetian guest said, "And we are good at bartering with Englishmen."

Having come to observe how well her actors performed, Lizzie judged that Michael Oakes offered a commanding performance as Signore di Bassanio.

But then a squeaking voice interrupted. "Signore, if I may advise. You must add maritime insurance to your investments. Too many ships come to naught, even with an English pass and an English flag."

It was that customs man from Bristol, with his thin nose, square jaw, and milky eyes, now hooded by a cheap satin mask even more out of fashion than Orlando's. The squeal of his voice roused ugly memories.

"Sir Bythorn Chudrakes." The duke greeted him, though not seeming to appreciate the interruption.

"My nephew," the signore gestured toward Felicity Oakes (in one of Rowland's best velvet suits), turning Sir Bythorn's attention across the room, "might be happy to discuss business with you." He spoke more intimately to the duke. "I admire your fresco. Is the artist from Florence? Rome?"

"No, signore," the duke said, apparently forgetting Sir Bythorn. "It's by an English artist. A Mr. Wijck, who hails from Cambridgeshire. Had a Dutch master, or so I've heard."

Perry, standing nearby, touched Ned's elbow, as if to awaken him. Wine glass in hand, Ned had been staring at another painting across the room. He roused at Perry's poke, yet didn't take the opportunity to approach the duke.

Meanwhile, like a frigate stuck in a blockade, Sir Bythorn could not sail past the duke to advance on the other Venetian merchant. He glanced around and found Orlando watching him. Yet he didn't recognize the person who'd insulted him in Bristol.

For the first time that night, Lizzie felt completely confident in her costume.

The talk about the fresco had caught Mr. Molewood's attention. He left Rowland with a curt bow and went to importune on the duke, asking about the fresco, because he planned one for his home and was in search of an artist.

"Mr. Wijck was recommended to me," the duke said, "by Simon Touchstone, the art dealer."

These words tickled Lizzie's ears. The duke, without knowing it, served as tout for her scheme to lure Molewood into the gambol. Knowing he was an art collector, she'd been striving to get Ned the painter into the man's house (with Perry following, to prowl). But before she could be sure of the duke's effect on Molewood, the forlorn customs man stepped close and blocked her view of Molewood. She did not want that man anywhere near her scheme. She tapped his shoulder.

"I believe we've met before, *senyor.*" She deepened her false accent and offered her hand in greeting. "I'm Orlando de Flores. It's Byspine Chudthorn, isn't it, of the Bristol customs house? We met when the *Skylark* came to port."

"It's Sir Bythorn Chudrakes, sir." His shoulders rose, then he must have decided not to take offense. "Of the king's customs commission here in London."

"Bless me, I promise not to forget again, Sir Bythorn. You gave my cousin Marborne advice about insurance."

"And you were the foreign cousin with a mad desire for African artifacts."

No, that was Ned, wanting Malaysian woods and minerals. I was the one burning in fury over the missing people.

"It was a disappointing night," she conceded, keeping her temper at a simmer.

"You should advise Lord Marborne," Sir Bythorn said, "to hire an agent and auction his insurance stake. It's a gamble, but better than waiting for an insurance syndicate to pay."

"Ha, such a jester you are, Sir Bythorn. Can you imagine the Earl of Marborne taking business advice from me?"

"Yet I hear that Marborne did well with the Venetian merchants, leasing them his two ships."

"They are Venetians? Not sure Marborne even knows which foreign merchants leased his boats," she said, as if ignorant. "Just between us, *senyor*, the Earl of Marborne has the kind of face that leads other men to take advantage of him."

She deplored the customs man as much as she disliked the farrago around the *Skylark's* insurance. Yet she let him repeat his advice before she said *bona nit* and wandered away, still believing he'd had a hand in the disappearance of the *Skylark's* people and their reappearance in London as indentured servants.

Ned and Perry soon made polite farewell bows to the duke. They had another chore that evening: to prowl the houses of investors who'd be staying late at the duke's fête. Only after the pair departed the fête did it occur to Lizzie that Ned might have helped her with the gentlemen's necessary. A missed opportunity. She looked yearningly down the long hall where several men gathered to smoke cigarillos.

Rowland was alone again near the foyer when she came up behind him. He caught her reflection in the mirror. His enquiring eyebrow arched. His lips twitched into a smile. Perhaps she was forgiven for coming here as Orlando and deceiving the duke. Perhaps she had her next opportunity for the gentlemen's room.

How you'll smile, Rollo, when I ask my next favor!

"My lord," she began, "may I importune for—"

"Marborne."

The Duke of Bagsham appeared suddenly. He seized Rowland's sleeve, stretching the earl's blue brocade coat down over the diaphanous French lace cuffs, which Lizzie had made.

"Where's your fiancée, Marborne? I'd hoped to have Miss Foxe's beauty and wit to enliven this evening."

7
A Mere Suggestion

— LIZZIE —

MONDAY NIGHT

VISCOUNT ORLANDO PREPARED TO greet the duke, but judging from the duke's nearsighted gaze, he hadn't seen that Rowland had company. Lizzie stepped back, but not out of hearing.

No use trapping Rollo into more than the usual number of lies.

Rowland said, "Miss Foxe contracted a bad cough at Christmas and remains at Revelstone House. She will deeply regret missing this fête."

"Sorry to hear it. At least your friends are here." The duke had made himself Rowland's mentor and closest link to King James. Rowland needed to keep the duke happy.

"It was kind of your grace to invite them."

"However, I must say, your Continental cousin, Viscount Orlando, was rather aggressive tonight, seeking introductions to the Venetians you asked me to invite. And that customs man your cousin was chatting with? Not a useful acquaintance. He won't rise further in the king's commission."

"I appreciate the advice, your grace."

"And I saw you with Gomfrey and his set." Though nearsighted, the duke indicated that trio across the room who now chatted with Molewood. "They are dissolute gamblers. Don't let your cousin drag you into such bad company."

"I treasure your guidance, duke. I see both the danger and the limited use of that customs fellow. However, Orlando is Miss Foxe's cousin. He and I don't seem to have much in common."

Rowland pursed his lips, eying Lizzie in the mirror. The duke, however, didn't notice, perhaps because her borrowed court suit blended in with the wallpaper.

"Ah, here's a man you must meet, Marborne. One of the five honest men in London." The duke again pulled Rowland's coat sleeve down over the delicate lace cuff. "Sir Oliver! I'm honored that you could join us tonight."

"Your grace." The man offered a deep bow. His eyes flashed to Rowland. Fortunately, Orlando still seemed to be invisible, since Lizzie wasn't sure she'd pass for a Continental lord if inspected by one of the most honest men in London.

"Have you met our new friend, the earl?" The duke put Sir Oliver's hand in Rowland's. "Rowland Foxe, the honorable Earl of Marborne, this is Sir Oliver Boxworth, England's best jurist."

"You are too kind, your grace." Sir Oliver shook hands without distressing Rowland's cuff. "I'm pleased to meet you, your lordship. I met your cousin, Mr. Thomas Foxe, last summer. He is quite a promising barrister. Is he here tonight?"

"Alas, no," Rowland said. "Tom's been struck low with croup. Half my family took ill at Christmas."

Their tête-à-tête continued, with Rowland being his charming self, his eyes flashing to Lizzie in the mirror only twice. Then a woman (the justice's wife or sister?) called Sir Oliver away.

The duke returned his attention to Rowland like an eagle on a hare, seizing that lace cuff as if to rip the life from it. Being two heads shorter than Rowland and comfortably round, he didn't typically appear to be a predator. Yet the pouncing eagle conceit seemed apt. The duke's jovial nature disappeared as he mashed his spectacles more firmly on his nose.

"Marborne, drop your insurance claim on that poxed ship."

"But it's a perfectly legal claim."

"Do not waste your time or reputation. The *Skylark* burned and then washed away on the tide. Forget about it."

Indeed, it had burned, which was why Rowland needed insurance to pay for its loss.

"I don't see—" Rowland began.

"Forget it!" The duke had a habit of interrupting. "You bring too much attention to the ship's African adventure. The king owns all attention to Africa."

"Yet my insurance claim is drawing out men who invested in Withersea's blind syndicate." His mouth set in an obstinate line; Rowland was not retreating from the powerful duke.

"Some of whom," the duke said, "are also investors in the Royal African Company. And who invested with Withersea only to keep a watchful eye on the marquess."

Heigh ho! Perry had not discovered that while prowling!

Rowland shook his head, refusing the advice. "Are all those men good watchers? Or are some playing both sides, investing in the king's charter while poaching on his monopoly?"

"Marborne, you waded into a murky swamp. Now you're thrashing in the mud." The duke gave a curt nod. "Give up on the *Skylark*. It was a gift. You didn't invest your own money."

Back in August, the same day Rowland resigned his commission as an intelligencer for the king's militia, the duke coerced Rowland into becoming a watcher for the king. That later grew into a guarded partnership between the duke and the earl, with Lizzie also promising service to the king, as the safest choice for the Foxes, for Marborne. Though neither held deep respect for this king, their Uncle Absolom had assigned service to the Crown to both Rowland and Lizzie as their duty.

The duke frowned. Rowland folded his arms, stretching his coat's brocade over his admirable shoulders that Lizzie very much admired.

I look like a withered leek in Rollo's suit. I need padding.

"Find new secrets, your grace?" Rowland struck his friendliest tone while rigid with anger. "I know one. Most of the House of Commons are annoyed that James prorogated Parliament. And another secret: Every man in England resents paying taxes while James spends English treasure on a standing army when there's no war here or on the Continent."

"I know you now, Marborne." The duke rubbed his small hands, then mashed his spectacles again, peering up at Rowland. "I know you'll express your pique to me, yet you'll never tell another soul about your grudge against the king."

"Pardon my temper, your grace." Rowland didn't sound at all sorry. "It's mere disappointment, not a grudge. Perhaps I shall instead investigate whether the *Skylark's* cargo was stolen from the king when customs men failed to seize it."

"Your fiancée speculated about that when you last came to supper with me."

"She thinks you and I should be suspicious that malefactors might be at play."

Suspicious? No, I'm absolutely certain of it.

"I have inquired quietly," the duke said.

"And I have dined with a few lords who boast new African servants. Hence, I shall proceed—"

"Please, Lord Marborne, do not seek to reveal that some of the king's closest advisers invested where they shouldn't." The duke plucked at Rowland's cuff again.

This time, Lizzie heard the screech of tiny tears in delicate lace. Which had taken her two days with bobbins and needles, another day to block and then stitch onto his best linen shirt.

"Come, Lord Marborne. Find new secrets to pursue. I *recommend* that you disassociate your name from Africa in the king's mind." He snatched away his spectacles, holding them between thumb and forefinger. "Now, excuse me. I must attend to my guests. It's too bad your lady-love isn't here for this splendorous Twelfth Night."

The duke raised his hand—a dismissal? a blessing? perhaps only a wave?—and walked away. He was soon kissing a lady's hand and then whispering in her husband's ear.

No grabbing cuffs and tearing lace among those guests.

"I have seen a splendorous woman," Rowland murmured. "That is Ysabel Foxe in the glittering gold gown she made with her own needle and wore to supper with the duke. Far more handsome than any woman here."

A balm to her ears. Still, the duke's words dropped like hot stones into the cauldron that had steamed inside her since that day in Bristol.

—

After the duke left, Lizzie applied every lesson she'd learned in Mary Stuart's court to keep any trace of emotion from her face. She twisted her lips into a civilized smile, so no one saw the enraged animal inside. A panther, perhaps. A bigger beast than the wild cat Rowland had called her.

When she could finally speak in a soft voice, rather than growl, she said, "Ah, my dear lambkin."

"'O, how full of briars is this working-day world!'"

"I'm relieved that you've unfettered your inner Bard. I've missed his sage words. Will you do as the duke suggests?"

Rowland faced her directly, rather than watching her in the mirror. "It wasn't a suggestion."

"No, but the duke cannot command your actions."

"It was a threat from higher than the duke."

"For all you've done for the Crown, Rollo, why must you be treated like a lowly servant?"

"Whatever the duke or the king might suggest, I will do what I must to protect Marborne. Our family. You."

Rather than pouring cold water on her fury, his words generated more steam. She said, "James wants to send every one of his enemies to the gallows. He's dismayed most of England by promoting his Catholic friends. He's a slavemonger who insists on his monopoly."

"Yet men worry the most about the king's growing friendship with Louis in France. However, let us cease such talk here." He touched her hand, as if to cool her heat.

"I am beyond sorry, lambkin, to have let the knot in my stomach get the best of me."

"Knot in your stomach? Some call that feeling anger." His quizzical brow rose. "Others might call it burning rage. But a princess's lady-in-waiting never has such feelings."

"Indeed. It was poor form, letting my ire spring free."

"What could have caused that accident?" Mercifully, he chose to tease.

"I'm unhappy that I cannot share my work with you, which I...which I..." She still didn't have that burning sense in her belly under full control.

"We both must do things in secret to protect everyone we are responsible for."

"But what will you do about the duke's warning?"

"I shall do the same as you. Will you leave off asking questions about Africa?"

"No. The duke's threat is only an impediment I hadn't foreseen. It's not insurmountable."

"I assumed as much," Rowland said. "I believe it's snowing again. Do you want to share a carriage back to Covent Garden?"

"With pleasure, my lord."

"Once we're in the carriage and on our way..." Rowland's brow rose toward the curls of his periwig.

"Yes, Rollo?"

"You will cease calling me 'my lord' and allow me to take off that accursed moustache. It holds no attraction for me."

"I will enjoy the carriage with you more, Rollo, if I can importune for a favor before we depart."

"Anything, my heart's gleam."

"Run a blockade, lambkin, so that I might I use the gentlemen's necessary."

Later, in the carriage and still laughing, Rowland removed her moustache. He said, "I cannot lie to you. I am worried."

"I hope you're fine with lying to the duke."

"Aye, have no fear." He clutched her hand. "But while you run your restoration gambol, Lizzie, please allow me to draw all attention from the duke and the king. And also..."

"What? I won't bite your head off for asking."

"Allow me to discover who among Hawkins' Heirs also invested in the Royal African Company. Then you must eliminate them from your gambol."

"Fine," she said. "Do you agree that Ysabel Foxe must remain absent from London for a spell?"

"Yes. I'll ask Lazarus to give Orlando a room at Xanthus House. And I'm sorry I was peevish tonight."

"And I'm sorry I couldn't forewarn you about tonight." She clasped his hand. "Also, your butler Lazarus already gave Orlando the blue bedchamber at Xanthus House."

"Yes, of course he did. His intuition and foresight are legendary. Come morning, I'll ask Lazarus to buy new clothes for Orlando, who cannot go around London wearing my suits. It'd cause a scandal."

When she didn't answer, Rowland sighed. "You already asked Lazarus."

"No, I wouldn't presume. And I have no money for the next fortnight." Just as he began to stroke her lip, she said, "Lazarus thought of that himself. He suggested I wear this satin court suit tonight, likely in hopes I'll ruin it, since he doesn't consider it a proper garment for the Earl of Marborne."

"Tonight? It's now tomorrow morning," Rowland murmured. "The glue on your lip has honey in it, doesn't it?"

Then they fell to doing what they most liked to do in carriages when riding together in the dark.

8
Xanthus Kitchen

— LIZZIE —

TUESDAY EARLY MORNING

AT ROWLAND'S HOUSE IN Covent Garden, the halls echoed with their footsteps. The servants had all gone to bed. Lizzie followed when Rowland beckoned her down to the kitchen.

"It's a household tradition," he said. "Mrs. Flurry worries about my strength when I stay out late."

This house and its staff came to Rowland from the Duke of Bagsham, who'd previously maintained it for his nephew, who had also served the king as a watcher, but had been killed the previous summer in the battle that stopped the Duke of Monmouth's invasion. The small household staff was more discreet than any Lizzie had ever known, even in Mary's court.

A covered plate on the kitchen worktable contained sliced beef and cheese. A china bowl held fresh rolls wrapped in a thick towel. Other dishes offered stewed apples, mustard, butter, and two honey cakes.

"I'm happy just for a drink of water, lambkin."

He found a flagon and a cup for her, then fetched pewter plates, spoons, and a knife from the cupboard. While Lizzie drained her cup of water, Rowland poured wine from a jug. "I noticed that you didn't drink anything at the fête."

"No, lambkin. I haven't had anything since noon. I knew Orlando would spend the night wishing for the necessary."

"'Silver dishes for thy meat, as precious as the gods do eat, prepared each day for thee and me.'" The carriage ride had awakened the poet in him. "Welcome to my house, my love."

Last summer, when their cousin Tom was reunited with Aurora Rôche, who was then Lady Withersea, the events led to the establishment of two households in Covent Garden. Felicity Oakes inherited Chalgrove House and invited Aurora and Lizzie to join her. The men all came to reside at Rowland's house, which at first included Tom, Michael Oakes, and Tom's ward, Jacob Rôche, the young earl who was Aurora's brother. Perry and Ned had moved in when they returned to London in October from Revelstone House. Perry's many young brothers had been employed as footmen among both houses. For this week, Viscount Orlando must live at Xanthus House.

"There's a letter for you." Rowland handed it to her. "Someone brought it over from Chalgrove House."

"It's from Tamsin." Lizzie broke the seal. "Three entire pages of news."

"Read it to me." He was building bites of bread, meat, and cheese. He put a bite in her mouth with his fingers, which were warm. It took a moment before she could speak.

"Tamsin begins with the date, January the second, and then is so helpful as to tell us she writes from Revelstone House in Marborne Parish. As if she'd be anywhere else in the kingdom."

Rowland offered Lizzie another nugget of food with his fingers, which was pleasant, if awkward. Between bites, she read aloud, beginning with "Dearest Lizzie."

> First, everyone is safe—and happy. As you foresaw, the woman you hired, Nadia Aguila, is a perfect teacher for the girls. She is called Tia Nadia among us and Madam Aguila when visitors are present.

> Rather than setting up a classroom, Nadia has made all the parish their schoolroom. So, their lessons are nothing like what Uncle Absolom subjected us to whenever he bade us sit down in his study.

Lizzie read more of the chatty doings at Revelstone, pausing when Rowland offered bites of cheese and buttered bread. She didn't enjoy reading the next part aloud.

> I am strictly advised by Camilla to ask if you and Rollo have decided when you will be married. Camilla wants a celebration that requires coming to London to order a new gown. I only wish to find that you are both happy and well.

"Ha!" Rowland laughed. "You don't have time to think about it until you finish your restoration. If I am wise enough not to ask you repeatedly, Camilla can show similar restraint."

"Thank you for that."

"Though you once said you'd be done by Twelfth Night."

"By this Friday, I promise. I'm only a few days late."

"Still, Camilla will have to find another excuse to come to London, since we will be married in Marborne Church. Can we manage it by Candlemas?"

Until that moment, Lizzie hadn't seen that he'd united the two notions: finishing her restoration gambol would free her to begin marriage plans.

How can I make myself be ready, even after Friday?

She said, "Perhaps February is a bit of a challenge."

"May-day then. That way, you'll have fresh flowers." He spooned honey on a bite of bread, lifted it to her lips, then licked his fingers after she took it. "'The shepherds' swains shall dance and sing, for thy delight each May morning.'"

He stepped away to rummage in the buttery for more mustard while finishing the next lines from his Bard. "'If these delights thy mind may move, then live with me and be my love.'"

Because it was too late at night for a serious discussion, Lizzie did not read the last part of Tamsin's second page aloud.

> Now, I must say this brutally. These girls do not need you to wreak revenge for them. No revenge that you might pursue will help to repair the girls' lives.
>
> We cannot fully mend the tear in the fabric of their lives, since they were so evilly taken from their families. But they have new friends who help quiet their nightmares and their fears of this new world.

"Any more news?" Rowland set the stone jar of mustard on the table, rustling the first page, which Lizzie had set aside.

"They're learning to churn butter. They already knew how to milk cows. Camilla is teaching embroidery."

He reached for the third page and read it while smearing the last piece of beef with mustard.

"God blind me!"

"What? Read it aloud, Rollo, like I did." Even though she hadn't read all of the second page to him.

"I'll be briefer than Tamsin was. Our neighbor Lord Hawksmoor came to Revelstone for a morning visit after he returned from Paris. He was surprised by your girls, Lizzie. Asked if they were indentured servants like his friends have in London."

Poynter, Lord Hawksmoor, had been their neighbor and childhood friend. Until last summer, he'd been known as Viscount Heydon. But then his older brother's title came to him after the Danvers Duncombe affair, although only the Foxe cousins knew the details.

"Good stars! Did Tamsin tell the story we agreed upon?"

"Yes, that they are visiting cousins from your great-grandmother's side. Tamsin, however, is certain Hawksmoor didn't believe her. She is unhappy about having lied to him."

Lizzie said, "I'll tell Poynter the true story when we see him in London. Of course, he's just the sort of man to be curious about where the girls came from."

"Hawksmoor can't be the last man to wonder." Rowland began to clear away the remains of their repast. "We should sleep. I rode many miles in the snow to return from Oxford. I'm fatigued beyond telling."

"Yes. I have a big day tomorrow with much to do."

"And I have new business of my own to worry about."

"I wish that..." Lizzie began to speak, but Rowland put a warm arm around her shoulder and then claimed her lips.

"That? What?" he asked when he stopped to breathe.

"I wish we could work together, without secrets."

"One day soon," he said, claiming her lips again.

It was several moments before she could speak. "After Friday, as I have promised."

9
Russell Street

— NED —

TUESDAY MORNING

AT FIRST, NED BELIEVED that his early-morning meeting at Simon Touchstone's gallery had gone as well as he'd hoped. Of course, his agent was always amenable to any business Ned proposed. It was only that Mrs. Touchstone had set obstacles, such that negotiations had taken five days. She'd finally agreed that morning. After that success, Ned also acquired two varieties of umber that he felt crucial for this day's work. Hence, the day began well.

But then, Simon dragged Ned away to show him a new Lely and a village scene by Jan Steen—not the kind of work Simon typically dealt in. However, Simon was in an excited state, which interfered with peaceful observation. Ned remarked on it.

"Ned, come another time if you want to admire the Lely in solitude. I have something I must share with you." He dropped his voice to speak confidentially, though they were alone in the warehouse. "I am to become the exclusive agent for the new Lely works, the ones that Dutch fellow is finishing."

"That's fantastic news!" Ned exclaimed. "No one in London deserves it more than you."

"It's good news that comes after a patch of hard luck."

Then Simon related a reversal that froze Ned to his bones.

"We sold a Lely sketch two months ago, with the best provenance, but the man came back two weeks ago and declared it a forgery. When I went to his house to examine it, I found that it was a forgery, and not a good one. However, it wasn't the sketch I'd sold him."

"Zooterkins!"

"My friend, far worse words fell from my tongue." Simon frowned, not a natural look for him. "I returned his money and carried the work away. It was a costly loss."

"You didn't argue?" Ned's fingers turned numb and his heart hammered. Any discussion of forgery disturbed his peace.

Simon said, "The same fellow destroyed Gosebourne's business last summer, drove the man out of town. And all over two Rembrandts he questioned. I cannot afford that."

"What man did this?" Among the ten thousand fears this story let loose, Ned felt sure Simon wanted something from him. Was it for Ned to confess? He'd never confess to his good friend Simon all the forgeries Ned had sold, with Simon as his agent.

"It's the same wealthy Mr. Molewood that your cousin the viscount wants to pursue. It's why Hildegonda agreed today to help that scheme."

"Why agree to pursue more business with the man?"

"He can't claim your work as a forgery, Ned, since you'll be painting right in front of him. And you can look about his house. I have a list of all the art I've sold him. See if there are any more substitutes."

"I can do that."

Ned had been enlisted by Lizzie to become involved with this Molewood character solely to gain entry to the man's house, so Perry could prowl the way he and Rowland had as king's intelligencers on the Continent. Ned would now add to his tasks: discovering any art forgeries in Molewood's house.

"And..." Simon hesitated. "Molewood kept the original provenance for that Lely. See if you can retrieve it for me."

After that shocking moment, Ned quietly took his leave, remembering how he'd felt the previous night at the duke's ball, seeing that the duke had acquired one of Ned's forgeries and hung it where all of London could see. Including Mr. Molewood, who'd asked the duke about his fresco by Eduard Wijck.

This new element of Lizzie's gambol, to pry into Molewood's business, differed from the many investigations Ned had undertaken with Perry and Tom since October. Now, Lizzie's victory over Hildegonda Touchstone, winning the chance to approach Molewood disguised as Touchstone's agent, threatened to open the lion's den.

—

Ned had left Lizzie in conversation with Mistress Touchstone, where his sister likely heard the same story about Mr. Molewood that had upset Ned. Yet he knew that would not deter her. He began to worry in the way that frets the mind and eats at the soul, if there is such a thing.

In the January cold, Ned walked with his worrying head bent down, letting his hat and scarf do the work his coat might fail. Camilla had sent him a fine wool scarf as a Twelfth Night present, and he could now afford good thick-soled shoes to brave the frozen streets of London. Still, he counted it fortunate that his destination had a warm parlor, providing what he most needed while painting: warm toes, warm fingers.

It being the first Tuesday in January, it should be a day in which nothing happened in London. With Twelfth Night over, no more entertainment could be expected besides the nightly wassailing down by the frozen Thames. Or a pie and hot ale at The Rose, Perry Frake's favorite tavern, which Ned liked because fights seldom broke out there. It was at The Rose where Perry struck up his crucial new friendship with Ezra Pelletoot. Ned had only listened while imagining the palette he'd use to capture the ancient fellow's happy bloom, and whose eyes sparkled with life although he was half blind. That Tuesday morning, Ned was, in fact, on his way to paint the old man, hoping it'd stave off worrying about Lizzie and Mr. Molewood.

When Ned crossed Russell Street, a carriage veered so close that its lantern brushed Ned's shoulder and tipped his hat further over his eyes. He pushed his hat back in place, startled. Being lost in a reverie was his common state, however often Perry cautioned about keen awareness on London streets. Ned took that caution seriously at night, but not so much while walking in the day, especially when it had frozen so hard that the sounds off every footstep and rolling cart or carriage echoed between the buildings and—

Thick hands grabbed Ned from behind, trapping his arms in their grip. Another hand opened a carriage door, and Ned was thrust inside. His hat fell to the floor, and his shoes slipped when the carriage door clicked shut, trapping the hem of his coat. Startled, his hands shaking and heart pounding, Ned struggled to untangle from his coat until he could shift onto the seat in the front quarter of the carriage.

He faced his kidnapper: a short, wide man huddled in a pile of furs, an ermine hat covering his head.

"You might wonder why a stranger would stop you on the street." The words were breathed softly through the fur muffler that enveloped half the man's face.

Ned did not wonder, since this was not a stranger. It was the Duke of Bagsham, Rowland's mentor. Ned's pounding heart quieted, while his curiosity roared. How had the duke recognized Ned on the street or even knew where he'd be? Despite having painted that fresco in the man's house, Ned believed he was invisible in all previous encounters with the duke, being only a member of Rowland's coterie.

"I do wonder at the kidnap," Ned said. "But I know you, having painted your new fresco."

"Then you are also Eduard Wijck, the painter? I am so sorry to make you worry this way."

In truth, Ned had first fallen into a quagmire of worry at the previous night's fête, because he'd overheard the duke describe a painting in his ballroom as coming from a famous Dutch master's workshop. No, it was from Ned Wijck's Revelstone workshop, created three years ago to earn enough silver to pay Marborne taxes. He'd been consumed since last night by the notion that his past might cancel his future. After Simon's tale this morning, Ned worried more that his devil-drawing might be revealed, what with his forgery of a famous artist's painting being hung so near a fresco signed with Ned's unfamous name.

To Ned's eye, even a child could see the two were painted by the same person.

"You haven't worried me, your grace." Ned offered a pure falsehood.

"Well, well. Eduard Wijck is Ysabel Foxe's brother. How did I miss that intelligence?" The duke was not expecting an answer. He began to rummage under the mountain of furs swathing him. "Now where did I…"

Ned's heart pounded again, all because Simon Touchstone did not know he had sold Ned's forgery to the Duke of Bagsham. If even one of Ned's forgeries were ever called out, he'd be the one to ruin the Touchstones.

The duke produced a letter from under his pile of furs.

"Here it is. Mr. Wijck, I'm asked by…" he paused, "an esteemed but anonymous acquaintance who wishes to employ you to protect Miss Ysabel Foxe."

"My sister Lizzie?" This was a greater surprise than being snatched off a street in London—surprising enough to knock the fear of discovery from Ned's thoughts for the moment. "But why ask me, your grace? The more logical protector is our cousin Rowland, the Earl of Marborne."

"I have it on good authority that Miss Foxe does not often take Marborne's advice."

So true! But to agree felt disloyal to Rowland.

The duke didn't wait for Ned to answer that. "I'm authorized to offer you two hundred pounds to protect Miss Foxe's safety until Easter."

"Two hundred pounds?" An astounding figure. Especially for work Ned believed that he performed as a matter of course.

"Guineas then. If you insist."

"What precisely do you mean by protection, sir?"

"You must ensure that someone follows her at all times in London. Preferably, that will be you. But it must always be a trusted man who can intercede with force if she's in danger."

While Ned tried to imagine Lizzie accepting such protection (she wouldn't), the duke produced what he'd been rummaging in his furs to find. "Also, you must deliver this letter to Miss Foxe at your earliest opportunity."

"How did you come to be the envoy for this anonymous acquaintance?" Ned spoke his puzzlement aloud.

"It came in a diplomatic pouch—" The duke stopped, seeming to have said more than he intended. "Never mind. Just deliver it to Miss Foxe, please."

"I will do my best. However..." Ned smiled at the thought of Rowland, just that morning, advising them that if anyone asked, Ysabel Foxe was at Revelstone House. "My sister remained in Cambridgeshire after her last visit. She is ill."

"I–I–That is..." His captor seemed baffled for a moment. "Ah, yes. That's what Marborne said. Dear me."

"Aye, your grace. I can do my best to deliver this letter."

"I appreciate that. And I will appreciate your discretion. This exchange must be a secret between the pair of us."

"Yes, your grace."

"You may go now, Mr. Wijck."

Ned gathered his coat and hat, but just as his hand was on the carriage door, the duke cried, "Wait!"

"Yes, your grace?"

"Since you know who I am, you must consider my demand for secrecy to be a royal command."

"Aye, sir."

Back on the street, Ned stood for a minute, considering. That encounter must have begun with Mary Stuart. No one else beyond the Foxe family knew Lizzie well enough to seek to purchase her safety.

He set off for his mid-morning engagement, then stopped dead in the street, such that a pie seller collided with him, cursing Ned foully. Ned could barely cough out an apology, struck so hard with one thought: he'd been made to promise to keep secrets from his sister and his cousins. From Perry.

Ned was commanded to choose between loyalty to Perry and his family or to English royalty.

After two deep breaths, he found it an easy concern to shake off. There was only one choice: He'd keep the secret—unless Perry or Lizzie asked.

10
Threadneedle Street

— LIZZIE —

TUESDAY MORNING

LIZZIE HAD BEEN APPEARING as Viscount Orlando at every visit to Threadneedle Street for the past week. At the end of Tuesday morning's meeting, Hildegonda Touchstone finally agreed to write a letter of introduction for Orlando, who was to act as the agent to contract Ned's services with Wolfric Molewood.

Hildegonda rose the moment Ned and Simon went to see new paintings in the agents' warehouse.

"Come to the kitchen for tea, Lord Orlando. And I've some caraway biscuits you might like. You look a mite peaked." She beckoned with a finger for Lizzie to follow.

"Thank you, Mistress Touchstone. We were up late and out the door early."

> *Out so early, I forgot Orlando's moustache, which Mistress Touchstone had remarked upon instantly upon seeing me.*

The kitchen was tucked into a corner of the warehouse that was the Touchstones' home. A big-boned woman, Hildegonda Touchstone moved through her kitchen with grace. Since Hildegonda grew up in Holland, the cozy kitchen was immaculate.

"Here be my biscuits, fresh this morning."

She set out the plate and pointed to where her guest should sit by the worktable while she prepared tea, spooning leaves from a tin cannister into an ornate ceramic pot, then pouring hot water from the kettle that hung over the kitchen fire. She clamped a lid on the ceramic pot.

I'm in for it now. Ned warned me this woman could be harsh.

Because the kitchen was a more intimate space than a viscount might be invited into, Lizzie prepared for a polite dressing down. Or at least a sermon. To forestall any lecture, Lizzie said, "Your biscuits are delightful, Mistress Touchstone. The caraway seeds are a brilliant notion. You are a wonderful cook."

"Nay, not a bit. We aren't heathens. I employ a cook. She and Sarah, the maid, are off to the market."

Hildegonda regarded her guest, studying Lizzie with extreme frankness. She had a square face and seemed judgmental, but her bright blue eyes revealed extreme intelligence. Also, she had a northerner's perfect complexion, which made it hard to judge her actual age.

Lizzie felt backfooted. Not a suitable way to prepare for what was likely to be an upbraiding.

Be bold.

"I surmise, Mistress Touchstone, that you invited me here for private conversation."

"Simon, my mister, always buys whatever Ned brings to sell, which has worked for them both. Now my mister has bought Ned's proposal that you serve as our agent, to convince Wolfric Molewood to employ Ned to paint a fresco."

"It was kind of you to agree. You have been most kind in tutoring me to advance our efforts with Mr. Molewood."

It had taken days to convince Hildegonda, so that the daily tutorials about art had been tentative preparation until the woman suddenly conceded to the request.

"Yes. I disagree with your strategy, as far as you've explained your goal. Hence, I want to know your true intentions so that I can offer you a better strategy."

Hildegonda lifted the lid on the ceramic tea pot, then sniffed and nodded, satisfied. She set out two white porcelain cups that were so thin as to be translucent. As she poured tea, she said, "Ned Wijck gave me these china cups, to thank me for a favor. But to my mind, it was he who did the favor, letting us know we'd mistakenly taken in a stolen Lely sketch. I'm so grateful to him for that." She set down the tea pot. "Now, I'm known to be inquisitive. May I have your full story?"

Lizzie busily looked into her teacup. "I'm not comfortable sharing more of our intentions."

Hildegonda pinched off a piece of her biscuit, savoring it. "And I'm not comfortable sending you to Mr. Molewood when I can see that you aren't Orlando. Ned must have forgotten that I met Viscount Orlando last summer. He's taller. And has more masculine features."

Lizzie kept guilt from her face, intending not to be bullied by this woman. Hildegonda, however, did not wait for a response.

"I'm sure you're Ned's sister, since we've sold two paintings that feature your face and graceful hands."

Hildegonda's dressing down is not proceeding as I expected.

"Ah." Lizzie folded her hands, then unfolded them, not meaning to adopt the portrait pose Hildegonda had identified. "The uncle who raised us, Doctor Absolom Foxe, gave us a set of principles to guide our lives. One is 'I never fool an honest man.' Which also encompasses honest women. And so, I apologize for the deceit."

"I appreciate the apology. But I'd also like to help you with a better strategy for approaching Mr. Molewood, if you will share your true motivation. You seek more than the commission for a fresco, don't you?"

Lizzie sipped tea. She'd kept secrets for the Touchstones' protection, the way she protected Rowland.

Time to give it up.

"The King of England rewarded our cousin the Earl of Marborne with a ship that proved to be carrying people from Africa intended for the plantations. After the ship docked in Bristol, the prisoners aboard were stolen away and, we believe, sold into indentured servitude in London. By great good fortune, I rescued six girls amid all the chaos."

"And Mr. Molewood is involved how?"

"He was the largest investor in the syndicate that funded that ship's African venture. We want to know more about his business, because I want him to pay for that evil."

"What will you do if you succeed?"

Lizzie couldn't tell if she was being judged or if the question rose from Hildegonda's inquisitive nature.

But I've embarked on the course of honesty and cannot stop.

"You may call me foolish, Mistress Hildegonda, but I seek to take those people out of indenture and establish them as cottagers and farmers, to repair the harm done to these people by English business and English law."

Hildegonda fussed with the tea pot. "I hope we haven't let it steep so long that it's gone bitter." She added more hot water from the kettle over the fire and set down the pot, then studied Lizzie again. Lizzie stared back but quickly felt compelled to break the mutual examination.

"Your lace collar is quite lovely," Lizzie said. "Is it your own handiwork?"

"Nay. I traded an ivory miniature for it. I don't wear jewelry." Prudence paused, then answering Lizzie's silent question. "Ned gave me the miniature. I'm sure it was his first effort at scrimshaw, not yet commercial quality. He brought me another in December, and his skill has greatly advanced. I sold that second miniature to Lord Gromley, who wanted a present for his wife."

While she told this tale, Hildegonda placed the tea pot on a tray with their two cups, added a third cup, and the plate of biscuits. "Come into my parlor. I want you to meet the woman who traded lace for scrimshaw."

—

The parlor was as snug as the kitchen, but felt grander, with paintings hung on every possible wall surface. Carpets overlaid the plank floor. Another carpet covered the low table where Hildegonda deposited the tray of tea things.

The woman Lizzie was to meet had her back to the door and did not turn around, staring into the fire. Lizzie prepared to take the seat Hildegonda indicated, then saw the face of the small woman seated before the fire.

"Miss Prudence Mott!"

That beautiful childlike face looked up from the fire, no trace of surprise in her peaceful expression, her porcelain complexion as translucent as the teacups.

Lizzie did not resist the impulse to embrace her, as she had when Prudence first came to Mary's court. Prudence, the third and very much younger child of an earl from East Suffolk, had been too young and too homesick to adapt quickly to the strange ways of life for ladies in waiting. She didn't tremble as much now, but in Lizzie's arms, she seemed to need succor. Prudence was also still thin as a child.

"Hello, Lady Ysabel Foxe. It is good to see you again."

"It is an unexpected joy to find you here," Lizzie said. "But I'm no longer Lady Foxe. Another cousin inherited my father's Marborne title last year. Now I'm only Lizzie Foxe."

"And what is this?" Prudence grasped Lizzie's sleeve; rather, the sleeve of a coat borrowed from Rowland.

Lizzie tugged at the coat's long skirts. "This is for the farrago I'd planned for today, with the Touchstones' help."

Prudence said, "Even in this costume, you'd make our former court proud. If only I had your talent with a needle. I always needed you to fix the curve of my bodice or to get the braid and ribbons right."

"You are exquisitely fitted out, as always," Lizzie said. "Now, why did Mistress Touchstone bring us together?"

Hildegonda said, "I didn't know you were acquainted. How convenient." She pursed her lips into her first smile that day. She poured tea again, handing the first cup to Prudence.

"Please, may we dispense with titles while we conspire together?" Prudence asked. The other two agreed. "When Hildegonda suggested someone who might help me, I had no idea it was you, or perhaps I'd have dared approach you on my own."

"Dared?" Lizzie said. "I hope you always feel safe coming to me anywhere in the world."

"Mayhap you do not know?" That hesitant question and her friend's modest smile about broke Lizzie's heart.

"I do know, my friend. Our mistress writes to me."

Their mistress, Princess Mary, was far more shocked than Lizzie when Prudence left the royal court to follow a portrait painter back to London and (as far as Mary knew) had not yet married her true love.

Lizzie said, "I regret not visiting as soon as I heard you were in London. Can I help you now? Has your family left you impoverished? Is your legacy lost?"

All the women in Mary's court knew each other's family and financial business. Prudence had an uncle, a younger brother of her mother, who'd become quite wealthy since the Restoration. He died without wife or child and left a large legacy to his niece.

"No, whatever quirks I might have, my family hasn't deserted me," Prudence said. "My legacy is secure. If I marry—

with my guardian's approval—before I am of age, my legacy comes to me, both money and property."

"You are fortunate." Lizzie's legacy consisted of an embroidered handkerchief that had been her mother's and a bed in a house shared with her cousins. "But if you marry now, won't all that wealth come under your husband's control?"

How often had the court ladies, shivering in their beds at night, discussed the availability and control of their wealth?

"Yes, but that's true whether I marry now or after I come of age. I am quite willing to remain unmarried, so that legacy becomes mine alone to control." Prudence laid her needlework aside and held Lizzie's hand in a familiar way, as if to better explain while she spoke. "Meanwhile, I receive a generous allowance through the legacy from my uncle. My solicitor, who is also my guardian, was my uncle's dear friend. He's helpful and understanding."

Lizzie returned the pressure when Prudence squeezed her hand, waiting to hear more.

"I have problems that my guardian has not been able to solve. We need help. You cannot imagine my relief that it's you Hildegonda found."

Why not marry the man you followed home? Any artist would leap to marry a lover with a fortune.

Prudence withdrew her hand, as if hearing Lizzie's unasked question. She folded them in her lap, the way they were taught to do at court if they didn't have work in hand.

Ah, not my business. And she knows that I will not pry.

"What kind of hero am I to be, dear Prudence?"

"You both have problems with Wolfric Molewood," Hildegonda said. "I have my own antipathies and fears about the man."

Prudence said, "Please begin, Hildegonda."

"Moge God de man verdoemen!"

Hildegonda damned the man. Lizzie knew that Dutch curse, having heard Ned utter it, although Hildegonda repeated it in her refined English accent.

"Yes," Prudence said. "Please share your grievance."

The stiffest lines of judgment settled on Hildegonda's lips. "We sold a Lely to Mr. Molewood. Later, he claimed it was a forgery. When Simon reimbursed him, what Mr. Molewood sent back was not the sketch we sold him."

Lizzie said, "Did you have provenance—no, of course you did. Why not fight him in court?"

That's what Tom Foxe would do if Ned were accused.

"Because," Hildegonda spoke carefully, "last year that man ruined our greatest competitor by claiming that Rembrandts sold him were forged. Neither our reputation nor our purse can afford that kind of fight. We also cannot afford to have Mr. Molewood sell a forgery that we'd attested to."

"That's when we met the Touchstones," Prudence said. "You see, my dearest friend is finishing paintings that Lely left behind. He is the known expert in verifying works of Lely."

Hildegonda said, "When Ned asked Simon about your proposal, Miss Foxe—"

"Please call me Lizzie."

"When Ned asked," Hildegonda said, "I began to think we might unite to fight the man."

"Am I to know your problem, Prudence?" Lizzie had over the years learned when to ask Prudence what bothered her, and when to refrain.

Prudence said, "Mr. Molewood wants property that's part of my legacy. He has importuned my guardian for the past year. My guardian believes it would be a mistake to sell, that I'll realize greater return in a decade. Yet Mr. Molewood seems incapable of accepting a refusal."

"What else?" Lizzie could see in her friend's limpid eyes too much emotion for her problem to be about real estate.

"He sent agents around questioning my friends and family, seeking information he could use to break the terms of my legacy, to find a way to acquire my land."

Hildegonda said, "In short, in many ways, the man does not conduct business as a gentleman should."

"To my knowledge," Lizzie said, "that is an understatement." Then she repeated for Prudence her own interest in Mr. Molewood's business.

Prudence sighed, dismayed by Lizzie's story. "I abhor that filthy trade. Can you therefore see me as a partner in your endeavor with Mr. Molewood.?"

"It's gratifying to think of us as collaborators again," Lizzie said, "as we often were during our lives in court."

"What do you intend?" Prudence said.

"For your own safety, I cannot share details," Lizzie said. "But I am gathering funds to settle those stolen people who were brought to England. I am working to understand all elements of Mr. Molewood's business. We intend to seize a portion of his wealth to assist with that."

Prudence gestured to the clothes Lizzie wore. "And you planned to approach him in that costume?"

"Yes, as an agent from Simon Touchstone. To urge him to invite my brother into his house as a painter. From that close association, my allies will learn how to breach his defenses."

Hildegonda said, "While you are doing your business, Miss Foxe, perhaps you can put a stop to Molewood's incursions against Prudence. Then, when Ned comes to paint at that man's house, he can seek more forgeries that Molewood might try to use against us."

"Lizzie, might you," Prudence said, "do your work while pretending to be Prudence Mott and divert him from prying into the details of my life?"

How delightfully preposterous.

—

As thrilling as Lizzie found the proposal, it had a severe deficit. "I look nothing like you, Prudence. I'm much taller and," she stated the obvious, "much darker."

"He has never met me. To my knowledge, he has never seen me. I don't live on the property he wants. Surely, Lizzie, his interest in my property can be used to your advantage."

"Are we agreed?" Hildegonda asked. "Do we trust each other to undertake this?"

Lizzie didn't need more convincing. She'd add their concerns to her plan. "My Uncle Absolom, who raised us, imparted rules for us to live by. Those rules are why you can trust me."

Prudence said, "I remember your rules quite well, Lizzie. You shared them with me the first week I came to court. Please expect me to live by them also."

Lizzie repeated the rules for Hildegonda's sake, beginning first, "I keep my promises."

"I agree also," Hildegonda said. "We must trust each other, both as confederates and as women."

"I'm so glad we are undertaking this together," Prudence said. "You were always good to me, Lizzie. I have treasured our friendship."

"I must offer one more warning," Hildegonda said, "before either or both of you agree to meet Mr. Molewood. He has had three young wives, all of whom died in childbed."

"Not so unusual," Lizzie said. "Are we to add it to his many crimes? In addition to the sins against each of us, he is known to cheat with mortgages and to build houses that fall down on their owners' heads."

"People say that none of his wives were happy," Hildegonda said. "Yet rich men want heirs. Hence, I predict that he will look on you, Miss Foxe, as more than the Touchstones' agent."

"And more than the owner of land he wants," Prudence said. "If you pretend to be Prudence Mott, your encounters with the man will differ from the business exchanges in your plan."

"I can adapt."

And I've practiced, going to fêtes as the king's watcher, which I loathe. But this is for Prudence.

Lizzie said, "I'm eager to begin today, but now I'm in the wrong costume.

Prudence said, "I was presumptuous and so brought clothes suitable for the false Prudence."

Hildegonda said, "I shall write an introduction that presents Prudence Mott, rather than your Viscount Orlando."

Lizzie said, "We must be quick. Didn't Mr. Touchstone set his meeting with Mr. Molewood for noon today?"

Hildegonda wrote the letter, while Lizzie dressed in severe clothes that weren't of the quality either she or Prudence wore.

"I look like a Puritan maiden in a Drury Street farce."

This isn't like flirting in party clothes for the king's sake.

Prudence said, "My guardian learned that Mr. Molewood was raised among Suffolk Puritans. His wives were Suffolk stock. He'll think you share an affinity with him. And this gown will refute any rumors the man has heard about whether my soul has been sufficiently washed in the blood of the Lamb."

Prudence helped with the rice powder and white bismuth makeup, then set an appropriate lace cap on Lizzie's head.

Hildegonda said, "There's a mirror in my bedchamber, so you can see the effect."

"I'd rather not," Lizzie said. "Prudence is a master at applying others' makeup."

"Any more tasks for this morning?" Hildegonda asked.

Prudence said, "Might I carry away a receipt for these biscuits? Our cook could put it to good advantage in our household."

Lizzie declined Hildegonda's receipt. There'd be the devil for suggesting new biscuits at Chalgrove House. The cook was Perry Frake's mother, with stern notions about her kitchen that were equal to the notions that Perry had about practically everything. At Xanthus House, Mrs. Flurry already produced a variety of biscuits superior even to these.

"It's the saffron that matters." Mrs. Hildegonda was saying when a nearby church bell pealed.

"I must go." Lizzie said. "Mustn't be late for my first encounter." No more time for dallying, and no time to let Ned and Perry know about the change in plans.

Prudence hugged Lizzie goodbye, as if she were going off to war. The miniature around her neck poked at Lizzie's breastbone.

"Be good," Lizzie whispered.

"Which means, in truth, don't be afraid." Prudence repeated succoring words Lizzie taught her when Prudence was fourteen and too young to be caught up in that hard world.

Lizzie held Prudence's sweet little face, stroked her hair.

She's still too young, too frail, for the hard world.

11
The Rose

— NED —

TUESDAY MORNING

NED HAD TAKEN CHILL while his coat was caught in the duke's carriage door. He slipped the coat on again, then found he'd left his new scarf in the carriage. Looking about to see where he'd been set down from the carriage, he spied The Rose and so entered the tavern to warm up.

The duke had sought to drag him into a puzzling intrigue. Taking care of Lizzie wasn't a challenge, but he wanted to consult with Rowland to learn whether the duke's senses might be scrambled. Scrambled senses or not, the duke had recognized him on the street as Ned, brother of Ysabel Foxe, and then the duke had wedded that name with Eduard Wijck. That left Ned again fearful of being exposed as a wicked forger who duped rich men.

While Ned swallowed a beaker of hot ale at The Rose, he studied the letterlocked packet the duke had passed to him. Ned intended to surrender it to his sister only if she allowed him to read it. In which case, he decided, he might as well read it at that moment. Of course, he'd never be able to reconfigure the puzzle of the letterlock. Yet it seemed both fair and appropriate that he read it, since he'd been kidnapped on the street for her sake.

However, he'd have to invent a story for how he came by the letter and why he'd read it.

He unfolded the letter and read flowing, spikey script, rather like Lizzie's own hand. It was dated just a few days earlier.

> *Carissime,* the truest friend of my heart—
>
> That heart has pounded with fear for you. I cannot do as you ask, and I beg you to remember how you and I are both led by God to do what is right.

Ha! Lizzie led by God? From the cradle, Lizzie did only what her own heart commanded. The rest of the letter did not reveal much more.

> Do not get crosswise with my father's advisors, who may be watching you. Palpitations of anxiety for you afflict me daily. I shall do more than only pray for your safety. Please take care. You are on a dangerous path.

The rest of the letter contained hashed scratching that did not form words. And it was not signed.

Yet he'd already surmised that the letter and the duke's proposed assignment came from Lizzie's friend, Mary Stuart.

Ned folded the letter and stashed it in his waistcoat, wondering why people around the king might be interested in Lizzie's gambol. Of the men marked for invitation to a Foxe-style restoration, no one was a member of the royal family. Or an advisor to the king. Had Lizzie secretly made changes to her plan that might alarm other men serving the king? The only way to find out was to ask Lizzie to trust him with all the details of her gambol. He'd have to ask, because he wanted to protect her from danger, even without the duke's proposed guineas.

He had every good reason to ask her. Although Perry often cautioned Lizzie to make safe choices, she often put herself in danger. Like donning Orlando's clothes and begging to go to Wolfric Molewood as an artist's agent.

Verdomme! At least they'd finish this gambol on Friday, so he'd have far fewer worries about his sister.

For now, despite declining the duke's proposition, Ned intended to ask Michael Oakes to join in the effort to watch out for Lizzie. If there were men employed by the king who were interested in Lizzie, Michael would notice them.

He laid out coin for his ale, then snagged a boy on the corner and gave him a penny to take a message to Michael, asking him to meet Lizzie in Bloomsbury and bring her home from her noon meeting. He'd have to explain later.

—

After lingering at The Rose, Ned was two shakes late to the locksmith's shop just off Oxford Street. At Ned's knock, the jolly Ezra Search-the-Scriptures Pelletoot opened the door and welcomed Ned into the pleasant home above his shop. The man wanted his portrait painted, to leave to his granddaughter. A pleasant chore for Ned. The warm house smelled of good cooking from the downstairs kitchen.

Perry had said of Ezra's portrait, "It must resemble one of the grand old men that the famous Dutch fellow painted."

An easy task, because Ezra ("we shall use our christened names as we are all equal before God") could be a twin of one of Rembrandt's rough fellows with a magnificent nose grown coarse and red with age, eyebrows like a chimneysweep's brush, and thick lips that could grasp a clay pipe while telling a story at the same time.

Ned and Ezra were joined by the man's daughter, whom he called Mrs. Pursglove, and who was old enough to be Ned's mother. She'd come from Windsor to visit for the twelve days of Christmas. And then settled in (Perry said) to poke her nose in her father's business, since he'd taken on a new partner.

Ezra obediently took his pose, with modest adjustments from Ned. The man said to his daughter, "Did I tell you how I met Mr. Frake?"

"Yes, Father. At least twice."

Ezra paid her no mind, which seemed to be the rule for how the pair communicated. "Lord Bagsham's man sent me to add new locks for a house the duke owns in Covent Garden, the one he got for his nephew. May the name of that departed soul ring bells in heaven."

"Is the duke well?" Mrs. Pursglove asked. "I haven't seen his grace since he came to Windsor last summer. He didn't recognize me in the press of the crowd, given that he's only ever seen me in London."

Ezra chuckled, shaking his head over his own memory, not answering his daughter. "While we installed locks for the new tenant at Xanthus House, Perry Frake followed me the whole length of the day that our Lord made. Watched all I did. Asked me questions as smart as Cromwell or one of Good Queen Bess's own spies. Not that I say Perry Frake was a spy. I would never."

Since coming back to England, Perry denied any rumors that he'd spent ten years as an intelligencer on the Continent. Perhaps men believed it when Perry said that he'd only served as guard for diplomats and visiting notables.

"Are Mr. Frake's changes to your business wholly proper and sensible?" Mrs. Pursglove asked, still dubious about her father's new partner. "He brought on his two young brothers, like Joseph installing his brothers to reign over Egypt."

The day's work proceeded with Ezra and his daughter talking past each other yet remaining in good humor, the old man being of an entirely different temperament from his child.

When Lizzie asked Perry and Ned to help her in London, they'd moved in with Rowland. When Perry and Ned weren't looking deep into the lives of the men who'd invested in the

Hawkins' Heirs syndicate, Ned painted. He also gave drawing and coloring lessons to Jacob Rôche, the Earl of Cloudesley, Tom Foxe's ward. His family had considered the lad to be an unteachable natural since infancy, but Perry and Tom discovered soon after meeting Jacob that he was capable of more than his meager education had covered. Only hunger or his dog would entice the lad away from a drawing lesson and its practice.

Besides the prowling of the Hawkins' Heirs investors that Perry undertook for Lizzie, he and Rowland chased down more malefactors from last summer's Withersea affair. That resulted in a new royal gratuity for Perry, which caused him to fret about what to do with so much gold. But that came around bright on the first day of Advent, when Perry met Ezra Pelletoot, locksmith to the king.

"What is it that stinks of pine in here?" Mrs. Pursglove asked, interrupting the meditation Ned typically enjoyed while painting. "Did you pay for bad coals, Father?"

"It's my turps," Ned said. He'd just used a drop to thin out a rusty shade of brown to get the tone right for Ezra's complexion. Some might think to try a rosy hue, but the elder Pelletoot had aged like brandywine, as if distilled by fire.

"We shall all be poisoned," she exclaimed.

Ned said, "It's only gum turpentine. Some ladies like a posey or a potpourri while sitting for their portrait. I can ask my sister for a recipe, if you like. She is good with scents."

"As am I." Mrs. Pursglove puffed up. She must have felt she'd been insulted.

But at least the woman was silent for a while, letting Ned fall into the reverie he desired while painting. That day, he meditated on how Perry had inserted them into Ezra's world. After Perry spent a day following the locksmith all around Xanthus House, Ezra accepted Perry's invitation to supper. Late that snowy night, the three of them were drinking ale at The Rose. Perry had urged Ned to try his singing voice.

Be merry my hearts,
and call for your quarts
and let no liquor be lacking,
We have gold in store,
we propose to roar,
until we set care a packing.

Ned, while singing, lost Perry's attention for a dog's age. Instead of joining in song, Perry dipped his head ever closer to his new friend Ezra. To Ned, singing didn't feel right without Perry's deep voice anchoring him. At last, the conversation with Ezra ended. They walked the ancient fellow home, without Ned attaining even a whisper of what the two had discussed. They said goodnight to the old man, then tramped over new-fallen snow, their boots squeaking on the fresh flakes. Perry, singing joyfully, urged Ned to join in.

Good fortune attend each merry man's friend,
That doth but the best that he may;
Forgetting old wrongs, with carols and songs,
To drive the cold winter away.

At home, after Peter the boot-boy took away their wet shoes in the foyer, they'd slipped upstairs in wet stockings. Not until they'd undressed and crawled into bed (with the brass warming tray Lazarus had prepared) did Perry explain his elation. Ezra's sole apprentice was sailing away to Pennsylvania, or one of those wild places. Ezra had a good business as a locksmith, but declared himself too old to start teaching a new boy his trade.

"You can perceive the cause of my joy," Perry said. "I've found the best place to invest my new gratuity from the king. I shall join Mr. Pelletoot as his partner."

"But why?" Ned felt slow in the head, cold in his toes. He'd been unsure about life in London, since Revelstone had always been home. This new business would draw Perry's time and attention away from Ned. Not a noble feeling.

"I can use my skills as an intelligencer while escaping that life. I shall invent a new Peregrine Frake."

"Can you not just begin your own business?"

"As a locksmith? Nay, there's no way I could purchase a place in the guild without a sponsoring partner. Ezra has the king's license to call himself purveyor to the Crown. I shall be both Ezra's apprentice and business partner. You and I couldn't have found greater good fortune if we fell into a dragon's hoard."

Perry bought three-quarters ownership of Ezra's business, with the option to buy the rest when Ezra made up his mind to quit it all. Within a week of the agreement, Perry brought two of his brothers along as apprentices. He hired a spritely housekeeper for Ezra and set about tidying, rearranging, and launching the business into new directions.

And so, for the fourth time since August, Ned rearranged his life for Perry's sake, happy because Perry found peaceful joy as a locksmith. Ned endeavored to settle into the peaceful painter's life he'd wished for. Simon Touchstone had accepted one of Ned's pastoral Cambridge paintings to sell under Eduard Wijck's own name and promised to secure portrait commissions. Given the ducal kidnapping that morning on Russell Street, it seemed that Ned would also have a large gratuity for doing what came naturally: protecting Lizzie.

Yet, while painting a good representation of Ezra's nose, Ned felt a nagging desire growing in his heart, to retrieve his old devil-drawn paintings sooner rather than later. The universe rang a major warning: Simon's story of his competitor being destroyed by accusations of forgery. Ned could not allow his past work to surface in a way that might destroy Simon.

However wealthy Ned felt (in comparison to past decades of poverty), he couldn't afford to buy back his own paintings.

The paintings must be retrieved directly, and Ned couldn't do that on his own. He'd have to convince Perry to help him to undertake his own modest heists, to remove his forgeries from London mansions. It wasn't like a pentimento, painting over images out of regret. Ned didn't regret what he'd done to survive. But none of those artifacts served a purpose now, only posing a threat to his future work and Simon's livelihood.

"Have you got the color right for the carpet on Father's table?" Mrs. Pursglove asked. "Isn't it more what they call almandine ruby? And isn't that jug more green than grey?"

"It takes several layers of paint." Ned saw just how Ezra's daughter pushed her way through the world. "Then there's a glaze overall. It will glow like a carbuncle gem when I am done."

"But that will take hours!" Mrs. Pursglove exclaimed.

"It always does," Ned said.

"I've nothing better to do," Ezra said, in his good-natured way. "Perry Frake has the hard work in hand each day. Never had a better apprentice. I can sit till supper if you want me, Ned."

"Not necessary." Ned began wrapping his brushes and palette. "We've lost all the good light that's to be had today. Thank you for your time, Mr. Pelletoot."

"It's Ezra, lad. I shall call you Ned because Perry does. And that's the end of it. What are you up to for the rest of the day, Ned? Fancy a spot of ale at The Rose?"

"It'd be my delight, except that I'm called to tend to business for my sister."

"You can't spend your days in a tavern, Father." Mrs. Pursglove had her hands on her hips. "You must attend to your apprentice, lest he rob you blind."

"I can spend my days however please, poppet. Perry Frake is an upright man, and my life is the better for it."

Smiling privately at this warm thought, Ned tucked his brushes in the small stone crock he used while painting, then made sure the crock's lid was snug.

"But his accent comes from Yorkshire," the Pursglove woman complained.

"Aye, by way of a grandmother, I think."

"His voice rankles, Father. I hear a man capable of deceit," she said, a viperish hiss in her pronunciation of deceit.

Ned knew Perry to be capable of deceit, though he'd never harm an innocent. Perry was profoundly upright in ways that made Ned's life all the better.

"Careful to watch your tongue, poppet." Ezra spoke lightly, yet shook a gnarled finger to admonish her. "Perry Frake is my good friend. I'll swear on my own name that he's a good man."

The old man slipped an arm around Ned's shoulder, stopping him at the door. "Perry thought we might make better use of those rooms on the third floor, but he's got the lads off with him on a job. Might you help me shift some boxes?"

Ezra coaxed Ned upstairs and told stories about the sources of various junk and watched while Ned served as stevedore to move piles of crates and lumber.

12
To Bloomsbury

– LIZZIE –

TUESDAY NOON

"WIST THA BIN, LASS?" the sledge driver called to Lizzie.

"To Southampton Square, please."

The driver wanted to be paid in advance to take her to Bloomsbury, as if it were the other side of England.

"Special prices in a hard frost," the driver said, likely accustomed to his passengers complaining.

She accepted this as the price of her impatience, not wanting to walk to a thoroughfare where more rides might be available. That sledge must have been dragged to town from a farmyard for the chance to make coin off Londoners who wanted to move over icy, snow-laden streets. She huddled under the heavy wool blanket, for which the driver had charged an extra penny. The beast pulling the sledge likely slept in that blanket last night, given its heady animal odor.

As a distraction from fretting over all she'd heard that morning, Lizzie pulled Tamsin's letter from where she'd tucked it up her sleeve, once more reading good news for the comfort offered. And to remember the reason for this week's restoration.

> All you wished for has come to be. The girls are learning English quickly, having a teacher in Nadia who under-

> stands them. For the widow Nadia, this work is a comfort after all she lost when her husband died last summer.
>
> Mrs. Hinxton and Mrs. Barton, our elderly boarders from the village, offer gentle lessons in sewing and knitting. Fortunata and Gloria have strong inclinations for needlework and asked me to write in this letter that you will be pleased to see their progress.
>
> Mrs. Bell is teaching kitchen skills. Thus far, Ines and Marta have achieved more with biscuits and bread than I ever did. Rebeca and Susana were already experts with milk cows, having learned in their former homes. They all take enthusiastic turns at the churn.

Lizzie closed her eyes, wishing to see what Tamsin wrote about, but it'd be many weeks until she could journey home.

They're happy. I will achieve their safe future.

After she tucked away the letter, the slow ride still allowed extra moments to arrange her costume before she began pursuing the day's goals: gain entrance to Jericho House for Ned and prepare the man to be lured into her gambol. She'd have to figure on the fly what she could do for the Touchstones.

"Here ye be, mistress!" the driver shouted.

He'd halted the sledge so precipitously that Lizzie slid from the rough seat. She tossed off the vile horse blanket and stepped down to the street, barely getting her balance before the sledge jerked away and a gust of icy wind tried its best to topple her.

Then, on that bitterly cold Tuesday, an austerely dressed woman walked along Southampton Square, a drab grey cloak over her head and shoulders. Her iron pattens crunched a rhythm on the frozen snow. Anyone on the street saw a woman who dressed with crisp care and managed her skirts with dexterity.

Lizzie stopped at a large brick mansion called Jericho House, which stood among the first houses constructed in Bloomsbury after the Fire. As brash as its name, the house presented an outsized front door with shiny brass fittings and shaded by a classical arch that did not match other elements of the mansion.

Nor did it match what Perry had discovered about the owner's Puritan family. Mr. Wolfric Molewood, the owner, was the only son of Job-Made-A-Covenant-With-His-Eyes Molewood, who came from a southern English village where children were christened with hortatory names to stimulate godly behavior. The senior Mr. Molewood's orphaned son Wolfric came to London when Charles II was restored to the throne. The younger Molewood wasn't the only child of Cromwell's minions who, misreading the Gospel of Matthew, set out ambitiously to lay up treasures on earth.

Lizzie dropped the brass knocker on the looming black door, presenting a figure as straightlaced as the mansion owner's Puritan mother was said to be. When a servant opened the door, Lizzie spoke as the incarnation of prim confidence.

"I am come from Simon Touchstone's gallery to keep an appointment with Mr. Molewood." Behind the servant, a clock struck noon at the same moment the neighborhood church bells tolled. "I believe I am on time."

As demure as "Prudence Mott" appeared, Lizzie's fierce heart was now in pursuit of the English businessman who'd invested in the Hawkins' Heirs syndicate.

She surrendered her bonnet and cloak to the servant, who didn't ask her name but took the introductory letter she offered and left her to wait. Offered no help with her pattens, Lizzie unbuckled and tucked them under the settee, then waited in the large, chilly foyer where the edges of everything—the picture frames, table legs, and chairs—were all gilded.

Clutching her satchel primly in her lap, she sat like a cat expecting a mouse, having learned the secret of calmly waiting when she first came to court. While practicing patience in the foyer, Lizzie espied a few paintings on the list Hildegonda had given her. One, which was in execrable taste, showed a woman beheading a man. Not what Lizzie would choose to greet guests. Two others were landscapes that she knew: scenes across a water meadow near Revelstone House that Jan Wijck had painted. A kind of sadness welled up within her, that they'd been so poor just a year ago that Ned had to sell his father's paintings.

After fifteen minutes of chill air sweeping over her feet and creeping up to the core of her being, she was escorted up the wide stairs. The serving man opened a tall, painted door and intoned, "Mrs. Mott," apparently having done a poor job of reading the title on her letter of introduction. He stepped aside to let her enter a large room fitted out for business, with the same flamboyant furnishings as in the foyer.

A voice rumbled from across the room. "Mrs. Mott, welcome. I hope you did not take a chill on such a cold day."

Not until you made me wait in your frozen foyer.

Lizzie assigned the man ten demerits for rudeness, the way the court matrons did, those witches who supervised Mary's young ladies in waiting.

—

"Not Mrs. Mott." Lizzie didn't add a greeting. "I am Miss Mott."

He didn't seem to hear her correction.

Mr. Molewood rose from behind a table stacked with papers and packets tied with ribbons. As menacing as an outsized hawk, his presence felt too large for this gilded room with its jumble of spindly gilded furniture. This day he wore a lush lavender silk coat that flowed like a dressing gown.

A devil. The only way to describe him, whether one grew up listening to hellfire sermons or (as Lizzie did) to philosophers arguing the enlightened detachment of philosophy from theology. A smoldering demon, abiding on the earthly side of creation, with those two smoke trails streaming down his pointed beard.

"I was expecting Mr. Touchstone." His voice rumbled, like masons dragging a large stone over pavement. "I am surprised to meet you."

He folded his arms in a commanding challenge.

"Mr. Touchstone is ill, sir. By luck, I was free today." Lizzie decided that Prudence the Puritan had an austere smile, and finally dipped her head in greeting. She knew the real Prudence Mott to be made of stiff fiber, a woman who never simpered. "Mr. Touchstone asked me to express his sincere gratitude that you have consulted with Touchstone's Gallery in your quest for an artist. We are honored to have your trust."

And you dare not speak of forgery tricks when I speak of trust.

While she recited her original speech and practiced her new smile, he was reading the introduction from Hildegonda. Lizzie tapped a foot, the way her friend Mary did when a subordinate wasted her time.

As Molewood read, his winged eyebrows rose in surprise.

His dark hooded eyes swept over her, frowning. Was that recognition? A quiver of fear wiggled through Lizzie's innards. No, he'd never met Ysabel Foxe. Nor Prudence Mott. He'd barely noticed Orlando at the fête.

Then his pouty lips slowly resolved into a thin smile.

No, a leer.

You warned me, Hildegonda.

"You are Miss Prudence Mott? The earl's youngest daughter?" His rocky voice became honey coated. "I am both surprised and pleased to meet you."

Molewood advanced, straightening into that posture men use to tower over others, his chest thrust forward.

Swifter and more graceful, Lizzie crossed the room and offered her gloved hand in greeting, not like men do, but in the way learned at court: hand angled downward, no pressure returned. Keeping four feet of distance.

"I am that creature, Mr. Molewood."

Then he put his other hand on her elbow and drew her closer, still holding her hand.

Sir, your demerits accumulate rapidly. No touching.

"Please, I beg you to have a seat, Miss Mott."

He fingered the chair he wanted her to take. She feigned not to notice and instead perched on a low, velvet-cushioned chair that forced her to look up at him. Of course, he'd arranged the chairs around his desk to disadvantage visitors.

But I learned power plays in a royal court. The game is simple draughts, not chess.

Lizzie sat as straight as she'd learned to do the first week in Mary's court, folding her gloved hands as primly as any old-time goodwife at Sunday services. She smiled like the innocent daughter of that goodwife.

He still studied her, his dark eyes flicking from her mouth to the lace cap that hid her hair and shaded her face. "May I be frank? I must express my surprise that Mr. Touchstone sent Miss Prudence Mott? I assume you are presenting proposals for the fresco I desire."

"Yes, I am here to perform that service."

"How unusual, to be served by an earl's daughter."

"Not so unusual, except until today I have only introduced artists to patrons who are personal friends. The Duke of Bagsham kindly introduced me to Mr. Touchstone, who begged me to assist patrons…um…"

"Outside your noble friends?" Molewood swallowed her teasing falsehood.

Lizzie lowered her voice as if sharing a confidence. "I cherish close friendships with several artists and often participate in salons where they debate techniques. Consequently, I am quite familiar with current trends in modern painting."

"Are you truly?" Perhaps he didn't mean to be so obvious, but he licked his lips, like a cat about to pounce.

Were I as innocent as this lace cap, I'd take caution now.

"Yes, sir. I was just now admiring two paintings in your foyer, among the many beautiful things in your house."

He liked the compliment. "My father often said, 'God smiles on those among the elect who help themselves.' I have been diligent, and God has been beneficent."

"You were blessed, Mr. Molewood, to have acquired that pair of landscapes by Jan Wijck."

"You have a good eye. He trained under Rembrandt, you know." He raised his brows, seeking another compliment.

"I've heard you were both shrewd and lucky to snatch them up, only a day after they came to Touchstone's gallery."

"You call such business luck?" Molewood again offered a thin smile. He began telling a story or preaching a sermon on his prowess. But Lizzie got lost in a sudden memory of seeing Jan Wijck's landscapes hang over the fireplace in the front parlor, just a few months ago.

Egad! Ned has his own forgeries hanging in this house.

Lizzie glanced around at the collection of paintings hung near each other on the walls, seeking any others she might know.

Molewood was saying, "So, at that point, I made a mistake. I said how much I wanted those Wijck landscapes for my mother. Hence, Touchstone drove me hard. After I won my bargain, you'd think I'd snatched food from his children's mouths."

"Your mother?" Lizzie indicated the miniature on Molewood's table of a dark-eyed Puritan woman, to which the portraitist had added not one glint of life. "Is that the good woman for whom you acquired the landscapes?"

"Yes." He glanced at the miniature. "That does not do her justice. I should commission a real portrait one day soon."

Lizzie leaned forward as if sharing a secret. "It is Mistress Touchstone who insists on bargaining in that hard way, for the sake of the artist. Mr. Touchstone prefers to do what's best for the patron, to ensure continuing trade." She sat back again. Molewood still blinked at her words. "Shall we begin? Or do we await your mother?"

"My mother? No, she will not visit London until Easter." He stared, as if seeking to see beneath Miss Mott's lace cap. Or perhaps to fluster her.

I promise, you will never see me aflutter.

"Pardon my confusion, Mr. Molewood. You said you sought those landscapes for your mother. I assumed that this new project is also intended to please her."

"My mother doesn't reside with me. I haven't yet had the opportunity to bring the landscapes to her." His smile showed a predator's teeth. "No, today, it's only me who will look at your artist's proposals."

"Then let us begin, sir."

13
Inside Jericho House

— LIZZIE —

TUESDAY NOON

RELIEVED TO PROCEED WITH the day's business, Lizzie removed the packet of proposed sketches from her satchel. He leaned closer to her. It wasn't often in this life that she'd felt such disgust for a man, even beyond his role in the Hawkins' Heirs syndicate. However, when she set out the packet of drawings, she touched his hand briefly, to draw his eyes away from her face.

"We are recommending an experienced prodigy who uses light to instill life in his work. Mr. Touchstone says that you are a connoisseur of the chiaroscuro effect."

"There's another term for the effect, isn't there, Miss Mott?" He tilted his head, and again smiled slowly. Testing her.

Alas, I only repeat my lessons. My brother has the talent. All I have is bravado.

"The Venetians say *tenebroso,* Mr. Molewood, but that's far gloomier than what you will see in these sketches."

"You intrigue me." He rested his chin on his palm, his elbow trapping the sketches, his eyes on her, not the sketches.

"Seeing your beautiful rooms, I understand why Mr. Touchstone asked me to recommend Mr. Wijck to your notice."

"I thought the man was dead."

"Wijck *fils,* not *père.*"

Molewood's eyes were blank, devoid of understanding.

"Jan Wijck passed to heaven a few years ago. We are presenting ideas from his son, Mr. Eduard Wijck, who has a distinctly English style that will complement your tastes."

"Um…ah…" He seemed confused. "Then Wijck *fils* painted the Duke of Bagsham's fresco? I must have misunderstood. Let's look at your sketches."

She tugged at the drawings to get him to move. Which he intended. She quieted the ire rising under her ribs. Molewood was the kind of man who forced others to bend to his will at every possible turn.

The animosity I carried through your oversized front door grows each moment.

She spoke low again, as if they were sharing a secret. "Mr. Touchstone thinks this first idea, *Apollo with the Muses,* will interest you, because your professional work has so stimulated new life in London."

"It's quite an extravagant scene, Miss Mott. But Apollo was the one with the orgies. My mother would not approve."

Apollo was the sun god. Did you not go to school?

"Then let us examine this one. *The Birth of Jupiter.* The artist can, of course, cloak the goddesses in the Greek style rather than…ah…undraping like the painter Rubens."

He glanced at the sketch with its jumble of nude putti, then at her. She rattled the paper, which drew a small, satisfied smile from him.

The paper rattled. I am not rattled. My loathing is silent.

She smoothed out the sketch to draw his attention away from her person.

"No. Too evocative. My mother would complain that I've lost my moral compass."

What moral compass? You invest in slaver ships.

"Your mother must take pride in all you've done for London. You've every right to be proud." More flattery to bend him to her purpose. She tugged the third sketch free of his elbow. "This sketch might adhere more to your family heritage and your own legacy. It's called *Achilles at Skyros,* and it shows—"

"This." Molewood tapped the sketch with his finger, tapping too close to her hand. "This is the one. When can your Mr. Wijck begin work?"

I win! Ned will soon be inside this house!

"This week. Mr. Wijck had engaged another commission, but the client sought a subject that was too…um, Catholic. The artist suggested Our Savior in a carpenter's shop with Joseph, but the client insisted the focal point be the mother of our Lord. Mr. Wijck could not support Lord Gomfrey's desires—oh pray, you did not hear that. We keep our clients' names in strict confidence, even if a transaction is not concluded."

A flame kindled in Mr. Molewood's dark eyes upon hearing that one of his public rivals had been denied Eduard Wijck's service. The man wore his desires openly on his demonic face.

"I should like to interview Mr. Wijck at his first convenience. I am so grateful for your assistance."

She repressed the heat of victory in her belly. Ladies don't celebrate their victories.

Even this lady, who always expects to win.

Then Molewood waggled his dark winged brows and rested his hand on hers when she reached for the sketch.

"I shall be more enthused about the project if you will agree to pose in the ensemble. You would make a charming Achilles."

One hand pointed to the figure of Achilles dressed as a woman. Molewood's other hand pushed at her calfskin glove, touching the back of her hand.

No touching. A thousand demerits.

—

Lizzie swept the sketches back under her control, like brushing pieces off a draughts board, and tucked them into her satchel.

"The artist can be available for an interview this afternoon. Is that suitable, Mr. Molewood?"

"Are you considering my proposal, Miss Mott?" He sugared his voice. "What do you think of my idea, of you appearing in my mythical fresco?"

"I will discuss it with the artist. He might like the notion, since it will save on model fees. However, if you want to know what I think, Mr. Molewood, may I be frank?"

"Please, Miss Mott." He raised his ridiculous brows, as if he expected to hear something salacious.

"If you want a large work with a mythological theme, consider a painting on canvas rather than a fresco. A fresco is mere household decoration. A painting is a prudent investment, its value sure to grow as a portable and convertible asset, should you need it to be."

"A shrewd notion, Miss Mott. I'll consider it."

She rose, hoping to appear imperturbable while she longed to flee the room.

"Before you go, Miss Mott, will you satisfy my curiosity?"

Am I that good a friend to sacrifice my time this way?

"Sir?"

"Pray tell, how did you come to be involved in this work? Few of England's noble ladies are engaged in commerce."

"Perhaps, because we must be discreet, there are more than you might think." She didn't sit down again, as he gestured. "I'm fortunate to have an independent living. But a portion of my funds was invested in a cargo of silk and spices that was lost to Levant pirates. I'm not destitute, but I must be wise for a year or so. Because my intimate friends are painters and patrons of the arts, I'm able to be useful."

She'd made that up in the moment and managed to sound both brave and pathetic.

"But surely your parents—"

"Sir, my independent living is a blessing beyond all others in the modern world. I need only borrow against my talents for a few months, not surrender my independence."

"May our gracious and loving Lord bless and save you, Miss Mott." His effusive language flowed, while she stayed busy buckling up her satchel, keeping her hands out of his reach. But he persisted. "What ship? Was it not insured?"

"*The Ridderschap*, a Dutch Indiaman, with no English pass to avoid pirates. No, the cargo wasn't insured. The captain tipped our silk and spices overboard."

"Insurance is the wonder of this age, Miss Mott." He laid a finger beside his nose, imparting wisdom. "When you next invest, dear lady, be sure your factor purchases insurance."

"Thank you, sir, for your advice." She presented demure resignation to her fate, masking how much she considered that endearment an impertinence.

"Would you allow me to help you, madam?" He'd believed her story, and so sought to drown her with his sugary concern.

"You are helping me. I shall receive two percent of the artist's fee for your fresco. More, if you seek a framed painting."

"Ah. Ah ha. Yet, if only you'd had insurance on your Levant cargo, my company would now be your rescuing hero."

"I thought you were a builder."

"A man seeks new challenges after each conquest."

As do I. As my next conquest, you will beg to join my gambol.

He reached for her hand again. She made it look like an accident that he missed. Time for one more compliment.

She said, "Mr. Touchstone said I must beg to view your *Jericho at Rest* fresco. Is that possible?"

And Mrs.Touchstone called it an abomination before God.

"Not today, madam. That fresco is in my mother's bedchamber. She can show it to you when she's in town at Easter." He brightened. "If you pose for the Achilles work, you can see it sooner than springtime."

A servant was at the door. "Nathaniel Sprottle has brought the carriage around for your appointment, sir."

"I'm coming. Please ask Ishmael to escort Miss Mott to her next destination."

"Thank you for your time, Mr. Molewood." She advanced to the open door, quelling a bubbling desire to flee. "You are all kindness, but I do not need an escort to Threadneedle Street."

"My mother would consider it a black mark upon my soul if I allowed a woman to walk out alone on the city street."

"No, truly, I—"

"And perhaps you might ask your guardian to discuss my business offer. I can help with your current straits better than can Mr. Touchstone or your artist friends."

What a lot of honey you poured until getting to this.

"Sir? My guardian does not involve me with business decisions he makes for me. I resolved long before now not to counter decisions he makes that are beyond my own wisdom. He understands my feelings."

"You must trust him greatly, Miss Mott, despite losing too much in shipping investments. I made an offer for property you own near Primrose Hill."

"Was that you? Then you know I do not want to sell the hallowed ground where my dear mother and family are buried. It is not worth two thousand guineas to disturb my forefathers' rest."

She cited a number three times what Prudence said he'd offered, and then noticed his rapid blinking because it occurred each time she'd surprised him in this conversation.

"I hope this is the first day of a true friendship." He touched her hand again. "Let your guardian know I will be contacting him again, to discuss how we can accommodate your concerns."

"I cannot do that. However, I will consider your request, that I participate in the new *Achilles at Skyros.*"

"Then I shall count the moments until we meet again, Miss Mott. Farewell until that golden hour." His stony voice rumbled deeper. "Ah, Ishmael, here you are. Please see to Miss Mott's safety. Walk with her until she's safe inside again."

"Yes, master."

Ishmael, who appeared to be a child of about ten, was as dark as the girls who now lived at Revelstone House. She followed him downstairs. When she sat to fasten her pattens and looked up at him, she saw that Ishmael was perhaps sixteen, but small for a young man. In addition to the suit of velvet livery he wore, a silver collar was buckled around his neck, locked with a tiny padlock.

Her belly revolted. Her heart broke.

14
A Silver Collar

— LIZZIE —

TUESDAY EARLY AFTERNOON

THE YOUNG MAN HELD out Lizzie's grey wool cloak.

"I do not need help, Ishmael. Do not go out into the cold."

"Master says."

He opened the door for her, and they were down the steps to the street, she in her cloak and he in no more clothes than what he wore inside the house.

As soon as they passed the first turning in the street, she asked in her rotten Portuguese, "Is Ishmael your Jesus name?"

If he was surprised, he didn't show it. *"Sim, senhora."*

"When did you come to London?" She had a tangle of questions and not enough Portuguese to ask them.

"Some time," he said.

She spied pie hawkers at the corner. "Are you hungry?"

"No, senhora. I had my dinner."

"Is your master…" Decent? Cruel? "Good to you?"

He looked up at her. "Where is the turning to your house?"

"It is just here. You can go home now. Get out of the cold."

She put a farthing in his hand, not knowing what else to do. He stared at it, then clenched it in his fist.

"Até logo." She called farewell when the lad jogged away.

She could not do one thing to help or fix anything, not even quell the jab in her heart when she saw stray light reflecting on his silver collar as he rounded the corner.

While she fumed about the devil Molewood's many sins, her iron pattens clanged on cobblestones as she stomped along in a manner unbecoming a woman who'd served Mary Stuart.

Tom and Perry would laugh at the story of her hour with Molewood. Ned would fret over what she'd wear while posing for the painting. Rowland—thank the heavy, dark, cloud-filled heavens—would know nothing about today. Her prudent plan would not entangle Rowland.

On the bare cobbles, her pattens tolled like dark bells while she had an unpleasant realization. She didn't want Rowland involved in this gambol because everything about Hawkins' Heirs filled her with anger, made her feel ugly inside. She had to focus on the righteous parts, on seizing justice and winning a future for those girls. And protecting Prudence Mott.

"Hello, Miss Foxe." Michael Oakes's voice broke into her meditations. "I didn't recognize you. In fact, Ned told me to look for Orlando. May I fetch a carriage for you?"

"Of course." She slipped her arm into the crook of his elbow, without thinking about it. She'd been too angry to feel the cold until that moment. "It is beyond freezing."

"Happy to be of use." He flung his woolen cloak over her shoulders, flagged a ride, and did his best to warm her on the ride back to Covent Garden.

It took a moment to find what disturbed her thoughts. "Ned sent you to look for me?"

"He said," Michael paused, "that you might have a message for him, and thought I could also get you home."

After a few moments, Michael said, "Here we are at Rollo's house. How do you want to come in?"

"What do you mean?"

"You left the house as Viscount Orlando early this morning. But now you are another woman. By the way, have we met?"

"It seems that I must be Miss Prudence Mott upon occasion."

"It's most often that it is you, Miss Foxe, who abjures us to keep our costumes and roles in regular order."

"Lend me your hat and cloak. I'll be you while I enter the house. Then, if you're carrying a message to Ned, tell him to be at Mr. Molewood's house at four o'clock today."

—

Inside Xanthus House, Lizzie inhaled faint odors from the kitchen while assaulted by Countess, who charged through the foyer and leapt to place paws on Lizzie's shoulders.

"Down, girl!"

The dog was called away by Tom's young ward, Jacob Rôche, who'd been making more progress with the dog's training than anyone else.

When Lazarus returned from delivering Michael's hat and cloak, he encouraged his son Peter to remove the livestock to the back terrace.

When it was quiet in the foyer, Lazarus said, "Apologies, Miss Foxe."

"No need. This house is wonderful to come home to." She considered the crypt-like sense of the mansion she'd left. The cheerful noise and homey smells of this frequently manic house were everything Molewood's mansion was not.

"Would you care for luncheon?" Lazarus asked, showing no surprise at her transformation into a Puritan lady since breakfast. After she agreed, he said, "His lordship left you a message, and you have letters waiting for your attention. I'll bring them to your room with your luncheon."

"Is Jane free?" Lizzie asked. The upstairs maid, Jane, had been helping Lizzie to dress as Orlando. "I can use her help, unless she finds that too awkward."

"I can say for a fact, Miss Foxe, that our Jane likes to help when she's allowed."

Upstairs, Lizzie read Rowland's message, which he'd scrawled on a scrap of paper:

> Orlando, I have good luck and want to share the news. If you have time this afternoon, come to my new listening post. Michael Oakes can bring you. Bring Countess, if you have the patience.
>
> — R (I swear on my Uncle Absolom's good name that you fill my heart.)

Better news than any other that day.

She considered her other planned chores: finish arrangements with the chef hired for Friday's event; meet with the new actors Felicity had found for the event. Lizzie simply had to ask for more help from Felicity and Michael.

And the actors were lynchpins in the coming event. They were all eager, Felicity said, for Friday and their first pay. Winter was a thin time for actors, besides whatever they could earn on makeshift stages at the Frost Faire.

With Jane's help, Lizzie washed off the bismuth-and-rice powder makeup. Together they performed the binding, tucked hair up under an ornate wig, and rearranged padding so that the inhabitant of a ruby-colored brocade suit resembled an exotic Continental noble.

By the time Lizzie finished dressing as Orlando, a plate with a hot meat pie and a dish of applesauce arrived from the kitchen. Beside the plate, Lazarus left a letter from her dear friend in the Low Countries. From the crossed addresses on the wrapper, her friend's letter had taken a journey to Cambridge and then back to London. Lizzie's heart rose upon seeing her friend's familiar spikey handwriting and the heading, "The Hague, December 10," which meant it had taken a month to arrive. Lizzie sought to remember the details of what she'd written to her friend six weeks earlier. Whatever the details in Lizzie's request, Mary's answer crushed hope.

> My dear Ysabel, I'm writing from the warmest room in the Stadtholder's palace. I cannot warm my bones in this country.
>
> My friend, I very much took your last letter to heart. However, I have discussed it with my husband, and we believe that there is nothing I can do to help you. My Dear One advises against taking any action that might set us crossways with my father. We must be conciliatory with him at this delicate point in our relations.
>
> Although I understand your grievance and wish that I could help, I beg you, please, do not drag me into the conflagration you intend. You know I have no power to snatch you from such a fire.
>
> I believe that you and I are led by God and our friends to do what is right to the best of our abilities. While I abhor that I am helpless to assist your quest, I send an armful of my love. Be safe.
>
> —M

Lizzie must answer immediately. Of course, there could be no way for Mary to confront her father about the Royal African Company. What was she thinking then? Now, Lizzie choked back a block of feelings: embarrassment at having importuned; remorse for alarming her friend; trepidation for whether she'd harmed her deepest friendship.

Also, at last Lizzie felt all that Rowland expressed about his helplessness, not being able to go against the king.

She prepared her quill. How to adequately express regret over alarming her friend? She decided on only one sentence:

> Please know that my affectionate and loyal heart would never take any action that might injure you in any way—politically, personally, or practically.

Then she added two more lines:

> I have met Miss Prudence Mott here in London and am working to be of use to her. She seems unchanged and as lovely as ever.
>
> —Y

That letter deserved an elaborate letterlock. Her other messages were not so precious: asking Felicity to manage the actors with her own discretion; begging off meeting with the chef until Wednesday.

She asked Lazarus to carry her crucial letter around to the Duke of Bagsham's house, with a note that begged for the missive to be added to a diplomatic pouch, so it might reach her friend as quickly as possible.

Then Jane came to say that Michael was waiting for her. She made sure Lizzie left the house with the warmest possible cloak from Rowland's closet.

"Where is Rollo's new listening post?" she asked Michael.

"Down by the customs house," he said. "It's a minor investment he's made."

Michael hailed a sledge and directed the driver to a street near the waterfront.

15
Achilles in Bloomsbury

—NED—

TUESDAY LATE AFTERNOON

AT FOUR O'CLOCK THAT afternoon, Ned set out to meet the richest man among the Hawkins' Heirs investors. It was now his job to get Perry inside the man's house so they could learn details of Wolfric Molewood's business. Lizzie needed to bait a hook to draw Molewood into her scheme to fish for recompense for the *Skylark* survivors.

When Ned knocked at the door of Molewood's Bloomsbury mansion, his eyes were assaulted by a host of architectural travesties. Angles and eves out of proportion to each other. Overhangs perched where there should be none. Windows set to look out at the street, then shuttered so none could see in or out. Inside the Italianate foyer, a baroque version of *Judith Beheading Holofernes* threatened to burn his eyes and torch his soul. Ned's Cambridge landscapes were hung far too high for anyone to get a proper look at them. Perhaps Molewood hung them high to be out of the reach of his dog—no, likely a cat. The house didn't seem to belong to a man who'd keep a dog.

But worst of all, the young man who took Ned's hat and cloak wore a silver buckled collar. The lad said only, "Hello, sir," when Ned introduced himself.

Ned wanted to ask, "Are you from the *Skylark?*" but didn't have sufficient Portuguese.

"This way, sir," the lad said in a heavy accent while gesturing for Ned to follow. The lad's appearance evoked the feelings that had flooded Ned's senses when they met those girls in Bristol, even though this lad was well fed and well dressed. But that padlocked collar!

Distracted by the lad, Ned followed upstairs to a sitting room while trying to regain his calm by tallying the defects in taste in each room he passed. Before he even met the man, Ned held high hopes that Lizzie might have the chance to fully vent her ire on the man.

"Mr. Wijck? So very happy you could come today."

The man in pansy-purple velvet was half a head shorter than Ned and not so broad as Perry. He offered a petulant smile. Ned extended his hand, said the necessary, and refrained from staring over the man's shoulder at the four forgeries on the wall behind him. One was another of Ned's work, an Italianate painting of Daniel in the lion's den that he'd sold a year ago. Back then, he'd been happy to know it'd hang on a rich man's wall. But now, a twinge of fear jolted through his hands. His left eye trembled. Would his past methods of survival destroy Simon Touchstone?

Ned prompted the fellow to show off his treasures. Besides the forgeries, Molewood possessed a few pieces of blue-figure chinaware and bright enamelware from Asia that appeared genuine, but not top quality. ("The man likes to find bargains," Simon had said.) Last year, Ned could not have discerned quality in anything other than painting, but it had been a year of many opportunities for profound learning.

"And which wall is to receive the fresco?" Every wall in the house was cluttered, and every hall was dimly lit.

"Mr. Touchstone's agent has convinced me that I should prefer a framed painting rather than a fresco."

Molewood then spent considerable time choosing which of his treasures should be memorialized in the planned painting.

"You must have made a huge investment in keeping out thieves." That was Ned's crucial statement for this meeting. ("*Get me into the house, chucking, so I can do your sister's bidding.*")

"All windows and doors have locks," Molewood said. "Safe as can be. As with every house I build."

Ned shook his head, tried to look mournful. "That's what the Duke of Bagsham said, just before thieves got his Gentileschi painting. I'm not one for the Venetian Baroque, but any man hates to think of such a piece gone to *banditti*. The Gentileschi is now likely in a French marquis's chateau."

Ned began a desultory list of the known thefts in the last year. "The old Dutch portraits have fared the worst at the hands of thieves. I'm sure Spanish grandees are paying robbers to get revenge for their military losses in the Low Countries."

It shouldn't take much more than that to further Ned's goal, but Molewood changed the subject. "I admired your fresco at the Duke of Bagsham's house in St James Place."

"You are kind to say so, sir. I was asked to repair another fresco from the time of the first Charles, damaged by thieves. I helped the duke find a locksmith then, just after his Gentileschi piece went missing."

Lizzie was right about appealing to a rich man's vanity.

"Who is it? I always hire locksmiths from the Guild."

"The duke hired the smith that King Charles used when he rebuilt Whitehall. The man works from Oxford Street. Has one of those old-fashioned Puritan exhortation names." Ned pretended cogitation. "Ezra Pelletoot, it was."

All of which was true, and Ned quickly sold the notion. As Perry and Rowland often said, always best to use a truth to advance a gambol.

—

The day's light was gone, and the servants were lighting candelabra. Quickly enough, Ned and Mr. Molewood had agreed on a plan for the man's mythological painting:

The room with the best light.

The pieces of art and antiquaries to be featured.

The number of human figures to include.

No mythic creatures.

"You'll be happiest with a realistic style," Ned said. "You won't want angels or putti in a painting with the hero Achilles."

Molewood frowned, pulled at his pointed beard. "Perhaps I should choose a biblical story. My mother might prefer that."

Ned, however, preferred not to paint such after having done Daniel and the lion. "But for your own legacy, shouldn't the allusion of the painting be to a man who has reached the pinnacle of his world though skill and wit? That is, you should stand as Odysseus in the painting."

"Ah, yes. Best not to think twice after a decision. That's how I do business."

"Speaking of which," Ned wanted to lead the man away from considering a Biblical story, "how much time can you take from your business to pose for the initial portrait? And when are you first available?"

Molewood seemed surprised. "Am I to appear, even though it's to be a mythic subject?"

"Do you not want to appear as the cunning Odysseus, the man who reveals Achilles's disguise?" Ned pretended greater surprise. "Every lord in London has himself or his lady in such pictures. Or perhaps you prefer the older style."

Ned pointed to a painting on the wall just above their heads, that lesser Italianate forgery he needed to take back before it caused the Touchstones any harm.

"The Venetians have long admired the notion of the patron who merely looks upon the scene from the side. Modern English painters of distinction, like Lely, prefer to place the patron at what we call the focal point. Perhaps our Stuart kings have encouraged that style."

Wolfric Molewood was not a man who'd look on from the sides in any situation, much less in a painting for which he was to pay what an ordinary man would consider a fortune.

"I am a busy man. I've heard a simple portrait can take fifty hours to paint. I don't have that kind of time to sit still."

"I begin work by capturing the face of the man that will draw all attention in the painting. After I gain your likeness, I can use a model to stand in for the rest. Can you give me ten hours, perhaps over two days?" Ned then began privately planning the palette for painting this client. Those hooded eyes with dark brows called for two parts common red mixed with four parts Devil-in-the-Head green. And a touch of pure soot.

Ned began suggesting which models he might bring to represent the Achilles and the daughters of Lycomedes.

"I'm planning three daughters, including the disguised Achilles."

"I believe," Molewood said, "I have convinced your agent to stand for Achilles. My servants can stand in for the rest."

Where, Ned wondered, would Lizzie find time for Orlando to pose at Molewood's house. Then he wondered more at the man's next claims.

"I was surprised when Miss Mott appeared as Touchstone's agent. She seems quite knowledgeable. Is it true—as an artist in London, you must know. They say she lives openly with the fellow who's finishing Lely's last works."

"I haven't met Miss Mott," Ned said. Zooterkins, why did Lizzie spring this purpose on him? "But there are no such rumors among painters with whom I'm acquainted. She's known as a learned supporter of promising artists."

At Molewood's insistence, Ned lingered longer, despite needing to learn what twists Lizzie had thrown into their plans. He felt forced to drink the man's Canary wine and toast their notions for the painting.

"You'll like this," Molewood said when his silver-buckled servant brought a tray with a decanter and small glasses. "It's the first of the Malvasia from Tenerife, from the year that King Charles allowed Canary imports again." He poured two sips for each of them. "It is a relief, is it not, to no longer pay Suffolk smugglers for Canary wine? They multiply charges worse than the king's Royal African Company thinks to add."

"I'm more of a genever man myself," Ned said, which he always said when any man tried to get him talking about the quality of one wine over another. His preferred drink was in fact small beer, cold from the Revelstone Hall cellar.

As a last push, he pointed his glass of Canary to the quartet of paintings above them on the wall. "I hope you did not think my little sermon about focal point denigrated your precious pieces. Styles change, but those old masters grow only more valuable each year that passes. Would that I possessed such treasures." He pretended as much consternation as he could manage, then said, sotto voce, "But if they were mine, I'd seek superior locks throughout the house."

The master of the house did not see the artist to the door. A small servant in blue velvet led Ned away. That lad allowed no familiarity or personal exchange. He said only, "Good day, sir."

On that winter's afternoon in London, the day's light was gone. The street had frozen even harder, making every step perilous. Yesterday's snow cracked underfoot with each step. Ned headed for Oxford Street, expecting to find Perry there.

PART III

THE LION'S DEN

—

CELIA

Why, cousin; why, Rosalind—
Cupid have mercy!—not a word?

ROSALIND

Not one to throw at a dog.

CELIA

No, thy words are too precious to be cast away upon curs,
throw some of them at me; come, lame me with reasons.

ROSALIND

Then there were two cousins laid up;
when the one should be lamed with reasons
and the other mad without any…
O, how full of briers is this working-day world!

CELIA

They are but burs, cousin,
thrown upon thee in holiday foolery;
if we walk not in the trodden paths,
our very petticoats will catch them.

ROSALIND

I could shake them off my coat:
these burs are in my heart.

— William Shakespeare, *As You Like It*

16
Samuel's Coffeehouse

– LIZZIE –

TUESDAY LATE AFTERNOON

THE BELLS AT ALL-HALLOWS-by-the-Tower rang the four o'clock hour. Lizzie hoped that Ned was now meeting Wolfric Molewood in Bloomsbury, while she and Michael waited for Tom under a newly painted sign: *Samuel's Coffeehouse.* The place was just off Tower Street, not far from the customs house. Michael insisted on staying with her until Tom came. Countess sat on her boots, once more borrowed from Rowland.

She peered through the steamy panes of the bowed front window of the coffeehouse. Inside, a swarm of men in wide-brimmed hats, feathers swaying, argued and gesticulated. They were businessmen from London shipping: merchants and chandlers, captains and shipowners, brokers and bankers. But there were no men dressed for work on the docks—no stevedores, dockwallopers, coopers, wrights, or bargemen.

Tom Foxe arrived, and Michael bid them farewell, returning to Xanthus House to finish a printing job for Friday's gambol. Tom coughed, still recovering from a cold in his head. He used his handkerchief then grasped Lizzie's elbow in greeting, grinning like a cat that has found the buttermilk. Countess stuck her nose in, to see if anything good was in the offering.

"It's nice to see you, Cousin Orlando. I hear we can enjoy your company in London for only a few more days."

"*Si, senyor*. I expect to be gone from Xanthus House after Friday. Perhaps I'll return to my own country."

"Not the best weather for travel."

"When it's time to go, one must be on the way."

Tom opened the coffeehouse door and stepped aside for her to enter, as if innately unable to pass through a doorway in front of a woman, even one dressed as a Continental viscount.

Inside, the room assaulted her senses. It wasn't dirty, with its well-swept plank floor, but tobacco pipes had stained the plaster walls. The tiles above the open hearth were streaky with smoke from the fire. And the noise overwhelmed her. Two dozen men did what men do when they must get the better of each other, their voices growing louder and louder.

Whatever Tom said was lost in the din. She'd walked far enough into the crowded room to see that one must order at a long table at the back. She stepped up to ask for a coffee, but Tom elbowed her ribs and spoke first to the steward.

"Good morning, Diggory. Two coffees. Is the earl about?"

"Yes, sir. No, sir." A soft puff of a voice. The coffee steward was shorter than Lizzie. He had a cloud of sandy curls, and his small brown eyes sparkled in a round, friendly, and young face.

Tom said, "Allow me to introduce you. Viscount Orlando, this is Diggory Crackbone, lately of Cadiz, now the steward at Samuel's. Viscount Orlando, our cousin, is from Catalunya."

"A cousin?" Diggory tipped his head with bright interest. "I always wished for a cousin. And a grandmother. I must pray that the saints will scrub my heart of jealousy."

Lizzie held out her hand in greeting, but he didn't notice it while rhapsodizing about his unrequited love for family and offering a distinctly Romanish prayer. Then he said, "*Bon dia,*" followed by a string of unknown words that might have been "pleased to meet you." Whatever he spoke, it wasn't Spanish.

Bother! He's speaking Catalan!

The faux viscount would be exposed as soon as she spoke a word. As if sensing her jangling nerves, Countess buried her muzzle in Lizzie's hand.

But Diggory returned to English. He went on blithely. "It's Barcelona, isn't it, your lordship? Your hat and that feather declare it. I came to your city after my ships were attacked by pirates. Barbary Muslims, they said, but I swear it was Genoese Christians. Yet landing in Barcelona was a wonder. The food! And every man there possesses the soul of a poet! Don't you agree?"

"*Si,*" Lizzie said, overwhelmed by his enthusiasm.

"Yet they say Barcelona is half what it was thirty years ago, before the Revolt and then the plague. The people hate that La Corona d'Espanya got its hooks in. Ah, ha ha. I didn't intend a pun. Never do."

Lizzie had no idea what his jest meant.

"Please believe," the steward spoke earnestly, "that I'd endure another shipwreck if it meant once again shaking my cloak dry in Barcelona. I am so pleased to meet you, Vescomte d'Orlando. Let us talk about Barcelona whenever you are homesick."

"It's kind of you to say so," Lizzie said.

Still enthusing, Diggory said, "It's only as we were taught by our Savior. I know what it is to be lonely in a strange city."

Tom interrupted the steward's rhapsody. "We'll be at the earl's table, Diggory." He steered Lizzie toward the far end of the room. "Sit with your back to the wall. Like Rollo always does."

She sat in the corner. Countess settled on her feet. "Who did I just meet? I was stunned by his instant friendship."

"Diggory Crackbone? He came to London skint from a failed mercantile journey. Took the job here and kips in the storeroom. And tells outrageous tales of his adventures."

"Those were tall tales about pirates just now?"

"I don't know. He's like cunning Odysseus, battling monsters at sea, but without a wife to come home to."

"Luckily, he didn't notice I don't speak Catalan."

"You impressed him, Orlando. That red brocade suit with all its embroidery makes you more notable than if you wore a silk gown. Everyone here thinks I'm with a he-strumpet."

"Not a gallant cavalier? No one ever takes Rollo for a rake or strumpet when he wears this suit."

"Because he walks like a man with notions of romance. That is, notions about one single woman."

—

Diggory manifested at the table and set down tin mugs for their coffee, startling Lizzie out of the conversation.

Impossible to guess what he'd just overheard.

"The Earl of Marborne has arrived," Diggory announced as he deposited a tin coffee pot. "Several men greeted him, but he's trying to make his way over to you. He's listening to those jobbers who have a ship set for New York. Who wagered that England would be the winner when the king gave Suriname to the Dutch in trade for that city?"

Rowland hovered behind the coffee steward. He wore a black brocade suit and a tall-crowned periwig. Countess sprung up and nuzzled Rowland's breeches, though they'd all endeavored to teach the dog not to do that. Rowland scratched Countess's ears, thereby rewarding her bad behavior.

"Hello, Diggory," Rowland said. "What news today? Did even one shipowner have luck with their insurers this week?"

"The captain of *The Asia* proved that he lost ten crates in a storm off the Cape of Good Hope. Two East India ships came into London on Monday, home from the Maldives, and the captains attested that one of their company ships sunk in the same storm off the Cape."

"*The Asia* captain was blessed!" Rowland said.

"Aye. Unusual, is it not?" Diggory said cheerily. "First time this year a London insurer paid out on a maritime policy."

"Unhappy day for that insurance syndicate." Rowland managed to squeeze past and sit next to Lizzie, pressing his thigh against hers.

That touch spread unreasonable comfort through her after the day's aggravations. If only she could tell Rowland about her meeting with Molewood while pretending to be Prudence. But they'd vowed to keep their businesses separate and secret.

"Some men claim," Diggory said, "the insurance syndicates only take in money, not pay it out. Ah, ha ha."

Again, Lizzie didn't perceive the jest.

"Maybe you'll have good luck, Diggory." Rowland exuded friendly warmth with the steward. "Maybe a captain will come to anchor in London and attest to all you lost."

"It's too late for me, my lord." Hands clasped behind him, Diggory rocked on his worn leather shoes.

"Perhaps. Never can tell," Rowland said softly. "May I have tea, Diggory? I'm not convinced coffee agrees with me."

"Of course, my lord." The steward scuttled over to his coffee bar and instantly began conversing with the men there.

Rowland said, "*Bon dia,* Lord Orlando."

"It's a good day, but cold." She sighed. "Whoever thought Ysabel Foxe would find true love with a London man of business? The gossip says she's hunting for an English title."

"I am now both men," Rowland said. "My vast holdings include a coffeehouse and the insurance policy on a burned ship that hauled illicit cargo."

Tom said, "Good idea, Rollo, investing as a silent partner. No daily business worries."

Lizzie dropped her voice. "Is this your gambol, Rollo?"

"I'm two weeks into this venture, which only Michael and Tom know about. I am learning more shipping news than an indolent king's watcher usually knows. Diggory Crackbone is worth his weight in shillings."

"Are his stories true?"

"I think so. What matters for my purposes is that he's invisible to others. People talk, and Diggory listens." Rowland still had no tea. He sipped Lizzie's coffee. Made a face. "I can also listen to Whigs and Tories plot with their allies."

"How?" Lizzie gestured to the noisy crowd. "I can't hear my own thoughts."

"It only works for certain tables, but it helps me satisfy the duke's craving for news with minimal effort."

Tom said, "This is how we found Sir Duxwold after I'd exhausted every other hope of finding that traitor."

"So convenient," Rowland said.

"And that fellow you had Captain Starbuck arrest last week? The one who wanted to blow up a church near the Tower?"

"He bragged about it here," Rowland said, "but he proved too muddled to do it. He had gone off his head and needed to be looked after."

Lizzie said, "So, this is your listening post, Rollo? A talkative coffee steward?"

"Diggory is priceless. But there's more. Show her, Tom." Rowland's eyes twinkled.

"Aye, come along, Orlando," Tom said. "Come this way, as if we're seeking the jakes in the alley."

She followed Tom into a dark narrow passage. When Countess rose too, Rowland called his dog back and, remarkably, she obeyed.

Midway down the narrow passage, Tom glanced both ways, then pulled Lizzie through a door she hadn't seen a moment before. They stepped into a space between two walls, scarcely wide enough to turn around. Like an old priest hole.

"Sit here," Tom commanded.

Lizzie sat on a narrow ledge. Once her brocade suit ceased rustling, she could hear Rowland speaking in a quiet voice.

"I can speak treason in this crowd, thinking the king will never hear about it. Yet it's not treason to confess that I love you, my Dark Lady. Your face, your ember-warm voice, your tender touch, they nourish me. It's almost as if I have a soul."

Her insides warmed; the day's chaos quieted.

She listened: A clatter of tin cups set on the table. A thank-you murmured. Metal on metal. Rowland stirring his tea? He slurped it, then exhaled an ungentlemanly but satisfied breath, as if the coffeehouse freed him from courtly manners. Yet, she did not hear what surely must be happening: Rowland running his gold angel coin over his knuckles. His persistent bad habit.

"You have a message, my lord." Diggory's voice clearly carried to the listening post. "May I speak, my lord?"

"Please, feel free." Paper rustled, which must be Rowland accepting the message.

"A customs house porter carried that message here. He prodded me with his thumb, which I found to be rude."

"As would I." Rowland spoke as mildly as Diggory.

"It made me long to warn you, my lord. If you undertake business with that porter's master, you will never be let free."

"What do you mean?"

"When I returned to London after my ill-fated voyage, my business was a mare's nest. That customs man named the exact price for releasing what remained of my Levant goods. But I didn't have the money. Every fortnight, the customs man asks again. His messenger, who prodded me with his thumb just now, says Tuesday is my last chance."

"Do you mean to say he solicited a bribe?"

"Yes, my lord. I'm told that is how ambitious men do business in London. I share my experience as a caution."

In the eavesdropper's cubby, Lizzie knocked Tom's arm and raised her brow. That porter must be Chudrakes' minion.

Rowland said, "Do you need a loan to pay this bribe?"

"By all the saints, no, my lord. I want only to warn you that once you take up business with those men, they'll never leave you alone."

Those words evoked a warmth in Lizzie's belly, because of Diggory's wish to protect Rowland. She noted again his mild but Romanish oath.

Rowland said, "I am most grateful to you for that warning. I hope to do you a similar good turn one day."

When Tom and Lizzie emerged from the passage, Diggory had left Rowland's table. The room smelled of wet wool that reeked of the original sheep. And coffee. Diggory must have burned a batch.

Tom said in a low voice, "You have a grievous amount of dust on your breeches, your lordship." He slapped dust from her rear quarters. "Unseemly for a lord who came all the way from the Continent to teach England haughty manners."

"I have perfectly nice manners, Tom. You," she said, "have pounce powder on your coat sleeves."

At his table, Rowland sipped tea and fingered the message Diggory had passed to him, not opening it.

Lizzie sat at the table. "Rollo, it'd be grand if Sir Bythorn solicited a bribe. You could turn him over to a magistrate."

Rowland said, "Why do you think it's—"

"Lord Marborne." A high voice for a man. Familiar. Irritating. "They said I'd find you here. I've been looking for you."

Vex me! The devil's own man, Sir Bythorn Chudrakes!

17
A Proposal

— LIZZIE —

TUESDAY LATE AFTERNOON

"HOW CAN I HELP you, sir?"

Rowland's voice was like warm honey and butter.

"As I noted in my message," the man whined, "I need an honest man who's sharp, but not known in London as a Captain Sharp. Ha. You see my meaning?" He plonked a bony finger on the message Diggory had carried to the table.

The devil is about to open a door to Hades.

"Oh?" Rowland glanced at the folded message. "I haven't had a free moment to read it. But we've met before, haven't we? Playing faro at the Earl of Gomfrey's house, am I right? The night I lost an entire flock of gold guineas? I regret teaching him the game. Seems Gomfrey has a genius for it."

Ah, Rollo is playing Merry Andrew.

"No, your lordship." His whine grated on Lizzie's ears. "Bristol. Last October. Sir Bythorn Chudrakes, at your service."

"Why, then it's no surprise seeing you here, just across from the customs house. Have a seat, sir. Let me signal for coffee. Or do you prefer the less bitter China tea? It's too bad that we are forced to pay the Dutch Indiamen a prince's ransom for the chance to drink it."

How do men tolerate it when Rollo plays Merry Andrew?

"Now, let me mind my manners. Sir Bythorn, this is my cousin Tom Foxe, the attorney who manages my affairs."

"Goob day, dir." Tom's cold left him red-eyed, red-nosed, and speaking with croupy hoarseness. He held out his hand in greeting, but that hand held his kerchief and was ignored.

"And, if I recall, sir, you met my cousin in Bristol. Viscount Orlando de Flores from Catalunya."

"Good day, sir." Lizzie chose English to be safe. She didn't stand in greeting or even offer a hand, yet made the effort to appear affable. She couldn't, however, match Rowland's skills at playing Merry Andrew.

Countess sunk her head back against Lizzie's knee, her eyes flickering with the same distrust that Lizzie felt.

"Your lordship, I came to discuss confidential business."

"Excellent," Rowland said. "These are the two men I rely on most in my confidential affairs. What can we do for you?"

Sir Bythorn glared down his thin nose at Tom and Orlando. But he sat and accepted coffee, without acknowledging the steward. He slurped worse than Rowland.

> *You look down your nose at Rollo, while wearing a suit that hangs on you like a feedbag. And brass buttons?*

"Lord Marborne, I've heard that your insurance claim has not progressed well for that ship the king gave you."

Rowland folded his hands, as if penitent. "I do confess, that ship still takes a great deal of my attention. And the lawyers are emptying a load of guineas from my pockets."

Rowland repeated his litany of grief over the contested insurance claim. Lizzie sensed that he rolled his gold angel over his knuckles as he listed problems that bored him.

First, as Rowland reported, the insurers denied the claim, saying the *Skylark* had been used as a slaver's ship, against English law. Rowland's attorney (he nodded toward Tom) countered with the captain's sworn statement, that the crew had rescued people off a foundering Portuguese ship. After that failed, his attorney made a claim against the ship's fire insurance. But the insurers insisted that witnesses in Bristol swore the owners had set fire to the ship.

Nay, six little girls torched it to drive out devils.

Rowland said, "I have better chances playing pharo, even against Lord Gomfrey, than playing the maritime insurers' game. It's all a fudge, you know. The insurers always win."

"Are you giving up the entire affair?" Sir Bythorn asked. "I'm sorry to hear it."

As if you've ever been sorry once in this life.

"S'welp me," Rowland's voice sharpened, "I shall not surrender. Now, tell me why the *Skylark* interests you."

"I pay attention for the king's sake, as is my duty." Snobbery dripped from Sir Bythorn's voice. He sat across from Rowland, arms crossed, a stern Puritan's expression on his pinched, thin-nosed face.

Sir Chudthorn, I wager the king does not know your name.

"Aye, of course." Rowland shrugged, as if conceding the notion. "How you must toil. Traveling to Bristol in the chill?"

"It's the complications I want to speak to you about." Sir Bythorn finally began the business he'd come for. "For the king's sake, I need your help to understand it all, beginning with Lord Withersea's investment syndicate."

You pompous rat! The king can just ask Rollo directly.

"Ha! The man is no longer *Lord* Withersea, is he?" Rowland offered a Merry-Andrew laugh. "The man now wakes every day, wherever in the world he fled to, knowing that King James gave away his assets and his title."

As if he were being friendly, Sir Bythorn said, "And the king rewarded you for uncovering Withersea's crimes."

The king never knew the half of it.

"That is where the complication begins," Rowland said. "The king's exchequer gave me three ships, believing Withersea owned them. Now a lawyer claims Withersea only launched the *Skylark* for a blind syndicate, which threatens—through an attorney—to sue me for any insurance payout, while claiming to have had no idea the *Skylark* was stealing people away from the Royal African Company. And I don't know who I'm battling, since the names of the syndic's members remain secret."

Rowland slapped the table. Countess whined.

"Lord Marborne, the king—"

"No, no, Sir Bythorn." Rowland smiled sadly, still wearing his foolish demeanor mask. "I beg you, do not tell our king that I am unhappy. Withersea's syndicate sought to cheat the king out of his African monopoly. It's not the king's problem that I ended up without all my reward."

"We share a mutual interest, your lordship, in advancing favor with the king."

I'd drink vinegar before sharing water with you in a desert.

Rowland said, "A chance to give lawyers more gold coin?"

"I propose, your lordship, that we work together to discover the members of that blind syndicate. In return, I will do all I can to help advance your insurance claim."

"How do we do that? My attorney hasn't cracked it."

You are a liar, Merry Andrew. Tom had a list of the investors before Withersea left England.

Sir Bythorn said, "Convene the men who helped you capture the traitor Danvers Duncombe. He created that syndicate."

"We cannot ask Mr. Danvers about the syndicate," Rowland said. "Lord Jeffries hanged him last November."

"Yet men in the Exchequer believe," Sir Bythorn spoke in the tones the original serpent must have tried in the Garden, "you have the skills to uncover what the king's intelligencers cannot."

Oh fine. Gossips in the Exchequer seek to plague Rollo.

—

Rowland raised his teacup high for Diggory's attention, then waved him over for service, taking a long time to reply to the customs man.

"We found ourselves in the Duncombe affair accidentally. None of us has a taste for adventure. We three cousins are not heroes." His open palm encompassed Lizzie and Tom.

Tom blinked as if innocent. Lizzie sipped coffee, bored.

Sir Bythorn gazed down his blade-thin nose at them. "Since summer, the king's intelligencers have worked to unearth new information about Withersea's business."

Tom covered a cough before he spoke. "What has been learned, Sir Bythorn?"

Sir Bythorn's milk-and-water eyes stared out from under tawny brows. "Their keen interest is in Withersea's syndicate, and how its members remain secret."

Tom had mastered an innocent, unreadable face. The king's people had uncovered very little, while Tom held Withersea's own original list of members.

"How can we help if the king's own men have failed?" Rowland was rolling his coin over his hand openly on the table. An astute person would see that he only pretended patience.

The customs man drew a paper from inside his coat. "The intelligencers collected this list of men who did business with the marquess. Find out which were members of that syndicate."

Lizzie coughed. Not like Tom's lingering croup, but from choking on Sir Bythorn's stale scheming.

Tom said, "Is your offer to help with the *Skylark* claim the sole reward for any effort we might make?"

Sir Bythorn proceeded to scare the devil out of everyone.

"We know that Miss Ysabel Foxe, your lordship's fiancée, meets with Quakers, who have preached since the Civil Wars that the African trade should be forbidden. You and I collaborating might bring Miss Foxe joy, because we will help the king to stop rogue slavers." Sir Bythorn grasped his clenched fist at the wrist, as if they were jointly defeating an enemy.

Who was spying on her? Was that why Bagsham warned Rollo to abandon the Skylark business?

Tom's hand lay on the table. His little finger twitched. Then his next finger twitched. He sneezed.

Rowland only rolled his coin.

Could Chudrakes destroy our delicate relations with the king?

Lizzie sipped coffee, hiding her sudden fear that she'd put Rowland in jeopardy by meeting with dissenters. One time!

The coffeehouse clock struck half past four, which meant they'd only been at this sham for ten minutes, yet Lizzie felt a tremendous enmity for Sir Bythorn. They'd be forced to cooperate with him, because of one risky conversation.

Tom picked up the list of businessmen. "How do we begin?"

"Invite each man to invest in a new syndicate. Hint that the syndicate will pursue trade in Africa. Then tell me who accepts your invitation."

"So, you advise," Rowland finally spoke again, "that we approach total strangers to invest in a new syndicate that transgresses a royal monopoly."

"Yes, you have it." Sir Bythorn squeezed his hands, happy with his childish idea.

You want us to set a badger trap—only to ensnare us. Why?

"And then," Tom said, "they go directly to a magistrate and report the men who propose to contravene James Stuart's Royal African Company."

"Lord Marborne." Sir Bythorn turned to Rowland. "Please, I hope you see—"

Lizzie smacked her hands on the table. Countess winced. She turned to Tom. "Is this man not wise about the world?"

Sir Bythorn puffed up, haughty and resentful. "I am offering you the chance to be of service to the King of England."

She spoke in a low voice, enunciating carefully. "Do you want to see us in Newgate prison, *Senyor* Bythorn? Or do you have higher ambitions for us? The Tower, perhaps?"

The customs man opened his mouth, didn't answer.

Tom said, "Are you implying that Lord Marborne caught Duncombe through an illicit business proposition?"

Yes, that's what Rollo did. How else to catch a rat?

"Ah, no, I—"

"*Senyor.*" Lizzie steepled her fingers. "I am not a citizen in your country. As a visitor, I cannot transgress English laws. And I cannot imagine my cousins doing so either."

Though my cousins had been England's nicest highwaymen, but we did it only to escape starvation.

Tom sniffed, the best prevaricator among all the Foxe cousins. "I swore before the bar to uphold England's laws. I cannot allow the Earl of Marborne to participate in any such scheme, unless..." He held up a finger. Sir Bythorn waited, seeming hopeful. "Will you swear before a magistrate to indemnify the earl and his comrades for any complications?"

Sir Bythorn quivered. "So, you will not help me stop the illicit African trade, Lord Marborne?" He seemed as crushed as a robin's egg fallen from a nest.

You suck words like a snake swallowing its own tongue.

Rowland pointed to Tom and Lizzie to answer.

"No, we'll help," Lizzie said, though she'd prefer to chase off the fellow, like shooing a woodpigeon from a garden. However, she had to prevent any bad effects that might arise from one visit with five Quakers. "Although not in your foolish way. Give us a week to see what we can do."

"And rather than your mere promise to help the earl," Tom said, "pay us for each name. Say, twenty pounds per name?"

"Guineas," Lizzie said. "In that way, no one can accuse you of soliciting a bribe. You will simply pay for services rendered."

"We will provide documents," Tom said.

"Do you require more of us, Sir Bythorn?" Lizzie said. "Discover other syndicates that impinge on the king's African monopoly? Or help you find officials who are being bribed to ignore such trade?"

"Uh, no, only the Withersea syndicate." Sir Bythorn stood, hands on his hips, as if ready to lecture, even though he'd just been schooled in a different lesson.

"I'll draft a contract for your review," Tom said. "Do you want me to include your commitment to help with Lord Marborne's insurance claim?"

When Tom uttered the word *contract,* Sir Bythorn shifted sideways, so he ceased looking down his nose. "No, just include the promise of compensation. I commit as a gentleman to helping with the insurance. No need for a contract for that."

Tom said, "Viscount Orlando will bring you a report on our progress. Shall we say, this coming Monday? Yes? Then we wish you good evening, sir."

Sir Bythorn wanted to shake Rowland's hand before departing, but Rowland had his hands buried in Countess's scruff, since she'd growled when the customs man stood up.

> *Next Monday? Perfect. After we take what we can from the Skylark's investors on Friday, the king can have the dregs.*

18
Smoke into Smother

— LIZZIE —

TUESDAY LATE AFTERNOON

LIZZIE CAUGHT PERRY'S EYE as he entered Samuel's Coffeehouse. He managed to appear just as Sir Bythorn departed. Perry held the door and greeted the customs man, abusing the Yorkshire accent he often borrowed from his grandmother.

"'Ow do, sir. Grand day, i'n'it?"

Sir Bythorn pushed past without answering, even though Perry cut a fine figure as a businessman. He wore an elegant businessman's suit, the color of a London fog, with twenty silver-colored buttons and a scarlet waistcoat that served as a reminder of his old military coat.

Perry went to order coffee at the steward's counter.

After the coffeehouse door closed behind Sir Bythorn, Tom said, "Thou pudding-headed malapert. Invite Hawkins' Heirs into a new investment? Who'd undertake such a bold notion?"

Lizzie laughed, though her insides churned. She tossed a button on the table, the one she'd stolen off the fellow's sleeve.

"Bones of me." Rowland picked up the button with a short, sharp laugh. "I'll wager three guineas that fiancée of mine might take such a notion. She's contrary."

He settled his hand over Lizzie's, his palm comfortingly warm. But also damp. Had Sir Bythorn unnerved him? Countess nosed her way between their hands. And licked. No, Rowland's hand was wet only because his dog loved him.

Tom said, "I could feel Lizzie catching on fire, but you didn't seem to care anything about Sir Bythorn."

"He's a powerless functionary," Rowland said, "with no power to affect our own business. I do not think he can help with my insurance claim. I expect I shall do as the duke advised me and surrender all claims. The king's reward has been more like a punishment."

"As your attorney," Tom said, "I cannot advise that."

"As your cousin," Lizzie began, "and partner, and—"

"Lover?" Rowland murmured, his eyebrow rising.

"All of that." She was furious about Sir Bythorn, but the man was only worth trifling ire, even with his threats about Ysabel Foxe consorting with Quakers. "He's an untrustworthy fellow who hangs on at the edge of the court, hunting for advantage."

"And, as Rollo's attorney," Tom said, "I shall ensure that we still keep to the leeward side of the law."

"If you think you are borrowing from the Bard," Rowland said, "the line you seek to quote is, 'Still you keep on the windy side of the law.'"

Lizzie said, "We do not want the law involved at all. English law cannot render justice for the *Skylark* victims. That's why those investors must contribute to a restoration."

Rowland rolled his infernal gold coin over the backs of his fingers. "You have softened, dear Lizzie. Your initial plan was to torch their houses and sell their sons to pirates."

"I convinced her," Tom said, "that it's too much work to seek out Mediterranean pirates. They tend to be elusive."

Lizzie said, "I continue to abide by Uncle Absolom's rules for enlightened people and our own Restoration Rules."

"Good," Rowland said. "For myself, I have not discovered how to use our rules for my part of the *Skylark* business."

"And I have not yet discovered the perfect scheme," Lizzie choked back bitterness, "which would end the African trade."

"Which," Rowland said, "will not happen, dear heart. Not even in our grandchildren's lifetime."

"Yet I do have one scheme, and I don't want Sir Bythorn interfering with it." Lizzie felt a stone of obstinacy form in her breast. "The king's only interest is to keep all African profits for his own. We have a higher purpose."

Tom drummed his fingers on the table. "And with or without insurance, I want the *Skylark* investors to pay out exorbitant sums that accrue to our Lizzie's plan."

"But," she said, "the customs man wants to please the king by doing the opposite of what the duke demanded of you last night, Rollo."

"Sir Bythorn won't entangle me in the king's affairs," Rowland said. "He's just an ambitious man of little talent who seized on a queer notion."

"Sir Bythorn is just an inconsequential disturbance," Tom said. "But also, perhaps a secondary source of income."

Perry joined them then, sitting by Tom. "So this is your listening post, Rollo? But, God's teeth, before you explain, I have a distressing tale to tell."

"Wait a moment," Tom said. "We are busy recovering from a compromising proposition from the king's customs man."

"Fine. Tell me all." Perry said. He listened as Tom explained Sir Bythorn's proposal, twice prompting for details.

"In the end, we agreed to seek out investors' names." Tom said. "After Lizzie finishes with my list of Withersea's syndicate members, we'll let the customs man have the dregs."

"I approve. It's straightforward." Rowland poured more coffee into Lizzie's cup. The clink of the tin pot on pewter mug rang loudly in the room.

"No one dies in my gambol," Lizzie said. "And we'll prevent Sir Bythorn from getting dangerous notions about us."

Rowland squeezed her knee. Countess licked her hand. Both reassured her.

Then Rowland said, "However, it's not clear that Sir Bythorn only seeks to please the king. He might have other goals."

"Mayhap," Perry said, "I should take a deep look into how Sir Bythorn lives his life."

"Not until you finish your work at Molewood's in Bloomsbury." Lizzie picked up her mug to sip the bitter brew.

Rowland ran his gold coin over his fingers again. "Tell us what you've been up to, Perry."

Perry said, "I went to prowl Sir Didlington's house again early this morning."

Lizzie said, "Why? We know all we need about him."

"Aye, but bones of me! It got my hackles up, how he insulted you at the duke's fête, Miss Foxe. And I noticed last night that Sir Didlington has an African page to wait on him." Perry reached inside his waistcoat. "Look what I discovered in Sir Didlington's lockbox."

He laid a paper before Rowland and Lizzie, which left Tom to read it upside down.

"That pestiferous peacock!" Lizzie cried.

"It's only the indentures for his servant. Except...A jinx on these pestilential fools!" Tom yelped. "It's signed by the Earl of Marborne and the Viscount Orlando de Flores. As if those two sold the *Skylark* people."

Lizzie felt a bonfire raging within her again. "This forgery proves that Sir Bythorn is the malefactor I believed him to be."

"No, it doesn't," Tom said. "We still have to prove he's behind the forgery and that he benefited from the indentures."

"I must go to Bristol," Rowland said. "We need Mr. Keckilpenny to swear that we had nothing to do with the people taken off the *Skylark*."

"I should go along," Tom said. "If oaths are to be sworn, then I—" He began coughing. Lizzie offered her kerchief.

"No, stay in London." Rowland said. "Lizzie needs you here, Tom. You too, Perry. I see what you're thinking, but I'll cadge a ride with the king's relay." He rose. "I need to take measures now, to go in the morning."

He began climbing into his greatcoat. Countess rose too and shook vigorously, like dogs do. Lizzie's red brocade suit acquired a fine coat of black hair.

Tom said, "Sir Bythorn had best not learn that Rollo's away from London."

"Perhaps," Lizzie said, "the earl succumbed to the disease that left his fiancée bedridden."

"Quite likely," Rowland said. "Rumors in London say they are intimate. Kissing in carriages and carrying on outrageously."

Perry rose too. "I'm off to meet Ned in Oxford Street, to hear if he gained entry into that house in Bloomsbury for me. I'll have to hear about the coffeehouse business over supper."

They all headed for the door, but Rowland stopped to say something to Diggory that Lizzie couldn't hear. A man in the coffeehouse crowd called, "Lord Marborne." Hence, Rowland lagged further behind.

Diggory was at her side. "Your cousin is such a good man. He has saved my life." At that, the steward brushed a tear from his eye. Then, a customer bellowed for service, and he was gone. But Diggory's words roused all Lizzie felt about the Bristol jaunt: fear for Rowland, dread for having to be without him, opening a gulf of loneliness.

Then she wondered how a bed in the storeroom could have saved Crackbone's life. Rowland must be doing more, even if only because this odd fellow collected gossip for him.

When Lizzie joined Perry and Tom outside under Samuel's sign, they were debating who had the duty to keep that reprobate, Orlando, out of trouble until supper.

"How very hilarious," she said. "I can call a carriage and see myself home."

Rowland came up behind her, as close as two men could stand. She felt his heat, since his greatcoat was still unbuttoned, and she smelled his spicy scent. She wanted to lean back into that warmth and comfort. He whispered, his warm breath brushing her neck, even with the weight of Orlando's periwig.

"What?" She needed him to repeat what he'd said.

He whispered in her ear again. "Quakers, Lizzie? You don't seem the type."

19
Frost Faire

— NED —

TUESDAY NIGHT

WHEN NED TURNED THE corner off Russell Street, Perry's arm snaked around his shoulder, which was so very welcome.

"Do not distress me for a moment, chucking. Your face is as stern as a monument. I cannot tell if you've won the day."

"Molewood will have a messenger at Ezra's shop before supper, I wager. It's the nature of the man and the presence of one of his servants that leaves me feeling grim."

"And now you must paint the fellow who makes your mood dark, while I must prowl his house. It's fortunate that you've a courageous heart."

"He promised only ten hours of his time to pose for a painting. Is that enough for your work, Perry?"

"I can prowl at my leisure with so much time."

"How much time do you have now? I should like a beaker of ale at The Rose. That man's Canary left a foul taste in my mouth."

Perry slapped Ned's shoulder, rather too hard. "You are a man of wise and sly humor, I avow."

After they had settled into their ale and a pie at The Rose, Perry again laughed. Ned felt thick-headed until Perry said, "His Canary tasted foul. Mayhap, he's a fowl that tastes like a canary."

"Ah." He finally caught the jest Perry mistakenly believed that Ned had intended. He swallowed his analgesic ale.

At Perry's urging, Ned told all he could about Molewood the man and the lad called Ishmael. Perry prodded him, wanting to know all Ned could describe about the layout of the man's mansion. Then Perry explained about Rowland having to go to Bristol and the new proposal from Sir Bythorn.

"The customs man we met in Bristol?" Ned considered what Lizzie might do in a second meeting with that man. Yet his first question to Perry was: "It's Viscount Orlando who sparred with the customs man today?"

"The same Orlando who's been all over London since the new year? Aye. Rollo asked your sister to stay at his house until her gambol is done, when she'll give up the Orlando fable."

"She was Orlando this morning, then I learned that the agent from Touchstone's who went to Molewood's house was Miss Prudence Mott. I have never met that lady in this life."

"We can ask Miss Foxe tonight about the unknown lady."

"No, not until tomorrow. She's bound to spend the evening with Rollo before he leaves town. And they agreed to keep each other's business secret until Lizzie finishes her gambol."

"Which must be the worst lovers' secret in England. It belongs in a play by Rowland's poet." Perry drained his ale. "We'd best get home for supper. Miss Foxe will want to hear your good news that we shall soon unveil Wolfric Molewood's secrets."

"Best send a messenger," Ned said. "I require your skills tonight, to help my own new plan."

He then explained Touchstone's jeopardy with Molewood, beginning with the false accusation of a Lely forgery.

"We must act tonight." Ned said, but Perry was still frowning over Ned's story. "To protect Simon Touchstone."

"But we must give priority to Miss Foxe's tasks for her plan."

Ned began his explanation again, still emphasizing the need to protect Touchstone's reputation. But this time, he admitted his personal concerns.

—

"Could you not have waited until I have a key to Molewood's house?" Perry whispered in the dark as they slid along ledges atop three adjacent houses in Bloomsbury.

"No, Perry. It cannot wait."

"It distresses me that we are required to risk our necks. And then the servants will be blamed for our actions. You know that's what rich men do."

"It took me an hour to convince Molewood to hire Ezra Pelletoot to replace every lock in his mansion. It'd be bad for your business if we fetched these paintings after you change the locks."

Simon Touchstone's predicament gnawed at Ned. A bonfire of desire had flared in his heart that morning. He'd explained to Perry why and how he wanted to act—immediately—to remove his faux paintings from Molewood's house.

At first, Perry had disagreed with Ned's entire notion. "It'll look suspicious. First, you make him worry about thieves, and then he's robbed that very night."

"I know you, Perry. You won't leave a trace that might cast suspicion on either of us. The greater worry is whether my old paintings will create tragedy for Simon Touchstone, who has been so good to me, as a friend and as an agent."

At last Perry agreed to help.

"It's beyond my ken, sweeting, but for the sake of your heart's desire, I must stir my bones, since I sense you'll do this with or without my help."

In Molewood's gallery of inferior paintings, it proved easy to take down *Daniel in the Lion's Den*. Ned folded that forged canvas and tucked it into his waistcoat. They could not reach the two false Jan Wijck landscapes in the foyer without a ladder, even if Perry, as tall as Goliath, boosted Ned. Worse, the house roused when Molewood returned home late and pounded at the front door. Hence, the only exit left for them had been out a window in the laundry drying room at the top of the house.

They crept across ice-frosted tiles and returned to the street using a series of lead downspouts as handholds. Kidskin gloves did not keep fingers warm, only prevented them from sticking to the frigid metal. When they rounded a corner and began walking south, Perry said, "Now, sweeting, I shall choose our adventures for the rest of the evening."

"Singing and ale?" Ned asked. His cheeks burned, either from cold or exertion. His heart pounded from the good kind of fright, when you get what you want at the end.

"Aye, my heart's dove."

—

They passed several taverns in a series of neighborhoods before Ned grasped that Perry was leading him to the river.

"Skating's not for me." Ned pulled back, though it felt like a childish motion.

"You haven't tried. And we'll only slide in our shoes. No one has skates to hire out for lads our size."

"That's because there's no real faire this year. It's not so cold this winter as past years."

Perry grew expansive. "There's no true frost faire, because James insists we still mourn King Charles. It's like the theatre. England is not allowed true happiness." Then coaxing quietly: "We'll only go along the river's edge."

"They say a man fell through just last Saturday."

"But that's much farther down the river than here. And it's been quite cold the last few days. Come, Ned. We shall be so merry. You've heard me tell of the joy we had skating the canals in Amsterdam, with ale and torches."

"A canal isn't the River Thames." Ned knew he'd lose this argument, but prolonged having to face the adventurous fate that came from being Perry's friend.

"I'll hold onto you, chucking. You won't fall. See, here are men all along the way, arm in arm. Torches, singing, and hot ale. It's just the thing to warm heart and soul."

It felt as uncomfortably frightening as swimming in a current, which Ned also loathed. He didn't like the twinges of fear when his feet were slipping out from under him, even with Perry's strong arm at his shoulder and elbow.

With no other choice, Ned imitated Perry until he came to feel the proper motion. They slid along the ice in a rhythm, like the dancing at May-day, except cold stung his cheeks. Perry warmed Ned's hands as they moved over the ice together. He sang, but Ned had to concentrate and so was too breathless to join in the song. His heart beat with a tremor of fright, as if they were committing a second dangerously criminal act that night.

Then Perry slipped and fell, taking Ned down too. Ned fell on top and couldn't get a toehold or handhold on the ice to pull himself off.

"Just enjoy it, chucking," Perry whispered as he wrapped his arms around Ned, holding him there. "You must have noticed more than one lover here ends up on the ice."

"You cheat!" Ned couldn't enjoy it, too aware of the painting inside his waistcoat, pressed between them.

"Yes, but now you know what it is to fall. And the Thames didn't open its ice mantle and swallow the both of us."

Indeed, after that hard fall, the slipperiness was no longer frightening. Just before Ned's toes froze, Perry pulled him over to where a huddle of men sang around a bonfire on the river banks. Since Ned had proved his mettle, he persuaded Perry to take up nine-pin bowls for their next joy, though even Perry wasn't thrilled with the difficulty of bowling on ice.

"We deserve more ale," Perry declared after he'd lost five shillings on an extravagant bet.

While Perry sought the ale vendor just a short way up the steps, Ned pocketed the shillings he'd won, and then managed to remove the folded canvas from inside his waistcoat. He fed it onto the bonfire, which quickly ate the faux Venetian canvas. The maw of the fire begged Ned to find more canvases to feed it.

As Perry predicted, the modest frost faire at the river's edge was not the danger Ned had imagined. He happily stood with Perry, drinking ale and watching the doings on the river and its frozen banks. Nearby, a square-framed man in a long red wool coat complained to a friend that it didn't come close to the glories of the frost faire two years before. He recalled, in a Kentish accent, when the games on the frozen river included carriage races and bull baiting, when tents and booths offered every treat, from mutton pie to gingerbread.

"That faire was a reward from God to cheer us in the cold," the man concluded. "Say it was so, Samson."

"Aye, Barnaby," his friend Samson said, a scrawny man in murky brown wool, speaking with an accent from the south side of the river. "God's reward after birds died in the tall trees and fish froze in the mill streams. People starved when the unharvested grain froze. Children and old folk had their frost faire in heaven, I warrant."

"But we're better now, praise God," Samson said. "We made it through. And we had such a grand faire that cold winter."

Perry nudged Ned away. "Do you believe that, Ned? Did we survive that bad winter by the grace of God?"

"I don't think of that time in such a grand way," Ned said. "My cousin Tamsin got every person into the fields the night the skies turned bitter cold. We stayed working till dawn by torchlight. And then brought all the harvest into the great barn. We managed to save more than half the usual harvest, which was better than many other villages in Cambridgeshire."

Remembering, Ned watched a quartet of boys sliding on the river, two dogs barking at their heels. That hard winter had been only a part of a very bad year.

"We all lived in only two rooms of Revelstone House, sleeping close to keep warm at night. Tamsin made us check on the villagers and cottagers, and we brought back to Revelstone House several of the old people and mothers with infants who couldn't keep warm in their cottages. We opened two more rooms, ones with hearths."

"You distress me, my dove." Perry dusted the shoulders of Ned's coat and adjusted Ned's second-best neck scarf. "I only remember that Rollo and I wore all the clothes we possessed to stay warm, and then slept most nights at a small tavern that was warmer than the barracks. I'm ashamed to say we only took care of ourselves."

"We had to care for the others because—"

A sledge glided past on the frozen edge of the Thames, bearing Lizzie and that fizgig actress Felicity Oakes. They'd dressed in men's clothes, but it was obviously Lizzie, if you knew her to see it. No sign of Michael or any other person to protect Lizzie.

It already proved to be his good fortune that he hadn't taken the duke's gold guineas, because Ned had already failed her.

—

"There's Lizzie." Ned tugged Perry's cuff. "We must protect her."

"Why?" Perry's voice lingered behind him, as if he weren't following when Ned took off in pursuit of Lizzie. But Ned could not look back while keeping Lizzie's sledge in sight. And keeping on his feet.

Running on ice in leather shoes was a hopeless endeavor, like in a frustrating dream where you must catch someone who's fleeing, but can never gain ground. To his great good luck, the sledge pulled up by a booth near the Whitefriars stairs.

Lizzie and Felicity emerged from under the sledge's blankets, then caught each other while slipping on the ice.

Ned arrived gasping and wheezing, his knees shaking like calf's foot jelly because of the effort to keep from pitching onto the ice. Felicity had removed a glove, offering a bite of gingerbread to Lizzie, who dipped her head to nip at it.

Too breathless to greet her, Ned merely puffed like a fish cast on shore.

"Ned! Hello! Where's Perry?" Lizzie didn't seem surprised to see him. "Have you tried the gingerbread?"

"Good evening, Mr. Wijck," Felicity said. "Oh, you've beat Mr. Frake in your footrace."

Perry arrived, not at all winded, with a smile left from the *why* he'd shouted moments earlier. He greeted the women.

"Why are you here?" Ned asked of Lizzie.

Gloved hands on her hips, and so looking nothing like a boy, Lizzie said, "Because we'd be fools to miss the frost faire."

"Even if," Felicity had her nose in the air, "it's less than half the faire we had when I first came to London."

"We'll take you safely home," Ned said. As soon as the words came out of his mouth, he heard they didn't fit with the niceties being traded.

"No need to go home so early," Felicity said. "The curfew isn't for hours."

"And no one's been enforcing curfew since the hard freeze." Lizzie spoke while looking past Ned.

Another sledge stopped at the stairs. Tom, Rowland, and Michael emerged.

"Hoy, everyone's here!" Rowland exclaimed. "Shall we find some food? I'm starving."

"After you admit that we won." Lizzie held out her hand. "And pay up."

"We let you win," Tom said. "And besides, there were three of us and only you two bird-weights on your sledge."

Ned had his eye on Michael, who Ned had asked to watch out for Lizzie when he could not. Michael shrugged, his open hands out as if helpless. A silent gesture that Ned understood: *Who can make Lizzie do anything other than what she wants?*

"They are roasting an ox just down the way," Perry said. "Serving it up on manchets. With mustard."

Their crowd set out to find the sacrificed ox, Perry and Ned acting as rearguard.

When Ned got near Lizzie, he said, "I succeeded with Mr. Molewood today. Perry can enter the house tomorrow."

"I know. He sent a message to the Touchstones, who sent a message to you at Xanthus House. You're to come at noon and bring Miss Prudence Mott as a model."

"Why is that you?"

"Yes. I'll tell you in the morning." She seemed distracted, watching Rowland come to her with a flagon of hot wine.

"Lizzie," Ned drew her attention back, "a messenger asked me to give you this."

She unfolded the packet and examined it under the blazing torchlight. "What messenger? When did you receive this?"

"This morning. After we left the Touchstones."

"And you waited until now to deliver it?"

"I haven't seen you until now." At least *that* was true.

"How did you come by this?"

"I'm not supposed to tell you," Ned said. "For your own protection."

"The letterlock is broken. And I wager it's you, Ned Wijck, who broke it."

"It was an accident."

She had Ned's hand and peeled off his glove. "I shall break your little finger, so it matches the one you broke last summer, if you do not tell me how you came to possess this letter."

"You're hurting me." He pulled away. "It was the duke. He gave it to me and asked me to protect you at all costs."

"The duke?" Lizzie found this bewildering.

"Yes, Bagsham."

Perry said, "Will you tell us what's in the letter, Miss Foxe?"

"Ned can tell you, since he's read it."

"I couldn't read the code," Ned said.

Foolish words, given the evil eye she cast his way.

"Thank you for bearing the message, dear brother. Now, forget what you read." She spit the last two words like poison, then turned away, her hand reaching out to Rowland. The wide skirts of her long coat whipped his legs.

"Mayhap that letter explains," Perry spoke close to Ned's ear, "why we had to run over the ice to protect Miss Foxe. I almost understand why you need to steal your own paintings. But I see no reason for us to protect Miss Foxe, when she has both Rollo and Michael at her command."

"I was cautioned not to say who asked." Ned disliked refusing to say, though he'd pondered this situation that morning.

"'Cautioned not to say.'" Perry repeated the words, then silently mouthed the words a second time. Light from a hundred torches flickered across his face, which appeared darkly stern. Not an expression that Ned could endure. "You distress me, Ned Wijck. I didn't know we had secrets."

An unpleasant, unfamiliar sensation gripped Ned's belly. "I was forced to pledge my honor to a lofty person."

"So much understanding you beg of me today, Mr. Wijck." Perry slammed Ned's shoulder, sounding jolly. "I shall trust you. But there's not one whit of difference between your honor and my honor. Not anywhere under heaven."

Ned had known that morning that he'd give in. He said, "We'll talk of it later, when we're alone."

"Do not distress yourself." Perry seized Ned's hand again, tugging him along at greater speed, sending Ned's knees into a quiver again when he tried to keep up. "I wager English royalty is involved. Mayhap I do not want to know more."

Zooterkins! Two people in this riotous crowd had regarded Ned solemnly.

The duke asked for secrecy. Yet Ned was not capable of being disloyal to the two people he treasured most.

By the time they'd climbed beyond the river, with Perry silent the whole way, Ned felt deeply what honor and loyalty meant in his new life. He tugged hard on Perry's sleeve to make him stop the march along frozen cobbles.

"It's from Lizzie's friend in the Low Countries, warning that she's on a dangerous path and that people around the king are watching her. The rest was all hen scratchings that I can't read."

Perry, hands on his hips, said, "You teased me into hoping for a big secret. But we already knew that Miss Foxe had created danger for herself. So, of course the king is interested. I'm not distressed that she goes about London dressed as Orlando. But this Miss Mott business presents a new quandary. And Miss Foxe didn't tell Rollo, did she?"

She hadn't even told Ned until the new sham had begun.

20
Cloud Fretting

— LIZZIE —

WEDNESDAY MORNING

LIZZIE WOKE WHEN THE hall clock struck five notes, ringing all through Xanthus House. She closed her eyes tightly against remorse, which she'd been feeling too much this week. She'd hoped to say farewell to Rowland before he departed for Bristol, but a miserable guilty dream kept her asleep too long.

She poked her nose out from under the heavy covers, intending to rise and begin the day's chores, but drew back under the covers against the cold, inhaling again the wood ash used in the Xanthus laundry. No, that was wrong. This house kept only a slim staff and so sent out the laundry. Whoever did the bed linens used too much stiffening and no scent in the soap. Living with Aurora Rôche at Chalgrove House, she'd grown used to soft linens, where the bed clothes were washed in-house, with sweet lemon balm and lavender scents.

Folding herself practically in two, Lizzie avoided the cold places, cleaving to the small space she'd warmed with her body. Cold might be an excuse for lingering in bed, yet it was no excuse for not planning the day. First, she had to write again to Mary and then again beg for it to be sent with a diplomatic courier.

Could she just ask Mary whether a rumor about meeting Quakers had prompted that cautionary letter? That might better explain why the Duke of Bagsham asked Ned to guard her—and warned Rowland to abandon the *Skylark* business.

Mary's letter was another reason for her guilty dream. If Rowland had any idea that his reckless fiancée had alarmed the Crown Princess of England, then…well, what?

He wouldn't scold her, like Mary had done. Instead, he'd try to fix the pickle she'd put them by letting rage overwhelm her, all while believing she was capable of more than she'd proved so far.

She stopped that thread of thought until she had a pen in her hand to write the letter.

Come breakfast time—which occurred much earlier here than at Chalgrove House—she'd check with Michael Oakes that all the letters and documents for the gambol were printed and ready to be delivered today to every man invited to the Friday event. He'd had done so much work that week, tending the printing press in the Xanthus House cellar:

> The final prospectus for the gambol's syndicate—the Balthazar-Levant Silk Merchants Association. The potential investors had so far received only tantalizing teases.
>
> The signing sheets for the investors' membership in the syndicate, with its pledge to secrecy.
>
> The ships' insurance pledges and English passes for protection against Barbary pirates.
>
> The elegant invitation to the merchants' final presentation, with a formal supper prepared by King Charles's former chef. (Had Tom sent advance payment as promised? She had a host of questions for Tom that day.)

That list alone indicated that she'd gone astray. Perry repeatedly insisted that the best gambol must be simple, able to strike the marks swiftly, and disappear like smoke. She'd made sure of the "strike and disappear" elements, but that list of documents whispered, "*Too complex.*"

But it wasn't. The gambol promised an outstanding return on investment while minimizing risk. It presented the sort of business every wealthy Londoner wanted to join in. And they'd finish in a night and be gone.

She needed to confirm that Lazarus had procured Orlando's new suit for the Friday event. Tom and Michael pleaded that, for safety's sake, Lizzie should not attend the event. However, she wanted Orlando to be the most eager investor, just before that false lord left London forever.

Also, she wanted to win—and to watch while she won.

She and Ned would have to return to Threadneedle Street that morning, with Tom in tow. Ned had to gather his paint trappings. Lizzie wanted more instructions for her charade as Miss Mott, and she wanted Tom to advise her friend. Although Prudence Mott's guardian was a solicitor, Lizzie had more faith in Tom's ability to attain all justice possible under English law.

That journey meant once more dressing as Orlando, since Miss Mott couldn't go in a carriage to visit herself. Being Orlando meant more binding and an outrageously heavy wig. She'd have to once more plead for Jane's help. Lizzie had never considered the discomfort Tamsin endured while pretending to be Tom for the many months when the real Tom had been deathly ill. It'd be such a relief to exile Orlando for all time. This Friday evening promised to fulfill so many goals:

> Economic justice for those made to suffer by the Hawkins' Heirs investors.
>
> The last of bound breasts and Rowland's shoes, which rubbed her feet sore no matter what stockings she wore.
>
> The last of so many long days planning miniscule details.
>
> The end of keeping gambol secrets from Rowland.

A shade of the morning's guilt dream haunted her again. She took a breath to be free of it. After the event, she'd confess all to Rowland. That she'd frightened her friend Mary. That she'd play-acted Miss Mott, whom Rowland had met in Amsterdam.

Yet—vexation!—she couldn't close all business with Wolfric Molewood by Friday unless she convinced him to invest in the Balthazar-Levant Silk Merchants Association. Before Rowland returned from Bristol, she had to empty Molewood's pockets, for her own needs as well as to solve Prudence's problem.

How long did she have for that? She knew how many days it took for a journey to Bristol in October, but that was by carriage. How long if riding with the king's courier? In ice and snow? Until the following Wednesday? Or even Saturday next?

The time after Friday seemed to stretch ahead like a vast frozen desert with no track through that empty land.

If only she and Rowland had never agreed to keep secrets.

Bones of me! I shall never be such a dulpickle again.

The door opened softly, and the snug, homey sounds of a fire being laid caused Lizzie to stir again, stretching so that her toes knocked against the now-cold warming pan.

After the strike of steel on flint and the whoosh of tinder catching the spark, Lizzie called, "Jane, may I beg you—"

"Not Jane."

—

"Rollo! Lambkin!"

He sat on the edge of the bed, his weight drawing the covers tightly over her. His finger trailed from her brow down her nose to her mouth, then lingered to trace her lips. She kissed his finger.

"Good morning, my miting, my turtle dove. I cannot leave without a better farewell than we managed after midnight. All business and solemn promises while still freezing from the frost faire. As if we had no poetry in our souls."

He bent so that his warm breath flowing over her eyes and ears smelled of cloves.

"Do you have a toothache, lambkin?"

"What? No. I didn't want to say goodbye while stinking of last night's frost faire mustard and ale. You, my ladylove, smell sweetly of mint and sleep."

"I intended to greet you, blithe-kin, but Morpheus kept me in bed. I wanted—"

"You can have whatever is in my power to give." He kissed her, more like a whisper. She could feel him smile in that kiss. "But it must be in the next five minutes. What is it you want?"

She saw only his outline in the dim light from the hearth fire. But her nose told her he wore riding leathers, which Lazarus must have oiled last night. He also smelled of brandy, thyme, and rosemary. Hungary Water.

"You aren't wearing that spicy French scent I gave you at New Year's."

"That's what you want? That I smell like a Frenchman? I don't need the king's courier to fall in love with me. Only you."

"I want you to be safe," she said. "Bristol is a long way to go in dire weather, just for a sworn piece of paper."

"But necessary paper, as we agreed." He kissed her again. It took longer and was more than a whisper. "I want you to be safe too. After you get what you want from your gambol, what I want is to wake up beside you every day."

While the fire in the hearth crackled, his fingers stroked her eyelids, her cheeks, her ears. She shivered at his touch. At the same time, his arms pinned her under the heavy covers. Maddeningly she could not return his caresses. He leaned so close she could feel his heart beat through his leather jerkin and the layers of covers.

"You're leaving for Bristol now?" Lizzie managed to speak without betraying all that she felt about the Bristol jaunt: fear for

Rowland, dread for all of them making do without him. And the sense that she was about to fly off a cliff into a gulf of loneliness. "This will be the most dreadful week."

"Aye. But it will be better by the time I return," he said. "We will both be fortified against any misfortune that the custom man wishes on us."

"I hope we are not talking only of dreams, lambkin," she said, then quoted his own poet. "'Which are the children of an idle brain, begot of nothing but vain fantasy.'"

"You are quoting Mercutio. Who dies halfway through the play. These are not comforting lines, dear heart."

He kissed her then until she could scarcely breathe, her lips hot and wet, and fingertips throbbing with the impossible urge to touch him the way he stroked her ears, her neck, her collarbone.

Then his deep voice throbbed against her throat as he spoke. "'Yon grey lines that fret the clouds are messengers of day.'"

"It's nowhere near dawn, Rollo. It's the dead of winter. If the sun appears today, it will be a few hours from now."

"Still, I must say anon, my own heart's root. Your Romeo must be off. The king's courier will not wait if I'm tardy. Which will throw my plans into chaos."

"'We that are true lovers run into strange capers.'" She repeated the line he must have used a dozen times while stealing from his Bard to profess his feelings for her.

"Oh, good line, my Dark Lady. I shall only say farewell, and I love you."

They parted then. No more promises or poems. His deep brown traveling leathers reflected no fire light, so only a dark shadow closed the door. She listened to his leather boots beat a fading tattoo against solid wood as he strode down the stairs and out of the house. The reverberation of each step tore away a piece of her heart.

I will never again let our royal masters and mentors be a reason for us to have secrets from each other.

—

It felt like a long time after breakfast to get Tom moving. Then the carriage made slow progress through the streets. Lizzie beat her gloved fingers on the carriage's window ledge.

Ned said, "Have you spent so much time with Rollo that you're adopting his gestures? Last night at the frost faire, you cried, 'Bones of me!' just like Rollo does."

She ceased that sign of her impatience. "There's so much to do today, and Tom is despicably late." She opened the window and hailed Peter, who often served as page. "Peter, please fetch Mr. Tom Foxe. Tell him the horses will catch cold if he doesn't come immediately."

In only a half a minute, Tom emerged, following Peter, and still pulling on his greatcoat, his neck cloth untied.

"Apologies to you both," Tom said. "Legal business to finish. Lovely suit, Orlando. But then, you always shine when you wear bright yellow. That copper wig that must cost Rowland several shillings each week for the barber to keep it looking so fit."

The carriage driver was skilled, so they were only caught twice in jams behind carts, sedan chairs, and carriages skidding over the icy streets. Tom failed thrice to tie his neck cloth. Impatient, Lizzie leaned across and tied it for him. He barely avoided coughing on her.

The journey to Threadneedle Street was long enough for Lizzie to inform Tom about her arrangement with Prudence Mott—which was also her first chance to share details with Ned, who asked more questions than Tom.

"Is it safe for you to be meeting with Molewood alone?"

Tom snorted. "Would it be any safer for Lizzie to be alone with him as Viscount Orlando? Who knows what the man's predispositions are? Lizzie is just as charming as a Puritan princess or a fey Ganymede."

Ned denied that with a shake of his head.

"I'm safe," Lizzie said. "But deeply annoyed with the man. Tom, I wanted you to come this morning to learn more about Prudence's inheritance. Perhaps you can find more ways to protect her from predators like Molewood."

"Is he pursuing her for marriage?" Tom asked. "I don't have much experience fending off fortune seekers."

"No, Molewood is pestering her to sell land that she treasures and wishes to keep."

By then, they were at Threadneedle Street. Ned departed for the warehouse with Simon Touchstone, leaving Lizzie to introduce Tom and face disappointment: Prudence Mott stood by her travel box, waiting for a carriage to take her home.

Hildegonda stood, arms folded, holding a letter.

"You've made great strides quickly, Miss Foxe."

Lizzie took the letter, noting that Hildegonda had abandoned their pledge to use christened names. The message was from Wolfric Molewood, praising Miss Mott's character and her beauty, and begging her to come with Mr. Eduard Wijck to join in his painting session at noon. The man made a too generous offer to compensate Miss Mott as a model.

Prudence liked the invitation. "If he's pestering the false Prudence, he cannot harass my solicitor-guardian."

"I've brought my cousin Tom, to help find ways to stop Molewood from harassing you about your land."

Tom bowed, lightly touching Prudence's fingers in greeting. "We met before, Miss Mott. I brought Jacob, the Earl of Cloudesley, to the house where you are living, He wanted to have a sketch of his mother and sister validated as truly the work of Lely the artist."

"I remember the earl. He was a charming young man who couldn't be separated from his little dog for a moment. He was so enthused about seeing the artist's studio."

"Yes, that's our Jacob. Presently, he's learning to sketch from my cousin Ned, who was with us that day."

"Your cousin has a great deal of talent," Prudence said. "When my friend brought me here a few days ago, Mr. Touchstone showed us your cousin's works for sale in the gallery. My friend wishes to introduce Eduard Wijck to several other artists who are our close friends. I suppose Simon will tell him."

Prudence's enthusiasm for Ned's art opened Tom to a real interest in Prudence's case. While sitting together in the little parlor where the Touchstones welcomed guests, Tom listened as Prudence told her story. He proposed that Lizzie try to learn more from Molewood while visiting with Ned that afternoon. And he promised Prudence that he'd undertake a thorough study of how the law might help her.

After Prudence departed, Hildegonda thrust a bundle into Lizzie's arms. "Miss Mott left another gown for you."

She seemed about to lecture Lizzie, but Tom began to admire the paintings and decorations in the foyer, which caused Hildegonda to unfold her arms and trade kind words with him. It had taken days for Hildegonda to warm to Lizzie, but Tom had a talent for making that happen quickly.

Then Tom said he had to get to his chambers, so Hildegonda sent a servant to fetch Ned from the warehouse. When Ned appeared at last, he was still leaving final instructions with Simon Touchstone for delivering Ned's trappings to Molewood's house.

On the street, after they said goodbye, the trio hailed another carriage. Inside, Ned studied a paper Simon Touchstone had thrust on him, ignoring both Lizzie and Tom. As they turned a corner to leave Threadneedle Street, Tom said, "That was interesting. What a great deal to have to understand so quickly."

"I just don't see," Lizzie's words sounded too passionate in her own ears, "why Prudence followed that artist back to England, abandoning Mary's court. Now she lives with him but won't marry him to gain possession of her fortune."

Tom said, "How odd, Lizzie. I wouldn't have expected such a prosaic view from you."

"Why odd? If her painter is worth loving, he won't squander her fortune or otherwise dictate the future for her life. He must be a worthy person for Prudence to have abandoned her old life to follow him to England. She possesses a brilliant intellect and a sensitive understanding of people."

"Some folks say that of you, Lizzie. Except..."

"Except what? Is there some rumor or insult you want to tease me about?"

"It's just that it was excessively obvious when I took Jacob to have that Lely sketch validated."

"What was so obvious that you are laughing at me? Miss Prudence Mott is an excellent example of English nobility. Kind, generous with her affections. Upright in all matters, social or private. I should be as good a person as she has always been."

"She didn't follow the artist back to England. She followed his sister, who keeps house for the artist, which is why Miss Mott lives in the same residence."

"Oh."

> *I am the most sophisticated of the naïve Foxe cousins. I see things others don't. Except for this.*

"That's likely why," Tom continued, "she doesn't want Molewood's agents snooping around the details of her life. It's not because she's living with an artist who, I might note, has never been judged as a seducer of gentlewomen. Rather, Ned says he's considered something of a Ganymede. Mayhap he'd get on well with Viscount Orlando. Rumor says the viscount is wickedly deviant."

"Oh."

"That's why I suggest to you that the false Miss Mott should lure Molewood into a honeytrap."

My honeytrap has already been laid. What did you think, Tom?

"Can we ride in silence for a while, Tom? I didn't get enough sleep last night."

"Sure, but how do you feel about all that?"

She couldn't gain his silence without first answering. "Ignorant. Blind. Blindly ignorant."

"Those are states of being, not feelings."

"My feelings are too overwhelmed with sadness for more."

"What do you have to be sad about? You have most everything any woman in England could desire. Your gambol is about to succeed, exactly as you dreamed it. One of the finest lords in England loves you and—oh."

"If you cannot stop talking, Tom, then tell Ned what Miss Mott said about his work."

"Mr. Touchstone must have told him," Tom said.

"Told me what?" Ned asked. "We spoke only of the Molewood project, which is now to be a framed painting."

Lizzie enjoyed the look on Ned's face when Tom explained that the artist managing Lely's estate admired Ned's work and wanted to introduce him to other artists.

21
A Pirate's Tale

— LIZZIE —

WEDNESDAY MORNING

AFTER THEIR JAUNT TO Touchstone's gallery, Lizzie smothered her impatience when Tom insisted he had to run a brief errand at Rowland's coffeehouse.

Ned said, "Perry told me about Rollo's venture, but I haven't had a moment to slake my curiosity."

After Lizzie, Tom, and Ned stepped inside Samuel's coffeehouse, she stood waiting for one of them to remove her cloak, then remembered she was dressed as Orlando and removed it herself, awkwardly draping it over her arm. She scanned the crowd until Diggory appeared to lead them back to Rowland's table. His well-worn leather shoes shuffled on the plank floor.

"Will Lord Marborne be joining you?" Diggory asked Tom. "He's usually here at an early hour."

Tom said, "He's been stricken ill. It may be several days before you see him."

"Ill? How sad. Will you send my condolences?"

"He caught a putrid throat." Lizzie pushed the fiction that was to keep people from knowing that Rowland had left London. "I blame Ysabel Foxe, since she had it first."

Pray Diggory doesn't notice Tom's and Ned's.

Tom said, "Ned, please meet Diggory Crackbone. Diggory, this is Lord Marborne's cousin, Ned Wijck."

"The painter? I'm quite pleased to meet you." Usually, Diggory's soft voice barely rose over the noise, but he seemed animated by that introduction. "I saw your painting in the customs house. The subject was Ruth and Naomi gleaning in the fields. As fine as Lely's *Susannah and the Elders,* to my mind. I was quite moved by it." He cleared his throat. "'Whither thou goest, I will go; thy people shall be my people, and thy God my God.'"

He spoke in an impassioned voice and set down the coffee pot to rub a tear from his eye, then disappeared into the coffeehouse crowd. It took a heartbeat for Lizzie to realize Diggory was quoting scripture.

Ned, bewildered, said, "I don't know what to say."

"You made the man cry." It was Perry. He slipped onto the bench beside Ned.

"Hallo, mijn man!" Tom's hoarse Dutch falsetto grated on one's ears. He shed his heavy cloak. After Tom finished coughing and clearing his nose, he tucked the kerchief into his coat cuff.

Perry said, "Pray do not cough on us, Tom Foxe. Your vile disease distresses me."

Diggory appeared again. He set a china pot beside Tom.

"Mr. Foxe, pray tell Lord Marborne that the ship's master is compelled to make good on the *White Swan's* losses."

"Tell us the tale," Tom said, though Lizzie guessed the steward did not need prompting.

"Its cargo loss is declared to be pilfering by the crew, so the insurers will not pay out. Same as with my failed voyage."

Tom said, "Thank you for that news. Diggory, do you know that Lord Marborne asked me to take up your case?"

"Yes, he informed me. But I believe you will only waste your time, Mr. Foxe."

"We shall see. Lord Marborne wants me to ask some questions, if you have a minute, Diggory."

"I have to serve the front two tables."

"Five minutes?" Tom pointed to the clock high on the smoke-stained wall.

"No more, Mr. Foxe." He left to carry coffee to a table.

Perry said, "What did Rollo put you up to, Tom?"

"Rollo met Diggory in the insurers' business chambers. He perceived that an injustice might be underway and asked me to investigate. It's clear that Diggory hasn't the funds or expertise to press his case further."

It was only two minutes until Diggory returned, bursting to tell Tom his tale.

"On our voyage," Diggory continued, "my cargo from the Levant was aboard two leased ships. For safety, we joined a pair of galleys sailing home to Genoa. Yet, in the dark of night corsairs came as if by magic. I swear on Our Lady's mantle, those Genoa men called those corsairs to us."

Lizzie again noted the man's Romanish oath but had no idea what to make of it.

"But you survived," Tom said, which begged more of the coffee steward's tale.

"By God's grace." Diggory's soft voice lulled like music. "I was coshed on the head and so didn't see the theft. But pirates never want large bails and barrels, only such goods they can pilfer and sail away in their light ships. More was lost when my ships foundered in a storm near Cadiz."

"What happened with your claim?" Perry asked. Lizzie had noticed more than once that Perry was always curious to learn from people.

"The insurers declared the losses to be from pilfering," Diggory said. "I am certain it was Genoese sailors and their friends who raided us. But only the captain was ever called to swear. He could not persuade our case."

Diggory was again hailed to attend to the service bar.

—

"How is it," Perry said, "that this fellow is the man Rollo relies on for his listening post?"

Tom said, "When Rollo purchased his share in the coffee-house, it proved to be almost bankrupt, despite being so popular. Rollo and I discovered that the two coffee stewards were robbing the store blind. Rollo persuaded Samuel to fire them. Just a moment later, Diggory came through the door, because Rollo had told him to come seek a job. Diggory became the coffee steward, and in the twenty days since, there hasn't been a need to hire a second steward."

Lizzie said, "While the man may be a good listener, his insurance claim is not like Rollo's. How is his case the best use of your time, Tom? We have so much pressing business this week."

Tom sipped his coffee. "Until this morning, I thought his case could be delayed for the sake of your gambol. But no, it cannot. You need me to undertake this, Lizzie."

"Why? How can—"

Just then, Diggory returned to their table. He carried a coffee pot and biscuits. "Mr. Foxe, do you have more questions?"

Tom said, "Please tell me more about your family. I want to be sure I follow the proper trail for your business."

Because Diggory loved to tell stories, he began while still pouring fresh coffee and laying out biscuits for everyone.

"I have no family living, sir. My father's name was Enoch. My mother died when I was born, which was in St Giles Cripplegate parish." Diggory didn't seem to notice that Tom was making notes with a plumbago pencil. "When my father died, I was quite young, so I have few memories of him."

His sad smile struck at Lizzie's core. She reached instinctively inside her sleeve for her keepsake, her mother's kerchief. But she didn't carry it when she dressed as Orlando.

Tom said, "It's the same for all the Foxe cousins," he indicated Lizzie and Ned, "as for Lord Marborne. We were orphaned quite young."

"That's what his lordship told me, when he first asked about my home and work. But luckily, he has cousins."

Tom said, "What became of you when your father died?"

"I was raised by his partner, Tristram Crackbone, an old bachelor who did me the honor of giving me his name. He had no family of his own, and like me, he'd wished for one. A grandmother and cousins. Although God does not always grant the fondest wishes of our hearts, Tristram and I found great comfort in our lives together."

"What did Mr. Crackbone tell you about your father?"

"Once, when Mr. Crackbone was sitting with me by the hearth one night, I recalled that my father said he'd been stolen by elves. Old Crackbone called that a tale for children, that in fact my father Enoch had been stolen by Irish travelers. When they tried to give Enoch back, his family wouldn't have him."

"Good stars!" The oath was out of Lizzie's mouth as a sudden reaction. "How could that be?"

"I don't know. That's the end of family stories. Tristram didn't tell tales from my father's life. 'Past is past,' he said."

This gnawed at Lizzie's heart. She—and her cousins—sorely lacked stories from their mothers and grandmothers. Uncle Absolom tended to tell stories from myths and poets. "Do you miss that? The stories, I mean."

Diggory splayed his empty hands. "No, you can't miss what you never knew. Tristram taught me his merchant business, pursuing whatever seemed a good line each year. A hose factor, woolen goods, wine. Before Tristram died—just over two years ago—he'd set us up as brokers, handling business between a few ship owners and prosperous shops in London."

"London city shops are a long way from the shipping lanes in the Levant," Tom said.

"Aye." Diggory's abundant natural curls bounced when he agreed. "I went off my head a bit when I saw the strongbox of twenty-guinea pieces that Tristram Crackbone left me."

"What luck for you," Ned declared.

Diggory cocked his head. "It was God's blessing, delivered through Tristram's careful ways. If only I had imitated Tristram's caution. Instead, I invested it all in the voyage of a pair of ships out to bring silk from Constantinople to the west." He laughed, as dry as Tom's cough, then shook his head. "Instead of caution, I indulged a foolish romance about Byzantium."

"Such a tragedy." Lizzie meant genuine sympathy.

"Kind of you to say." Diggory poured more coffee. "I believed that I'd learned so much working with Tristram that I could make a plan to cover all exigencies. I procured English passes and we flew under the English flag. I even purchased the best possible shipping insurance."

"Then lost it all to betrayal, piracy, and shipwreck?" Tom said.

"And an insurance syndicate," Lizzie added, managing the deeper tones of Orlando's voice.

"Here's what I've learned, Diggory." Tom unfolded a paper that he'd had in his capacious sleeve. "Your father wasn't carried away by travelers. His father was a Puritan's son with the portentous name of Job-Made-A-Covenant-With-His-Eyes. He died when your father was only two years old."

"Then our early lives were too much alike." Diggory had that sad smile again. His curls shook.

"Indeed." Tom unfolded the paper a second time, but Diggory still hadn't taken it from his hand. "But your father Enoch had a family. He was raised by his grandfather, who had been given the High Puritan name of Fear-God."

"Why have I never heard of him?" Diggory blinked, now beginning to understand that Tom had an important story to share. Lizzie still didn't see what it had to do with her plans.

"Your great-grandfather lived not far from London. He died two years ago at the significant age of ninety."

"Why did Tristram say my father had no family?"

"Because," Tom said, "when your father Enoch came of age, he married a woman who was Catholic and converted to her faith. Your great-grandfather disowned and disinherited Enoch."

Diggory was silent for a moment. He traced something unseen on the tabletop. "That's why Tristram always said that the wars between Puritans and Catholic Royals were the worst of sins. A travesty against heaven."

Lizzie touched his hand, an impulse to offer comfort, but likely not what Orlando would do.

But then, Tom also put his hand on Diggory's. "I'm sorry to tell you such a shocking tale."

"How did you learn this?" Diggory asked.

Tom said, "When I approached the insurance agent about your claim, he said that you first had to prove you are Diggory Crackbone. I've been doing that through parish records."

"Yes, that added to the impossibilities," Diggory said. "I was barely able to return to England from Cadiz."

"It'd take a barrister who knows how to get answers in the proper courts," Tom said. "By luck, I had my supervising barrister to consult."

"I'm grateful." Yet Diggory seemed overcome by the news. He swiped at his eyes, like a man who doesn't want others to see him weep.

Tom said, "We learned that your Great-grandfather Fear-God died without a will."

"Pray God his soul rests in heaven," Diggory said.

"The law offers me no guidance about that," Tom said. "But your father's next younger brother has been in court since then. Family lore may have disinherited Enoch, but no documents ever reached court. The inheritance flows through the elder son's line. That," Tom tapped the back of Diggory's hand, "is you."

Lizzie swiped at her own eyes. Ned was watching Perry, who never wept but looked like he might. Yet Perry found his voice first. "Could Tristram Crackbone have known?"

Tom said, "He knew part of this story. Mr. Crackbone was the leaseholder on a farm and Enoch was his landlord. When Enoch was disowned, Crackbone was kicked off his land."

"I can well guess," Diggory said, "that he didn't want me to waste hopes on a false legacy. Other men have done so."

"He couldn't have known about the disputed estate," Tom said, "since he died before your great-grandfather did."

"Mayhap," Perry said, "Mr. Crackbone was the kind of man who'd want naught to do with your Great-grandfather Fear-God, who'd disowned your father."

A voice in the coffeehouse hailed Diggory, who looked about, and called, "Anon, sir." Then he closed his eyes, his face disarmingly peaceful. "I should have liked to have known that great-grandfather though."

"What else do you remember?" Tom asked.

"I remember Father saying that he'd never let me be stolen by elves. And I remember flashes of sunlight between trees on a hot summer's day. I rode in a carriage to a house that Father called the elf hold. The door knocker was a gold lion. Father let me knock it, though it was so heavy I could hardly lift it."

Lizzie said, "That's just the kind of ancient memories I have about my mother. Sometimes I can remember more if I squeeze my eyes tight."

Diggory squeezed his eyes tight. "I was given a boiled candy that looked like a flower. Father said I wasn't allowed, but he didn't take it from me. I sucked on it while Father fought a witchy woman who cursed him as a sinner. Father swept me in his arms and cried, 'You'll never have him.'"

"How terrible," Lizzie murmured. She never thought herself to be sentimental, but she felt her heart would break at the thought of such a wretched family.

"I remember that candy flower and the door knocker, and my father saying he'd never let the elves have me. I believed that angry woman was an elf."

"Did you never ask Mr. Crackbone for that story when you were older?" Ned asked. He looked severely pale.

Ned must be thinking of questions he'd never asked his father.

Diggory said, "Tristram didn't know that story. But I was thinking of it at the very moment when the pirates came upon us in the Mediterranean. I lifted the pistol the captain gave me, and it felt the same weight as that gold lion door knocker."

Several men hailed for the steward to bring coffee.

Tom said, "Let us meet Saturday after the coffeehouse closes. We can discuss how you might best pursue this business."

"Thank you. Please, excuse me, gentlemen." Diggory swiped at his eyes again and left to answer the hails for coffee.

—

"Do you think that knocker is still on the door?" Tom looked thoughtful. "I suppose we'll know when we find the house."

"What house?" Ned demanded.

Tom said, "The house Wolfric Molewood has been suing for possession of since the death of his grandfather Fear-God. His mother and grandmother still live there."

"Vex me!" Lizzie grabbed Tom's cuff. "You couldn't say that before now?"

"I was putting most of it together yesterday. Then I heard your story about Miss Prudence Mott. I think the properties are near each other at Primrose Hill."

"Remind me again," Lizzie began, then adjusted her voice into Orlando's range, "how and why 'shun revenge' became one of our rules."

Tom said, "It's what Uncle Absolom said, whenever he explained what could be done about the Marborne title not being returned to us."

"It's sad," Lizzie said, "that Absolom didn't survive to see us reap justice. If he were here now, I'd ask him to offer more philosophy about why revenge is not to be considered."

Tom said, "His view seems to contradict certain basics in the human spirit."

"Will one man pay the fare for all?" Diggory appeared suddenly. "Or each his own?"

Ned laid out a penny for his coffee.

"It's two pennies each, sir."

"People who told me about this house said it cost a single penny." Perry felt in his waistcoat pocket for coins.

"Lord Marborne suggested prices be raised during the morning rush," Diggory said. "His idea hasn't affected trade one jot."

Tom laid a shilling on the table. "Here's for everyone. I will see you again on Saturday, after business hours."

"Thank you, Mr. Foxe." Diggory shook Tom's hand vigorously. "And please give Lord Marborne my very best wishes for his recovery. I am praying for his lordship."

Lizzie was out the door with the others before she understood that Diggory did indeed believe Rowland was seriously ill.

With luck, that rumor would be all over London by nightfall.

22
Lycomedes' Daughter

– NED –

WEDNESDAY NOON

NED SLASHED A SWATH of Sops-in-Wine brown to establish the lower edge of the picture's perspective, then he furiously mixed Bristol red and slashed the top of the curtain behind Odysseus, all while listening to Wolfric Molewood in the outer hall as he angrily chastised his servants over the previous night's theft. The servants' predicament was entirely Ned's fault, and he felt for the poor beleaguered souls, but that retrieval had to be done for the Touchstones' safety. And his own.

Then Molewood thundered at his steward because Mr. Peregrine Frake of Ezra Pelletoot's lock shop was not free to attend business at Jericho House until two o'clock, and then only to consult. That wasn't Ned's fault; it was his problem. Ned and Lizzie came there to distract Molewood, but Perry wouldn't be prowling that day. Hence, Molewood's outrage was contagious.

Ned used a charcoal stick to outline where Achilles. as Lycomedes false daughter, would stand in place at the bottom right. "Hold still," Ned commanded Lizzie, who dressed as Achilles pretending to be a woman in white linen, though she'd come into the house in grey wool, pretending to be Miss Mott.

His sister shouldn't be here at all. She should have stuck with the plan: plead (while dressed as Orlando) for Ned to paint here, then go away and leave Ned and Perry to deal with a man as dangerous as Molewood. But in a white-hot passion, she'd come dressed as Miss Mott.

Just before they'd entered the house for their first portrait session, she'd ranted at Ned. "He plagues dear Prudence. He seeks to steal Diggory's inheritance. He heads the insurance syndicate that's cheating Rollo and Diggory. And he holds poor Ishmael as if he's a slave."

Ned sought to caution her because of the intensity of her passion. "That's true, but our plan is to—"

She'd waved away Ned's grip on her arm. Her last words before the Jericho House door had opened for them: "When I'm done, I'll put a silver lock on *his* collar and lead him through London on a brass chain."

Had Lizzie never listened to Perry and Rowland lecture on the rules for a successful gambol: simple, sudden, secret? Instead, she'd let her gambol grow outrageously large. How many of Felicity Oakes' actor friends had been hired on for the Friday event, and so knew too many secrets? Then Lizzie had added Miss Mott's plight as a problem to be solved.

Ned added two drops of Mortal Sin black to the dark pool at the center of his palette and hacked in the unpopulated edges of the picture. The scene would be bright amid a halo of darkness; Lizzie-as-Achilles would glow in the righthand focus.

Lizzie had that white-hot glow all winter. Her outrage had compelled her to create a righteous gambol. And Tom wanted Lizzie to double down, like a reckless gambler, by dragging in Diggory Crackbone's case. It simply wasn't the time for Lizzie to complicate the original gambol. Lizzie's only goal for the act of painting the disguised Achilles should be to lure Molewood in as an investor at Friday's event. The rest of her many goals—help

Diggory and Miss Mott, free the boy from the *Skylark*, help Ned protect the Touchstones from Molewood's schemes—all that should be saved for later, after running Friday's gambol.

He didn't understand how Lizzie intended to advance any of her goals by pretending to be Miss Mott instead of Orlando. It seemed like she was doing what she said she'd gone to Bristol to escape: flirt with a rich man, intending to break his heart. He jabbed the Mortal Sin black heavily into the dark pool, building up thick paint. He hadn't intended that, but he'd begun that stroke just as he suddenly understood.

Lizzie was following Tom's advice, to set a honeytrap. She intended harm to Molewood's feelings while taking a portion of his wealth, using the Miss Mott disguise to stir up dark chaos.

Well, then.

Molewood came into the room.

"Pray pardon me, Miss Mott, Mr. Wijck. Last night's calamity distracted me. But I'm now ready for business."

Ned fumed. Lizzie consoled Molewood as he seethed about his stolen painting, her voice more than politely kind.

"Don't apologize for showing your heart, sir. People who don't understand the power of art cannot know that losing a beloved painting is as hard on the soul as losing kinfolk."

Verdomme. Lizzie quoted words Ned once said.

Too bad about Molewood's feeling of loss. Ned hadn't taken *Daniel in the Lion's Den* for purely selfish reasons. He needed to solve the Touchstones' dilemma.

Lizzie's honeyed voice penetrated Ned's black ire. "My heart goes out to you, sir. A theft of a precious thing from inside your home? It's much like a bodily violation."

Now, while preparing to pose as Achilles, his sister cooed like a dove and sweetly talked business, as if syndicates and insurance were the language of flirtation. This, from the same sister who'd fled to Bristol in the autumn chill to avoid playing flirtatious maiden as the king's watcher.

"I admire that you are leading London's men of business to invest in art and beauty. Such investment will advance England's place in the world."

"It's not an investment, Miss Mott. I seek no return on funds expended, only a consolation for promoting the wellbeing of artists whose works make my home a retreat from the world."

Ned coughed, about to choke on his own bile.

The purported Miss Mott said, "I believe the lords in England should invest all they can with the new class of London businessmen. That is the path to increasing England's power."

Gah! She used the same tone of voice as when she spread the sugared cream of love in conversation with Rowland. How was Ned to endure this?

"Mr. Molewood, Miss Mott. Are you prepared to take your positions while I sketch the outline for this painting?"

He only looked up then from the canvas to fully realize that his patron proposed to pose in a hideous suit, coat, waistcoat, and breeches, all in a vile Love-longing purple.

—

Ned made no headway with the argument for his planned color palette. His new patron had insisted on the purple suit and velvet Italian hat. The fictitious Miss Mott agreed, adding flattery.

"You see such attire in the best of classical paintings. And that deep purple connotes royalty. Wasn't Odysseus a king?"

All Lizzie knew about classical paintings she'd learned from Ned. Did she have to use what she'd been taught by her own brother to make love to this tyrant?

Ned positioned Molewood to the far left of the scene to play the cunning Odysseus. Then he indicated Lizzie's position. "Miss Mott stands here as Achilles, the picture's contrasting form."

"Can she not be placed here?" Molewood pointed to his end of the table.

"That would destroy the balance of the picture and hide the artifacts you wish to show. Remember the picture's story?"

"Yes. I am Odysseus, presenting a sword and shield among other treasures. I want to unmask Achilles, who's pretending to be one of Lycomedes' daughters to avoid the Trojan war."

Lizzie, in that cloyingly sweet, warm voice said, "Playing the crafty Odysseus suits you, Mr. Molewood. I'm at a loss for how I am to be a warrior dressed as a woman."

Ned had his back to Molewood, so only Lizzie saw Ned roll his eyes. He draped a red velvet cloak over Lizzie's shoulders, leaving her shoulders bare except for an edge of her gown.

"Is that linen gown suitable for Miss Mott's comfort?" Molewood asked. "She may well take a chill."

Molewood stopped everything to bid a pair of servants, who awaited their instructions as background figures in the painting, to build up the fire already crackling in the hearth.

Ned said, "She'll be swathed in this cloak." He waited until Molewood's attention was elsewhere to tug both linen and velvet down to bare Lizzie's shoulders, the only element of her beauty, besides her face, to appear in the painting.

She tugged it back up, whispering, "I didn't make up my dark shoulders to match my pale face today."

He placed a shield on Lizzie left arm, buckling it in place. She'd been warned, so didn't complain about the shield, the helmet on her head, or the sword, which Ned had procured by begging Felicity Oakes to raid the props at her theatre. The armor was paste-and-paper, so only the sword had any weight.

"Am I to hold this weapon the whole time I'm posing?" Lizzie asked.

"No. Only for a few minutes while I sketch things in place. Then you'll hold it only when I'm painting its details.

While Ned was arranging the servants in the background, Molewood stood far too close to Lizzie. His excuse was to show her the artifacts laid on the carpet-covered table, the treasures that Odysseus used to entice Achilles to reveal his warrior nature. As Molewood explained at length the provenance and cost of each, Ned could see Lizzie's backbone hardening under the velvet draping. He called them into their poses to stop that which most annoyed Lizzie.

Ned didn't believe that either the real Miss Mott or the future Countess of Marborne could be beguiled by that parade of common artifacts, Molewood's purchased glory. To Ned's way of thinking, only one carved piece of ivory was worth more than a glance. Last summer, he'd begun his own collection of engraved and carved ivory, most of which he'd verified as having come from China. The lovely piece on Molewood's table of treasures was an ornate, fanciful bird with a lengthy crest and painted neck-bands and wings. It came from a world far away from China and the spice islands. It had to have come from Africa.

Ned went to work, rapidly sketching the position of each model, capturing the perspective for the whole picture. He became sure of how the light must fall on each figure, even while he sketched with charcoal.

Lizzie and Molewood had been discussing business, which Ned found boring. He focused on properly capturing the curves in his under-sketch. Then he heard an impertinent question about how Miss Mott came to accept a modeling fee. Apparently, the two had moved on to a deeper intimacy while Ned sketched.

The warm, friendly Miss Mott spoke. "As I said when we first met, I am compelled to live separately from my family. I have funds to live, but I must stretch what I have by assisting artists in finding patrons and selling their works to worthy men. Your fee helps my freedom."

"Now you have made me even more curious, Miss Mott. Compelled to live separately from your family?"

"If I share my reason, it must remain a confidence."

"Please, I'd consider it an honor if you would trust me."

She said, "My father, I regret to say, is meeting with a priest to study, intending to convert to the king's faith."

"God's bodkins!"

"You may well imagine my dismay. My grandfather and his father followed the path of righteousness. I cannot account for this new whim of my father's. Just as I cannot account for God having made a Catholic our king. To think, in this modern day and age!"

Molewood seemed struck dumb for one blessed moment. Then: "We've been sitting here with nothing to do but talk. The result seems to be that you've come to treat me as a friend."

"I consider it good fortune that you consider me a friend."

"I do, Miss Mott. It is astonishing, don't you think? We come from entirely different worlds, yet share ideas about faith, business, and the management of wealth."

She sighed and looked wistful. "I spent a few years in Princess Mary's court. I learned quickly how to know whether to trust people upon first acquaintance. You are the only man I've met in London that I feel I can trust."

Ned's charcoal stick made an unplanned squiggle along Odysseus's backside.

When the clock's chimes and the echoing church bells signaled two o'clock, Mr. Molewood excused himself. "I must meet with my locksmith to direct his work." He said to Ned, "I'll need my servants."

"I have their places sketched, sir. I won't need them again for a few days."

Molewood again stepped too close to Lizzie. "I'll be only a moment, Miss Mott. Please rest in my absence."

Lizzie turned her head to him, just a bit. "Thank you, sir, but I'll keep my pose so Mr. Wijck can continue his work."

—

The door had scarcely closed behind Mr. Molewood and his servants when Lizzie completely broke her pose. "Can you tell him I've taken ill and must go home? This room is so warm, it's melting my bismuth-and-talc makeup."

Ned said, "Perry's here. It's too late to change the plan."

"This is excruciating," she said. "Whose idea was this?"

"Following your plan, I am to paint while Perry prowls. But then suddenly Miss Mott came to seduce Molewood into your gambol. Now you want to give up?"

"No, I want you to nag me into persevering," Lizzie said. "The way I've been nagging everyone else all winter."

"Did you take on too much?" He repeated what Perry said privately the previous night.

"I'll never admit that."

When Molewood returned, his first words were an apology. "Pray excuse the interruption, which was scarcely worth it. The locksmith fellow cannot start work until tomorrow."

His new friend Miss Mott kept up bright, beguiling patter, though Ned guessed he shared her dismay. She explained Ned's methods to his patron as if she were indeed an expert, noting how Mr. Wijck had sketched all the figures in the painting, to define their proportions and the shadows they cast.

"Then he'll work on details later, perhaps when we aren't posing. He'll hang your costume on a form when he paints the texture of the cloth. He will do the same when depicting this crimson cloak. After today, he'll want us here only to capture the details of our faces."

"And hands," Ned said. "Especially Odysseus's hands."

But Mr. Molewood seemed too entranced with Prudence Mott to pay attention to anyone else.

Ned repeatedly chided Miss Mott for losing her pose, while never reminding his patron. He'd nearly finished the basic sketch when Ishmael, Molewood's servant, knocked and begged to deliver a message.

"Pray, excuse me." Molewood left for several moments, then rushed back into the room.

"I have such an idea. I should have thought of this before now. My servant Ishmael must also be in the painting. Here he is, in his best page's suit."

Ishmael stood by his master, expressionless, dressed in a brushed blue velvet coat, his silver collar polished to a shine.

"But, Mr. Molewood, I've finished the basic composition." Ned, seeing Lizzie's expression turn grim, drew Molewood's attention to himself. "There's no place for him."

"Nonsense. He can stand by me. We'll move the Chinese bronze lantern."

Ned knew he could not debate this patron. For the sake of why they were in the man's house, Ishmael had to appear as one of Molewood's prized possessions, along with gold and ivory pieces from Africa. Ned didn't dare look at Lizzie, sure she struggled with anger greater than his own.

To Ned's great surprise, Lizzie said, "It will make a lively addition. It shows Odysseus as a lord, not merely a merchant."

"I shall adjust the sketch tomorrow," Ned said. Then, to relieve Lizzie from the Hades where she'd trapped herself, he added, "We are out of good light for today."

He meant it as an immediate relief for Lizzie. How could he know that Molewood would take an entire half hour to offer solicitous goodbyes?

23
Preparations

— LIZZIE —

THURSDAY MORNING

IT SNOWED AGAIN AFTER midnight. The wind rose, and the air turned stunningly cold again. Ice flowers painted the window.

The whistle of the wind woke Lizzie, and she immediately worried about Rowland on the road in such weather. Yet he'd laugh at her for such concern, since he was on the road with the best riders in the kingdom.

She should rise and go to work, in solidarity with Rowland's endeavors. Yet any human alive would prefer to stay in bed on such a day. Lizzie burrowed under the heavy covers, thinking she could claim to have done more work over the last few days than most any woman in England. For a moment she inhaled the comfort and solace she'd sought when she'd crawled into bed, exhausted from the previous day's performance.

She'd slept in Rowland's bed.

No one would know except Lazarus and Jane, the upstairs girl. And Rowland's staff was more than discreet. No one had to offer an explanation to this staff for anything. Which was good, because she couldn't explain to herself why she'd been overcome with a deep sense of loneliness.

She'd long been a grand master of fending off loneliness. She'd been ten years in a royal court, a world where you cannot have real friends or fully trust a soul. That was a world so far removed from Revelstone, where she'd been raised, that she might as well have been sent to Java or Tortuga. The language in court was so different from home, it was like English spoken in the elven realm. The manners practiced in court seemed to come straight from *The Faerie Queen,* every gesture an allegory.

Yet she knew why. Rowland was gone from London.

She'd crawled into his bed when the only comfort to be had was the scent of Hungary Water that Rowland left behind. Rosemary, thyme, and brandy. She peeked at the comfort she'd used all week, tucked under the pillow: that letter from Tamsin, which was a cheery, reassuring start to the day.

> The teacher you found for the girls, our new friend Nadia, turns English lessons into songs and games. To join in, Camilla and I are learning Portuguese. We learned that the girls each have different dialects beyond Portuguese. We now all count and sing in several languages.
>
> Sometimes, I wake late at night, thinking I can remember my mother singing to me. So we encourage the girls to teach us their songs and tell their stories in their own dialects, because that's where memories abide. Do you think that's the right thing to do?

Having found as much comfort as she had time for that morning, Lizzie pushed back the heavy covers and dressed before she could freeze. Lazarus had (as was his way) laid out choices: a shiny suit for Orlando or Puritan-grey gown for Miss Mott. Lizzie longed to transgress and climb into one of Rowland's narrow black suits and, again, his second-best boots. But this was another day of playing Prudence Mott.

She went in pursuit of Michael Oakes, finding him in the dining salon eating a bowl of cooked oats and reading a book. "I have a list for this morning." She sat beside him, a plumbago pencil in hand, prepared to annotate the list.

Michael pushed a basket of bread toward her. "Please have breakfast before we begin."

She broke the bread over one of Rowland's mallorca plates. While buttering the crust, she asked, "Can you help me with freight I want to send to Revelstone? It's just a few bolts of wool, warm boots, and other odd bits. I'll ask Jane to run to the market, so I can add measures of flour and a pair of sugar loaves to supplement Mrs. Bell's pantry."

"I'm sure Revelstone can use the comforts you plan to send. But Lazarus should help with that chore, Miss Foxe."

"I have a regiment's list of tasks for him. You can ask the two Frake brothers to help with those freight tasks. I have more for you today."

"I'll ask Lazarus. It's his duty to assign their tasks."

"Of course, it is."

What was I thinking, impinging on Lazarus's duties?

"Do you want tea?" Michael asked.

"My list of tasks seems too long to be drinking tea."

Lazarus was at the door then. "Mrs. Flurry has a hot breakfast for you, Miss Foxe. It'll be ready in a moment. And there's a message for you, sent over from Chalgrove House."

The message had been through a circuitous route. It came to Chalgrove House, where Lizzie usually lived with Aurora Rôche, by way of Mrs. Touchstone from Threadneedle Street.

Egad! Does Molewood have agents prowling at Touchstones?

The outer wrapping was a message from Hildegonda Touchstone, saying that Miss Mott had an admirer who'd sent a package. Hildegonda's message enfolded another:

> Miss Mott, I have sent herbs and a tincture in care of your employer, out of concern that we exhausted you in our first day's work. If I can do any single thing for your

> comfort, please send a message. I will happily reward your messenger and fly to your assistance.
>
> Given the kind of modest woman you are, I estimate that you'll prefer I act with moderation. Will you consent to allow me to call you Prudence? Could any woman have received a more perfect name at her baptism?
>
> — Wolfric Molewood, Jericho House, Bloomsbury

She considered all that had passed between them since Tuesday morning, not believing for a moment that she'd charmed Mr. Molewood, only that she'd opened a new path for him to pursue Prudence's inherited land. There'd been times at court, before Rowland came to Amsterdam, when she'd flirted for the sake of...What? Power. That's all she'd done with Wolfric Molewood.

You loathly, goatish nithing!

Would she regret that she'd gotten the Touchstones involved in this gambol? Yet Prudence's predicament made it a righteous deed to have undertaken her own quest in this way. Besides, it would all be resolved tomorrow, Friday, when her gambol concluded. She did feel annoyed that she hadn't found a better way to deal with Molewood than flirting over art and business deals.

Lizzie crushed his letter, not wanting to be made mifty. She needed energy to address every item on her list.

"Ready to work, Michael?"

"In a minute. Mrs. Flurry expects you to eat breakfast first."

"Mrs. Flurry?" She frowned. "Why does she think I need to be cautioned to eat properly?"

"Rollo left instructions," Michael said.

—

Michael complained that her list of tasks was interminable. However, as the morning passed, Lizzie found pleasure in their progress, which brought her that much closer to the apocalypse she'd planned for the Hawkins' Heirs investors.

They worked through most tasks by eleven o'clock. Lizzie had confirmed Felicity Oakes' work, hiring actors and costumes, delivering scripts, and rehearsing actors for Friday's event.

Michael had printed all the invitations and prospectuses. Lazarus had deployed messengers to deliver invitations to potential investors. He'd joined Tom to finish arrangements for the rooms hired for the event, including food and servants.

Lizzie sat quietly at the dining table, the headquarters for their morning's work. Most everything had been cleared away, but she reread the foundation for Friday's work, designed to draw rich men into gambling wildly with Venetian merchants they scarcely knew.

"Too many words," Michael had complained on Monday, when he began pulling letters from the type case tray.

"More words, stronger lure," Lizzie had argued, until they settled at last on the text:

> Those indulging in the popular madness for African trade—or who are new to mercantile investment—are forgetting that they have missed opportunities to bring silk, ivory, jade, and novel treasures directly from China.
>
> One Venetian house has been bringing China silk by way of the Black Sea since the Romans ruled Europe and Africa. The French empire procures its silk in this way.
>
> Le Casa Mercantile del Fratelli Gratiano invites a privileged few to join an opportunity to bring new silk trade directly to England by investing in a newly incorporated entity, the Albion-Byzantium Company.
>
> These elite will choose to participate by funding voyages with English passes through the Mediterranean, thereby gaining the opportunity to sell rare goods to premier London merchants.

> Le Casa Mercantile del Fratelli Gratiano offers the opportunity to discuss the investment prospectus for the Albion-Byzantium Company at four o'clock on Friday, January 11. Present this invitation for admittance at Mercers' Hall on Fredericks Street, London. Supper will be served.

The list of invitees was the Hawkins' Heirs list, minus Lord Withersea and two names Rowland, Tom, and Perry had hunted down and revealed to the king as Withersea's confederates.

Tom and Perry hadn't yet identified who on the list also invested in the king's chartered monopoly. Thursday, the whole list would be invited. Friday, the Venetians would decline the membership requests of any men the duke wanted to see protected. Lizzie didn't like that, preferring notions of equal justice. But she'd tread the safer path.

Come to me, you vile, greedy creatures.

Now, time to call for Jane and dress as Prudence Mott.

24
Falser Than Vows Made in Wine

– LIZZIE –

THURSDAY NOON

LIZZIE AND NED ARRIVED at Jericho House at precisely noon on Thursday. The day began tolerably, since their purpose came to fruition: Perry had arrived to begin his survey of Molewood's house. Lizzie had planned ahead and wore Rowland's *longues jambes,* keeping them on under Achilles' Greek gown.

Molewood again dressed in dark velvet, a deep purple that flattered his dark coloring. However, to Lizzie's tastes, Rowland wore such suits better. She also believed that, despite the cost of his clothes, Molewood was still the son of a country Puritan come to London with the Restoration, not fully integrated into the dissolute ways of lords' sons.

Molewood clearly accepted the notion that wealth indicated God's favor. That seemed to why he had no need to muck about with old-fashioned precepts of honesty.

Lizzie playacted Prudence Mott as a wise soul who championed art and thoughtful investing. She conversed with Molewood while imagining a wild painting Ned would never make.

I see grey blobs with only that purple velvet Italian hat in focus.

By the second hour, Lizzie had answered two dozen of Molewood's inquiries about her life and refused his solicitations for her comfort. She asked flattering questions, so that he could wax forth about his successes and talents. Molewood tended to move his hands when he talked, but Ned murmured only kind reminders to hold a pose.

As the day wore on, Lizzie's chore wore on her: playing Achilles who looks in a mirror yet holds a sword and shield, while also playing Prudence Mott, beguiling Mr. Molewood by talking business. Ned had posed her with one knee on a stool, so she'd lost most feeling except for a point of pain on her knee the size of a guinea coin. Her hand fell asleep holding the sword. When she complained, Ned let her pause, which then meant sharp needles jabbed her fingers as blood flowed to her extremities again.

She guessed that Ned, Tom, and Perry thought this a useless way to spend her time. Yet she believed this was the path to Molewood's ruin. She'd seen men forget rational thought for a chance with an unattainable woman. Molewood was just such a man.

Ned said, "Please hold still so I can capture the hand holding the sword."

"Why," Lizzie asked, then moderated her voice to sound like Prudence, who was never a termagant, "is the hero clutching a sword while admiring himself among ladies?"

"Why wear a helmet on a battle-free sunny day in Greece?" Ned looked up from his painting. "No, don't hold it like that. It's a weapon."

Lizzie had to console her restless spirit and endure Molewood's bragging patter. Then Perry came to the parlor where they worked and professed his tasks done for the day, that he'd return Saturday with more hardware to begin the fortification.

"Saturday?" Molewood's thundering anger echoed from the hallway where he had gone to do business with Perry.

"I have other clients who requested work long before you. And I must order the necessary metal work and locks."

"I was just robbed, yet you cannot fortify my home before Saturday?"

"I have provided your steward a list of actions that can be undertaken without new accoutrements." Perry sounded so mild for negotiating with a shouting, angry client.

Molewood returned and took nearly fifteen minutes to climb out from under the cloud of his anger and return to the pose Ned wanted. For half that time, he didn't listen to Lizzie's attempts to return to their former conversation.

Frustrated, Lizzie repeated advice Rowland and Tom shared over supper, though neither cousin regarded the other as a wizard of London investment. She hoped to make such business talk sound beguiling, coming from a woman who offered warm, kindly compliments. In truth, Perry's departure removed any need for her to distract Molewood in order that Perry might freely snoop.

I want to go home. Or be anywhere but here.

Then Molewood's anger at Perry receded, like a rapidly outgoing tide. "Miss Mott, our conversations have been so intriguing. I've never met a woman so astute about business."

"I have to be," the gracious, overly friendly Miss Mott said. "My guardian is very good at protecting my inheritance and fending off gentlemen with lesser fortunes than mine. He invests modest sums for me and has done well enough, but he demands that I understand the decisions and outcomes."

"Very wise." Molewood nodded and was chided by Ned to hold his pose. "I would do the same for any ward of mine. How is he currently investing for you?"

At last, my chance to lure you into my scheme.

"He wants me to join an exclusive syndicate that's investing in a shipping venture. Would you be interested in joining if I can manage an invitation for you?"

"I'm a cautious man." His voice thrummed with hesitation. "I am always compelled to investigate new ventures for myself."

"You wouldn't care to take a risk with me, Mr. Molewood?" She ladened her voice with an entire loaf of sugar. "After all our talk, shall I be bold and offer you a challenge? We shall both invest in this new proposal, so that we can encourage each other."

"An intriguing challenge." The hesitancy left his voice.

"My guardian has approved the proposal I will bring for you tomorrow. I am sure he can secure an invitation for you, Mr. Molewood." The alleged Miss Mott shifted her voice to wheedle. "Shall I beg you to engage in my challenge?"

"Egad, I will do it!" His voice suddenly warmed with enthusiasm. "What right have I to hesitate when you, who must guard your inheritance, are willing to take the risk? If you can gain me an invitation, I shall join in the venture."

At last! The week's labors are now worthwhile.

"A champion decision," she said. "It will be a jolly undertaking between new-made friends."

But given that success, she experienced an extreme loss of will to persevere in her Achilles pose. It felt rather like a baked pudding losing its height.

First, Lizzie let that infernal sword clatter to the floor. Then she sneezed. It was the talc, which had the chore of hiding her true complexion.

"Please hold your pose, Miss Mott," Ned said.

She sneezed again. "Apologies, Mr. Wijck. I feel an ague coming on." Hand to her head, she sneezed again.

Ned, this torturous posing is pointless. Perry's gone.

As if he heard her thoughts, Ned said, "We are taxing Miss Mott. We must stop, else she will fall ill."

That illness is seasickness. I've sailed beyond my wit's end.

Molewood began to make repeated solicitations for Prudence's wellbeing. She responded with modesty and bravado. Then she sneezed again.

"I'm afraid it's true. I must be excused for the day."

"Of course, my dear," Molewood exclaimed, breaking the barriers of propriety with an endearment.

"We'd best dismiss our star model," Ned said. "But, Mr. Molewood, let us continue with your Odysseus portrait. We still have good light. I only need a moment to prepare my palette for your complexion."

"Let me first say goodbye to Miss Mott and ensure she's safely on her way."

—

A Shakespeare tragedy unfolded once she'd changed back into Prudence Mott's walking dress. In her haste to change, she'd streaked the Greek veil with her whitening cosmetics. After she tied Prudence's Puritan-like cap in place, she wrapped a woolen scarf around her face. She turned to leave, but found Molewood just outside the dressing screen, blocking her way and proceeding to importune on her time and her very soul, that velvet Italian hat in his hand.

"Allow me to help you with your cloak and pattens, Miss Mott. I long to kneel before you."

Lizzie, grasping her iron pattens so hard it hurt her hand, nearly lost control of her Prudence. "Mr. Molewood! You cannot kneel to me. I command you to stand."

Though he obeyed, Molewood said, "You take my meaning, Miss Mott?" Rather than kneeling, he folded his hands as if in prayer. "I would be honored if you would allow me to court you."

"We've only just met, sir."

"We have spent hours in rapt conversation, touching all that is most important to our hearts," Molewood said, his face and voice far too earnest.

Lizzie lifted her head, let her lips part as if speechless in the face of his passion.

You want Prudence's lands. That's what's dear to your heart.

He wrenched his hands, as if his heart were touched. "Dear Prudence, from the first moments of our acquaintance, I have admired you for your kindness and goodness."

"I'm not..." Lizzie stopped.

Not Prudence. I'm Achilles in a gown, sword in hand.

So, she wasn't kind or good, but Molewood used words of love with the calculated actions of a businessman. A business-man who was used to getting whatever he wanted.

"Yes, yes. Your guardian will believe it's too soon." Mole-wood grasped her hand. "But do not say it's shocking. Please, I beg you to consider me as your best offer for a secure future."

"I cannot think." Lizzie lied. "Your notion is so surprising."

"That's your modesty speaking. Which I find charming. Our differences in station are not great, and I can offer the kind of protection that a good woman such as yourself deserves."

"It is too much for me to think of at this time, Mr. Mole-wood." Lizzie sneezed, then coughed out a few more words. "It is vastly kind of you to ask this."

And I'm not good. I'm "falser than vows made in wine."

"Yet you do not say no. I beg of you to think on it. We will grow to know each other while Mr. Wijck paints your likeness."

"Yes, but I cannot entertain such a proposal. Please think of me only as a model for Achilles while we work together, lest it become awkward."

"We shall remain in friendly harmony. When the painting is done, I hope you will let me plead my cause to your guardian. He will at least recognize that I am not seeking your fortune."

No, you seek the land that holds Prudence's family cenotaph.

"It is beyond my powers to deny you hope." Saying that, Lizzie truly felt ill.

"My hope, Prudence, is that your kind heart will bring you to see this house as your home. I wrote to my mother about you last night. When she meets you, she will believe as I do, that God intended for me to find such a kind, good woman."

Lizzie dropped one of her pattens on the floor. The clang of metal brought servants into the room, searching out the sound.

"I am," Lizzie choked back the words, "overwhelmed by the honor you do me."

If I had Achilles' sword, I'd remove you from my misery.

Though she'd pleaded illness, she still had to tolerate a quarter hour of Molewood begging to take care of her, to let him fetch his carriage, to bring her wine.

Molewood did at last yield to her insistence that she preferred to go home on her own. But he commanded his servants to fetch a sedan chair for her. Then he called for Ishmael.

"See Miss Mott to her chair, Ishmael."

After she climbed into the sedan chair, Ishmael paid the bearers with coins from Molewood, then said to her, "Good day, madam." He quickly mounted the portico and slipped inside and closed the mansion's front door.

"Not a good day." She muttered as the porters lifted the chair. "Except for my hard-won victory."

After the porters crossed two streets and turned a corner, she demanded to be set down. She felt too angry and irritated to sit still, though the agitation had shifted in the past few moments from resenting Molewood's importunity to dark despair over Ishmael's servitude.

Upon my soul! What if I cannot conjure justice?

She stomped down the street toward Covent Garden, her pattens ringing whenever she crossed bare cobbles. She began chanting the chorus of that Tom O'Bedlam poem.

While I do sing,
Any food, any feeding,
Feeding, drink, or clothing;
Come dame or maid,
Be not afraid,
Poor Tom will injure nothing.

Lizzie stopped chanting.

What if Poor Ysabel injures nothing, like Poor Tom O'Bedlam?

No, she could not allow Mr. Molewood to shake her confidence. She was only angry at that pretentious bully coming so close. Breathing on her. Proposing marriage like a lover in one of Rowland's preposterous theatre plays.

All Molewood wanted was Miss Mott's land.

The patten on her left foot caught on a cobble. She tripped, almost fell. By the time she stood upright again, Lizzie's better self had claimed her consciousness. She'd won her day's goal: Molewood committed to joining her gambol.

Friday will be the last time I have to meet that man in this life.

25
A Bold Theft

— NED —

THURSDAY AFTERNOON

WHEN THERE WAS NO more good light for painting that Thursday afternoon, Ned caught a carriage at the corner down from Molewood's mansion and directed the driver to take him to Touchstone's warehouse.

There, he found Lizzie, now dressed as Orlando, in conversation with Mistress Touchstone who, upon seeing Ned, went to fetch her husband.

"Why are you here, Lizzie?"

"To assuage Hildegonda's ire over having to forward messages from Molewood. And to pay my debt for being allowed to serve as their agent while meeting Mr. Molewood."

"She didn't ask payment for that. They get a commission from Molewood's fee."

"I'm not paying with gold. The collar and cuffs of her gown show that Hildegonda likes lace. I have a pretty length from Amsterdam to share with her."

"Lace?"

"Don't look so puzzled, Ned. The reward must be truly lovely when you convince a woman to offer falsehoods in support of someone else's gambol."

"She now knows you're my sister, but here you are, playing Orlando again."

"I told her we're going to the frost faire later, and that I find the faire too rough to attend as a lady."

"When you stand like that, *Orlando,* no one sees a man."

Lizzie conversed with Mistress Touchstone, while Ned joined Simon, who was tallying the paints and brushes Ned had requested. Together, they stashed Ned's trappings in a crate.

"You must intend a great deal of red, Mr. Wijck." Simon's smile always hinted that he knew more than was being said. "And all this white lead and black carbon? Do you plan a great deal of armor in your vision of Lycomedes and his daughters?"

"Just enough for the disguised Achilles."

"So much light ochre!" Simon exclaimed. "Are the daughters wearing few clothes? Just red sashes?"

"I'm painting in half light, and I want the image to be convincing. As my father said, *'Het draait allemaal om kleuren.'*"

"'It's all about the coloring.'" Simon grinned. "You said that each time you sold me one of your father's paintings."

"And he impressed me on it," Ned said, "from the cradle."

"My wife is happy with how well your sister did with Mr. Molewood. Talked him into a greater investment than a fresco. If the man tires of your *Achilles at Skyros* in ten years, I'll have another commission when he sells it."

"Does he do that often? Sell art he tires of?" Ned's heart thumped. What if Molewood sold one of the forgeries before he and Perry could retrieve it?

"Yes, but not anything he's had from me in the past few years. It's been pieces he got directly from the artists."

Ned sighed. "Will you let me know if he offers you any pieces to place?"

"If you wish. Molewood tells me he intends to have a reputation as a collector."

Ned almost said it: many of the artifacts in Molewood's house are trash. Instead, he asked, "Does he have that sort of a reputation now? Will 'art from the collection of Wolfric Molewood' be interesting to other collectors? Raise the value?"

"Why? Do you want something he has?"

"A couple of pieces that you had from me, like those landscapes that were my father's."

"I remember," Simon said. "Yes, I'll give you first look if he tires of them. But why should he? They are nice pieces, especially for the kind of collector he wants to be considered."

"I'm hoping to convince the Earl of Marborne to build a collection and—"

Hildegonda Touchstone's voice rose, tinged with anger. "You cannot just come in here with such extravagant demands. We aren't servants!"

"Wait, Mistress Touchstone." Lizzie's voice pitched too high for the faux Orlando. "The lad doesn't speak English. Likely, he doesn't know what that note says."

Regaining a deeper voice, Lizzie spoke in another language. Portuguese. Ned didn't understand the words but recognized who Lizzie spoke with.

That unfortunate servant from Molewood's house. Looking even smaller and lost.

"*Deixe-me ajudá-lo.*" Lizzie spoke to the lad in Portuguese, then repeated the words in English. "Let me help you."

The young Ishmael offered Lizzie the note he'd shown Hildegonda. The expression on his face was so hopeful, yet not conquering his fear of Hildegonda Touchstone's scolding.

"He sent another package to Miss Mott?" Lizzie expressed disdain. Ned and Mr. Touchstone had crossed the room to join them, just as Lizzie read aloud the note Ishmael handed her. It wasn't for Prudence.

> Mr. Touchstone, My sincere apologies that business takes me away, such that I cannot meet you personally with my request. First, pray give this package to Miss Prudence Mott, with my kind thoughts.

"Today is the second," Mrs. Touchstone said. "He seems taken with Miss Mott. Read the rest of the note."

Lizzie cleared her throat and read.

> My house has come under attack from thieves. Until I can properly protect my property, I must beg you to take my treasures under your care, for safe protection. I've sent as much as my carriage can hold. I'll come tomorrow to settle your charges for this protection.
>
> —W. Molewood, Jericho House, Bloomsbury

Ned glanced at Lizzie, who was looking for his response, because of what they both knew: Perry promised to install locks at Molewood's house on Saturday, the day after tomorrow. This was nonsense.

"Bless me!" Hildegonda exclaimed. "How are we to manage this? Our lads have gone home for the day."

This further frightened Ishmael, though he likely didn't understand what she said, only her tone. Lizzie spoke in Portuguese. "Don't worry, Ishmael. We will fix this."

He looked up at Lizzie, still startled. *"Você conhece-me?"*

"Yes, you and I met before." She continued to reassure him, that she'd met him at his master's house.

Ned offered to help. "You and I can shift his parcels, Simon. Perhaps the carriage driver can help too."

Ned and Simon headed for the street. Lizzie, Ishmael, and Hildegonda followed.

Lizzie must have asked Ishmael to help. He shook his head vigorously and answered in English. "Not to touch. Only messages." On the street, Ishmael pointed to the other side of the warehouse. "Carriage down there."

Ned and Simon rounded the corner first, with Lizzie and Hildegonda close behind them.

"Zooterkins!"

—

The carriage doors were open, the canvas boot cover torn, the boot empty. The driver lay on the icy cobbles, senseless.

Ned knelt beside the driver. There was no blood. The man was alive and breathing.

"Liz—uh, Orlando, ask Ishmael the driver's name."

When she did, Ishmael said, "Nathaniel. He's new."

Ned bent close. "Nathaniel? Are you awake?"

The man's lids fluttered, but he didn't open his eyes.

Lizzie said, "Hildegonda, please find a surgeon."

"Simon?" Ned said. "Best fetch a constable."

Ned loosened the driver's neckcloth, with no other idea of what to do. But Lizzie spoke to Ishmael, who stepped away and returned with a fist of snow from the drift under the eaves.

Lizzie made a snowball. "Haven't done that for fifteen years. Rub it on the driver's temples, Ned."

The driver's eyes fluttered again but opened this time. He struggled to sit up. Ned said, "Be easy, Nathaniel. Let's wait for the surgeon."

"My carriage." When the man tried to rise again, Ned pressed him down.

"It's right here. Truly, you must wait for the surgeon."

"The lad." Nathaniel became agitated. "The Moor—"

"He's here. He was with us when you were attacked."

The driver sighed.

The surgeon and the constable came at the same time. While the surgeon knelt by the driver, Simon and Ned together began to tell the constable about the situation. Lizzie rose.

"His name is Nathaniel," Lizzie told the surgeon.

"Aye," the injured driver said. "I'm Nathaniel Sprottle."

Ned motioned for her to come to him, but she stood by Ishmael, who'd retreated into the shadow of the eaves. He was shivering, likely from the cold, because his velvet suit didn't seem enough for that frozen day. At least the snow had stopped, and no wind had started.

"Where is Mr. Molewood?" Lizzie asked Ishmael, first in English, then Portuguese. "We must send him a message."

"Don't know." Ishmael shook his head.

Ned joined them. "Call a chair and go home…uh, Orlando." Why did it matter? The Touchstones knew it was his sister.

"I'd best take Ishmael back to Molewood's house," she said. "No one here will understand him."

The constable came over. "I'd best ask the boy what he knows." He had a deep voice, like distant thunder, out of character with his small, podgy frame. "What's your name, boy?"

"It's Ishmael. He doesn't speak English," Lizzie said. "He was inside with us, and so saw aught."

"But he must know—"

A faint rustling drew Ned's attention from the constable. Ishmael was running—and often slipping and sliding—around the corner, hurrying away from the scene.

"Now you've frightened the lad." Lizzie ran after him.

Ned started too, but immediately slipped on the ice and fell catastrophically, only managing *not* to use his hand to break his fall, so at least he'd be able to paint the next day. What he could not do was rise and regain his balance rapidly enough to catch Lizzie before she disappeared.

And once again, he proved incapable of protecting his sister from herself.

26
Ishmael in the Wilderness

– LIZZIE –

THURSDAY LATE AFTERNOON

WHEN LIZZIE CAUGHT UP with Ishmael, the church bells were chiming four o'clock and the winter light failing fast. She reached him only because he fell twice on the ice while she, in Rowland's second-best boots, had more sure footing. As Ishmael scrambled to get up, she held out her hand to help him while reassuring him in Portuguese.

"It's all right. Let me help you. Do you know the way to Mr. Molewood's house?"

Given the flash of his eyes and the deep frown, he did not. But he accepted help up from the snowy street, his gloveless hands like ice.

"Please don't be afraid, Ishmael." She stripped her gloves and handed them to him. "Let me help you get home. Let's go to the main street and find a ride."

The first driver to respond to her hail had a horse-drawn sledge, rather than a carriage. But it seemed a good idea to get Ishmael under the sledge's heavy blanket (which smelled of horse and hay). Enough snow had fallen in the morning that the sledge didn't bump much over exposed cobbles and ruts.

"Are you warm enough?" She tried to make conversation.

"Not since I came to this land."

"I'm sorry. Are you hungry? We can find bread and cheese along the way."

It took a moment, but Ishmael began to say more as they slid along the road to Bloomsbury. "Hannah the lady cook at home will let me warm up by the fire and give me soup. She is kind that way. Does it always snow here? How do you live like this?"

"It's only a few weeks in winter. It will melt and then spring will come."

"Spring?"

"When the leaves come out on trees and flowers bloom."

"That will be nice." He said it in a dreamy sort of way.

"Ishmael, can you trust me? Tell me where you came from."

"What's your name? I don't remember meeting you."

"Call me…" Oh, ah. She'd met him as Miss Mott. "Orlando."

"You are a lord? Do I bow down?"

"Just bend your head. Will you tell me, please, did you come here on a ship? The *Skylark?*"

"A devil ship, yes. I don't know its name."

They arrived at Jericho House. Lizzie paid the fare and stepped onto the portico with the lad. She asked, "Was there a good woman on that ship called Tia Angelina?"

Ishmael looked over his shoulder at her, eyes wide with wonder, but tinged with fear. "How do you—"

The door opened part way. A man, perhaps a butler that she hadn't met before, stood in the archway, fists on his hips.

"Good afternoon," Lizzie said. "I'm Viscount Orlando de Flores. And I'm—"

But the fellow was intent only on Ishmael. "What are you doing here, boy? Where's Nathaniel?"

"He hurt. By devils," Ishmael offered in English.

"Nathaniel Sprottle was attacked while Ishmael was in Touchstone's gallery," Lizzie said. "He was with the constable when last I saw him. I wager they'll be along shortly. I was there when it all happened. I shall be happy to recount the entire affair for Mr. Molewood's edification."

"A constable?" The butler still held the door only half open, but it was enough for Ishmael to slip in.

"Yes. Might I come inside to await Mr. Molewood? I'm sure he'd appreciate hearing the story."

Before the butler could decide on any question of basic hospitality, Molewood's carriage arrived, driven by one of the constable's companions. The doors opened, and the constable, Ned, and Nathaniel descended to the snowy pavement. Ned clutched a narrow wooden box, about as long as his forearm. The constable introduced himself but didn't wait on the butler's decision for admittance. He bowled his way in, offering his broad-brimmed felt hat to the butler.

"I must speak with Mr. Molewood about today's calamity."

Nathaniel entered too. Ned and Lizzie trailed behind.

Molewood was descending his ostentatious staircase. Surprisingly, Perry came down the stairs behind him, saying, "I shifted my other commitments. I can start tomorrow, to make your house safe as the king's castle."

Then Perry noticed the crowd and paused on the stairs. "Hello, Mr. Graveley. Are you here about Tuesday's robbery?"

Perry knows the constable. Perhaps through Ezra Pelletoot?

Molewood spotted Ned. "Mr. Wijck! Were you at Touchstone's warehouse when my gift for Miss Mott arrived? How did she receive it? Is she well? I fret for the return of her good health."

"I'm sorry, Mr. Molewood." Nathaniel spoke before Ned could answer. "I was coshed while delivering your treasures."

"Dash doggone it." Molewood rapidly repeated words that were meant to be curses. "Why do I pay servants for failure? Now I've lost my greatest treasures."

Strangely though, Mr. Graveley hadn't yet announced that there'd been another robbery.

—

Lizzie glanced at Ned, who'd been watching Perry but flicked his icy blue eyes her way. With a brief nod, he let her know that he too had noticed that lapse.

"I thought Mr. Touchstone would keep my treasures safe." Molewood, hands on his hips, shook his head, as if regretting the misbehavior of a child. "And he didn't even come to explain how it happened."

Ned said, "Your treasures never came under Touchstone's care. The carriage was down the street while Mr. Touchstone was reading your note."

Molewood frowned deeply. Then scolded his driver. "But Nathaniel, how—"

"It distressed us all," Lizzie began, pitching her voice low, "when we found Mr. Sprottle coshed and as still as a dead man."

The constable bent, hat in hand, as subservient as poor Nathaniel. "We have an inventory, which your servant carried to Mr. Touchstone." He held it out, and Molewood took it without a glance. "We searched the carriage as thoroughly as can be, sir. My comrades came on watch early and questioned any man in the neighborhood who might have seen it."

"Threadneedle Street was strangely deserted," Lizzie said. "This London cold is keeping everyone at home by the fire."

That brought Molewood's icy gaze to her. "Who are you? How did you come into this business?"

Though grateful to be dressed as Orlando, still, she hadn't thought this through. How close a tie with Ned to claim?

"Viscount Orlando de Flores, sir, at your service. I was negotiating business with Mr. Touchstone when we were drawn into the tragedy on the street."

"And Lord Orlando was helpful," the constable said. "Caring for the driver until I arrived with the surgeon."

"Appreciate it, sir." Molewood tipped a brief acknowledgment in Orlando's general direction, then dismissed the viscount from his consideration. He waved the inventory list, as if it were a kerchief. "Thank you for this, constable. If you could, please, uh…pardon me. It's Mr. Gravesend, is it not?"

"Graveley," the constable said, still humble as a servant.

"If you could, please forward a report to me of your investigation and other efforts. Is tomorrow convenient? I'd like to submit the inventory and your report to my insurance people as soon as possible. I've lost everything that I loved and valued."

"Not quite," Ned said, stepping in front of the constable. "We found one box in the carriage, either missed or abandoned by the malefactors."

He opened the box. It contained that intricately carved piece of ivory that had been set before Achilles as part of the composition for *Achilles at Skyros.*

"Thank the merciful heavens for that," Molewood said, though his voice was flat rather than pleased. "But they did seem to have absconded with my servant. Poor Ishmael."

Was Molewood concerned? No, she decided. Lizzie intended to take Ishmael under her protection as soon as possible.

"The poor lad is in the kitchen, getting warm," Lizzie said. "He'd like to have perished from fright or frozen to death, but we got him home safely."

Molewood didn't show relief. Instead, his face seemed clouded with dislike for Orlando's interference.

Rowland as Orlando had always earned people's trust and friendship. When Rowland returned to London, she needed to beg for a lesson on how to avoid active distrust. She never made friends with anyone while wearing Orlando's fancy clothes.

PART IV

NO WHIG MAJORITY

—

ROSALIND
O Jupiter! how weary are my spirits!

TOUCHSTONE
I care not for my spirits, if my legs were not weary.

ROSALIND
I could find in my heart to disgrace my man's apparel, and to cry like a woman; but I must comfort the weaker vessel, as doublet and hose ought to show itself courageous to petticoat; therefore, courage, good Aliena.

CELIA
I pray you bear with me; I can go no further.

TOUCHSTONE
For my part, I had rather bear with you than bear you: yet I should bear no cross if I did bear you; for I think you have no money in your purse.

ROSALIND
Well, this is the forest of Arden.

TOUCHSTONE
Ay, now am I in Arden: the more fool I; when I was at home I was in a better place; but travelers must be content.

— William Shakespeare, *As You Like It*

27
Trick for Trick

— LIZZIE —

THURSDAY EVENING

AFTER THEY LEFT JERICHO House, stepping out into the early night, Perry joined Lizzie and Ned beside the thoroughfare, around the corner from Molewood's house. Lizzie wanted a carriage but was prepared to settle for a sledge.

"Good evening, Mr. Frake," she said. "If we ever manage to hail a ride, let's hurry to Xanthus House. I'm beyond weary after such a day."

Perry raised his hand for an approaching sledge, but it slid right past them.

"I need to go to the frost faire first." Ned said.

"Whatever for?" Lizzie wanted only the warmth and peace of Xanthus House. "You didn't seem to enjoy it last night. Too cold, you said. Too crowded. And you bruised your bum falling on ice."

"It wasn't so bad. I have business to attend to."

She'd seen Ned that cautious before. "What are you up to?"

Ned glanced at Perry. "I intend to recapture all the devil-drawn art I sold in London."

"The artwork that staved off starvation at Revelstone the last three winters?"

"Now that's over, I want those paintings back, especially after Molewood cheated the Touchstones, claiming forgery when there was none."

"You won't find them at the frost faire." She waited for Perry's response, but he was hailing another sledge, this one too far away to notice him. He seemed to be keeping his distance while Ned spoke with Lizzie.

Ned said, "I stole one from Molewood last night, and then burned it at the frost faire. And today," he tugged at his waistcoat, "those two forged landscapes were left behind in Molewood's carriage. I took them, and now I need to destroy them where no one will notice."

"You sound," Lizzie said, "as unhappy as when one of the barn cats went missing last winter. You liked those paintings, because you so successfully copied your father's style. You hated having to sell them. Can't we just hide them until they can be sent safely to Revelstone?"

"I know how," Perry raised his hand again to hail a ride, "to hide things so they can't be found. I'm especially happy to do it if it means Miss Foxe doesn't freeze by the river while Ned destroys his worries."

A sledge came down the street. At Perry's hail, the driver pulled to a stop, the sledge's rails screeching on the ice.

"Where to, gentlemen?"

"Covent Garden." Perry gave directions to Xanthus House.

The driver offered a horse blanket for two more pennies. Lizzie felt warm again before she got used to the sledge's bouncing. Then she asked what had been burning inside her.

"Wasn't it odd that Molewood guessed he'd lost Ishmael long after he mourned his treasures?"

"It did seem," Ned said, "he was less concerned for his servant than for his stolen treasures."

"Yes," Lizzie said. "Also, he seemed unhappy when you returned his box with the ivory."

"If I'd known it'd make him so sad, I would have just kept it." Ned sniffed. "As consolation for all the ivory that was not aboard the *Skylark*."

"I was only distressed," Perry said, "because Molewood sent his treasures away for safety. On Wednesday, I gave his steward clear instructions for fortifying his house. Yet he didn't trust or follow my advice."

"Did Mr. Molewood hurt your feelings?" Lizzie asked.

Ned laughed, though it was more of a snort.

"I possess a strong heart," Perry said. "It strikes me as irregular that he would both hire a locksmith and send his treasures to a secure warehouse, but then he did not rend his garments and weep when all was lost."

"He was quite in possession of himself," Lizzie said, "while the constable told him what was lost."

"You'd almost think…" Perry pretended to be thoughtful.

"That he expected to be robbed." Lizzie finished the thought.

"It's natural. We did rob him last night," Ned said.

"Not that kind of expectation," Lizzie said.

"Ned is too pure of heart to conceive of what we suspect, Miss Foxe." Perry threaded his fingers through Ned's.

"What?" Ned sounded bewildered.

Lizzie said, "Mr. Molewood robbed himself."

"I'm distressed at having to make such an accusation, Miss Foxe," Perry said. "Was the servant lad—"

"He's called Ishmael."

"Did he help advance Molewood's scheme?"

"No, not on purpose," Lizzie said. "He was quite frightened by it. And when I brought him home—"

"Whyever did you do that?" Ned asked. "I was so worried when you disappeared."

"Ishmael was lost, cold, and afraid. Had no idea how to get home. When I knocked on Molewood's door, the butler was unpleasantly surprised to see the lad."

"Mayhap the lad was supposed to be taken in that false robbery. You've invested an interest in the lad, Miss Foxe?"

"After rescuing him, I learned that he was on the *Skylark*. He's a pure innocent in Molewood's affairs."

Ned said, "Me, I'm not so pure, whatever Perry claims. I'm busy stealing back my past transgressions."

"I wish," Lizzie said, "that I could steal back my past sins, burn them in a fire, and cast the ashes in the Thames. However, I wish you wouldn't burn yours."

As the sledge bumped wildly across the icy street, Lizzie peeked out from under the horse blanket, but she couldn't determine how close they were to Xanthus House.

"You've convinced me," Ned said. "I'll stash these at Chalgrove House." Ned took a package from inside his coat.

"I'm glad you have those landscape paintings. I want us out of this engagement with Molewood by tomorrow afternoon."

"How will you do that, Miss Foxe?" Perry sounded interested. "I applaud the effort, though my locksmith business does require payment."

Lizzie said, "We'll take compensation from Mr. Molewood at the gambol tomorrow night. I want nothing more to do with the man after that. We can let the king punish his greater sins. I can't bear to think of him for more than the next day."

"What will you do?" Ned asked.

She decided at that moment. "I'm reporting Wolfric Molewood's name to Sir Bythorn. Tonight. I'll give up a few names from the list who haven't wealth to contribute to our gambol."

Ned shook his head, violently at first. But Perry crossed his arms and said, "I see your meaning. You can't be the avenging angel for all the man's sins."

"You agree with her notion?" Ned asked in surprise.

"Aye, but I'll leave you two to that task," Perry said. "I must stop at Oxford Street to chat with Mr. Pelletoot before I conclude my day's work."

Even before Perry was out of sight, Ned complained about their sudden errand at the customs house.

Lizzie said, "You'll see Perry at supper."

"It's not that."

"Then why are you glowering?"

"What did Perry and Rollo teach us about planning a gambol? Make a simple plan and follow it as if it were a narrow path across a wilderness. You, however, are now wandering all over England, the colonies, and the foreign ports."

"No," she protested. "It's all simple. The gambol is poised to run. I have engaged Molewood in the gambol, and I'll be done with him tomorrow. It will take time for customs to convince the king's men to take action, so it'll be next week before Molewood will have to answer to the king about his African investments. That will absorb his attention and free Prudence from his importunities until Tom finds a legal solution for her."

Ned scowled, quite unhappy. He wrapped his neck scarf tighter, then sat in silence after Lizzie redirected the sledge driver to the customs house.

—

Ned and Viscount Orlando stamped impatiently in the freezing foyer of the customs house. They'd come in the inky dark that settles early in the winter, just before most London businessmen depart for their supper. Sir Bythorn had made it plain at the coffeehouse meeting that he always stayed late. Yet Lizzie received no answer to the verbal message she gave the porter about their arrival.

"I should have claimed to be Rollo," Lizzie whispered. "Lord Orlando's Catalan title is getting us nowhere."

"Rollo warned not to tell obvious lies," Ned said.

"He didn't mean for us to be made into fools by a customs lackey with a title far beneath Marborne's."

"When did you become such a snob?" Ned said.

"It's not snobbery to want the Earl of Marborne to be properly respected."

With her best importuning smile, she spoke with the porter again. In five minutes, Orlando had ink, quill, and paper to leave a message. She wrote briefly, then begged the porter for pounce. When the ink was dry, she folded a letterlock and wrote, "Orlando de Flores, acting for the Earl of Marborne," in her best imitation of a masculine, Continental hand.

"Sir Bythorn is awaiting this crucial information from the Earl of Marborne," she said to the porter. "If Sir Bythorn doesn't appear in the office this evening, please send it to his house." She insisted upon a receipt and left the message, with two pennies. "In case you need to employ a message-boy."

Then they were on the street again, hailing a sledge for a ride to Xanthus House. Lizzie huddled deeper into the coat she'd borrowed from Rowland's closet.

"Thank you for doing this with me," Lizzie said. "I'm sorry you had to come out into the cold tonight. We're only on this journey because Mr. Molewood is so perverse."

"We are only in this gambol," Ned said, "because the wrath of Ysabel Foxe was stirred by men like Molewood. Though I admit, that man continues to justify your wrath."

"We're done with him after tomorrow night." Lizzie folded her arms as part of her final declaration. "I shall take his money. Tom will release Ishmael from his indenture. We shall free Prudence. Next week, the king's men will bring him to account for his sins against the Crown and the people of England."

At the corner across from Samuel's Coffeehouse, Ned held up his hand to hail a carriage.

Once inside the carriage, Ned said, "I don't see how any of our deceptions might be uncovered. Hence, I have no reason for what I'm thinking."

"Which is what?"

"That we must not be caught out, because Rollo isn't here in London to save us."

"Rollo not being here," Lizzie said, "will at least protect him if, in the impossible case, we are discovered."

Rollo not being here makes every hour hard to endure.

28
A Savory Pie

— NED —

THURSDAY NIGHT

NED AND LIZZIE STEPPED into the foyer at Xanthus House to find Perry had already returned and was shedding his greatcoat. Lazarus the butler left off assisting him to help Lizzie out of Rowland's heavy coat.

"Miss Foxe, you have a message just now brought from the Touchstone warehouse in Threadneedle Street."

Lizzie broke the seal. It proved to be one message wrapped around another. She glanced at the outer message. "Mr. Molewood has sent another missive to Miss Mott. Hildegonda will need a greater reward than that strip of Holland lace."

The message from Hildegonda was wrapped around a love letter from the Bloomsbury swindler.

Ned said, "When did he have time to write? Before or after robbing himself and chastising his servants?"

"You read it, Ned." Lizzie handed him the letter. "I fear choking if I read it."

Ned scanned it, then read it aloud. He choked on some of it but made it through to the end.

> My dearest Prudence, Prithee forgive me for being so forward, to press upon you how I feel. Meeting you put me

in the upper boughs, because I have never met a woman like you. As my mother says, London is full of gadding gossips, all ready to play goose-cap to a man, especially a man who can provide wealth in the way I can.

It was bold of me to approach you unawares today. I beg that you will consent to my notion that we write to each other, to learn to know each other better.

To begin, I long to introduce you to my mother. Next, I long to give you everything you need for comfort and joy in this life. You have seen how God has smiled on this faithful servant. I beg you, write to me to say you will think on it. I shall endeavor to wait patiently and not chafe over the time it takes to learn if your feelings have grown, ready to bloom, as mine have.

— Deeply and truly yours, Wolfric Molewood

Perry asked, "What is he apologizing for? Why must Prudence meet his mother? Does that mean you, Miss Foxe?"

Ned answered, because Lizzie was again fuming. "My new patron asked my chief model to marry him. My model is not pleased about it."

"Great bones!" Perry exclaimed. "What good luck! A man wants to share his fortune, and his high place in society."

"I already have a suitable place in society," Lizzie said. "And a fortune."

"Aye," Ned said. "But your fortune has to be renewed every few months by a gambol in pursuit of righteousness."

"I'm going up to put on a gown," Lizzie said. 'I'm done with Orlando for today."

—

When Ned and Perry came to the dining salon, Lizzie and Tom were already seated at the table. As they entered the room, Perry said, "That foamy blue velvet looks well on you, Ned."

Ned liked the sensation of Perry's compliment but would have preferred to hear it while they were alone on the third floor.

"It's called Sea Water blue. Found it in Portugal Street." He pulled back the collar to show the purple lining, but then felt too shy to tell Perry that the color of the lining was called Love-longing, especially since Lizzie was close by. Though she was deeply absorbed in her own thoughts.

"My dear Ned," Perry said, "you look to be the king of winter tonight. You'll dazzle the crowd while gliding on the icy Thames." He murmured rather too close to Ned's ear, sending shivers down his spine. "Are ye ready now, my man?"

Ned felt unsure about more frost faire adventures. "It's been such a day. I don't think I can make it to the Thames."

"I mean," Perry held out a chair for Ned, his breath still flowing warm over Ned's ears and neck, "are you ready for us to take up our new life in London, as men with respectable reputations? Who wear nice clothes." Perry took the seat close by Ned. "I'll help with your paint trappings. And you'll help me," Perry cupped Ned's thigh under the table, "pick some arduous locks. Now, I'm gutfoundered. I'll eat everything before me."

To Ned's way of thinking, the quality of food at dinner far exceeded the fussy tidbits served at the duke's fête last Monday. The cook modestly claimed to offer only winter fare: onion-and-mutton broth, a savory chicken pie, a bread pudding with bits of dried apple, cinnamon, and mace. Hot rolls.

They were still devouring supper when Tom asked to know everyone's business that day.

Perry said, "If you are so intent on talking instead of eating, you go first, Tom. What have you been up to?"

"Preparing papers to help Diggory Crackbone claim his inheritance. Spending money through an anonymous agent to pay for Lizzie's gambol. Lizzie, will you earn enough to offset these expenses? And do tell us what you were up to."

"Since noon," Lizzie said, "we've been in Bloomsbury, on Threadneedle Street, and back to Bloomsbury before going to the customs house off Tower Street."

"Our Lizzie," Ned said, "got a proposal of marriage."

"Oh, do tell," Tom said.

"I will not." Lizzie remained irate about that proposal. "We also rescued a coshed coachman and hunted Mr. Molewood's servant after he ran off, frightened by the robbery at Touchstone's."

"After that," Ned said, "Mr. Molewood's revolting ways with his servants put Lizzie out of sorts."

Lizzie clapped her hands. "I hope the king seizes the miscreant's land and transports him to some wild, uninhabitable place like Massachusetts or Virginia."

"Yet you have to go back to his house tomorrow," Ned said.

"I'll go as Orlando," Lizzie said. "I can't bear any more romantical proffers. Especially since all he wants is Prudence's land. Now, can we talk of anything else?"

Perry summed up his day of prowling.

"Tom gave me an onerous list of things to find in London this week. I found forged indentures in Mr. John Cokayne's house and the Earl of Gomfrey's townhouse in St James Place. Those documents are identical to the one I found at Sir Didlington's house, forged with Rollo's and Orlando's names."

"Good stars! Rollo did nothing to deserve that."

"I fear," Perry continued, "I have yet to connect any false indentures with Sir Bythorn."

Tom said, "We need clear proof of how these people passed from Bristol to London mansions."

"We do not need that," Lizzie said, "unless we want the king to punish them for investing in the African trade. We can punish them by way of their purses."

"But we need to clear Rollo's name from the forged indenture scheme," Tom said.

"I have faith that Rollo will manage that in Bristol," Lizzie said. "That's not a goal for tomorrow's gambol."

Tom said, "Yet I must assist Rollo in solving other problems. I've gathered insurance records for English ships that account for payouts and denials."

Perry asked, "Did you learn more about Hawkins' Heirs and the battle with Rollo's insurance claim?"

"In past years, the wealthiest syndicate members have received big insurance payouts against shipping losses. Perhaps they feel they deserve to always win."

"'God smiles on those who help themselves.'" Lizzie said.

"I wager Bythorn Chudrakes is part of the insurance scheme and the forged indentures." Lizzie said.

"It's improper for ladies to gamble." Tom said.

"You know nothing of what ladies do." Lizzie tossed her head. "But we need to save the insurance problem for later. Tomorrow's gambol is a more elaborate scheme than we've done before, for both setting the bait and closing the trap."

Tom said, "I'm especially interested in ensuring we do not get caught in our own trap."

Lazarus was at the door. "Mr. Oakes is here with his sister. They believe you expect them. Shall I prepare a punch bowl?"

"What could be better in this life?" Tom said, enthused.

—

After a long, trying day, Ned longed to sit by the fire and sip hot spiced wine from a copper mug. But it took thirty minutes for Michael and Felicity to report on the plan with the actors. Finally, Lizzie stopped asking questions and Perry declared that all contingencies were covered.

After the Oakes siblings departed, the four of them sat by the fire, but every five minutes Tom found a new way to plague Lizzie for her rash decision to give Molewood's name to Sir Bythorn.

"We still possess too little information about Sir Bythorn," Tom complained. "I haven't yet found who his parents are or what he desires beyond money."

Lizzie said, "I'm sure he also wants a more powerful title. We should find ways that he can be used for our purposes."

Tom said, "You mean, beyond giving him Molewood's name in a rash fit of revenge?"

Lizzie said, "I am disgusted with Molewood's existence on this earth. I persuaded him to join in the gambol. I think it's a rational way to let the king deal with the man's other iniquities."

"It grieves me," Perry said, "that you've run to Rollo's enemy and asked him to take revenge for you. That contradicts the Restoration Rule to shun revenge."

Ned sought a last cup of hot punch. Tom passed his own punch cup for Ned to fill.

Lizzie said, "I'm not seeking revenge, only recompense for the *Skylark* people."

Perry shook his head, looking dour. "I've kept my own counsel about this, but it's a puzzle to me how your gambol serves the English Crown, as you've sworn to do. And you are transgressing on the duke's warning to give up on the *Skylark.*"

Ned fidgeted with his now-filled punch cup. Had he been too easily persuaded by Lizzie's justifications? It was unpleasant, sitting between Lizzie and Perry when they challenged each other, as if a cold wind blew from both directions.

Lizzie shrugged. She'd long before abandoned her punch cup. "I serve future rulers and a future parliament who believe it is wrong to put people in chains. For the man sitting on the throne now, we'll give him the list of Hawkins' Heirs when we're done with them. Except for names the duke wants withheld."

"I cannot quarrel with that." Perry set aside his punch cup and held up his hands in surrender. "We should call it a night, since Lizzie's big day is tomorrow and we must be busy soldiers."

29
Odysseus the Cunning

— NED —

FRIDAY MORNING

ON FRIDAY MORNING, NED stopped by Samuel's Coffeehouse along with Perry and Lizzie, it being too early to knock on the door at Jericho House in Bloomsbury and resume painting Mr. Molewood as a Greek hero. When the trio came to Rowland's usual table, they found Tom with his head bent, listening to the story Diggory told while he signed papers where Tom pointed.

"It's sixty days since James prorogated Parliament." Diggory continued his tale, as if not noticing the trio taking seats at the table. "And now there is no Whig majority."

"How can that be?" Tom asked.

"Early this morning, three members declared for the Tories, abandoning the Whigs. And two of those have declared themselves studying to join the Roman faith."

Without knowing what the others heard, Diggory recited the names, as if reading them in order from the list Orlando had sent to Sir Bythorn the previous evening.

Then Diggory straightened. "Ah, good morning. The good dog Countess isn't joining you today, Lord Orlando?"

Lizzie blinked at Diggory twice, as if she didn't realize he'd addressed her.

"No, it's just us," Ned answered for his sister. "May we have coffee, Mr. Crackbone?"

"Ah, ha." Diggory chuckled. "Perhaps I'm not Mr. Crackbone at all. Better just call me Diggory."

Then Diggory set off for his coffee bar, which relieved Ned, who wanted to discuss the distressing news Diggory just told. However, Lizzie wanted to talk about something else. "After Diggory shared his story on Wednesday night, I feel duplicitous, not sharing my true name. I should tell him."

"It distresses me," Perry said, "that you'd seek to complicate Mr. Crackbone's view of the world merely to ease your private feelings. You feel duplicitous because for the past fortnight every version of Ysabel Foxe that has appeared outside of Xanthus House has been a fabrication."

"What distresses me," Ned said, still anxious to discuss the news they'd just heard, "is that last night we gave Sir Bythorn those names, all of whom sit in the House of Commons."

Tom said, "Who could guess that the king might be waiting for those names?"

Perry said, "Molewood bought his way to a seat in Parliament as a Tory. What do you think the king, or Sir Bythorn, will do with that investor's name?"

Ned said, "Lizzie had guessed that the king wouldn't act until Monday at the earliest. But this morning, three of them have suddenly become Tories."

Perry said, "Mayhap the king only seeks to offer other investors a cautionary tale."

"Whatever else the king intends to do," Lizzie said, "he hasn't arrested those men. So, the king's action opens an opportunity for us. Tonight the other investors can show the king they are turning away from Africa and investing their funds with the Venetians and their imports from China."

Tom rose. "I shall see you gentlemen—and Orlando—at the Venetian investors event this evening."

Perry also rose. "If we are as lucky as we wish to be, we can celebrate later at the frost faire."

"We will succeed through skill," Lizzie said. "Not luck."

After Tom and Perry left, Ned paid for everyone's coffee, then rose with Lizzie. They had their own work to do.

—

Friday noon at Jericho House in Bloomsbury, Ned gave Molewood a message from Miss Mott. Molewood beamed at receiving it but pocketed it to read later.

As Ned was setting up to paint, he caught over his shoulder that Molewood kissed the message, then pocketed it again. He had to remind the man of where to place his treasures on the carpet-covered table.

"You can see that I've sketched each in their places." He pointed to the table in the foreground of the painting. That lovely carved piece of African ivory was back on the carpeted tabletop, glowing like white gold among the silver bracelets and trinkets.

"I do see. Each piece must always be in the same place to properly capture the angle of the light," Molewood said. For someone with poor taste in art, the man did strive to know what a painter did.

"You have such beautiful artifacts," Ned said. "It's a shame that you lost so many to thieves."

"Aye." Molewood did not sound at all dejected. "I replaced one yesterday. By great good luck, I picked up a Jacopo Bassano painting. It was a bargain, since I didn't have to pay a broker. Do you want to see it?"

He dragged Ned upstairs to an overly decorated salon to show off the painting, *The Good Samaritan.* "Do you approve?" he asked, obviously seeking only praise.

"It's magnificent. You are a lucky man. Bassano was a master of brushstroke and form." Ned inspected it closely, hands behind his back. He didn't learn much from that inspection, given that he'd painted it. In the fall of 1684. The apple crop had been particularly fine, but not enough to save the Foxe cousins or the village from the wolf coming for them that winter. And Molewood had missed one detail: the signature on the back was dated a year after the artist had died.

It'd be a shame to destroy it. Lizzie had the right idea: hide all rescued paintings until they could be carried to Revelstone, back to the studio where they'd been conceived.

"I believe," Ned said, speaking sagely, "you should add it to the wall behind us. I'll include it in *Achilles at Skyros*, to add a Christian note. And it's even more beautiful than these artifacts to show your material and spiritual worth."

Molewood leapt at the notion. "I've heard of such. It's like one poet quoting another in a new poem."

It wasn't a large piece, scarcely an ell in width. Ned volunteered to move and remount it in the salon that had been devoted to the painting project.

"I do hope Miss Mott will like it." Molewood pointed to where Ned should hang it. "I had her in mind, especially, when I secured it for my house. Do you think she will be here soon?"

"I apologize, sir. Did you not read her message? She's quite ill. That's why my cousin, Lord Orlando, came to model today."

The model had been waiting in the salon, already in costume as Achilles. Molewood didn't cast a glance at the model while he fretted, expressing dismay at Miss Mott's absence, asking Ned how the work could possibly progress before the lady's good health returned. Ned showed him the sketched form of Achilles, with the reassurance that he'd finish the details when Miss Mott recovered her health.

"Today, sir, I plan to advance the figure of Odysseus."

Molewood stiffened. "Can you simply work on Odysseus's costume? I have pressing business today."

"I can," Ned said. Lizzie would be happy, since Odysseus wore the warmest costume.

"Must I give you my African servant for today?" Molewood asked. What Ned heard: the shine went off the project with Miss Mott absent. Lizzie, unseen by Molewood, was signaling a need to keep Ishmael for the day.

Ned said, "I need your servant here and posing to keep perspective and shadows."

Molewood left his purple velvet coat, then summoned his driver and left for his business chambers across town.

Lizzie had dressed as Achilles but now had to be Odysseus.

"Can we have a warmer fire?" Lizzie asked after Molewood left. "I'm sure these Greeks never endured a London winter."

She must have then asked the same thing in Portuguese, because Ishmael went to add fuel to the fire.

Ned made four thin slashes to indicate where *The Good Samaritan* would appear in the background. He pondered when it'd be best to carry that painting out of the house.

"We have no reason to be here," Lizzie whispered when she mounted the stool to be Odysseus. "No Molewood to distract. No Perry prowling."

Ned said, "Molewood might return. We need to stay to protect our investment."

And if Ned accomplished nothing else that day, he'd ask for Perry's help to protect the Touchstones from the danger posed by *The Good Samaritan.*

30
Achilles at Skyros

– LIZZIE –

FRIDAY MIDAFTERNOON

LIZZIE BEGAN TWO HOURS pretending to be Orlando, standing in for the famous builder Wolfric Molewood as the cunning Odysseus at the moment before he unveils the disguised Achilles.

This was the safest character she'd played in Molewood's house. This costume meant a morning without worries about being revealed as a double fraud and without being harassed by Molewood. Unfortunately, it also meant wearing the purple velvet coat that smelled of the man whenever she moved in the slightest way. Ned folded his overcoat with sleeves inside and made her wear it under the coat, to emulate Molewood's bulk. She also had to wear that floppy Italian-style velvet hat which Molewood thought looked Greek.

Ned took a break. "I need to attend to personal business." He put his suit coat on over his waistcoat, claiming it was freezing cold out in the gentlemen's necessary. While Ned was gone, Lizzie shook her limbs to restore feeling. In Portuguese, she suggested to Ishmael that he rest and stretch, but the lad scarcely moved from where Ned had placed him.

Lizzie used those few moments to take solace by reading Tamsin's last missive, which she'd tucked into the shift under the purple coat.

> In December, all the girls came down with head colds, with shivering, shaking, and fevers. What luck that Dr. Oakes stayed here after you summoned him in October.
>
> The girls are well again, and Winwood has helped Gloria, Ines, and Marta with skin problems that Mrs. Bell could not cure with her potions. The nightmares have lessened, but Winwood denies that anything he did affected that.

When Ned returned from his personal errand, Lizzie resumed her pose, though Ned had to nudge her limbs into place. "Can you hold that comfortably?" he asked.

"I can. I am strengthened," she crowed, "by the joy I took when Molewood departed in a dark mood. And all because Prudence Mott isn't here to elevate his spirits."

"I should just send you home," Ned said. "I can keep up the pretense should Molewood return."

"I know I wanted to leave, but you are right. Molewood is likely to come back to check on you, as if you were his servant. He's the type to patrol and pester to ensure he gets full effort from his workers."

"At two o'clock, you can go. I know you need to join your gambol at Mercers' Hall."

The closer it came to two o'clock, the more impatient she became, until she shivered so violently that Ned came over to adjust her pose. He said, "Wasn't that green vase on the list of treasures stolen yesterday? That's the ivory I rescued from the carriage."

"Yes. And the little iron statue of the world's ugliest demon? Wasn't an African statue on the list of what thieves took from the carriage?" She switched to Portuguese. "Ishmael, do you know anything of this statue of a demon?"

"Not a demon," Ishmael said. "He's called Nyame. He has many stories."

"Can you tell one of his stories?" Lizzie asked. "Is there a song you know?"

That's how they came to endure the early afternoon's tedium. While Ned painted, Ishmael sang. He described the stories of his song, which Lizzie translated for Ned. Several times, a pair of servants drifted to the doorway to hear Ishmael sing. There did not seem to be many servants in the house that day.

"The song is better with the kora," Ishmael said. He turned wistful. "My kora surely misses me. Someone in my last village must have claimed it now. Someday, I will—"

A heavy pounding thundered on the front door of Molewood's house.

A servant's voice could be heard—not the usual butler—answering the thunderous knock. "Mr. Molewood is not at home. You cannot—"

"Open for the king's warrant!" A deep voice growled. The door banged open. "The king's customs commission has a warrant to seize smuggled goods hidden here. Call Mr. Molewood."

"He's not here." The servant's voice quivered.

Several men tramped into the foyer. The door to the salon slammed open. When it bounced back, the customs man who seemed to be the leader kicked the door open a second time. The man wasn't tall, but his deep voice came from his barrel chest.

Startled, Ned shifted, as if preparing to do battle.

Ishmael went rigid with fear, then shook his head and removed all emotion from his face.

Lizzie prepared to have her masquerade pulled apart, for which she had a story ready.

The leader again growled. "Please provide the keys to all the locked doors. Now, sir."

The servant, whom Lizzie had never seen before, kept protesting. "Mr. Molewood has the keys. He's not here."

"He's here." The leader grinned, pointing at Lizzie. "Our warrant says he's the one being painted in the purple coat." The fellow held out his hand. "The keys, Mr. Molewood. Else, we batter down every door and open every box."

"I don't have the keys," Lizzie protested. "And I'm not Wolfric Molewood. I'm—"

"You, sir, are refusing to comply with the king's warrant."

"I'm not—"

The leader tipped his head. A pair of men grabbed Lizzie. One stuck a kerchief in her mouth, gagging her. Then he held her while the other bound her hands. She kicked out. The two lifted her, as if she were freight from a barge and tramped down to the foyer, all while Ned protested loudly.

The leader loudly instructed his men. "Take the African boy. He must be more of Molewood's booty. Take the painter too. Our captain says he was seen carrying African booty yesterday. Look, it's right here on this table."

Seen? Did Sir Bythorn have them watched at Touchstone's that day when Molewood's carriage was robbed?

She was still pondering that question, more annoyed than frightened, when she was shoved into a sledge with Ned and Ishmael. A heavy sheet of canvas was tossed over them.

—

Lizzie struggled to spit out that kerchief, fearing what was on that rag more than this dire situation.

"It's a trap! Sir Bythorn set a trap."

"For Molewood?" Ned asked. He wasn't gagged.

"And Viscount Orlando. Sir Bythorn must have had someone follow me, to know Orlando was at Molewood's house."

From listening to the customs men's chatter, Lizzie judged they were headed for a local lockup. One customs man began reciting their crimes when the sledge pulled onto a wider street: holding smuggled goods; refusing a rightful warrant; assaulting a customs officer.

Ned argued. Their captors laughed.

The entire sledge ride, she burned with anger, hot fury that threatened to consume her in flames from her bewigged head to the toes of Rowland's boots. Jammed against Ned on one side, on her other side she was repeatedly elbowed by a customs man who smelled of boiled cabbage and tobacco. She clenched her teeth hard enough, it seemed, to crunch them to pieces.

Ned said, "Breathe. We'll be fine."

Lizzie breathed. She had, after all, vowed to Rowland that she wouldn't act out of rage. That she'd retain a peaceful soul while reaving the Hawkins' Heirs investors for their sins against the people from the *Skylark*.

Now, she could not act. Her hands had been bound in fetters by smelly customs men who repeatedly told her to shut up in the name of King James and God Himself.

Her own voice called out in the fire that raged inside, castigating herself: she'd given Molewood's name to Sir Bythorn. All because Molewood had offended her. Now, two repulsive men stood in the way of her efforts to reap justice.

As the cart rumbled along, heavy enough that it seldom swished on patches of ice, a local church bell struck three o'clock. If something didn't happen immediately to free them, she'd miss her own gambol.

Ned kept whispering, "Perry will come," while Lizzie chastised herself: wise Prudence Mott had refused to return to that house, but hare-brained Orlando couldn't resist.

Perry did not appear.

When the sledge skidded to a stop, one of the customs men jerked her onto the street. His leader untied the fetters binding her wrists. Then she was thrust into a cold, dank room. She fell to the floor, her face dropping onto soggy, filthy straw laid over stone flags. Ishmael was tossed in behind her. Ned staggered in, didn't fall, and offered a hand to help Lizzie up.

The heavy door clanged shut.

"Are you hurt?" he asked.

"I'm fine. Where are we?"

"It's that half-ruined old priory off Holborn."

"Will they sell us again?" In the dark, Ishmael asked in Portuguese, his voice quavering. Alas, Ishmael had been caught up in this debacle because of Lizzie's anger with Mr. Molewood.

Lizzie sounded as reassuring as she could. "No. Our friends will come for us soon. Don't be afraid."

"Master said if I meet soldiers, he must put me on the block and send me to the plantations. That means—"

"No, Ishmael. Don't worry. We'll keep you safe." Silently, Lizzie vowed to see Molewood in Hades before Ishmael saw the auction block again. In English, she said to Ned, "I promised to keep Ishmael safe. This is my fault."

"It's the fault of Misters Molewood and Chudrakes," Ned said. "And another stroke of bad luck for Ishmael."

Ishmael understood his name. "I was to take a message to Miss Mott after Mr. Wijck finished his work today. Master will surely send me to the plantations."

"Please trust me, Ishmael. Our friends will come. You'll be safe." She had to make that right. She repeated Ishmael's worries for Ned.

"Zooterkins!" Ned wasn't assured. "Will Rollo have to buy our new friend if Molewood tries to sell him?"

"We'll deal with Mr. Molewood later. Ned, we must get the lad warm. He isn't wearing half the clothes we are, and he has no cloak. Can't you hear his teeth chattering?"

First, she made Ishmael take the wig she wore while posing, since keeping his head warmed seemed critically important.

That ridiculous Italian velvet cap might have been better, but it was lost somewhere, likely in the cart that dragged them here. Lizzie removed Ned's heavy overcoat from under her purple coat. Ned took off his long suit coat, keeping only his waistcoat. He tugged at the waistcoat to get it in place. Lizzie reached over to help him, finding he presented an unnaturally stiff and bulky front for a man who was stick thin on his heaviest days.

It was too dark for Ned to see the question in her eyes, but he said, "I liberated *The Good Samaritan*."

"Oh. That's why you were so long in the necessary."

They shuffled and chided each other to find an arrangement where everyone was warm, with Ishmael perched across their thighs. At least they had a wooden bench under them, rather than the frigid, rush-strewn stone floor.

While they warmed each other under the huddle of cloaks, Lizzie silently conceded that the hour for her gambol had passed. Her only hope was that Tom and Michael might salvage enough from the event that they could lure people back later. All that effort to obtain a room at the Mercers' Hall, hire servants, print invitations, rehearse everyone: all for naught. She yearned to turn her mind to formulating explicit revenge, even though revenge was forbidden under their Restoration Rules.

Ned insisted they try his father's methods for how to stop shivering. This meant trying every possible distraction to avoid thinking about being cold. Ned sang tavern songs, with Lizzie translating for Ishmael. Then Ishmael sang songs from his home. The effort wasn't working well for Lizzie. Ned kept admonishing him for shivering. "You must relax."

Ishmael proclaimed that singing warmed him to the bone, with all glory to Our Savior. His new friends, he said, had been sent like angels for his salvation.

No, they'd caused him to be dragged into this dungeon.

31
A Bad Night

— NED —

FRIDAY NIGHT

"TELL ISHMAEL THAT WE'RE no angels." Ned felt a frantic need to distract both Lizzie and Ishmael. She didn't seem to believe it, but Ned felt sure that they just had to endure until Perry found them. "Ask about his home. He'll take chill again if we don't divert him with talk."

To begin, Ishmael said he could sing his story, since his father had intended for him to become a singer of stories. He used a word that Ned didn't know, then said he had yet to master songs in Portuguese. He sang, then told his tale in Portuguese.

"When my father was a child, my village was under the protection of the great queen Nzinga. The black-robed priest in our village, who taught us his tongue and gave us Jesus names, said Nzinga had been as great a queen as Isabel in Spain and Elizabeth in England. When we said no one knew those queens, he drew in the dust to show us where those queens had ruled. Nzinga had a greater country."

"I never heard of a queen called Nzinga," Ned said. "It must be a very big world."

"Yes, I didn't know then how big it is." Ishmael was quiet for a moment, before resuming his story. "The priest was called

Father Benedito, but he had no wife or children, so I never understood why we called him father. When he was in the mood to teach, we sat at his feet, and he called us his children. Then my mother and father died of the spotted fever, along with my sisters and little brothers. Besides the children, many others died that year. Those alive left the village for elsewhere, burning down all the houses and leading the cattle away."

He snuffled for a moment. Ned drew the coat closer around Ishmael, waited for him to speak again.

"Father Benedito took me to a village near the Great Sea. He was growing old and needed me to carry water and make his food and fetch his medicines from the priests in the next village. He was teaching me to read. At night it was too dark to study letters, so I sang the old songs and sang the stories my father taught me. Father Benedito praised my reading each day and how well I made my letters in the dirt. He said I might go to the priests' school in Luanda. But I didn't want to leave him, because the priest had been good to me, and he could not get by on his own."

"That was kind of you." Ned remembered how much he'd liked it when his father praised him for even the smallest thing.

"One cannot choose otherwise." Ishmael wiggled under their pile of coats and cloaks, then righted the wig that kept his head warm. "Then Father Benedito caught the sweating sickness. When he died, the chief of our new village sold me to the first trader who passed through. They sold me at the water's edge in Luanda, where we had to stand on a block in chains. I'm small, so I was with the last to go on the devil's ship, along with a bundle of crying children, all younger than me."

Ishmael went quiet for a long time. Ned searched for something to say that could be helpful. It was beyond him to know how to comfort a soul telling a nightmare story. "It must have been very frightening." He made Lizzie translate.

"I wasn't supposed to be afraid, because Father Benedito taught me to pray. I tried hard to beg Our Father in heaven, day after day. But no angels came for us. We cooked like little fish in the hot, dark hold. They took away those who died only every third day. We had water each morning. I was the last of the little children, who had only half rations."

"What did you eat?"

"Hard bread. A bite of fish every other day. That's it. When they brought us to the cold country, new devils took us away to the city. They gave us food and clothes, and a man said we must thank God for our salvation."

Ned coughed at that thin notion.

Ishmael finished his story. "Then I came to my master."

"You were sold to him?" Lizzie's gut wrenched.

"No. There was no auction block. No one spoke Portuguese, but I quickly understood the rules. Cook, in the kitchen, is kind and has taught me the ways of this cold country."

After Lizzie translated Ishmael's answer, Ned said, "Ask how it was when they were rescued from the Portuguese ship. Was the second ship better, with English sailors?"

"Second ship?" Ishmael sounded puzzled.

Lizzie translated Ishmael's answer, her voice hoarse again. "Ishmael says there was only one devil ship, and only one man on the devil ship who spoke Portuguese. The rest spoke the tongue of this cold country."

"Then the *Skylark's* captain lied to the customs men." It must be because of the freezing cold, but ideas came together slowly. "They did not rescue people from a Portuguese slaver. They bought their captives in Africa."

Ned felt Lizzie shaking beside him. She wasn't shivering from the cold. Her voice sounded strained, hoarse. "Wolfric Molewood and all of Hawkins' Heirs hold servants they gained through their syndicate." She cleared her throat. "And that wretch Chudrakes is helping to preserve their investment."

"But why did Sir Bythorn send customs men to arrest Molewood?" Ned had too little information to make sense of this.

Lizzie again translated his words for Ishmael's sake.

"*Senhor* Bythorn?" Ishmael said the man's name with only a hint of an accent.

"Do you know who he is?" That must be what Lizzie asked. Ned felt impatience rising as he waited for Lizzie to translate what the young man said.

"He comes to the house often. Late at night. And last night at midnight, when Sir Bythorn came, they quarreled."

Lizzie translated that, then listened for more.

"Ishmael had to stay up quite late last night, to rouse the chair bearers, open the door, and escort Sir Bythorn to his chair."

Ned folded his arms, comforted by the sense of *The Good Samaritan* safe inside his waistcoat. But his movement disturbed their careful arrangement of coats and cloaks.

"Does this change how we understand all this?" he asked.

"Yes. And it makes me even more eager to get out of here," Lizzie said. "That had better be soon, because I'm not about to use that filthy slop bowl in the corner."

"I can hold my overcoat as a curtain," Ned said. "I did it for Tamsin many times when we played highwayman."

"That's nearly the last thing I'd do," Lizzie said.

"What's the last thing?"

"Throw this whole chaotic mess at the king's feet and ask him to fix it." Lizzie paused. "No, that's not the last thing. Rather, it's something I'd never do. The king's monopoly on African trade is at the root of all this misery."

They were all quiet. Cold. Miserable. Listening to water dripping down the stone walls. Straining to hear beyond the bolted door, not discerning even the ever-present London street sounds.

"Perry will come." Ned said it again, having kept the idea beating in his heart the whole of the dark night.

"I'm not in the mood for false hopes," Lizzie said.

But the door opened, and Perry had come.

"God's teeth!" Perry's deep voice echoed against stone walls. "The long moments without you have distressed me, chucking. Ah, good morrow, Miss Foxe. Mayhap you require assistance?"

The guard at the door was arguing with Tom, who croaked, "If you cannot read this writ, can you at least recognize the judge's seal? Read the words *habeas corpus.* In the grand English tradition, this writ demands that you deliver these prisoners directly to Sir Oliver Boxworth's chambers."

—

Ned asked, "Have we met Sir Oliver before now? Why is his name familiar?"

The carriage stopped near what Tom said was the judge's chambers.

"He's the judge," Tom said, "who issued a warrant to arrest the Marquess of Withersea, when I swore to that man's crimes."

Before they alighted from the carriage, Lizzie asked Tom to help arranging the auburn wig that belonged to Mr. Molewood, since Orlando's name appeared on the warrant. Then she asked directions to the necessary, which Ned and Ishmael also needed.

When they returned, Perry elbowed Ned. "Mayhap you want my assistance putting your neckcloth in order. Tom did promise the judge that the prisoners to be released were men of quality, from the Earl of Marborne's household."

"I would be most grateful." Ned said. Perry scrubbed at Ned's face with a kerchief from his pocket, like Mrs. Bell used to clean the cousins' faces before Sunday services.

Tom inspected each of them, tweaking a neckcloth, tucking away stray locks. He studied Ishmael. "I'm not sure how I explain the third man in our party. His name isn't on the warrant."

Lizzie spoke to the lad, who answered quietly.

"He says we must allow him to hold our coats," she said, translating. "He'll be Perry's page."

While they were piling cloaks into Ishmael's arms, covering half his face, they were called into Sir Oliver's chambers.

The judge was an older, withered man, who sat at his table amid a clutter of papers. When his visitors entered, he straightened his periwig and looked at the clock on the mantel. The clock (Dutch ceramics) showed forty minutes after eight o'clock, and Ned didn't know whether that meant they were early or late. The judge's eyes bore down on Tom. Milk-and-Water blue. That's the color Ned would use to paint those eyes.

"These are the prisoners you wanted freed from the customs men, Mr. Foxe?" He shook his head. "I can tell they've not been in their own beds this past night. Which one is Eduard Wijck?"

"I am," Ned said, stepping forward.

"You, Mr. Wijck, were also a ward of Doctor Absolom Foxe? You are a cousin of Tom Foxe and the Earl of Marborne?'

"Y–Yes, your honor." Ned was not in any proper shape to be representing the Foxe cousins, but he was struck hard with the notion of the judge associating Ned's shoddy self with Uncle Absolom. "I had that good fortune, until only last year."

"Doctor Foxe was my tutor in Latin at Trinity."

"Mine also, but at home, not at Trinity," Ned said. "Our uncle had not the success with me that he did with Tom Foxe."

The judge's milky eyes darted to Tom, then back to Ned, and must have noticed they didn't look like cousins. "What did the customs men want with an English artist who has no ties to shipping or importing?"

"I don't know, sir. They claimed to have a warrant, but I never saw it. I was only in Mr. Molewood's house because he contracted with me to paint a significant picture for him. He is a collector and supporter of the arts."

"Please offer a guess, Mr. Wijck."

"The composition for my painting included several artifacts from Mr. Molewood's collection, which the customs man claimed were smuggled from Africa." Like that piece of carved ivory Ned had lusted after so heartily that his palms itched to snatch it.

The judge studied the paper before him. "Mr. Wijck, are you related to the Dutch painter, Jan Wijck?"

"My father, sir. He lived in Marborne parish for many years. He was a more successful tutor for me than was Uncle Absolom."

"I shall believe you have talent then. I have a landscape by your father in our dining salon at home."

Zooterkins! Would Ned's heroic work as a forger pursue him everywhere?

"My father was a talented artist," Ned said, "with much to teach me."

"That landscape has hung there for more than twenty years," the judge mused. "It must be almost as old as you are."

Ned became busy rolling under waves of relief while staring at the judge's Dutch ceramic inkstand, which also seemed to be genuine. He couldn't pay attention to how the judge queried Lizzie, which seemed to call for her to once more put on Ned's overcoat to show how it padded out the purple coat and therefore allowed the thin Orlando to be mistaken for Molewood.

After fifteen minutes on the judge's Dutch clock, Sir Oliver waved them off.

Ned wanted out the door. He could guess from Lizzie's darting eyes that she wanted the same. But there was Tom, stepping up to the judge's table.

"*Quod infortunii!* Your honor, is there any chance we can bring an action against those who fostered my cousins' arrest?"

"I'm sorry for the night of misery," Sir Oliver said, "but it's my judgment that you shouldn't try it. From my inquiries this morning, the warrant came from a judge the customs commission relies on. The mistakes likely came from chaos when those men brought the warrant. And the original warrant, which was only to search the house, was set aside early this morning."

On the street, while Perry waved the carriage over, Tom said, "That's a relief. I dreaded having to plead that you are all king's watchers on secret assignment."

"No!" Lizzie cried. "You must never do that. Calling on the king in this case? It's the worst thing we could do. It'd create a tragedy for Rollo."

"Vero, vero," Tom said, as if humbled. Ned was too weary to ponder if he'd ever learned what that bit of Latin meant.

They retrieved their cloaks from Ishmael and stepped back into the morning cold. When they moved toward the carriage, a small band of street urchins swarmed them, calling for pennies. Perry loomed over them, calling threats, but then reached into his pocket and tossed a handful of pennies further down the street. With shouts, the urchins ran to grab pennies from the cobbles, then shouted at each other over issues of fairness and theft.

In the noise and confusion, Ishmael disappeared.

Ned saw emotion sweep over Lizzie's face. Despair? Failure?

Ned had her elbow. "Into the carriage with you, dear sister. We'll find him. He's likely gone back to Molewood's house."

"He'll freeze."

"It's just a few streets from here, so the lad likely knows the way home."

They were all in the carriage, Tom at Lizzie's side and Perry at Ned's, all reassuring Lizzie that they'd find Ishmael.

"I have another question." Lizzie held up her finger to quiet their assurances. "What in the name of every imaginary saint happened last night that kept us in a freezing cell?"

"Mayhap," Perry said, "a great deal. More than most nights."

32
A Better Morning

—LIZZIE—

SATURDAY MORNING

ON THE WAY FROM the magistrate's chambers, Lizzie felt a chill breeze flow through the carriage. She let Tom swaddle her with his coat.

"Mayhap I should tell my tale first." Perry adjusted Ned's coat, pulling the collar up close around his friend's neck. "It's a tale to warm hearts and souls."

"If you believe in souls," Lizzie said. The past night left her especially dour.

"For my part," Perry paused to again assess whether Ned was adequately wrapped, "I came early to Lizzie's gambol and played my part as the guard at the door."

"We welcomed your guests at four o'clock. I must say, the rented room was perfect for the occasion. Silk coverings on the chairs. Crystal glasses in people's hands.

"I wish I had seen such glory." She did not care that she sounded bitter.

"Your friend Mr. Molewood came," Perry said.

"He's not my friend." Lizzie's insides revolted at hearing the man's name. "And because of Molewood's bad behavior, we rotted in gaol while he drank my wine. Who else came?"

"All the invited guests," Perry said, "except three who suddenly became Tories yesterday. Out of everyone present, Sir Didlington, Mr. Cokayne, and the Earl of Gomfrey were the most pleased to be invited, as excited as lads at a pleasure garden."

"You can imagine my regret at having missed my own gambol." Lizzie indulged in a childish sulk. Yet her wish to hear Perry's tale was stronger than other longings.

"Tell them the rest of the story," Tom said before Lizzie could beg the same.

Perry said, "When Miss Foxe didn't appear at the meeting, Michael Oakes, as Signore di Bassanio, continued to lure the investors further into the gambol. He described two ships, *Galatea* and *Medea,* leased in England and rechristened for the Levant trade."

Lizzie said, "Did Michael convince people to commit to joining our syndicate?"

"No," Perry said, "we all feared having our skins stitched to the wall if we proceeded without you. Michael called for the guests to submit written bids to join the syndicate. He opened three bids and began shaking his head, crying, '*No, no, troppo poco,*' in a passion. Then he sent people home, promising they'd receive new invitations when Mercutio's health improved."

"Good," Lizzie said. "We'll write new invitations tomorrow morning."

It seemed a small detail, but as the carriage jolted along, she noticed that Ned was stroking the back of Perry's hand. A flood of longing washed over her. If only Rowland were here now. All she could conjure, though, was his voice reciting his Bard: "*O, how bitter a thing it is to look into happiness through another man's eyes!*"

Then her imagined comfort washed away in an instant when the carriage bounced around a corner and splashed into standing puddles where the ice crust had broken. The passing splash onto the carriage cast the stink of night soil into the air. She covered her nose and mouth, held her breath. The memory of their filthy gaol washed away any thought of Rowland.

Perry was saying, "After the guests departed, we all went to search for the two of you. Felicity went to Chalgrove House."

Tom said, "Michael met me at Xanthus House. We searched all the taverns Ned visits. At Samuel's coffeehouse, Diggory said he last saw any of us that morning."

Looking out of the carriage window, Lizzie thought she saw Ishmael in the crowd along Theobalds Road. But it was a dark child in a ragged cloak. Ishmael didn't have a cloak. Why hadn't she pressed one of their coats into his hands? As wretched as the previous night had been, it wasn't an excuse for failing to rally her mother wit. She should have expected him to run.

She again wished Rowland were there. Yet, he wasn't and—

The carriage halted.

"We're at Chalgrove House," Tom said. "I directed the carriage here because Lizzie needs resuscitation."

"What I need is the rest of the story!" she protested.

"I aver, I shall not forget any of it while you are restored," Perry said.

"Go, Lizzie." Ned glanced up for a moment before his eyes again stuck on Perry. "Have a washing and breakfast."

As Lizzie descended from the carriage and the front door of the house opened. Aurora Rôche stepped onto the stoop, holding her hands, goggle-eyed behind her thick spectacles. Lizzie grasped her friend's warm fingers, aware that hers were as cold as the icicles hanging from the eaves. In Aurora's thick spectacles, Lizzie could see her reflection, hair askew, Molewood's purple coat, and Rowland's *longues jambes* an unholy mess. Ned's woolen overcoat, which hung from her shoulders, had fended off frostbite but would never again be fit for more than a dog's bed in a stable.

"I had faith Tom would find you," Aurora said.

Lizzie would never say how often her faith had wavered. She'd spent the night reassuring Ishmael that people she trusted would rescue them. But it took so many horrible hours.

"We have water heating for a bath," Aurora said.

Those felt to be the best words Lizzie had heard in this life, given that she was filthier, hungrier, and more fatigued than she'd ever been.

"I don't want to press my own ideas on you," Aurora said, "but wouldn't you enjoy this day more in skirts? That nice yellow silk? It's warm, and you could wrap up in the wool shawl you knitted at Christmas. I'll have fresh under-linen warmed while you bathe."

Lizzie still had the words "bread and butter" buzzing in her ears. She said, "You speak to me in the tongue of angels."

—

Linen sheets lined the copper tub. Lizzie sank deep in the heated water, letting it wash over all the parts that had been bound up and itching, or that had been freezing for a day and a night. Lavender scented the water. Not her favorite. She'd smell like someone's aging grandmother for the coming week. No matter. She wiggled to let the water wash over her, wishing for bread and butter, but then dozing in the fragrant hot water.

Twice she woke with a jerk, fighting anger and dark despair. The warm water washed away the fear that had clotted in her veins during the long night. Perhaps she couldn't always rely on luck, or English justice, but she could rely on her friends. The bath reheated her confidence, or at least her courage. She could still run the gambol and seize justice for those who'd survived the last voyage of the *Skylark*.

Aurora's voice roused Lizzie, begging to wash and braid her hair. Then Aurora wrapped Lizzie in a soft dressing gown warmed by the fire. A dozen steps into the next room, and Lizzie sat before a plate of toasted bread heaped with butter and marmalade. A coddled egg. A cup of hot chocolate prepared in the French style. Consoled by these comforts, Lizzie sighed with pleasure, swallowing the last of the chocolate.

"But Ishmael!" She suddenly remembered him running away into the icy morning. He didn't have these comforts.

"Peace!" Aurora stroked Lizzie's hand. "Perry's brothers went searching. The lad is already at Mr. Molewood's house, where the cook was feeding him by the kitchen fire."

"Come, Lizzie. Each time you blink, it takes you longer to open your eyes. Tom and the others will return at three o'clock. Enough time for you to indulge in sleep. Now, here's what my mother would do when I was worn to a nub."

Humming, Aurora folded down the bed linen, tucked a warming pan under the comforter at the bottom of the bed, and then laid another woolen blanket over Lizzie's feet. "Time for dreamland. That's what my mother would say."

Instead of the solace of privacy when Aurora left and the door clicked shut, a sense of loneliness swept over her. A ridiculous emotion. She'd been surrounded by her brother, cousin, and good friends, who'd either succored her through the night or come to her rescue. For a decade, she'd felt alone in Mary's court, which was different from feeling lonely. Now Rowland had been gone less than a week, and she felt loneliness at her core.

She instead remembered how toast and marmalade had made her belly happy, while every exhausted fiber of her being searched for dreamland.

33
A Tale Best for Winter

— NED —

SATURDAY AFTERNOON

AT XANTHUS HOUSE, NED devoured the lavish breakfast Mrs. Flurry set out. Perry and Tom did as well, though they hadn't been penned up for the night. By the end of the repast, Lazarus had arranged sufficient hot water for a bath in their bedchamber.

Ned emerged from the bath, the last of gaol filth washed away. He declared, "I am too simple a creature, my chuck. Given food, fire, a clean shirt, and my friend close by, I'm succored to the core. I should be ashamed to be restored so easily."

But Perry had fallen asleep, though that had the benefit of warming the bed. Not even unhappy with Perry for dominating the bed covers, Ned fell quickly asleep, with no dreams.

Instructed to rouse them at two o'clock, Lazarus knocked. He carried yet more sustenance from Mrs. Flurry and the news that Winwood Oakes had returned to London and was tending Tom Foxe. On the food tray was another message from Mistress Touchstone, who again complained that Wolfric Molewood persisted in seeking Prudence Mott.

Though Ned begged to hear more about the previous night's doing, Perry urged him to dress so they could be on their way.

"I dare not risk my health and safety by telling you anything before Miss Foxe also hears it."

Tom joined them for the walk to Chalgrove House. Winwood promised to come along after he'd examined Jacob Rôche, to ensure the lad's Christmastime cold had done him no harm. They found Lizzie and Aurora Rôche in the large parlor. For the first time since Twelfth Night, Lizzie sat as Ned was used to seeing her. She wore a soft silk gown, its creamy white casting a glow, and was embroidering with a length of silk dyed Maid's Blush pink. Aurora, as usual, was buried deep in a book, and so took a moment before noticing the trio of men had joined them.

"Gentlemen! Come in and be at home."

"Are you in good repair, Lizzie?" Ned asked.

"I'm sufficiently fine to hear the rest of your story, Mr. Frake." Lizzie rearranged the fabric on her embroidery hoop. "We left off with Michael and Tom searching for us."

When Perry declined the wine and biscuits the serving girl had brought, Ned did the same, since they'd eaten at Xanthus House. Also, Ned would never admit it to a soul, but Mrs. Flurry was better in the kitchen than Perry's mother.

"Aye." Perry said. "After the gambol event, I followed Molewood to Bloomsbury. Of course, he called chair-bearers, but I'm faster on my own two feet. He was inside his house for only moments, then the front door opened, and he stood there berating a pair of his servants. One lingered, watching his master leave on a sledge. After the door was shut, I waited a moment and knocked, claiming an appointment with Molewood. The servant said, 'Mayhap it's a misapprehension, sir? Mr. Molewood is gone for the night.'"

Tom said, "I wager he went to ask Sir Bythorn to return his servant and smuggled goods."

"Mayhap." Perry agreed. "I argued with the servant that I had crucial business information for his master and asked where

I might find him. To emphasize the seriousness of my request, I fingered a silver half crown, which the fellow took up, saying, 'The master has gone to his mother's house on Primrose Hill.'"

"Can you imagine," Tom said, "Lazarus revealing where Rollo could be found for half a crown? Tells the world what Molewood's servants think of him."

"But then," Perry said, "if servants respected their masters, how could intelligencers in England do their work?"

"Is there more to tell?" Lizzie's foot tapped the carpet. Ned felt the same impatience.

"The best part is to come." Perry said. "With that news, I had another half-crown in my hand, asking if anything had happened. It was a waste of coin, for this fellow could hardly stop talking. 'Customs men raided us,' he said. 'Took away the artist fellow, his model, and one of our serving men.'"

"That's when," Ned said, "you set out to rescue us."

"It did help," Perry said, "to solve the mystery. I found a lad at a tavern on Holborn Road and gave him three pennies to carry a message around to Xanthus House, to report what had happened to you."

"However," Tom said, "it took most of the night until we knew enough to beg a judge for your release."

Ned said, "Perry, what did you do next?" He bit back against adding *instead of finding us.*

"I believed Tom would find you, so I went to Primrose Hill. I hired a sledge, since it's a solid four miles out there, with icy roads not fit for riding a horse at night. The driver knew his way along a road that follows the Tyburn."

Perry paused to sip wine, watching Ned with a teasing smile. Ned sipped his wine, trying not to show his dismay, that Perry chose to chase after Molewood. Perry winked, then continued.

"When my sledge came into the neighborhood, I stopped at a public house, where I learned which house belongs to Miss

Foxe's friend, Mr. Molewood. It's called Shiloh House. Another good Puritan name, like his Jericho House."

"He's not my friend."

"Aye, as you have said." Perry shifted, sitting back as he spoke, leaning near to Ned. "I left the sledge driver to wait for me and walked up the lane. The abode is called Shiloh House now but was built when Elizabeth was queen. I guessed it best not to knock in the dark of night but peeked through windows like a hedge thief."

"I beg you, Mr. Frake," Lizzie said, "for a faster story."

"I shall endeavor to please, Miss Foxe. I believe myself to possess good sight for spying in the nighttime, but no one moved around on the darker lower level. Given my snow-wet boots, I judged against breaking in to prowl."

"Then you saw nothing?" Ned said.

"Naught to see. I returned to the public house. My sledge driver had warmed his horse in the stable and went to put the beast to harness while I conversed with the publican. You can imagine my thirst as well as my cold feet, and the publican was happy to have my custom. He took a bad shot to his leg in our English king's last tussle in the Low Countries, so he—"

"I'm sorry for the man," Ned said, "but it's not the story to tell now."

"Patience, sweeting. I told the publican that Shiloh House was the sort of manor my master was looking to buy in the country. The fellow said it was the home of an older lady and her mother-in-law, who might be Methuselah's bride. He claimed the old mothers had comfort enough, given a load of goods was carried into the house every fortnight. Just this Thursday night, a whole wagonload was unloaded."

"The goods stolen outside Touchstone's gallery!" Ned exclaimed. "Now safely stored on Primrose Hill."

"Not a surprise," Lizzie said. "Adds a dash of color to what we know about Molewood. What else did the publican say?"

"He said, 'Your master don't want that house. Molewood's men built that new wing. All his houses fall down.' I promised to heed his warning but noted that it seemed fine for an old-built house. And the publican said that 'Sir Bythorn hired village lads to give it fresh paint last spring. So, I said to him—"

"Sir Bythorn!" When Ned croaked the custom man's name, Lizzie's eyes flashed and her face flushed red.

Perry held up a hand. "I'll finish my story. The publican said the household keeps a tight purse, with stiff reins on its servants."

Ned murmured, "We know Molewood isn't generous with his servants."

Lizzie pressed her lips into an angry white line, then said, "Ishmael claimed that pair quarreled at midnight Thursday."

Tom said, "Are you not seeing it, Lizzie? Ned? Perry followed Molewood to his mother's house. The publican says Sir Bythorn's mother lives there. That means—"

"They have the same mother," Ned said. "We're fatigued after last night but did not turn blockheaded."

"Why didn't we discover it before this?" Lizzie stabbed at her embroidery. "We've dug deep into all their business."

Perry pursed his lips, as if considering it, but then hared off down another path. "The publican said that another new set of people come to serve every few months, with none hired from the village. And there's a new woman, black as a Moor. He claims his missus never gets a chance to say hello at church before the cook hurries that woman away."

Lizzie drew a sharp breath, like a quiet cry. "Tia Angelina!"

"We'll go back in the daylight to find out," Perry said. "Mayhap tomorrow is a good day for it."

—

"I never liked either man." Ned watched Lizzie, who he knew despised both men. "Slippery as glass eels, both of them."

"We should have known," Lizzie repeated.

"We didn't know about Primrose Hill," Perry said. "And we don't yet have all the pieces."

"We can guess much more now," Lizzie said. "Sir Bythorn first." She spoke the custom man's name as an expletive. "He's hated Orlando since Bristol, where I called him out for bribery."

"And by association," Ned said, "Sir Bythorn hates Rollo."

Lizzie said, "He must be responsible for the false indentures that sent Rollo to Bristol in the frozen winter."

"And got us jailed by customs men," Ned said. "Do you think Sir Bythorn knew Molewood wasn't at home when he sent his men to raid the house?"

"Like as not," Lizzie said. A scarlet red flushed over her, though her voice remained steady. She seemed about to catch fire. Her eyes blazed. "Poor Ishmael. He suffered through cold and hunger only because I didn't watch my tongue in Bristol."

"Or other times since," Tom noted.

Ned asked, "Shall we pull Sir Bythorn into Lizzie's gambol?"

Perry said, "Or shall we wait until Rollo returns, to be sure we choose the proper course?"

"We know what to do," Lizzie said. "We'll destroy both men as quickly as we can, and sow salt on any patch of England where either man has ever set foot."

The room was quiet for a moment.

"Neither Molewood nor Chudrakes has a son," Lizzie said, "so we need not sell anyone to the Barbary pirates."

"Aye, Miss Foxe. We'll not make it complicated," Perry said. "We need to learn more about Sir Bythorn's deepest desires and how Wolfric Molewood is involved in Rollo's insurance business. But we can do all that in England. The Barbary pirates are of no use to us."

"Do you agree, Tom?" Lizzie prompted. He'd fallen quiet.

"For the most part," he said. "I definitely agree about the pirates. But I don't agree that we knew nothing about Shiloh House. I told you about it on Wednesday night, though perhaps I didn't name the house or the neighborhood." He seemed to relish that everyone looked puzzled. "It should belong to Diggory Crackbone. Or I'd best say, that will belong to Diggory when I finish crossing the last T in my pleading."

"Mayhap," Perry said, "we shan't sow salt there."

"Now you know what Perry did last night," Tom said, "shall I tell you what I did while you lolled away the night in gaol?"

—

Tom said, "When Perry sent a message that the customs men took Lizzie and Ned away, Michael and I began to search the customs lockups. It was five o'clock when we convinced the guards to tell us who was in the Holborn Road lockup."

Ned took a sharp breath, thinking that if Tom hadn't persisted through the night, they'd still be in a dank stone room.

"That's when we visited Sir Oliver," Tom said. "I lifted his brass knocker at six-thirty, long before dawn. Since we possessed a righteous call to justice, he gave us our *habeas corpus*."

Ned's veins flooded with brotherly feeling. "You are a blessing from the gods, cousin."

"Don't chafe me with your teasing," Tom said. "I'm sorry it took all night."

Ned said, "For all you've done, Tom, I shall leave off teasing you for all times."

"Now you're serving me a big bowl of botheration. You'd never be able to resist."

Instead of arguing, Ned considered what gift he might make for Tom at his next birthday. Perhaps that portrait of Aurora and

Jacob he'd been working on since November. Then Winwood and Michael came into Chalgrove House. Behind them, Jacob Rôche and Neriah Frake shouted to Countess and Pip, Jacob's dog, calling them back from whatever the dogs had chased down the alley.

The original confab was broken up by the chaos that followed Jacob and Neriah when they brought the dogs inside. Countess wanted to ruin Lizzie's cream silk dress by burying a snow-wet nose in her lap.

Aurora invited them all to join that night's meal. At supper, Ned and Perry made up for the meals missed the day before. Mrs. Frake had prepared a savory mutton-and-turnip stew and served it with fresh bread, plus a sweet almond cake with quince paste.

Aurora, always attuned to Jacob's needs, excused him as soon as he'd put away the last crumbs of the almond cake. He left with Neriah to visit in the kitchen. Pip followed Jacob, but Countess remained at Lizzie's feet.

With the noise gone, Tom summed for Winwood all their doings. As he concluded, Tom said, "It's not like they were in a real prison. Just a temporary lockup that customs people use."

"It felt real." Lizzie said. "The door was quite firmly locked. Malodorous straw on the cold stone floor. Vermin."

"And we learned," Ned said, "that Mr. Molewood is one of the scoundrels who gained servants from the *Skylark*."

Lizzie said, "It must be by way of Sir Bythorn Chudrakes."

"That's a great deal to have learned," Winwood said. "I'm still not sure I understand how Miss Foxe was arrested."

Ned said, "We believe Sir Bythorn sent customs men with a warrant to search Mr. Molewood's house for smuggled artifacts."

Lizzie said, "Except Mr. Molewood stole his own African artifacts on Thursday."

"He kept that one beautiful piece of African ivory." Ned intended to filch that ivory. Would Perry stoop to help?

"But Michael says Miss Foxe has been going around London as Viscount Orlando." Winwood seemed confused. "Where does Orlando fit in last night's story?"

"I came to Molewood's as Orlando and ended up posing for Ned's painting dressed as Mr. Molewood. The customs man demanded the house keys for his search. He thought I was Molewood and locked me up when I didn't produce the keys."

Ned said, "I wager Sir Bythorn knew Orlando was in the house, and that's who he wanted to arrest. You as good as accused him to his face of corruption. Twice."

Lizzie, of course, insisted on the last word. "We can only speculate Chudrakes wanted to punish Orlando."

She settled back, which roused Countess. The dog got up, begging for more attention. When Lizzie wasn't quick enough, Countess turned to Perry for an ear scratch.

"Is that all of the story?" Winwood asked. "It's a lot."

Lizzie said, "Perry learned last night that Mr. Molewood and Sir Bythorn are brothers. We don't know how Molewood's insurance business and Sir Bythorn's customs work are connected. But they must be."

Tom said, "We do know that those two own a house where their mother lives. In truth, the house belongs to the steward at Rollo's coffeehouse."

"Rollo bought a coffeehouse?" For the first time, Winwood showed surprise.

"He's a partner with Lazarus's cousin Samuel," Tom said.

"I know Samuel," Winwood said. "I treated him for a sanguineous crust last September. He thought it might be infected, but it was just a scab."

"That's a relief," Tom said.

"Are we done sharing?" Lizzie said. "Ready to fix the plan?"

"I assume," Michael said, "that I'll get scrivener's palsy tomorrow, writing new invitations to the new event."

"'Tis a shame to be working on the Sabbath," Perry said.

"I am aware of such notions," Lizzie said, "but new invitations must be delivered Monday morning. The new event will be midday Tuesday. And Perry, you and Ned will also be busy on Sunday. You need to explore Shiloh House and the land around it on Primrose Hill. Learn everything you can."

Ned sighed again, but happily this time. Lizzie had given them a task to do together.

Perry said, "Mayhap my mother will take a significant piece of my hide if she learns I went prowling on a Sunday."

Lizzie said, "Go to church with her in the morning. Then just take a sledge ride in the country."

"My Sunday work," Tom said, "will be to study the papers Perry found in Molewood's house. I'll think how to investigate Sir Bythorn, short of giving evidence to the king's intelligencers."

"I also need you to find someone," Lizzie said. "Remember Cornelius Rosewurme?"

Tom said, "He left England for a wilderness in the colonies."

Perry pointed his finger at Lizzie. "You want the man who took over his business."

"The very being."

"Nathaniel Merryboy." Tom snapped his fingers. "There's a problem, besides not having even a vague idea of how to find him. We have a rule against that."

"Which rule?" Michael asked.

"No one dies," Tom said. "Merryboy is an assassin."

"No one will die," Lizzie said. "I merely require extra chaos. Also, one more thing, Tom."

"Not to grouse, but you've already asked a lot."

"At the subscription event on Tuesday, you will have to play Mercutio di Bassanio. I cannot play that part, since I'll have other chores."

"Mercutio died in the Shakespeare play, didn't he?" Tom asked. "And I don't speak Italian. That won't work."

Michael said, "Felicia can help with your accent."

"Excellent," Lizzie said. "Each of us will do things in the coming days that were never dreamt of in your philosophy."

"You've spent too much time with Rollo," Tom said. "Now you're quoting his Bard."

"Mayhap that's true. When he returns, we can confirm whether I got the quotation right." Lizzie likely intended her smile to support the jest, but Ned saw her smile tremble at the edges. She must sorely miss Rowland.

Tom said, "Do I have to wear one of those sad velvet hats like the Venetians wore who leased Rollo's ships?"

"Ask Felicity. She's our costume-master." Lizzie had more to assign. "Perry, after Tom finds Nathaniel Merryboy, you'll direct the man and his minions in their work."

"Shall I help?" Ned asked. He wanted more time with Perry; this week's work for the gambol had separated them too much.

"No," she said. "I have a letter that needs your help."

"Not Tom?"

"No, I need your special talents."

"Perhaps we should wait for Rollo," Perry said, likely the only timid words Ned had ever heard him speak.

"*Carpe diem.*" Lizzie tossed her head, denying his suggestion. "And the day we are seizing is Tuesday. We have two days to ensure a sound plan."

Jacob burst into the room, Pip trailing behind. That aroused Countess, who leapt past Lizzie, disturbing her skirts, and then came too fast at Pip. Hence, mutual barking commenced.

After Jacob finally quieted both dogs, he said, "It's raining. And snowing. Both at the same time."

Lizzie said, "Mr. Frake, may I put you in charge of accounting for mud? I have only been calculating for ice."

34
Littlecote House

– LIZZIE –

SUNDAY NOON

SUNDAY MORNING, LIZZIE ACCEPTED a breakfast tray in Rowland's bedchamber. Jane, instead of helping her to dress, encouraged Lizzie to have a lie-in while the staff went to church.

"If 'twas me done to by clodpates declaiming the king's name," Jane said, "and no comrades gave 'em a bollocking, I'd go live in a Yorkshire hovel, just to be safe. And I must tell you just how much—"

"How much you loathe the country," Lizzie said, having heard this declaration before.

"Aye, Miss Foxe, that I do. But hide there I would."

Jane had only just closed the chamber's door when Lizzie stopped thinking about how she also loathed the country—the dire lack of informed, convivial company; the dearth of quality fabric and decent silk floss for embroidery—and instead she pondered which friends could be enlisted to administer a bollocking. Yet the situation required more than slagging in the street and more than a good bonking in an alley. Perry and Ned and Tom would assist, but she needed a force greater than her own cohort.

She slipped from her bed, finding the room sufficiently warm since Jane had laid a fire, and then she enjoyed the ewer of hot water for a wash in the basin. Still in her night shift, Lizzie began opening the packages Lazarus had procured for her. She had only opened two when she found what she felt might best serve the day: a fine white wool suit with well-padded shoulders, the coat falling to her knees and the silk lining a good match with that waistcoat she'd embroidered for Rowland in September. She'd used the finest scarlet and lapis-blue floss, though Rowland insisted it was far too fine for him, of course. Because he didn't perceive what a striking figure he cut when he wore good clothes.

Before dressing, given that Jane had gone to church, Lizzie applied her own whitening makeup, bound her own breasts, put on the new silk shirt and suit, tied a lace neckcloth, and tucked her hair into a new wig that proved to be as fanciful as the one Rowland had bought out of pawn last year in Paris.

She had to borrow Rowland's shoes again, better ones than she usually took from his closet, because those that Lazarus ordered for her hadn't yet arrived from the shoemaker. No matter. She'd have them back in the closet before Rowland returned to London, and it wasn't as if she'd parade through the streets in them. Just a step into a carriage, then out, and home again at the end of the afternoon.

After pulling on a pair of Rowland's kidskin gloves, remembering how she'd been teased for the size of her hands among Mary's ladies, Lizzie followed Daniel Frake when he went out to hail whatever carriage might be free between taking people to church and driving them home again. The previous night's rain had been followed by an early-morning refreezing, so any piles of snow had sloughed from roofs, battered but not yet defeated. The carriage that stopped for Daniel cracked the new crust of ice formed over puddles of melt.

Daniel gave Lizzie a hand up into the carriage. "Lazarus has been teaching me how a man is supposed to take care of a lady."

She appreciated the help and found she'd retained the habit of ducking properly while stepping into a carriage when wearing a tall wig and a wide hat.

Riding in the carriage that crushed ice on her trip across London, she needed to boost her courage. She fished in the deep cuff of her coat sleeve for Tamsin's last letter, which always raised her spirits.

> There was the chaos at Christmas. We were sorry to miss you, but Tom came and, of course, brought along Jacob Rôche and Neriah Frake, who seems more like Jacob's friend than his valet. The young earl joined in the counting and songs the girls are learning.
>
> Tom had explained to Jacob about the girls being orphaned in a strange land, so Jacob brought two puppies. The girls had already made pets of the barn cats, but Mrs. Bell allows only one mouser inside the house and only at night. We are still grieving the loss of Caesar, our dear and ancient dog, and so Mrs. Bell allowed Jacob's gift puppies inside the house, though she'd sworn on her mother's name that it was the last thing she'd ever do.
>
> Until New Years, when Jacob and Tom returned to London, Jacob stayed busy teaching the girls how to train young dogs. With Jacob gone, the girls are chasing the dogs up the stairs and through the hallways, calling commands the puppies haven't properly learned. Hence, there's never an hour's quiet in the house. (I must see to the repair of all the bannisters, for safety's sake.)
>
> I think Tom and Jacob might have caught the cold that everyone has been passing about since early December. If either Tom or Jacob suffers too long, please write. Winwood would want to go back to London for them.

Lizzie pondered that Mrs. Bell had had an easier time doing what she'd sworn she'd never do than did Lizzie that morning when she'd risen from bed and set out to do what she'd sworn she never would.

—

Daniel had come with Lizzie as a footman. He lifted the brass knocker. As it banged against the plate beneath it, he exclaimed, "It's freezing cold. Like to make for chilblains."

The footman in blue livery who answered the door must be new and hence was on duty when most staff had Sunday afternoon free. The flouncy lace cuffs of his livery fell over the invitation when Daniel handed it to him. The footman had to pull his cuffs back to read the card. He accepted that the guest at the door was the person named on the invitation, then left Lizzie to wait in the foyer no more than two minutes before reappearing to say, "My lord, please come." He escorted her to a salon on the first floor, while Daniel remained behind on a bench in the foyer. Upstairs, the walls were covered with blue silk that matched the footman's livery.

"You came, Marborne! I didn't think it possible." The host made as if to rise, but in a lazy, uncommitted way.

"Pray, your grace, do not get up. It was excessively kind of you to invite me."

Lizzie liked to believe she'd mastered Rowland's voice, as long as she coughed and feigned winter hoarseness. One thing was certain, the Duke of Bagsham was so blind, he only saw the Earl of Marborne before him, not Lizzie Foxe in a padded coat, bismuth-and-rice-powder makeup, and an overwrought wig.

The duke rubbed his spectacles with his neckcloth, then jammed them in place to inspect his guest. "When I sent that invitation, your man Lazarus returned a messenger that it was unlikely you'd be here. Then I heard you'd left town from my…" He trailed off, waving a hand.

"Your watchers?" Lizzie said. "I'm not offended that you care enough to observe my business."

"It's only that," the duke paused, "there's been so much tumult since your Spanish cousin came to town and your affianced bride went into the country."

"Catalan, duke. Not Spanish." That was the way Rowland used to correct anyone who misinterpret the disguise he'd used to escape from the Continent to England.

The duke ignored the correction. "He seems a turbulent sort of fellow, bringing chaos everywhere. But that's to be expected of Spanish gentry. He's your cousin's cousin, isn't he? They're both dark. Do you in fact have him under control, Marborne?"

"Miss Ysabel Foxe," a voice said behind her.

"Yes, that's the cousin I mean." The duke clasped his small hands as if congratulating himself. "A descendent of the Flores woman who served our Good Queen Bess. Married the elder Samuel Foxe, I believe. Who sired the son who saved Charles Stuart from the Roundheads."

"I mean, duke, to correct who you are addressing." It was Poynter, Lord Hawksmoor. "This is Miss Ysabel Foxe, not her cousin Rowland."

"Yes." Lizzie didn't intend to dodge it, but her eyes burned at feeling exposed and...and...but no, not embarrassed, either for playing Rowland or for doing everything she could for her girls and the *Skylark* people. "I was about to remove that misconception, your grace. Ysabel Foxe stole your kind invitation. Rowland has indeed gone to Bristol."

"To meet another ship from Africa?" The duke frowned in confusion.

"No, to enlist the harbormaster's aid in denouncing the rumors Sir Bythorn Chudrakes is fostering about Rowland trespassing on the king's African trade." While she answered, she bore with equanimity Poynter's inquisitive stare.

The duke shook his head, then removed his spectacles and pinched at his brow. "I warned him."

"It isn't anything Rowland has brought on himself," Lizzie said. "But it is why I've come to ask your assistance."

Poynter, who'd previously invited her to address him by his christened name, took a place on the settee beside the duke. He must have only recently left it, for a glass of sherry stood on the small table by his hand.

"Perhaps," Poynter said, "we'd best put our heads together to understand and find solutions."

Poynter tipped his sherry glass to salute her. This was far beyond what she'd expected when she resolved to come here. She intended to make better than the best of this twist.

—

Poynter, Lord Hawksmoor, looking his usual fine self in an understated grey wool suit, had the divine skill of small talk, the kind that puts people at ease. He'd long been Tom's good friend, especially during Tom's tedious years clerking under a barrister in Cambridge. Poynter had been kind to Tamsin while she managed the Foxe family business (though he'd believed it was Tom). He'd often visited while Lizzie was in service to Mary Stuart in the Low Countries. Last summer, out of his characteristic kindness, Poynter (then Viscount Heydon) had offered to marry Lizzie to give her the title she needed to return to service with Mary, though he wasn't a man with an interest in marriage. And Poynter had offered Rowland sufficient funds to buy back the Marborne title from King James. When both kindnesses proved unnecessary, Poynter bowed out without hurt feelings.

In sum, Poynter was neighborly, worldly—and as intuitive and incisively intelligent as anyone Lizzie knew, even Rowland and Perry Frake.

She'd rehearsed on the way to St James Place what she'd say to persuade the duke to act as she needed. Now, amid polite pleasantries, she had to recalculate how much recent history to reveal and how best to formulate her argument for action.

Because she was undertaking that which she'd sworn she'd never do.

Now, Poynter's presence demanded bold attack.

Right after Poynter surmised that a bitter London rain was bound to break the frost sooner rather than later, Lizzie said, "The king is being cheated by his customs commissioners. And the Earl of Marborne is being set up to be falsely accused of those swindles."

The duke removed his spectacles, cloudy with fingerprints, and massaged a crease that crossed the bridge of his nose.

"It's about Africa, isn't it?" His grace sighed. "I warned him to let go of that business, given all the rumors the king hears." He began to mash his spectacles back in place again, then stopped, once more rubbing that crease.

Lizzie, who'd taken the velvet-covered chair closest to the duke, put her hand on his knee, knowing his hand would be placed on hers not far into the conversation.

"Your grace." She gently took his spectacles, retrieved the kerchief from the cuff of her coat, and polished the lenses, then handed them back. "I'd like to help you see the truth."

Poynter turned his head, likely just enough so the duke wouldn't see the thin, knowing smile he couldn't repress.

"Oh ho, Miss Foxe." The duke shook his finger, admonishing her. "You finagled your way into my salon with an invitation I addressed to Marborne. And now you offer me a Sunday sermon on truth?"

"Yes." She tucked away her kerchief, the only keepsake she had from her mother, and which she took from its satin-lined box only on days when she needed either succor or courage. "You must act for the Crown of England. And while you are doing that, you must also protect the Earl of Marborne—and not just because you are known to be his mentor. Do it because it's the proper thing."

"What is it that you proclaim to be proper?" The duke had his spectacles mashed in place again, inspecting her through new finger smudges. "While you come dressed in that fine suit."

"Warn the king that he's being lied to." She took a breath, hoping her dramatics impressed the duke. "It will otherwise take us too long to stop the rumors. You can help the king identify the swindles within the customs commission."

"That requires irrefutable proof," the duke said.

"We shall en..." She began to say *entrap,* but quickly found better words. "The Earl of Marborne will ensure the king has a precise list of the men who invested in Withersea's illegal African trade. And he will identify which commissioner cheated the king by selling the people seized from the *Skylark.*"

"How," Poynter asked, "can Marborne do that when he isn't even in London?"

Lizzie folded her arms, hoping for the same effect as when Rowland made it clear he was adamantly acting on principle. "He's been making enquiries all winter. He'll return to London shortly, prepared to take all action possible."

She tapped one impatient hand on her arm, but she was only impatient about having to attribute all that work to Rowland. He'd been wrestling with insurance people and buying a coffeehouse, while she led the effort to track down the evil that the Marquess of Withersea had loosed on the world with the *Skylark.*

"Duke, I am not begging a favor. I previously promised you that I'd do whatever I can to support the Crown." She wasn't confident about admitting to being the king's watcher with Poynter there. "Please warn the king that his own men are cheating him."

"How can the king intercede?" Poynter asked.

"Clearly, your lordship," she still tapped her arm, "James can use existing laws. We have proof that the indentures for the

Skylark people are forgeries made by the customs officials who seized them."

The duke placed his tiny hand on her knee, as she'd expected. "I cannot do this today, Miss Foxe. Or even Monday."

She put her hand on his and smiled brightly, because his disclaimer wrapped itself around an agreement to act. "But you can do it by Tuesday, can you not?"

"It's Tuesday that you want?"

"Yes. Let's say, midday? And when you ask, please convince the king to guarantee the safety of the *Skylark* people stolen and illegally sold in England."

The duke wiggled his fingers and extracted his hand from under hers. "And here, I'd been led astray by a warning from our friend in The Hague." He made a gesture to indicate he meant Mary Stuart. "I was told you were in danger because you'd gone mad and were in a passion to stop all of the Royal African Company's business."

If only I could.

"My dear friend misunderstood my passion, likely because I didn't tell her all of my story, to spare her distress."

"What story?" Poynter looked concerned—and curious.

"Indeed, what story?" the duke said. "All of London knows Marborne is disappointed about the king's gift of three ships."

"In Bristol last fall, I..."

Am I doing this? Trading on that tragedy to gain sympathy? To win a collaborator? Yes, yes, I am.

35
An Old Friend

— LIZZIE —

SUNDAY AFTERNOON

LIZZIE BEGAN HER STORY. "When we arrived at Bristol harbor, the customs men had already seized all the people from the *Skylark*. While Rowland spoke with the harbormaster, I undertook a foolish act."

"That's not believable, Miss Foxe," Poynter said. "I have known you to do only one foolish thing in your entire life."

"No, Lord Hawksmoor." she said. He referred to their extremely short-lived engagement. "*That* was only mistaken strategy. On both our parts."

"Ah." Poynter said. The duke glanced between them, too nearsighted to detect what his guests exchanged. "So, in Bristol last fall, what was it you did?"

"The duke kindly gave Rowland a good dog. It ran off, and I followed, calling for it to come to me."

"I shall speak to Lazarus," the duke said, mentioning the butler who had originally been hired by the duke. "You and Marborne should have proper serving people when you travel."

"You may be right." Lizzie was bent on being agreeable. "When I ran into the Bristol fog, I was grabbed and thrown into a rotting warehouse where crimping fellows had imprisoned six little girls taken off the *Skylark*."

"No!" Poynter, such a good friend, was alarmed.

"How could that be? You, a lady, imprisoned?" The duke, though too old to be so innocent, frowned and shook his head.

Lizzie peeled off Rowland's glove, baring her hand, displaying it where the duke touched her knee. Given her white wool suit, her hand seemed quite dark. "They mistook me for one of the people taken off the ship. I believe the blackguards' intent was to sell the girls. And me."

"Jupiter!" Poynter exclaimed. "Yet, of course, Rowland rescued you?"

"After a long, cold hour, the girls and I rescued ourselves." Lizzie decided in an instant to skip the part where the girls set the *Skylark* ablaze. "Meanwhile, Rowland was held in wait for the customs man, who wanted to know if he'd had anything to do with the *cargo* brought to Bristol."

"I find it painful to imagine," Poynter said.

"Yes, but my pain was brief compared to my companions' pain and grief. While we shivered in the dark warehouse, I learned the girls' stories about being captured and put on the auction block, then shipped off with sick and starving people until they ended up…" Lizzie was not thinking about those dark hours just then, but about what she could gain here, given the stricken look on the duke's face. "Until the girls found themselves on 'this blessed plot, this earth, this realm, this England.'"

She named and described each girl and how they'd suffered between leaving their home villages and arriving in Bristol.

"Those are the girls living at Revelstone?" Poynter said. Tamsin had written that he'd met them. "I didn't for a moment believe them to be your cousins from Portugal. Such was the story Miss Thomasine put about in the neighborhood."

The duke had been silent through the whole story. Lizzie hoped she'd led him to where this story must next go. At last, the duke said, "I see now that you never wanted to convince the king to give up the Royal African Company."

"I cannot prevaricate with you, duke, I'd destroy the Royal African Company if I could. I know I can't."

"You want revenge for those girls, don't you, Miss Foxe?"

"Not revenge. Only a modest restitution," Lizzie said. "I need your help, duke, to protect the Earl of Marborne plus those unfortunate people who came to England on the *Skylark*. Because of wild lies spread about Marborne's role in this, I'm hoping the king will help do what is right."

"Thus far," the duke paused to pour another thimbleful of sherry, down it, and set the tiny glass on the table beside him, "the king has been happy with Marborne. I have an audience with the king on Tuesday morning. For all this evidence you claim Marborne has in hand, he'll need to deliver it to the king personally. Can you promise that?"

Time to hedge.

"I promise. Rowland will speak to the evidence personally."

"Excellent," the duke said.

"But not on Tuesday," Lizzie said. "It would take a miracle for him to return from Bristol before next Friday. You will have to take the evidence I have in hand to the king on Tuesday."

"But Miss Foxe—"

"My word, my honor, and my commitment to England are as deep and genuine as that of the Earl of Marborne."

She felt sure about having just committed Rowland to act, but less sure that weather and fate might bring him back to London in time. She'd worry later if fate failed to comply with her wishes. She wasn't reckless enough to appear before the king in Rowland's clothes in order to confirm the veracity of information it had taken this entire frozen winter to gather.

Because, unlike the duke, the king wasn't half blind.

"Please taste a sip of my sherry before you go, Miss Foxe." The duke poured for her. "And please have a biscuit. However, I must warn you that they are so sinfully delicious, I shouldn't serve them on the Sabbath."

—

"You and Rowland both serve as king's watchers. Will you confess it, Miss Foxe?"

Poynter had offered to see her home, for which Lizzie expressed genuine gratitude. His carriage had appeared as if by magic, though, of course, the duke's footmen had performed the magic. He'd gracefully seated her inside the carriage before springing that question.

"You asked me once to call you Poynter, and I asked you to call me Lizzie. I acknowledged Miss Foxe as my name in the duke's salon. But here, when you ask that question, please call me Lizzie, like a true friend."

"Fine. Don't answer my question, Lizzie. It's surely such a state secret that it'd place my wellbeing in jeopardy."

She managed to laugh, though she was still making peace with herself over having just done what she'd sworn she'd never do, asking for the king's help.

She said, "I confess, Poynter, I always understood that you were merely a visiting Englishman on a Continental tour every year, visiting Paris and the Low Countries."

"I'll grant that I asked the wrong question just now. What I want to know is what was in the letterlocked missive you handed to the duke when you said goodbye."

"I am capable of the best letterlocking," she said. "I wager the duke hasn't got it open yet."

"Ladies shouldn't make wagers, Miss Foxe."

"You agreed to call me Lizzie. And don't scold."

"What was in the letter?"

"The names of the men who invested in Withersea's illicit African expedition. And the name of the man in the customs commission who sold the people from the *Skylark* into indentured servitude."

"Will you tell me the names? Or must I await a well-crafted letterlocked missive?"

"Will you help me with other ways in which I am seeking retribution for the stolen people?"

Poynter folded his hands and studied her. He'd given her the rear seat and sat opposite, more careful to avoid bumping knees or treading on her feet than anyone she'd ever traveled with. "I wager that Marborne has a scheme cooking, like he did with Danvers Duncombe last summer. When he used my house to swindle my brother's dishonest in-laws."

"I own this scheme. Not Rollo. If you want to help, I'll send you an invitation to a presentation being made to potential investors, where the perpetrators of that African nightmare will join in making it right for their victims." She paused. "Though they won't know that's what they are doing."

"Will this turn into a debacle in any way, like Rowland's scheme did last summer? Assure me that no one will be sentenced in the Bloody Assizes."

"Rollo merely exposed a traitor. And the king chose to hang such men. It was you, Poynter, who made a debacle that day, sending your brother and his relations off to Barbados. No, I want you to come and play Doubting Thomas. You can say that the investment syndicate cannot succeed without an inside man in the king's customs commission."

"Are you entrapping anyone I know?"

Lizzie recited all the names, speaking rapidly and clearly. She'd gone over the list so many times, forever grateful for what Tom had learned last summer about Withersea's business dealings. "But there are two men in whom I have certain interest. One is Sir Bythorn Chudrakes."

"That dry chaff is your felon in the customs house? The one King Charles made a knight for adding to the royal coffers?"

"Yes, that man. He came to Rollo, claiming to be in pursuit of Withersea's syndicate, asking for help to identify the investors. We gave him a few names just days ago. Almost immediately, three of them suddenly became Tories in Parliament. I assume they were persuaded by the king. Meanwhile, Sir Bythorn is responsible for the forged indentures that placed the stolen people into servitude with Withersea's investors."

"Do you want me to learn more about what Sir Bythorn might be doing?"

"I have the necessary information in hand, but thank you for the kind offer."

"Who's the second man you want to…um…allow to participate in helping the *Skylark* people."

"Wolfric Molewood."

"The builder?"

"He wants to enlarge the ways in which the world knows him. He bought a seat in Parliament. He has new business interests in insurance, which started with fire insurance. Now he's excited about the profits in marine insurance."

"And you dislike him because of his investments?"

"No, I met him while I was working to learn about his business." She paused. But she'd already dragged Poynter deep into her story. "I was posing as Miss Prudence Mott."

"From Princess Mary's court?"

"Prudence came back to England last year. But it will take me until Monday morning to explain all of that to you."

"What are Molewood's sins, besides his business dealings? You must know he has a muddy reputation as a man who made all his money building shoddy houses after the Great Fire."

"He holds one of the indentured the *Skylark* people. And he had the unmitigated gall to ask Prudence to marry him, though he only wants property she inherited."

"I felicitate dear Miss Mott. Does his mother approve? He's known in town as a man who owes much to his mother and his Puritan forebears."

"Except his business smells of dead fish, and Sir Bythorn seems to be in league with him, over customs and insurance."

"And that adds up to more jeopardy for Rollo?"

"Yes, but also for me. If you promise to help me, then come to supper at Xanthus House, I'll tell you about spending Friday night in a lockup off Holborn Road because of Sir Bythorn."

Poynter rubbed his upper lip, like a man in thought. He had not once revealed any sense of shock or disgust. When he took his hand away, she saw he was trying not to laugh.

"I'd forgotten how much more interesting life can be when I'm abiding in the same district at Ysabel Foxe."

"You'll come to supper, Lord Hawksmoor?"

"I cannot choose otherwise."

PART V

CROOKED PASSAGEWAYS

—

DUKE SENIOR
Dost thou believe, Orlando, that the boy
Can do all this that he hath promised?

ORLANDO
I sometimes do believe and sometimes do not:
As those that fear they hope, and know they fear.

ROSALIND
Patience once more, whiles our compact is urged…
I have promised to make all this matter even.

—William Shakespeare, *As You Like It*

36
Shiloh House

– LIZZIE –

TUESDAY MORNING

AT MIDMORNING, LIZZIE SET out on her Tuesday business. It had rained in the night and felt too warm for any snow to fall again, yet not warm enough to speed the melting of what lay on the ground. Which was good, Lazarus said. They must hope for a delay in the melt-water floods.

The rain might have added more for Lizzie to worry about, except she lived in England, where weather and especially moisture required contingencies for all plans. The promise of a thrilling day's work tingled in her fingers, because she'd resolved to change course. Beyond directing a gambol while secretly hidden, she'd decided to confront her enemies full on, to show herself. Ned badgered her about the wisdom of that undertaking. "How would Rollo feel about such rash action?"

"Rollo has his business. I have mine." She replied so sharply that Ned held up his hand, beseeching peace. Yet she too had worried about how Rowland would feel about this new action before she took stock of her own feelings.

She'd awakened that morning (in Rowland's bed again, for the simple comfort of it) knowing exactly how she felt: tremendously excited. As exhilarated as when she'd first arrived in

Mary's court. She was sallying forth today, not as an avenging angel, but as plaintiff, lawyer, and magistrate seeking justice, with justice to be served to the benefit of the people torn from Africa, loaded onto the *Skylark*, and dumped into servitude in frozen England. The only reward she wanted for herself was to know the guilty suffered for what they'd done.

She intended to enjoy this day's work. She wouldn't be cold because she wore a neat, serviceable woolen gown and a drab, grey topcoat over at least two layers of linen and woolen underthings. She also had gloves, knitted stockings, and serviceable ladies' boots. Rowland's boots remained in his closet. A scarf, a linen headcap, and a large Puritan felt hat minimized the amount of bismuth-white makeup and rice powder she had to apply.

That tingle in her fingers must be a harbinger of the day's success. The patter of a heartbeat beneath her flannel waistcoat must be the fluttering thrill from starting the day's undertaking. Beginning this day, she never again had to bind her breasts to play Orlando. Lazarus never revealed his feelings, but she saw his shoulders lift and his lips twitch when she asked him to put it about London that Orlando was leaving for the Continent. She knew he didn't respect the clothes Orlando wore. She suspected he didn't like Orlando residing in the Earl of Marborne's world.

Lazarus had advised a sledge for this day's business, but Lizzie insisted on a carriage. He helped her in, and Countess bounded after her. Lazarus called the dog, but Lizzie surrendered to the dog's choice. "Countess can keep my feet warm."

Her first stop was to fetch Diggory Crackbone, where Tom Foxe waited to introduce them.

"Miss Mott, this is Diggory Crackbone, whom I have persuaded to act as your escort and chaperone today. You have my solemn oath that he is an upright man, as respectable as any righteous gentleman in England."

"You are kind, Mr. Foxe," Diggory began. "Miss Mott, I can only attest that I—"

Tom held up a hand. "I must be on my way, since I have an imminent engagement. Miss Mott, Mr. Crackbone has been presented with your predicament and is prepared to act in support of your best interests."

Diggory expressed mild amazement about traveling by carriage. "Shouldn't we take a sledge, Miss Mott?"

Lizzie said, "The miniscule cunning I possess about weather was learned in Amsterdam. I can tell in my bones when it's best to forego traveling by sledge."

"In Amsterdam? Is that—"

"Get in, sir, if you are ready for our adventure." She let her impatience escape, then reined it in. "We'll chat along the way."

"Yes. I…um…" Once inside, he seemed anxious and had a hard time finding a comfortable position on the rear-facing seat. "Was it in Amsterdam that you met Lord Marborne? That is how Mr. Foxe persuaded me to join your adventure. He says you and his lordship are old friends."

"Yes, since childhood. We've both led different lives since then." She couldn't have him this excitable today. As if to help with that, Countess thrust her head in Diggory's lap and nosed under his hand in search of an ear scratch. She said, "I hope you are comfortable with our adventure. Do you understand from Mr. Foxe what we are doing today?"

Tom went the previous night to seek Diggory's help, claiming that if Lizzie initiated the request, she'd either overwhelm or intimidate their new friend.

"I believe I do, Miss Mott. We are going to meet a man who asked you to marry him and who wants you to meet his mother. I am accompanying you because you have no male relatives and require an escort for your safety. I hope you will correct me if I fail to support you properly."

"Do you feel anxious about this adventure?" She'd judged that he did, yet once Countess stuck her nose in, Diggory's usual calm seemed to be at least partially restored.

"Oh no, Miss Mott. I'm a good traveler. I tend to have the fidgets before a voyage. But once all provisions have been made, we have only to trust the saints to guide us. I am mostly surprised to be riding in such a fine carriage."

"What I meant to ask is whether you are anxious about undertaking this action with me. I hope Mr. Foxe explained that a chief goal of this journey is to persuade my admirer to stop pestering me for marriage. I cannot entertain notions of courtship."

"Mr. Foxe did say that was why he wanted you to have a chaperone."

"I must beg you to allow me to introduce you as my relative, for the protection that might afford me. I hope that prevarication will not offend you. You can be frank, Mr. Crackbone."

"From my time in the Mediterranean, I know that sailing under false colors can be the wisest action. Also, I am sure I can trust you, like I do Mr. Tom Foxe, because you are both the earl's friends. I embrace this adventure, even if it's unpredictable."

"Mr. Crackbone, before we leave London, I must share one more fact, so that you can decide whether you want to proceed."

"But I have already committed to the adventure, because you are Lord Marborne's friend in need of an escort."

"Thank you. However, I must tell you that our destination is the house on Primrose Hill, which is part of the inheritance that Tom Foxe is seeking to restore to you. The man I am meeting is a brother of your father—that is, a half-brother."

Diggory blinked twice, his eyes wide, but then he smiled. "It shall indeed be a great adventure. I thanked Our Savior for leading me to meet Lord Marborne, who brought peace and safety to my life. Yet now, that divine-inspired meeting has brought about another upheaval. Thanks be to the blessed saints, I already know how to ride rough waters when the tide turns."

Before Diggory could say more, Lizzie said, "Then you and I agree that Lord Marborne is an upstanding, good-hearted man?"

"Aye, madam. I've never met a better man."

I need not miss Rollo wildly just because I heard his name.

—

It was five miles along the Tyburn to Primrose Hill. Diggory chatted while Lizzie mused.

"I felt the hands of Saint Cajetan interceding the day I met his lordship. I'd prayed for a change in my personal fortune—I mean to say, I prayed for better luck, not great wealth, since we are taught to trust God and not to pray merely for eternal riches. The saint brought Lord Marborne to me, he who has changed the course of my life."

"I wish he were here today." Lizzie repeated a too-personal notion to a man she'd barely met. She needed to eradicate that sense of loneliness plaguing her.

"Mr. Tom Foxe told me that his lordship had gone to Bristol. It'd take a miracle to return from Bristol so quickly." Diggory took up a new stream of thought. "Though perhaps the saints might intercede against weather, ice, and muck. We could pray together for such good travels."

He paused, looking out the carriage window where they had passed into the open country. That pause lasted two heartbeats.

"And yet, my dear foster father, Tristram Crackbone, considered it an affront to the Almighty to pray for personal miracles, rather than beseeching blessings for all people. It's not as if we're heathens who seek unnatural miracles to prove that God rules the universe."

Lizzie murmured tones of agreement, sure that letting Diggory talk aided his comfort. She fended off any further indulgence in missing Rowland or wishing for his help with her gambol. Everything had been extraordinarily well planned, across every hour of the day, with essentials and contingencies understood by all players.

She stopped Diggory's reflections on beseeching divine intervention and instead taught him what he was to say at the coming meeting. He listened without comment—Rowland did pay him to serve as a listener. He said, "I shall do my very best," and repeated precisely the speeches she'd taught him.

Then he turned to talk about the weather. "The ice on the river broke last night. Did you hear it, Miss Mott?"

"No, I must have slept too soundly."

Diggory said. "Stopped my heart for a moment. A rabbity sense inside me believed it to be a pirate's cannonade. Then men in the street cried, 'The frost faire is ended!' Thank the blessed saints, most vendors had the wisdom on Sunday and Monday to move their tents and booths off the ice."

They rode along companionably, Lizzie prompting Diggory for new expositions, the carriage cracking ice over puddles and sometimes sticking for a moment where there'd been enough travel that morning to churn mud. All of England was destined to suffer that fate in the coming weeks: churning through mud.

When the carriage drove up to the house, Diggory exclaimed over the beauty of a bare-limbed orchard that unfolded within his view from the carriage. But from Lizzie's position in the carriage, she saw an arm extended from an upper window on the north side. A very white, gloveless hand tossed out seeds. More than a dozen birds fluttered down from nearby trees to where the seeds fell on a crust of snow in the shade. It seemed, from the middle distance, to be wrens and tits until a magpie landed among them, scattering the nervous tits back into the bushes. The wrens fluttered to the side, but then hopped back, seeking their share of the feast cast out for them.

When the carriage stopped at the front of the door, Lizzie said, "Mr. Crackbone, the driver has been paid for the day. Ask him to wait several moments, in case we need to return to London immediately. After a quarter hour, he can retire to that inn we passed down the lane."

Diggory helped Lizzie down from the carriage. She'd worn a tall Puritanical hat, which meant bending low to descend. Countess bumped against her, almost before she found sure footing. After Diggory spoke with the driver, she said, "Can you trust me, even if you find this meeting perplexing?"

"Aye, Miss Mott. Mr. Tom Foxe warned me to be prepared."

"Then let us begin. Will you knock for us, Mr. Crackbone?"

She stood behind him in what appeared to be great propriety, and which also gave her another frisson of joy that she no longer had to play Viscount Orlando.

Diggory placed his hand on the knocker, then turned to her.

"This…this is the gold lion knocker in my memories of my departed father. I have been here before."

"We are about to learn more. Knock the door, please."

His face presented pure joy.

Now I'm responsible for one more person's fate today.

—

The door opened with a hideous screech, like a crying child or a hawk falling on its prey.

The young footman who opened the door regarded them with haughty reserve. At least, he tried to look down, but Lizzie was as tall as the footman and had been trained in a royal court on the ways to appear several stations above a footman. He took the invitation that Lizzie offered and closed the door on them.

Lizzie and Diggory were made to wait.

Even though the invitation she presented was clearly signed by the footman's master.

Even though the carriage that waited in the sweeping drive bore the master's initials (painted by Ned yesterday).

Even though the wind and moist air made for a raw day.

It did give Lizzie a moment to instruct Countess to wait on the stoop. At last, the door opened again. The footman bowed and led them into a salon off the foyer.

The woman who stood to greet them had given Wolfric Molewood his widow's peak and bestowed her shovel-shaped chin on Bythorn Chudrakes.

"How do you do, Mrs. Chudrakes. I am Miss Prudence Mott, come at the beseeching invitation of your son."

Humility Chudrakes was (by Tom's calculation) in her sixties and wore clothes redolent of pre-Restoration Puritanism, with mud-dark colors and simple lines, topped with an immaculate starched collar that bore only a thin edge of lace. The woman's linen cap had been bleached with wood ash and sour milk to within the limits of its life. But when the woman crossed the room to greet her guests, Lizzie heard the rustle of silk. Lizzie had made a fair guess at dawn about how she might dress like this woman, given the miniature she'd seen at Molewood's London house. But Lizzie had not guessed about silk undergarments.

Instead of hello or any other welcome, the woman said, "My son gave me no indication he'd invited you. And he was just here for the Sabbath."

The woman had the voice of a practiced scold, or perhaps Lizzie was only hearing her prejudices about Puritanism, because of all the grief it led to in the civil wars. No, it was more than that. This woman's type matched the four strict, unloving matrons who'd supervised Princess Mary's ladies in waiting when Lizzie first came to court. Those women encouraged talebearers and enjoyed punishing rule-breakers. Lizzie enjoyed it when Mary's new husband William had sent those termagants packing.

"In your son's note, he was quite insistent that I come meet you. Today." Lizzie spoke in her most honeyed voice and extended her gloved hand in greeting, disregarding the woman's rudeness. She motioned vaguely to where the carriage stood in the sweeping half-circle drive. "He sent his carriage."

The woman stared with the same cow-eyes as her son.

Meanwhile, that gold lion knocker had reduced Diggory to silence. He glanced around, his lips parted and hands folded behind him, like a man who'd suddenly found himself in another world. His only motion was the rapid blinking of his eyes.

"Madam, do you mind if I sit down while we discuss this predicament?" Lizzie said. "This journey was quite tiring."

"Who is that man?" The impertinent Mrs. Chudrakes indicated Diggory, who offered a mild smile when she darted her finger in his direction.

"This is Mr. Crackbone. He's my half-brother. It felt improper to come without a chaperone and protector."

"I am most happy to make your acquaintance, madam." Diggory bowed. And roused his voluble tongue to cite what he'd been taught to say at the beginning of this encounter. "I have not yet had the pleasure of meeting your son, but Miss Mott says he has a reputation as a great man of business in London. Further, I have read his letters to my sister. Your son presents himself as an honorable man with noble intentions."

Lizzie had first thought of him as dusty, but he was merely sandy colored. His linen tunic was freshly washed, his neckcloth properly tied, his hair brushed into a cloud of curls. He was, in fact, better looking than either of the two men Mrs. Chudrakes spawned—and utterly lacking in vanity.

Mrs. Chudrakes continued to study Wolfric Molewood's letter inviting Miss Prudence Mott to visit the family home at Primrose Hill and to meet his mother.

Lizzie spoke before the woman could voice any thought. "My apologies, madam. I did not expect to impose upon you. Your son has repeatedly and fervently expressed how much he desired that I meet you. I came at his request, but I'm desolated to see that I've inconvenienced you. I feel I've transgressed against everything my mother taught me, about how to behave when meeting important people."

Lizzie clasped her hands, as if in prayer, thinking she'd found the proper words and put them in appropriate order.

"I am simply at a loss for what to do," the woman said, she who had spawned the extremely resolute Wolfric and Bythorn.

"I should go," Lizzie said. "I cannot bear the thought of inconveniencing you without—"

Diggory's soft voice interrupted, as he'd been instructed during the carriage ride. "If I may be so bold as to make a suggestion." Of course, he didn't pause for an answer. He never did. "Perhaps a servant can fetch your son from London. Or at least advise the gentleman of his forgotten invitation, so that he can judge what's best to be done." Diggory continued in his anodyne voice about the distance and the quality of the roads that day, with an estimate of the time it would take to fetch the absent son, until Lizzie believed the woman had to either agree, in order to stop him, or else fall into a stupor.

"But my servants have no way to travel." Mrs. Chudrakes wrenched her hands.

"We came in your son's carriage." Diggory pointed out the window. "It was sent to bring Miss Mott here."

"Bless me!" Lizzie spoke in alarm. "He sent his carriage for me. Then he hasn't forgotten. Perhaps there's been an accident." She clutched at her throat. "Can you not put his own carriage to work, to solve this puzzle? Now I fear for his wellbeing."

"I can send Solomon and Theophilus." The woman begrudged the concession. "They'll know how to find my son."

Then, more to herself than anyone in the room: "But they'd best ride up with the driver. Wolfric does not hold with servants riding inside his carriage."

Lizzie tweaked Diggory's elbow as a thank-you, though he probably didn't feel it since he wore so many layers of clothes. And she managed to neither sigh with satisfaction that a hurdle had been crossed at last nor to fret that they were a quarter of an hour late starting this part of the plan. Lizzie coughed, covering her mouth with her gloved hand.

Diggory came alive again. "Madam, my sister, Miss Mott, has been ill. Can I beg you to spare a hot tisane for her health, as a Christian gesture? And perhaps we can become better acquainted while we wait for your son to join us from London."

Lizzie said, "Will you tell us about this beautiful mansion, Mrs. Crackbone? It must be so much work for you to maintain, to have to direct a regiment of servants. Is it not an enormous burden for you?"

"No, not at all. We have only the kitchen people, the footman, and our maids."

Diggory walked out with the footmen to instruct the driver. Upon his return, Countess bounded in ahead of him, and there were moments of chaos before the dog could be coaxed outside again, for Mrs. Chudrakes screamed, which caused Countess to bark, and it took Lizzie's firm voice and firm hand to get the poor creature back on the stoop. Lizzie took long enough to console the dog that her nose was cold by the time she returned.

Diggory and the Chudrakes woman sat as far from each other as it was possible, given the arrangement of furniture. Diggory was recounting a dog he'd had in his youth who had the best heart and sweetest disposition, while the woman tapped her foot, arms folded firmly over her bosom.

Lizzie launched the first tedious conversation to sustain them while waiting for the next action.

The woman remained suspicious and distracted by Diggory.

"What do you think this change in the weather will bring, Mrs. Chudrakes?"

"Whatever the Good Lord intends," Mrs. Chudrakes said. That she was a dour woman had carved itself on her face, nothing softened by the silk chemise she wore under her severe woolen gown.

"How very true, madam," Diggory said. "We've learned over the years—I would say, beginning when the Spirit of God first moved on the face of the waters—that we might expect in the month of January to endure the rains that make England a green paradise. For that is how we are blessed and challenged by our Lord." As he spoke, Mrs. Chudrakes began nodding in agreement, as if transfixed. "I was absent from this green island two years ago when our Lord and Creator challenged us with the hardest winter anyone remembers. That year, baptized and saved children were carried to heaven because our Creator chose to preserve them from suffering in the cold. In such times, we mourn for our loss while also thanking our Lord for all that we do not understand about His Creation."

The woman presiding over this house searched for opportunities to argue, but all slid off Diggory, who had an innate ability to let obstruction slide away from him.

When a steaming pot was at last delivered on a tray, Lizzie sipped from a thin, translucent china cup to find the bitterest of healthful tisanes. Over the rim of the cup, she caught a glimpse through the open door that must lead to the kitchen.

Through the passageway, a tall, dark woman peered, as if curious: a strip of linen tied around her head to hold back abundant black curls.

37
Broken and Infirm

— NED —

TUESDAY MORNING

AFTER LIZZIE LEFT THE house Tuesday morning, Ned and Perry enjoyed a leisurely breakfast, well-earned after all the work they'd executed, dawn to midnight on Sunday and Monday. Mrs. Flurry had provided a breakfast for sending workers off to their toil:

Rashers of back bacon, beautifully sliced.

A nutty oat porridge, with honey and cinnamon on top.

Bone marrow, the bones still hot from roasting in the fire.

Figs, preserved in brandy last September.

Bread, fresh that morning, fried in beef drippings.

Marmalade (never on the table in Ned's youth).

For the first few moments, they ate in silence.

Then Perry said, "This feast distresses me."

"You never cease to surprise me." Ned loaded his plate, since it'd be long after sunset before they found a meal again. "Mrs. Flurry is like an old-time alchemist, turning dross into gold."

"That's the problem." Perry set down his knife. He touched Ned's hand. "Heartling, Ezra Pelletoot offered me the upper half of his house. I told him I'd discuss it with you."

"Leave Rowland's house?" They'd only come in October, but they'd settled firmly in Xanthus House.

"You will inspect Mr. Pelletoot's upstairs when next you work on his portrait. The north third floor has a bank of windows over a handsome space where you could work. And it has a masonry stove, built by a Dutchman, or so Mr. Pelletoot says. So, you will be as warm as you like while you work."

"Warm would be nice." Ned wanted to join in Perry's enthusiasm. "But I have seen the upstairs. He beguiled me into moving lumber for him last Tuesday. I agree that it has good light."

"Were I to speak truth, I am deeply seduced by the notion of you and I regulating life as we want it."

"That was the plan for our life at Revelstone." Ned began to understand Perry's proposal.

"Exactly. Now, that's why this feast distresses me. How shall we find a cook as good as Mrs. Flurry?" Perry said.

That wasn't the first consideration, in Ned's mind. "What about Tom and Rollo?" He'd always lived with Tom, and he'd found it grand to have Rowland in England again.

"We'll be ten minutes away," Perry said. "And you wouldn't be at their call at any time of the night when they need you for devil-drawing. If we have our own house, it might break their bad habits, so you could be free of that."

"Our own house." Ned repeated it. The notion felt right, like trying on a new coat and finding that it fit quite well.

"You do want to escape your Foxe cousins' demands for forgery, do you not, Mr. Eduard Wijck?"

The use of Ned's formal name meant Perry was in a teasing mood. They both expected to find a great deal of joy and amusement today, despite the unexpected rain.

Ned said, "What I most want—"

"Help! We are doomed!" A woman shrieked.

Felicity Oakes rushed into the dining salon, her brother Michael following. Her cloak trailed behind, its hem inches deep in mud. Lazarus struggled to take it from her. The tiny actress's face was as stark white as her shift's collar, save for scarlet roses burning on her cheeks, from either cold or excitement. While Lazarus pried the muddy cloak from her fingers, she spoke hurriedly, her accent slipping between French and "London actress" in the way it often did. Ned usually heard her accent shifts as pretentious. At that moment, he heard panic.

"Each and every one of the actors is lost for today's work," she said. "Broken and infirm, to a man. And I promised Miss Foxe faithfully that I'd supply and manage her actors."

Ned choked on a spoonful of stewed fig, every thought about moving house wiped from his mind. He instantly shared Felicity's alarm.

His sister's gambol was ruined once more. And myriad immediate tasks lay before them: rescue Lizzie from where she'd gone into the country; send messages to all the investors to cancel the event; warn the caterers; call back the mercenaries who'd been hired to—

"Sit down and catch your breath, Miss Oakes." Perry tugged a chair out and pointed to it.

Perry grasped Ned's knee under the table, as if he sensed Ned's deep alarm and knew how to steady him.

"It's not that dire," Michael said. He strongly resembled his sister Felicity, but their temperaments were wholly opposite. "We can find replacements quickly enough."

Ned felt reassurance surge through his gut and limbs.

"Except," Felicity said, her voice sharp with panic, "for the key actors with speaking parts. We cannot replace them."

"Coffee, Miss Oakes?" said Perry, still gripping Ned's knee.

—

Ignoring Michael's reassurances, Perry chatted until Felicity came back from her panic. "It's not that coffee is new to this house, but Mrs. Flurry has introduced chocolate in her preparation."

"My sister Lizzie calls it decadent," Ned said. He'd caught on to Perry's direction, to help reduce Felicity's panic. His dear friend had taken the most sensible path, as always, by approaching the problem in pursuit of strategy. Getting everyone in line. Ned mustn't add to the alarm.

"No coffee." Felicity sat in the chair, shaking her head, tawny curls flying about. She hadn't tied back or even combed her hair. She caught her breath. "Our actors were doing a shortened version of *The Disappointment.* They've played it on a makeshift stage every night since the frost faire began. However, don't tell our maestro, because they haven't collected sufficient coin from the crowds to pay the author."

"That secret is safe with me," Perry said.

"With all the rumors flying, that the ice wouldn't hold, most vendors had moved their tents and carts off the ice. But our stage was on the bank, not on the river."

She stopped, staring at the floor, as if watching a scene.

"Then the ice broke at midnight," Perry said, as if to pull her into the story again.

"The ice broke just as the actors pitched into the last scene. Chunks of ice lurched onto the river bank, knocking out the barrels holding up the platform, and every one of the actors fell into the water. Anthony broke his arm. Martin threw out his collarbone. Roger was knocked senseless, didn't rouse for quarter of an hour." She went still again, which was unlike Felicity.

"And the rest?" Perry prodded. He took her hand and began to stroke it, as if to offer comfort.

"Sprained ankles. Bruises and cuts. They all look very battered. Several were sniffling and sneezing last night. This morning they are now all coughing like lungers."

"I'm truly sorry to hear it." Perry still held her hand.

Michael spoke again. "There's only us two who are fit for the gambol today. We've been seeking other actors. I roused the four Buckworth brothers, who doss near Drury Lane. They want the coin offered, since it's winter. They are so very large but might be able to squeeze into the costumes."

"How about enlisting my brothers?" Perry asked. "They aren't doing any kind of noble things today, just carrying tea and chopping wood, both here and at Chalgrove House."

"Aurora and I can give them the day off to help," Felicity said. She seemed to be starting to rally.

Michael said, "I think we can persuade Winwood."

"Persuade me of what?" Winwood Oakes stood at the door, suppressing a yawn, his clothes and hair already tidy, his tawny mane drawn back with a leather string. He'd spent the last two days in the kitchen at Chalgrove House, creating concoctions to defeat Tom's long-time ailment. He glanced over the breakfast offerings, then took the chair beside Ned and reached for the bowl of porridge.

Felicity answered Winwood's question. "Our hired actors are now off today's playbill due to an accident at the Thames stage last night."

"Do they need a doctor?" Winwood asked. "I can come straight away."

"No," Felicity said, "we need replacement actors for Ysabel Foxe's charade."

Winwood sat back, hands in his lap, his face stern. "Tamsin…Miss Thomasine has always insisted that I not be involved in your…ah, restorations. It's one of her rules."

"But now," Ned said, "along comes an exception that puts that rule aside."

"What rule are we breaking?" Tom came in, not yet dressed in his periwig or waist coat, his nose red from the remains of that grippe he'd suffered since Christmas. He sneezed, then coughed until he'd turned red from the neck up. When he could speak again, he said, "We've been walking a narrow, cautious pathway, attending to every rule, whether it's our Restoration Rules or Uncle Absolom's rules for enlightened people. Or most of the laws of England."

Ned said, "We are abiding by all Foxe family rules. Although Lizzie had Perry and me breaking so many English laws, they'll likely have to invent new ones."

"If the king ever lets Parliament sit again," Perry said.

"But what rule are we breaking?" Tom repeated.

Ned said, "Tamsin's rule that Winwood Oakes doesn't participate in our restorations."

"Or have any knowledge of them," Winwood said.

"Why are we breaking that rule?" Tom asked.

"Because," Felicity exaggerated the word, "our actors all fell into the Thames last night."

Michael said, "So we need every possible recruit."

"And we need to train them by eleven o'clock," Felicity said. "Winwood, you must join us."

Perry said, "What part can he be taught to play without having any actual knowledge of Miss Foxe's gambol?"

That was just like Perry, solving the problem and making quick order out of chaos.

Felicity and Michael exchanged glances. Felicity said, "He could guard the door. We need someone of significant size."

"Absolutely not," Perry said. "I shan't even explain why that's a bad idea, because you aren't none of you addlepated. We cannot push him that deep into Lizzie's gambol."

"He's too tall for a page," Michael said. "Perhaps he can serve as one of the merchants' attendants."

"Fine," Winwood said, seeing that Perry and Ned had folded their arms, signaling an affirmation that he was joining them. "I'll dress the part if I do not have to speak any untruths, and as long as no one else ever knows, especially Tamsin."

Tom said, "If we have Perry's brother and the Buckworth brothers and Winwood, what else do we need?"

Michael said, "A customs man, the main guard, and a replacement for Viscount Orlando."

"That's why we hired Anthony, Martin, and Roger," Felicity said. "We need true actors. Perry's brothers are too—"

"Too young and insubstantial," Ned said, "for any of those parts. They are fine for the liveried servants."

"And my friends, the Buckworth brothers, are too Goliath sized," Felicity said, "for any role save for the footmen."

"I am deeply distressed," Perry said, "that we must take on so many new actors this late in the plan. We need to ensure that those in the crucial roles can be trusted. Who among us is thin enough to play our customs man for two brief moments?"

Everyone turned thoughtful. Winwood supped his porridge. Perry pried the last of the marrow from a roasted bone with his knife. Tom spread a thick layer of marmalade on the last piece of toasted bread.

Then Lazarus the butler, who appeared and disappeared as if by magic, coughed softly. "I believe I can serve your need for a thin man."

Perry and Ned traded wary looks, with Ned sure that neither of them believed Rowland would agree to involving the Xanthus House butler. However, Tom said, "Excellent! Now, who do we find to replace Orlando?"

"It's too bad Miss Foxe abandoned that role so late in our preparations." Perry said. However, Ned still appreciated Lizzie's decision to choose safety, and not to attend the event.

"There's one more actor you haven't roused yet, Felicity." Michael folded his arms. "I know you want to avoid being in company with Geoffrey Shadwell, since he had the misfortune to fall in love with you. But he's a match in size for Orlando."

"*C'est naze!*" Felicity wrinkled her nose in disgust. "Mr. Shadwell is the greatest coxcomb in London—nay, in all of England. And he'd charge us a small fortune for his time." She shrugged, resigned to making the request.

"Can't Winwood do it?" Michael said. "It's only two lines and two minutes. Then Orlando disappears from our pageant."

Winwood was shaking his head.

"Come, doctor. You can do it," Tom said. "You've seen Orlando in all his vain glory. You can ape that for two minutes. And we'll all of us swear to never tell Tamsin about the broken rule."

"We must depart for the meeting house," Felicity said. "I need to make sure everyone knows their roles and can be in place on time."

"Miss Oakes," Perry said, "tell my brothers that their compensation is dinner at Xanthus House on Sunday. We shall not pay my kin as if they're real actors. And they are responsible for returning their hired costumes in pristine condition."

Michael, Felicity, and Winwood were out the door. Lazarus supplied Felicity with a mud-free cloak.

Tom said, "That leaves only the chore of teaching the door guard his lines and getting him in costume."

"I have the costume," Perry said.

Ned hoped Lizzie truly appreciated all that Perry did for her scheme, how calmly and selflessly he prepared for every eventuality, beyond anything the Foxe cousins had done in planning their own restorations, before Perry and Rowland returned to England. He stabbed the last rasher of bacon, claiming it before Tom could snatch it, when he saw that Tom and Perry were staring at him. He sat back, no longer intrigued by the bacon.

"But I was to be with Perry today," Ned protested. "I've looked forward to our adventure." Perry was leading a raid on Molewood's London house during the hours of the meeting.

"We'll be parted for but a few hours," Perry said. "And you, Ned Wijck, will look particularly fine in the guard's clothes."

Tom agreed. "But you'll need gloves to hide the paint stains on your fingers."

Then it struck Ned that they'd forgotten the role Lizzie had added late in the plan. "We need a man to play Miss Prudence Mott's solicitor."

Lazarus cleared his throat. "I can ask my cousin Samuel. He has experience."

"As an actor?" Felicity asked.

Lazarus denied that with a slight shake of his head. "As an intelligencer in Holland, before Charles signed the Peace of Westminster. But you must not spread that news about."

38
Beauty Provoketh Thieves

– NED –

TUESDAY BEFORE NOON

ALL THE MORNING DECISIONS meant that at midday Tuesday Ned stood at the meeting room door inside Mercers' Hall on Ironmongers Lane, though serving at the subscription event against his preference. However, the work needed doing. The hired room would soon hold wealth that required a professional guard.

And Ned could pretend to be a silent onlooker better than any of the actors. Yet every few minutes he winced in discomfort. He never felt agitated when Tamsin led them out to act as land pirates in a Cambridgeshire country lane. Or when he sold art signed with another artist's name, to earn silver for the mortgage and taxes.

It was the russet wig and the tight black leather suit that provoked his agitation. The leather suit creaked when he moved. Being what Perry called "bone thin," it'd be a challenge to move at all if Ned had to actively guard anything.

Ned also had to avoid catching the eye of any footman bustling about Mercers' Hall lest the servant under the periwig and liveried coat prove to be one of Perry Frake's brothers. Ned could carry out this charade, but he didn't want anyone he knew smirking while he performed "strongman in leathers."

He stiffened the stern look on his face, but that made his lip itch behind the false mustache.

Somewhere down the road a church tower struck eleven. Every player who'd been bustling about (or tossing dice, like Felicity's actor friends) snapped into place. The false Venetian merchants adjusted their velvet suits and righted their floppy hats. The hired servants adjusted their borrowed periwigs and straightened their lace cuffs.

Tom, in his elegant Venetian disguise, stood at the meeting room door. He repeatedly snapped his fingers, claiming he'd seen actual Venetian merchantmen do the same, but Ned estimated those merchants had been commanding servants without masking their agitation.

The first potential investors to come down the hallway were, of course, the Earl of Gomfrey, Sir Didlington, and Mr. Cokayne, the trio that Michael Oakes had described as most eager at the failed Friday event.

Behind them came Wolfric Molewood, strutting in Dragon's Blood red velvet, his hawkish cheeks shaved and shiny with balm, cuffs dripping lace. The scent of pomade and sandalwood as the man passed struck Ned like a physical blow, right where his ribs joined above his belly. The day's most crucial moment was now at hand.

Ned enjoyed a rush of sensations for this moment. Perry had once described it to Ned: the thrill of confidence and well-being when all the parts of a plan move into play, and a man need only observe as success unfolds.

Except the lad Ishmael trailed Molewood, carrying the hat and cloak that Molewood had shed at the door. As if he were still confident, Ned pointed Ishmael to the far end of the hall, where the pages had a bench to await their masters.

Ishmael wasn't supposed to be here. Lizzie's plan needed Ishmael to be at Molewood's house in Bloomsbury.

Tom was busy playing his role. And no one else here knew this part of the plan, to rescue Ishmael from his master as part of the day's business. How was Ned going to fix this? The day's business demanded that he guard the door at Mercers' Hall.

The thin body inside the guard's leather suit roiled with dread, wanting to take action, when there was no way to act. Ned's mind raced over every possibility. Perhaps he'd have to reveal himself to one of the Frake boys currently playing footman. But how? None of them spoke Portuguese.

Before Ned could pry his clenched jaw free to open his mouth to call to Daniel Frake, a dry, elderly voice spoke nearby.

"Mr. Molewood? I beg a moment of your time. I'm Josselin Kidwelly. I am solicitor and guardian to Miss Prudence Mott."

This must be Lazarus's cousin Samuel, a diminutive fellow who more closely resembled a penny-paper hawker in Drury Lane than a man who might spy for the king.

"Sir!" Molewood bowed. "I am at your service. Is Miss Mott attending today?"

"No. She confided her needs to me last night, believing she'd still be indisposed today."

"I am alarmed." Molewood did sound concerned, though Ned had heard from Lizzie that what the fellow wanted from Miss Mott was her land. "Has she seen a physician?"

"I believe that is in hand," the solicitor said. He held out a folded package. "I am commissioned to ensure that she meets her part in your mutual challenge to invest in this venture."

"Surely, if she's ill, we can defer our sporting challenge."

"No, Miss Mott insists on meeting her obligation to you. I cannot attend today's presentation, because I did not receive an invitation. It's…" The elder fellow paused. "The new offering is too rich for my thin pockets. Miss Mott asked me to give this to you, so that you might advance her participation in the scheme on her behalf."

"I am astounded at her trust." Molewood looked surprised.

But the solicitor didn't give him another moment to respond. "Out of my duty as the lady's guardian, I must ask you to sign this receipt."

As if Ned were invisible, the solicitor heralded one of the footmen—Daniel Frake—and asked for a quill and ink. Molewood stood behind the solicitor, staring at the thick packet as if an elf had handed him fairy gold.

When that actor left the Mercers' Hall, Ned wished he could smile at the day's first success. Yet the plan to rescue Ishmael from Molewood's house dangled precariously.

—

Ned's lip itched. He reached up to smooth his false moustache and beard, then stopped just in time. When Felicity glued that hair in place, she repeatedly warned him not to touch his face.

However, Wolfric Molewood stood close, demanding attention, as if addressing a servant, breakfast ale heavy on his breath. "What room will hold this day's meeting with the Venetian merchantmen, sirrah?"

Without speaking, Ned pointed to the door to the room for the day's event. Molewood didn't offer a nod in response, much less any common expression of gratitude.

Ned couldn't bear another day glavering to that sneaking cur. He abhorred the cheating man so much that he didn't even care that the gambol's final act meant that the painting of *Achilles at Skyros* would remain unfinished. He didn't even care about abandoning his brushes and colors in the Bloomsbury mansion, since everything that came close to Molewood risked corruption.

"Good morning. It's Mr. Molewood, isn't it?"

That familiar voice fired a sense of dread through Ned like a muzzle-ball shot. It was their Cambridgeshire neighbor, the new Earl of Hawksmoor, but who'd been Viscount Heydon for most of the twenty years that Ned had known him. Ned couldn't think of who might be more out of place here. The men invited to this event had all been Hawkins' Heirs investors. Neither Viscount Heydon nor Lord Hawksmoor had appeared on that list. That judder of alarm tingled in Ned's fingers, which sought to check his beard. But Ned resisted. He'd been worrying about every unknown actor pulled into this gambol on short notice. He could deal with a Cambridgeshire neighbor.

Hawksmoor held out his hand to Molewood in greeting. "I'm Poynter, Lord Hawksmoor."

An overly familiar way to introduce himself. Lizzie, Tom, and Rowland called him by his christened name, but here was Hawksmoor giving it to a cheating London builder as if they were to be friends.

Lord Hawksmoor politely greeted his ornately dressed Venetian host—Tom—without either offering his christened name or recognizing him. He didn't look Ned's way twice. Ned had no more time to ponder Hawksmoor's presence, because the day's crucial moment was at hand.

The door to another meeting room down the hall opened. A high-pitched male voice called for Mercutio di Bassanio. That door remained open just enough to reveal a figure that disappeared when Tom entered. After only a moment, Tom emerged from the room and called, "*Grazie, grazie mille,*" to the unseen figure behind him.

Ned had a view into the other room, and believed he saw a figure like Sir Bythorn Chudrakes. Molewood, standing nearby, had to have seen it too, given his surprised expression.

The man better have seen it, since this charade was wholly for his benefit.

Tom unfolded the paper he held, trailed his finger over the words, mouthing them silently as if he struggled to read. He looked astonished for a moment. He approached Ned, then glanced around, seeming to see no one, although Molewood had stepped just inside the meeting room door. In an Italian accent, as false as Ned's beard, Tom said, "You give to viscount."

Ned tucked the paper inside his thick black leather jerkin. Tom patted Ned's arm, then entered the meeting room, exclaiming, "*Benvenuti, amici!* Welcome," and vigorously shaking Molewood's hand. As the other dozen men arrived, Tom shook their hands and invited them to take a seat.

At the quarter hour, Tom began the presentation as Mercutio, the leader of the trio of merchants.

"Le Casa Mercantile del Fratelli Gratiano welcomes you to this presentation for the Albion-Byzantium Company."

After that, Tom made several attempts to speak but coughed too much to be understood by the audience. In better English, Signore di Bassanio, his brother, spoke.

"It is good that my elder brother Mercutio can join us at last. On Friday night, we described a rare opportunity to participate in our new venture to bring oriental rarities directly to England. For generations we have imported silk, rare artifacts, and other things of beauty to Europe. If you choose to participate in this venture, it means great profit with no French or Genoese agents adding costs in the middle."

Lord Hawksmoor asked, "What about the East India Company? And the Royal African Company? How will you compete with those large entities?"

Mercutio boasted, in a wretched accent, that his family had their own trade monopolies from the Great Silk Road through the Mediterranean. "It has been our family's monopoly for generations. And we have a second shipping business from Egypt. We only need," Mercutio said, "your English partnership. With an official English ship's pass, we can sail through Gibraltar with no fear of pirates."

More questions, more reassurance. Ned had never in this life attended business meetings, yet he could see from Tom's beaming face that this was going well.

Lorenzo said, "If you have decided to join this syndicate, please give your banker's draft to the guard at the door. We will hold your reservation safely in trust. There is one member who cannot join us until four o'clock. So, we shall all sign the syndication documents then."

While Lorenzo passed around copies of the syndicate documents (printed in Rowland's cellar), Mercutio said, "And now, *signori,* please join us for dinner in the chamber next door."

However, as all the men rose, the Earl of Hawksmoor said, "We should elect one of us to account for all the funds paid into the syndicate. And to serve as paymaster when the ships return to England."

"*Buona idea!*" Tom said. "Whom will you elect?"

"I nominate Wolfric Molewood," Hawksmoor said. "He has more experience in business than all of us in total."

Murmurs of agreement rumbled through the room. Molewood bowed to the acclaim. "I'm humbled by your trust in me. I shall do my best to serve your needs, gentlemen."

Ned tugged at his stiff leather collar, as if that might relieve the itching beard. He wasn't a newborn babe found under a cabbage leaf last month. Lord Hawksmoor obtained an unexpected invitation to invest, and then stuck his oar in to steer the business. This was Lizzie's surprise for the day. No use resenting that his sister hadn't shared all details of her plan. He should have known to expect it.

Hawksmoor said, "I can submit a large draft on my bank. However, I'd like to see all the appropriate sureties. Neither an English ship's pass nor an ancient monopoly can prevent thieves or customs officials from interfering with the course of our business. As the Poet says, 'Beauty provoketh thieves.'"

"We have shared," Lorenzo said, "our insurance charter."

"But do you have a written surety with the customs commission?" Hawksmoor asked. "Do the king's customs men agree that you are not infringing on other companies' charters?"

Of course. Except Lizzie hadn't asked Ned to create such a document. And she must have composed Hawksmoor's script.

"Indeed, your lordship," Lorenzo was saying. "We'll present all sureties when we reconvene at four o'clock. If you are not happy then, we will return your banker's draft immediately when you demand it."

Ned unfolded his arms and set a stern demeanor as he accepted letterlocked papers that contained the attendees' banker's drafts. The men, chattering with each other, were eager to participate in this trade venture—which was only a tailor's dummy clothed in Tom's legal craft and Ned's forgeries. And Michael's work with the printing press in Rowland's cellar.

Wolfric Molewood left the meeting room with Hawksmoor at his elbow, the last men to exit. They both gave their banker's drafts to the guard and stepped away.

A gloved hand tapped Ned's shoulder.

"*Hola,* varlet. You hold a message for me? I am the Viscount Orlando de Flores."

Varlet? Worse than the insult, the voice didn't sound like Winwood Oakes, or even a timbre that Winwood might falsify. Across the hall, Neriah Frake, in his Venetian footman costume, grinned at Ned like a bedeviled jackass.

Whoever Felicity had enlisted to play Orlando, the man knew his lines from the script for the day's next crucial scene.

Ned stiffened his spine and hardened his demeanor. Which again made his lip itch so badly it threatened to involve his nose.

"I am at your service, your lordship."

39
An Error, Sir

— NED —

TUESDAY NOON

WHILE TRYING NOT TO turn his head, Ned glanced around to ensure that Mr. Molewood watched. Yes, still in the doorway with Hawksmoor at his side.

The new Orlando stood with his back to Ned, as if watching the door where Sir Bythorn had appeared earlier. He wiggled his fingers behind his back, wanting the message.

The actor managed a grand achievement, so like the Orlando Ned first met last summer, down to wearing a shiny court suit, inappropriate at a business meeting. The actor posed as a better Orlando than Lizzie had ever managed, since her version incarnated a dissolute Ganymede. Although she'd had all winter to practice, she never mastered a man's way of movement.

Ned pressed the "customs" note into Orlando's hand. The actor never faced Ned, which nicely increased the sense of devious action. As they'd hoped, Molewood stepped up to impede the passage of the so-called viscount.

"You, sir, besmirched my good name, telling customs officials that I am a smuggler. I shall demand satisfaction through my attorney."

"An error, sir. On your part." Just like Lizzie, this Orlando stood in stiff reserve, as if this actor also hated Molewood too much to let him hover too close. "You have clearly mistaken me for some other man."

"No mistake." Molewood grew red in the face. "You are Orlando de Flores, who came to my house to return my boy. You sent a note to the customs house, condemning me."

"Get a grip on your garters, man. You are mistaken. If you apologize, I shall let this insult pass."

Orlando sauntered toward the exit. He reached to put the letter Ned had just given him into a capacious pocket of his shiny court coat. However, the letter missed finding the pocket and drifted to the floor.

Molewood bent to retrieve it. He glanced after the retreating Orlando but didn't call out to him. Instead, he unfolded the paper and read it. His bulging eyes fluttered, opened wide.

Ned tapped Molewood's shoulder, knowing the man would find it impertinent. "That belongs to Viscount Orlando." He reached to take the paper from Molewood.

"No, it's mine." Molewood slapped at Ned's hand, as if flicking away a bothersome fly.

"But I saw him drop it, sir," Ned protested.

"Are you calling me a liar?" Molewood scowled. "Varlet."

When the actor playing Orlando spoke that word, it was a jest. The same word was vile in Molewood's mouth.

"I shall fetch the viscount and—"

"Master! Master! You come." It was Ishmael, begging Molewood's attention, inserting himself between Ned and Molewood. "Boys here from Madam your mother. You come."

Molewood, flushed from confrontations with Orlando and Ned, followed Ishmael to the front door while pocketing the letter he'd picked up. "What boys?"

When Molewood reached the front door, Hawksmoor called after him, "See you at four o'clock, Mr. Molewood. Neither of us wants to miss this opportunity."

—

Ned wished Lizzie could know that her plan was succeeding. Each element of play in the Mercers' Hall had been executed perfectly, like a longways country dance, with a strict dance master keeping it all correct, each interchange passing down the line, just as the gambol master…uh…mistress had planned.

Except Ishmael was here instead of being at Molewood's house, where Perry's hired crew was supposed to intercept him. Such a small lad and a big complication. Rescuing Ishmael mattered more to Ned in this gambol than the rest of Lizzie's machinations, and not just because they'd suffered together in the customs lock-up. The events later that day might create such chaos as to make it hard to find another opportunity to rescue the lad.

Perhaps Molewood would leave Ishmael at home before going to his mother's house. Ned bit at his lip in both hope and consternation, then had to spit out a false hair.

Yes, that's what Molewood would do. He wouldn't ride out into the cold with an unneeded page.

No, here was Ishmael back again, without Molewood. He stood before Ned and held up a message.

"Master sends for Sir Bythorn. What room?"

"He's not here." Ned had no reason to say otherwise. "Likely he's at the customs house."

"What to do?" Ishmael looked puzzled. "Mr. Wijck?"

"I–I, uh…" Ned faltered at being recognized. But then, they had endured an entire night together.

Orlando came up behind Ned again, just as suddenly as before. "Did it work? Did he pick up the letter?"

Which seemed a bad question to ask in front of anyone, even when it was Ishmael, who had little English. This Orlando wore dark makeup, badly applied, so his face seemed fuzzy, indistinct, like a badly aged painting.

Ned said, "Orlando, do you remember Mr. Molewood's page, Ishmael? He wants me to take a message to Sir Bythorn at the customs house."

An actor gives another one a cue. That's what they do in the theatre, is that not true? Ned very much hoped that the new Orlando would pick up the cue and understand that Ishmael had a part in the day's play.

"Does he?" Orlando, hands on his hips, frowned as if thinking about that problem. "Mayhap I should go instead."

Ishmael studied the actor. "You are not my Orlando."

"Oh?"

"My Orlando is a woman." He looked up at Ned. "Isn't she, Mr. Wijck?"

"Yes." Ned had to adjust Lizzie's plan quickly. The translator Lizzie had hired was in Bloomsbury now, prepared to give Ishmael the choice to come away. How was Ned to explain that plan to Ishmael while possessing so little Portuguese?

"*Hola,* Orlando." Hawksmoor was there, his hand on the actor's shoulder. "I'd heard the viscount was leaving England."

Orlando turned to him. "Do you speak Portuguese?"

"*Um pouco.*"

"Good. Help the guard here with this page."

Then Orlando was gone. That, at least, had been the plan: an actor shows up as Orlando, then leaves, first the building, then England. Therefore, the departure was not a surprise. The need for a new plan about Ishmael must be created there on the spot with Lord Hawksmoor.

Ned said, "Miss Ysabel Foxe intended to ask Ishmael if he'd like to leave his master, to live with her family. And if so, we hope that Ishmael can also help to fetch a woman called Tia Angelina to join us."

Hawksmoor agreed with a slight nod. "I'll try, with the ten words I know."

Ned said, "Ishmael, this is my friend. Call him—"

"Hawksmoor, *al tuo servizio.*" After introducing himself, the earl chatted with Ishmael for two moments.

The lad nodded at each question Hawksmoor asked. Then he answered one question in English. "I know Tia Angelina. I'll go meet her. With Mr. Wijck?"

"No, I cannot go." Ned couldn't abandon his part in Lizzie's plan. "I must be here until late. Your lordship, can you take this lad to Bloomsbury? We have a translator there who was hired to take Ishmael to meet Tia Angelina at Primrose Hill."

"I cannot," Hawksmoor said. "Likely for the same reason you cannot leave. We all serve at Miss Foxe's pleasure. But I will run after Orlando to see if a solution can be found."

While Hawksmoor pursued that mission, Ishmael asked in English, "Mr. Wijck, you will take my master's message?"

"Aye. I'll find a messenger."

Hawksmoor returned and motioned for Ishmael to come, which must mean that the false Orlando, whoever he was, had agreed to go to Bloomsbury. Ned exhaled in relief, then found another false hair on his tongue.

Ishmael was barely out the door when Ned opened Molewood's message, written in plumbago pencil on the back of a scrap of paper. Hawksmoor took it from Ned's hands and read it, then passed it to Tom, who appeared from the room where dinner was served.

> Brother, What did you intend by the large figure you gave the Venetians? Be at the Mercers' Hall event at four o'clock to let me know why you offered that number. Meanwhile, beware that foolish Viscount Orlando.
> —WM

"Ha!" Tom said. "Ned, you'd best find a messenger who can get this into Sir Bythorn's hands. This is better than our plan for luring the customs man to where he needs to be."

Ned grabbed his cloak and was out the door, down the steps, and onto the street immediately, happy to escape the meeting hall and begin his next assignment.

Alas, it was raining.

Ned tugged his cloak's hood close, to protect that beard.

40
Reunion

– LIZZIE –

TUESDAY AFTERNOON

LIZZIE NEVER ONCE LOOKED out the window of Mrs. Chudrakes' parlor. She resisted straining to listen for a carriage.

Countess barked, the one sharp sound she always made when impatient. She served as an animated clock, barking once each quarter hour. At each yap, Mrs. Chudrakes darted dark eyes to the door, her chin shoveling out in annoyance.

It took great resolve for Lizzie to swallow a bite of the overbaked gingerbread she'd been served. Diggory had no problem with it. However, he'd said before now that he ceased being choosy about his food while stranded in Cadiz.

Setting aside the little mallorca plate of gingerbread, Lizzie returned to her efforts to make conversation, though only to pass the time. "Please tell me about your family, Mrs. Chudrakes. Are you from this neighborhood?"

"My people are from Suffolk," the mother said, clearly reluctant to engage. "An uncle introduced me to my first husband, my oldest son's father. Like the men in my family, he had an old-fashioned name, Job-Made-a-Covenant-with-His-Eyes. You young people will laugh at that in this age."

Lizzie said, "No, not at all, madam. My grandfather also came from Sussex, and he too had the sort of name that good people in those days gave their children to guide them along the righteous path. You might say that my christened name, Prudence, follows in that tradition."

Lizzie did not possess such a guiding name. Or a Puritan grandfather. She didn't follow a righteous path, only precepts learned from Uncle Absolom and her cousins' Restoration Rules. That is to say, she felt free to prevaricate as needed.

Yet her nonsensical depiction of virtuosity pleased Mrs. Chudrakes, who twisted her mouth into a smile, if it could be called that. "It was the first grief in my young life, to lose Mr. Molewood when his son was not yet a year old. I have done my best every day to shape that son into the man that his righteous father would wish him to be."

Lizzie smiled, as if agreeing that the lost husband wanted his son to become a greedy, wicked sort of person who got rich by way of others' losses.

The mother said, "We were blessed, of course, that the elder Mr. Molewood—I mean my son's grandfather—remained with us until just five years ago. He was our bulwark through all misfortunes. We are thankful that God has shown His shining face upon us, raining down blessings."

"All praise to the Almighty."

Is that what people say?

Lizzie's eyes drifted to Diggory, happy that he remained quiet. This interview would not hold up well under a discussion of saints and intercessions. But it drifted along well enough with Lizzie asking questions to which she already knew the answers. "You must have been quite young when you lost him."

"Aye, Miss Mott. But another good man did find me. However, we enjoyed only four years together until God chose to take him too, into Abraham's bosom. He gave me another son, and I have enjoyed many years, taking care of my children."

"And now," Lizzie said, "you are being taken care of by your sons. Or so I understand from Mr. Molewood."

Mrs. Chudrakes shuddered. Lizzie couldn't interpret that expression. Before she could decide, the crunch of wheels echoed from the drive.

All gratitude to the gods of Olympus! We progress.

Diggory stood. "Can you please excuse me, Mrs. Chudrakes? I saw your facilities in the back when we came up the drive. I need only a moment."

And, without awaiting an answer, he was out of the room, headed in the direction of the kitchen.

A door in the back closed just before the front door squeaked opened and then squealed again as it closed. Lizzie regretted that she'd met the man enough times to recognize Molewood's padding footsteps across the wood floor.

"Miss Mott!" he exclaimed as he stood at the door to the parlor. He held out his hands to her, but she kept hers in her lap. His mother held out her hands though. She rose to embrace him with greater speed than she'd greeted Prudence Mott.

Lizzie was used to seeing Molewood in his elegant velvet suits with braid and lace. Today he wore a fine blue wool suit and the most sober of neckcloths, no lace at his cuffs. Had Molewood dressed to appear Puritan to his mother? Why would a fifty-year-old man dress to please his mother?

"I'm so sorry, son," his mother said, "that you had to come out here in the cold for this terrible mistake."

"Not terrible," Molewood said. "I am always delighted to see Miss Mott. I'm only surprised. I was stricken to hear that you have been ill, Pru...Miss Mott."

Lizzie hoped she didn't look as predatory as she felt. "I've been ill, sir, but I felt compelled to answer your plea to meet your mother. No man has spoken to me as you have, with such passion and constancy."

Picking up the letter from the table, Lizzie cleared her voice and read it aloud. With trembling passion.

> I beg you to lay open your soul to my earthly conceit. Come meet my mother today. If these earthly pleasures may thee move, come live with me and be my love. Teach me, dear creature, how to think and speak.

She held out the note to him but spoke to his mother. "Do you see why your son's plea moved me, Mrs. Chudrakes? Such heartfelt poetry."

Molewood took the letter and studied it, shaking his head.

"Please be kind, dear lady, and call me Wolfric. You promised once that you would try." He mumbled words she couldn't hear. "Oh, no, it's…it's very like my hand, but I never wrote this."

"Then you do not have such feelings for me?" Lizzie wrenched her hands, distressed. Rowland never composed such words either, but he recited the Bard often enough that it was easy to tell Ned what to write.

"No, Prudence. I long to be such a poet. But I didn't send for you today. I would any other day, but not today."

"Who would play such a cruel trick? To make me think a man cares for me so much as to bring me out into the cold? To prostrate and embarrass myself before your kindly mother?"

"I do care. And you haven't embarrassed yourself, Prudence. We are wild to have you here. Aren't we, Mother?"

Mrs. Chudrakes first shook her head, but then nodded, quickly catching the error in revealing her feelings.

"Oh, hello. It's Mr. Molewood, isn't it?" Diggory returned. He advanced on Molewood smiling, his hand out in greeting. "I'm Diggory Crackbone. I am so pleased to meet you, uncle."

"Good lord!" Molewood dropped the love letter.

His mother gasped, dropping her embroidery hoop.

—

"Enoch!" Another voice at the door, this from a tiny, ancient woman in grey wool with a modest lace collar. "I thought I heard your voice, dear boy."

Perry didn't warn me about the grandmother!

The elderly woman wrapped her arms around Diggory, even though she was too tiny to close the embrace. Molewood tugged at his hair, seeming to forget he wore an elaborate wig. "Whatever—"

"No, Mother Molewood." The Chudrakes woman stepped up as if to part the embracing pair. "It's only a guest. Enoch's been dead these twenty years. You know that."

"I know my own son's voice."

"I'm Diggory, Enoch's son," he said. "From what I've recently learned, you must be Great-grandmother Molewood. I remember stories my father told me, Grandmother."

"Granddame, please!" Molewood's voice squeaked as he tried to interfere. He'd flushed red—no, purple as a beet.

"You must call me Yaya." The little woman was only interested in hearing Diggory. "Enoch always did."

"Are you Greek, Yaya?" Diggory bent low and smiled into her face. The grandmother proved the perpetual smile was an inherited trait. "When I was in Greece, the children called their granddames yaya. It made me long for my own grandmother."

The grandmother still clutched his forearms. "Yaya is what Enoch called me. Every babe's first word is mama, but she passed to the Lord when Enoch was born, so I taught him to say yaya instead. You say it's Greek, my dear lad? That's as great a gift as you appearing here, like an angel bearing God's message."

Though eager to begin the day's assault on Wolfric Molewood, Lizzie enjoyed how Diggory's sudden appearance had befuddled Molewood and his judgmental mother.

There could be no doubt about how Diggory had fallen heir to his decided tendency to belabor every story. He and his grandmother were the only people in the room finding joy in that moment. Lizzie wished to see herself on their side. Warm hearted. Gently kind. Perhaps she'd feel that way if she were here with Rowland, instead of this greedy malefactor? Lizzie was stuck here, fending off all emotions save for impatience for the day's business to be done.

"I always knew this to be Enoch's son's house," the grandmother said. "I promised God to greet the day with joy if that child ever appeared. And here you are!"

Molewood had been struck dumb with dismay. Unable to interrupt the reunion, Mrs. Chudrakes forgot about Prudence Mott. Diggory had supplanted Prudence as the target of her quiet malice. She tugged at Molewood's sleeve.

"You said he was dead." To Lizzie, the Chudrakes woman said, "You said he was your brother."

"Foster brother," Lizzie said. "He lived next door for years after he was orphaned. I feared we'd lost him at sea. So, you must imagine my joy, my thanks to the Almighty, when—"

"How can that be?" Molewood said, having taken such a shock that he forgot to pretend to adore his Prudence. "He was raised by that infernal papist, the Crackbone fellow. And they said he died in Cadiz."

"Left for dead," Diggory said. He chuckled the way he did when things were ironical but scarcely humorous. "Yet, thanks to the indulgences of the blessed saints, here I am, with the grandmother I always longed for."

"Mr. Molewood," Lizzie said, "I had no idea you were related. Pray, do not think I had nefarious intentions bringing Diggory Crackbone here. I only wanted a male chaperone, rather than coming to your house alone."

Oh, I'm beyond nefarious.

"Wolfric," his mother shook a thin finger at him, "do something. Make him go away."

Molewood looked at Prudence, intelligent enough to know he was not appearing in the best light before his beloved.

"Sir, I'm uncomfortable," Lizzie said, "at being swept into your family affairs. And I apologize for my unwitting part in it. I should depart."

"Do you want to see Shiloh House?" the grandmother asked Diggory. "So often, the voices of angels have whispered that it should be yours. I've prayed for you to come, though the world unfolds only as God intends for those to whom he has offered salvation."

"Wolfric, I—" The mother's eyes flashed with fire.

"Prudence, I—" Molewood sounded even sadder than his eyes looked.

"Dear Enoch…ah, Diggory, all praises to our Heavenly Father that I was born to be your yaya."

Amazingly, Diggory said nothing. And Lizzie didn't join in the confusion because she had nothing to add. Rather, she was distracted for a moment, curious about how the day's plan was progressing in London with Molewood absent.

Then the front door screeched open again. Didn't this house have tallow or linseed oil? Did they never have visitors and so didn't know how hideously their hinges screeched?

A pair of large men came in through the front, a quartet more came in through the back, all in thick black leather clothes, masked like highwaymen.

"Nah then, Mr. Molewood!" The tallest of the men called in a heavy Yorkshire accent. "Whot yer up t'? Care t' talk business? I've got nowt to do today 'cept this reaver work that needs your help to be done right."

"Lord in heaven, protect us!" Mrs. Chudrakes shrieked.

Lizzie choked back what might be heard as a womanish scream. A jolt of fear wrenched her belly. An invasion of thieves at Primrose Hill was not in the plan. Rather, varlets hired by Merryboy were to invade the Bloomsbury House, to take everything Molewood hadn't stolen from himself.

From the look of shock on Molewood's face, this was decidedly not another instance of the man robbing himself.

41
Reavers

— LIZZIE —

TUESDAY AFTERNOON

"TIE THEM UP," THE tall leader commanded of the two men in masks at his side. He dangled a handful of leather fetters.

Lizzie felt wild elation as soon as she identified Perry's voice. She checked Molewood's reaction, hoping he did not recognize Perry. But the invaders wore leather face masks that showed only their eyes. And long black locks flowed from under Perry's hat. Even his mother wouldn't recognize him.

Perry came to steal what Molewood stole from himself! Why didn't he tell me about this plan?

"This is an outrage!" Lizzie cried out, feeling it imperative to protest amid the tumult. Miss Mott had already complained about being swept into the Molewood family affairs. "What have you got me into, Mr. Molewood?"

"Do not touch me!" the imperious Mrs. Chudrakes cried when one of the reavers seized her hands. Her attempts to wrench away were to no avail. "In the name of God—"

"Peace, woman," Perry growled. "Does not your Good Book command a woman to learn in silence with all subjection?"

Molewood said, "Be patient, Mother. I shall handle this."

"Aye, ye will be the hero," Perry said. "Tie up the pretty one with the master of the house."

He gestured that Lizzie should be bound with Molewood.

"No," Molewood cried. "Do not insult this good woman's morals. Place her with my mother."

"I prefer not," his mother said. Then she adjusted the horror she'd let show. "We are not well acquainted. I won't be bound with a stranger."

The grandma said, "I don't mind if you tie me with Enoch's boy. He's a good man."

Diggory, although not warned about this complication, remained calm. "Thank you for believing that of me, Yaya." He offered his hands up to the closest man holding fetters.

"He's an infernal papist!" Mrs. Chudrakes cried, her subsequent words muffled as a reaver bent over her, tying her wrists. Apparently, the new jeopardy had not overwhelmed her revulsion to Diggory.

"God has forgiven far more significant transgressions," said the grandmother, who'd declared her alliance with her new-found great-grandson. "Surely it's only a misunderstanding. This lad shows no sign of having been thrown out of God's company and the promise of heaven. And wasn't the disciple Peter the first pope? Hence, Peter must have been Catholic, or he couldn't be called a pope or a saint."

Perry shook a finger at the tiny old lady. "Learn in silence with subjection, madam."

Molewood said, "Get on with robbing me, and stop alarming these women."

"Rob you?" Perry stood over Molewood, hands on his hips. "You distress me, sir. But if you insist, I shall command my lads to do as you ask." He motioned to the masked reavers. "The master of the house wants you to rob him. You must please follow his command."

What is Perry up to?

"You fiend!" Molewood cried.

Perry pointed a finger at him. "All you possess is insured, is it not? No matter what these men help themselves to, you'll claim insurance. Unless there's a problem making a claim a second time for goods you already claimed were stolen."

Bright scarlet with anger, Molewood threatened to have the king's men after them. Perry laughed.

Lizzie made her voice quaver with fear, though she believed the real Prudence to be made of sterner stuff. "Mr. Molewood is a good man. Born of godly people. He would never cheat or rob."

Molewood turned to her, his face perspiring. He was violently red with anger, yet the edges of his lips were white with fear. "Thank you, dear lady, but—"

"If your ladylove says you are godly," Perry said, "far be it for me to castigate you for transgressions she is willing to overlook. I'm inclined to leave guilt and judgment as a private matter between a man and his God."

"Such perjury!" Lizzie exclaimed. "And you a robber."

"I believe you mean blasphemy, madam," Perry said. "And we shall only rob Mr. Molewood because he commanded us to do so. He and I have other business. And we must proceed without interruption." He motioned to his lads. "Gag them. Except for my friend Wolfric."

"I pray," Diggory said, "we only have to pray to God and endure a few moments together in silence."

He and his yaya chatted happily, disregarding all around them, until the reavers made speech impossible.

—

Once bound and gagged, Lizzie gave Mr. Molewood her best beseeching and vulnerable look, even though Prudence Mott had never let anyone think she was a beggar. Or helpless.

Perry rubbed his hands, relishing this. "Now, my dear friend Wolfric. You will call me Robin, since you are joining my band of merry men. Perhaps they'll write a ballad for us."

"We have no business together in this world, sirrah."

"You distress me with such denials. I have it on good authority that you are the prime example of a London man who seizes new business opportunities."

"What do you know of business?" Molewood bravely scoffed. "You've brought a dozen robbers into my house."

"It's only six of us inside. The others are outside. But we're only reavers, like the old-time Scotsmen, robbing the men who robbed them last year."

"I've never robbed any man. I certainly never robbed you. I don't know you, sirrah."

"Let us say 'cheat,' then, I'm sure we can find a score of men in London who know for certain that you cheated them. Another four score who have guessed it. And a hundredfold who were struck on their blind side."

Lizzie enjoyed watching Perry at work. She'd only witnessed it once before, when he'd taught them how to plunder the house of a bad man. Her enjoyment this day was enhanced by the perpetual evil looks from Mrs. Chudrakes.

Molewood cherished his own indignation. "You know nothing about me that could give you reason to call calumny on me. Or upon my reputation as an honorable businessman."

Perry laughed as if Molewood had shared a jest. "Even if I knew only that a Puritan boy came to London and got rich off his dada's money, then I'd know that plenty of men were cheated along the way."

"I shall not debate this with you." Molewood turned his head—he couldn't turn his body away—and gave a haughty toss of his chin. "Take what you will and go. I shall have no truck with a picaroon who tortures women."

"I say again, we are not robbers. I shall, however, claim to be ruthless. I needed to call you here, in the presence of all your women, so that I might enjoy your full attention."

"Call me here?" Molewood's periwig shook with his astonishment. "You blackguard! You lured Miss Mott here with that false note."

"And managed to get your attention, didn't I? Now, you will cooperate with our business to avoid losing that which you treasure most." He grinned broadly when Molewood shuddered. "You see, we have at our mercy your greatest treasure."

"Do not harm these women!" Molewood cried.

"Ah, as I guessed, you are the sort of lover and son who will protect his women." Perry took up Mrs. Chudrakes' embroidery scissors and snipped a lock of each woman's hair. He folded the three locks into the note that brought Prudence Mott here, then tucked it into Molewood's waist coat. "Carry this near your heart, Wolfric, so you remember with each heartbeat what's at stake."

"You fiend!" Wolfric pulled away from Perry's touch. "I will not commit crimes for you."

Mrs. Chudrakes seemed about to choke in her efforts to express her anger. One of the reavers shook a finger, admonishing her to silence.

Perry tipped his head, studying Molewood. "You object, Wolfric? Let's ask Miss Mott what she thinks." He tugged Lizzie's gag free. "If my friend Wolfric's new crime will free you, will you admonish him to commit yet another transgression against society and the king's law?"

Lizzie coughed. "No, Mr. Molewood. Prove that you are a good man. Do not sully your soul with a crime for my sake."

Perry said, "Should he agree to my scheme if I promise that your friend Wolfric won't be caught in any wrongdoing?"

Molewood perked up. "I would, to protect these ladies."

Lizzie shook her head. "No, Mr. Molewood. One must do right for its own sake, not out of fear of punishment. You must not do as he asks if it will sully your soul."

"There you have it, Wolfric," Perry said. "If you feel unsullied, then you are free to do as I ask. Though if you refuse to do so, I cannot control these men if they are not paid as promised. Though, I suspect they'll leave your mother unharmed. She's a bit dry for their tastes. Not nearly as tempting as Miss Mott."

"Gadzooks!" Molewood writhed with anger. "You cannot harm this lady. You pestilential hellhound! You accursed fiend!"

"Such strong language, Wolfric! And they say you were raised in the ways of righteousness. Now, you'll be wanting to ask what crimes you must commit to prevent transgressions against the women you love."

Molewood didn't look as if he'd entirely agreed to his tormenter's demands. But what Mrs. Chudrakes tried to squeal must be understood as *Do! Do!*

"First, Wolfric, we'll return together to the Mercers' Hall. For our first mutual crime, you'll ask the guard to hand over the investors' cheques for you to hold. Then you'll sit through the Venetians' meeting and offer a surety for an insurance bond, which I will supply to you. After the other investors have departed, my men will enter the meeting chamber and you'll surrender that paper horde to me."

"Then you'll rob me, as well as my fellow investors."

"To all appearances. But after that event, I shall release your women and return your own banker's draft. So, the day will not be a loss to you as it will be to the other men."

"That's it?" Molewood seemed struck at the simplicity of the crime he was to commit. "You want me to steal from my friends and business associates?"

"We're taking the syndicate's money and sharing it between us, you and I." Perry said. "They're rich men who can always find new money, so they won't be destitute. Most important, they won't know you took their money."

"It's not…It's not…" Molewood turned to Lizzie. "This isn't the kind of man I am, Prudence. You must believe me."

Lizzie made her eyes as wide as she could. Mimed the best possible chin quiver.

I know what kind of man you are. We studied you deeply.

Lizzie said to Molewood, "Nothing these bad men force you to do can possibly change my feelings for you, sir, even if they rob you of my own money." At that, Perry tugged Lizzie's gag back in place.

I will always despise you to depths you cannot conceive.

"Bless you, Prudence. When that horde is taken from me, I shall return my own banker's draft to you."

"So kind, but—" The gag was over Lizzie's mouth before she could offer more false flattery.

"Prudence, does this mean"—

Lizzie cried out as the gag was tied.

"Do not hurt her!" Molewood cried.

"Nay," Perry said. "I shall treat her as my sister. If I had any. How will you treat her?"

"As the most blessed among women. Will you promise, Prudence, that you will be mine, no matter what happens? That we shall tie our fortune and fates together?"

Lizzie whimpered like a frightened woman should.

Gadzooks! You won't get Prudence's land. And all this belongs to Diggory after Tom hauls his case through chancery.

Molewood dropped to his knees. "All that I do today will be for your sake, my dear lady."

Oh, it will, sir. It will.

Perry nudged Molewood.

"Let's be on our way, Wolfric. I'll explain the details on the way. Oh, and you'll want to return here tonight with new servants, since the ones from this house have all taken new positions since we arrived."

Mrs. Chudrakes screeched behind her gag.

"I'd find it embarrassing," Perry said, "to learn how little coin it takes for a servant to choose another master."

Perry has freed Tia Angelina!

All the tension left Lizzie's body. The bonds on her wrists loosened. As she wiggled her fingers, she denied in her own mind that she'd feared failure. Yet she hadn't known until that moment the burden of trepidation she carried for Tia Angelina and Diggory.

I don't fear for myself or the day's plan. Or whatever all of the day's plan proves to be.

"Never let it be said," Perry seemed happy with the progress of his day, "that the milk of kindness doesn't flow in my veins, left from nursing at my mother's breast. Comrades, take off their gags when I'm gone. Let them chat while waiting for Mr. Molewood to conclude our business in London. Give them water or a tisane every hour. And take anyone to the necessary if they ask."

The mantel clock struck two as Perry, having a firm hold on Molewood's bound hands, led him from the room. Molewood had cocked his head to listen to the explanation of the crime he was to commit.

The front door was left open, which allowed a cold wind inside. Countess also found her way inside the house and burrowed her nose in Lizzie's lap, ecstatic at the reunion.

Perry's voice was lost for a moment, then in the yard, his voice echoed back through the open door.

"Do you sing, Mr. Molewood? We can entertain ourselves with ballads to make the time fly. Do you know the Robin Hood song? Won't that be appropriate?"

His deep voice echoed over the sound of the carriage wheels until all was lost in the distance.

But Robin Hood so gentle was,
And bore so brave a mind,
If any in distress did pass,
To them he was so kind
That he would give and lend to them,
To help them at their need:
This made all poor men pray for him,
And wish he well might speed.

When the carriage could no longer be heard, the reavers at Shiloh House removed gags, first releasing Lizzie.

As soon as she could speak, Lizzie said, "Would you be so kind as to poke up the fire? And please make sure the other ladies have adequate shawls against the cold."

"My Diggory is keeping me warm." The grandmother displayed no sign of fright at all from the reavers' attack.

When the gag was taken from Mrs. Chudrakes, she immediately launched a host of Biblical invectives. Rather, Lizzie guessed that her diatribe came from the Bible, though the stream of words were to condemn rather than save souls. The reavers complained about having to play nursemaid to haughty, scolding women.

"Where I grew up," said the reaver who stood over Mrs. Chudrakes, "the elders liked to dunk a scold. Just pointing to the cucking stool made for peace in the village."

Another said, "In my village, the precisionists used the scold's bridle. That's what my gran'fa said whenever he tired of his wife and her sisters haranguing him."

"When we have a Protestant king again," the first said, "perhaps he'll bring back the old ways."

"It's a queen we'll have then," the second reaver replied, "as soon as the papist one runs to the French king for safety. And he will, you know. It's what they all say."

Another reaver in leather came inside the house. He bent to cut the ties on Lizzie's wrist, though she had nearly worked her hands free.

"I'm to take Miss Mott to London, to help ensure Mr. Molewood does the right thing."

But Perry wants me to be far away when the gambol unwinds.

"I cannot go," Lizzie protested. "These women have no servants or transport. I must stay to care for them."

The grandmother beamed. The mother scowled.

"I'll stay," Diggory said. "I'll be sure they are safe. After all, they are my family."

That is also not the plan.

Countess danced around the reaver and followed when he led Lizzie out of the house.

"I'm rather tired, Lizzie. Can I convince you not to complain about riding down to the inn where I have a carriage waiting? I know that neither you nor the horse will enjoy it."

This was definitely not the plan.

"As Perry and Tom advised, I'm not supposed to be in London on the day of the gambol. For my own protection."

"Yet, I know you, Lizzie. You'd give two drams of your own heart's blood to see Molewood's expression when your gambol succeeds. That's why I made Perry change his mind about what's best for you."

Rowland mounted one of the reavers' horses, then held his hand down to her. "Up you come, Miss Foxe. You must suffer on your way to rejoicing. But it's only until we retrieve the carriage you left at the inn."

42
Thereby Hangs a Tale

— NED —

TUESDAY LATE AFTERNOON

IN EXACTLY THE WAY his sister's plan specified, one of the hired knights of the post took Ned's place at the meeting room door. This new man was the right height and, mayhap, with his leather helmet and large neckcloth, no one would notice he had red hair. On a positive note, the man's beard looked genuine.

From the day's experience, Ned had another assurance that no one would notice the replacement: no one had paid attention to the guards by the door.

Ned covertly handed the new guard the packets of banker's drafts. "The packet count is fourteen. Make sure of that whenever anyone demands to see what you hold. Count again at the moment you hand them to the men's treasurer."

Then Ned took his place beside one of the mercenaries who guarded the inside of the meeting room. Now sans beard and with a leather helm, Ned felt the prospect of joy in performing the coming tasks. However, the leather suit remained too tight, which Ned seldom experienced from his clothes, as he was among the narrowest of men in England.

A few minutes before four o'clock, a gaggle of men returned from the dining chamber to the meeting room. All seemed in the best of moods, but then Lizzie had insisted on spending coin for good wine. Two men returned through the front door, followed by Viscount Orlando, who had gained a leather-clad guard as a footman. Orlando did not hail any of the men he passed, did not glance at any servants or guards.

"*Hola,* Viscount Orlando!" Hawksmoor called. They fell into deep discussion. The topic seemed to be a series of guesses about when the Dover Road might again allow travel.

Molewood was the last to return, accompanied now by a tall, brawny guard with long black locks and the kind of raggedy, wispy beard one saw on forlorn Cambridge scholars. His long black coat, buttoned up tight, made the fellow appear massive and threatening, as if Molewood required the most severe of men to protect him.

And who winked at Ned.

Zooterkins! Ned had known the man nigh on six months. The longest they'd been apart since the day they met was for the duration of the Bristol journey. Ned felt in his heart, in his head, at the bottom of his shoes, that by now, he would recognize Perry when his little finger came into sight, even before the rest of the man entered through the door.

Molewood's voice rose, creating a ruckus. "I was chosen as banker for this syndicate. I shall hold the investors' drafts."

The guard argued for one of the Venetians to confirm this. Lorenzo materialized. "It's true," he said. "Signor Molewood is the banker for the Albion-Byzantium Company investors."

As if reluctant, the guard fished that packet from deep inside his thick leather vest. "There's fourteen, by my count when men passed them to me before your dinner." He counted them out into Molewood's hand. "Do all you gentlemen agree that I delivered all fourteen?" He glanced among the men who stood near, which included Lord Hawksmoor, who strongly agreed the count was correct.

"I see mine at the top," Hawksmoor said. "Let me inspect it, and I will confirm all is well."

After Hawksmoor showed his banker's draft to the others gathered around, Molewood put the packet inside his waistcoat, patting the bulge it created in the line of his Puritan vest and coat.

When the other men continued into the waiting room, Perry waved an admonishing finger at Molewood. He spoke in a low voice, "It's all over in the next half hour, my friend. Then you will be free to rescue your ladylove. Mayhap, she will give her hero her heart."

As the afternoon script played out, the clock on the wall tracked the minutes, yet Ned felt sure it mysteriously ticked several extra minutes, advancing too slowly toward the plan's zero hour, not just the fifteen minutes allowed for this last act of Lizzie's gambol.

The men had gathered around the table in the front of the chamber, taking turns signing the participation agreement.

"Have we seen the new insurance commitment?" Hawksmoor commanded attention, once again amazing Ned that Lizzie had made him her puppet.

A few men murmured that they too wondered; others muttered that it wasn't worth holding up the proceedings.

Perry dug a finger into Molewood's side. Molewood jerked, took a false step forward, almost stumbling before Perry caught him. Molewood took a packet from inside his coat and showed it around the room. His eyes darted around the room, seeming to land on Mercutio, standing to the side with his Venetian brothers.

Molewood said, "I will fund a greater insurance bond. I do this because I believe so strongly in this venture."

"How much surety?" Hawksmoor asked.

"Three hundred pounds, as a draft from my banker." Molewood showed Hawksmoor the draft.

Ned didn't think he imagined it, but Molewood's hands seemed to be shaking. The man was much paler than he had seemed just days earlier. Whatever Perry did to threaten the man was all well and good, but Ned felt the need to also begin trembling, given that the clock was counting down the minutes, while all the players were not yet present.

Hawksmoor inspected the banker's draft. Rather than handing the packet back to Molewood, he laid it on the table near the pile of signed agreements from the participants.

A voice from the gaggle of men beside the table asked, "Lord Hawksmoor, are you satisfied now? Or shall you withdraw your participation?"

"The insurance bond is sufficient," Hawksmoor said, "but I have not seen the commitment from the king's customs house."

"Why does it matter?" Mr. Cokayne muttered. "It's not as if we need to offer a bribe. We aren't bringing in African goods."

A few men agreed, but not all. Rowland and Perry had both claimed that Cokayne was an idiot, likely from birth.

Hawksmoor said, "Without a pre-voyage customs declaration, this venture with the Albion-Byzantium Company presents too much risk for my tastes. I'm just a poor country gentleman."

Ned didn't laugh, though he knew Hawksmoor to be among the richest of Cambridgeshire's landed gentry.

Mercutio said, in a thick Italian accent, "I beg you to wait, signore. The assurances you want are at hand."

Three minutes behind the day's schedule, by the clock in the chamber, a commotion arose with the guard. It was Sir Bythorn, thank the gods of Olympus, at last demanding entry.

Mercutio went to the door to greet him.

"*Ciao, signore.* This is a private meeting. Who do you seek?"

"I'm an invited participant in this investment opportunity." Sir Bythorn squeaked in his high thin voice. "Here's my invitation. The king's business kept me from joining you until now."

Lorenzo came over, with better English than Mercutio. "Do you intend to participate in this venture?"

"I have my banker's draft." Sir Bythorn waved a packet he'd retrieved from his waistcoat pocket.

Lorenzo received the packet, then handed it to Molewood. "If you are here to participate, there's still time to sign the agreement. We regret missing your presence earlier."

"Sir Bythorn?" Hawksmoor mused over the man's name. "Are you not from the customs commission?"

"Yes, your lordship." Sir Bythorn bowed low. Ned judged it to be fawning. "I serve on the king's customs commission."

"Then are you the man we've been waiting for?" Hawksmoor asked. Sir Bythorn might be fawning, but Ned judged his Cambridgeshire neighbor to be needlessly friendly. But then, Ned had no idea of what script Lizzie had given the man.

Yet Ned felt satisfied that, as the clock chimed the quarter hour, neither Molewood nor Sir Bythorn perceived what was happening. Sir Bythorn, however, was murmuring with Mercutio and Lorenzo, all of them standing close to Mr. Molewood.

"With which of you am I to exchange the details for the requested customs clearance?" Sir Bythorn held another packet that he'd produced from his pocket.

"I accept, signore." Mercutio held out a hand to receive it.

Hawksmoor said, "May we all see it?"

Several men gathered close to peer over Hawksmoor's shoulder as he read. The Earl of Gomfrey seemed most eager to have a glimpse of the letter.

Hawksmoor shook his head, then cleared his throat. "May I ask that the participants be left to discuss this for a few moments? If we are to unite, we need a minute to confer."

Ned glanced at the clock.

A minute was about all they had.

Lorenzo agreed and became busy herding guards and footmen and brothers from the room. The disguised Perry was herded out alongside Ned, abandoning his grasp on Molewood.

The meeting room door was not yet closed. While Ned was being herded away from that room, Ned heard Hawksmoor declaring a possible loss of faith.

"I'm tempted to demand the return of my banker's draft. All the customs declaration from Sir Bythorn offers is a belief that the goods will not come from Africa."

Then there was a knocking at the front door of the Mercers' Hall. No, more of a banging than a knocking.

Zooterkins! This was too soon for the next act. They had too few minutes to clear out. But then Perry pulled shut the door of their room, and the Venetians, servants, and guards were all pressed into their next act.

"You know the way out, gentlemen." The so-called Gratiano spoke without an Italian accent. "Get away quickly."

—

The way out involved people rapidly tiptoeing down the servants' stairs to the kitchen. Hired servants and guards who had no concept of a gambol were paid off and sent packing, including the chef who'd served the previous king. The actors, however, left in pairs, walking down the malodorous alley to Ironmongers' Lane, then dashing to the next corner. Perry directed people to the corner where they were to turn and find carriages.

Lazarus had, of course, hired enough carriage drivers to be waiting to take actors along various routes to Drury Lane. It was raining again, so the packed carriages smelled of wet sheep. Once the carriages stopped and doors opened, Ned felt they all fell to the street like clumps of sugar broken off a loaf.

By then, rain was bucketing down. A handful of people knew the destination and led the others to the warehouse. When the doors closed, most inside were too wet to get warm quickly.

Lanterns were lit, but the large space swallowed half the light. And the room soon smelled of wet sheep.

Felicity Oakes stood on a barrel and commanded people to remove their gambol costumes and get into dry clothes, which proved to be threadbare theatre costumes. People followed her orders to pack their wet costumes in barrels. The actors who played at being guards, like Ned, had the hardest time stripping, since leather stuck to skin.

Felicity began peeling off her velvet Italian suit, stripping down to chemise and drawers. She caught Ned watching her.

"Look away if you must." she said. "We're all players here, and a player knows to strip and dress for the next cue, before the curtain raises." She then pulled over her head a dusty and badly creased gown in a light purple color called Pansy. She tucked up the trailing hems at her hips and then was busy closing the barrel into which she'd stuffed the wet Italianate costume.

A short, roundish fellow stood on the barrel and shouted, "I am the maestro today. We have been rehearsing *As You Like It* for the Earl of Marborne's birthday feast. You'll have to share scripts. I'll point out your parts as we go." He pointed to Ned. "You are Duke Senior. Start with Act II since we've been at this since noon."

Ned shared a script with Neriah Frake, now in a hodge-podge of a costume. He found the place and began reading.

> Now, my co-mates and brothers in exile,
> Hath not old custom made this life more sweet…

When Ned finished his first lines, Tom whispered, "But where's our Orlando and his bodyguard?"

"They say," Perry spoke, "the viscount has left England."

"I mean," Tom whispered, "where are they really?"

Perry said, "They were right beside Ned in the meeting room. Didn't you follow them out?"

Lazarus pulled at Perry's arm. The rail-thin butler stood only as high as Perry's elbow. "The Earl of Marborne told he'd be discarding his Orlando court suit and returning to the hall with a quartet of king's men."

"Ah," Perry said, "sorting goats from sheep among a dozen transgressors to the Crown."

"With Lizzie too?" Alarmed, Ned spoke louder than a whisper. "But we all agreed that she—"

The little maestro clapped his hands. "Your attention please, gentlemen, to the task at hand."

The task was to provide cover for everyone, so they could never be associated with the day's events. But who most needed to not be associated with this gambol? The pair who had chosen to stay behind.

The dread beating of Ned's heart lasted through the rehearsal. Ned had to be reminded of his turn to read a speaking part. If any asked, he couldn't tell you the name of the character he'd been assigned.

Long after his heart had beaten a deep hollow in Ned's breast, Lazarus showed a note to Perry, who then grabbed Ned's elbow and led him away, weaving through the rehearsing actors, to a back door that led to a narrower alley than the one that took them to the warehouse.

"We have an invitation to supper," Perry said. "But we should warm ourselves mean time."

That led to a calm reckoning at The Rose tavern, drinking hot ale and waiting for supper time.

43
Housework

— LIZZIE —

TUESDAY EVENING

LATE THAT AFTERNOON, LIZZIE'S favorite moments played out like the concerto she'd heard at the duke's palace in November: slow, quick, slow.

The theme of this afternoon's concerto began when Poynter, Lord Hawksmoor, asked the merchants and their servants to leave the room. Molewood started, surprised that his captor followed the Venetians from the room. Lizzie lingered by the wall near where Viscount Orlando stood, hoping she correctly imitated the posture she'd seen Perry take when he most wanted to be invisible.

While the last of the Venetian crew departed the meeting room, a small, dapper man entered with a liveried servant behind him. He hung in the back, waiting patiently as Molewood delivered a speech to assert that he was providing the surety bond personally for the Venetians' voyage.

When Molewood paused to allow the investors to discuss insurance and customs declarations, the newly arrived man stepped forward. He must have known Molewood on sight, because he walked up to the man directly.

"Mr. Molewood, I am Josselin Kidwelly."

Molewood glanced at the man, not comprehending for two breaths what had been said, then frowning deeply.

"I'm sorry, sir," Molewood said. "I met another man earlier who introduced himself as Kidwelly, a solicitor."

"That's what I've come to speak to you about. I had a message from Mr. Simon Touchstone, an art dealer in Threadneedle Street. You know the man?"

"Yes, I—"

"He bade me seek you out with dire news. He has learned that the woman introduced to you as Miss Prudence Mott is a charlatan. Because I am Miss Mott's guardian, Mr. Touchstone asked me to warn you, so that you are not deceived any further by that impostor."

Lizzie wanted to carry forever in her memory a catalog of images: how Molewood's hands tremored at his sides; his lips parting as if to speak when he had no words; his bushy brows climbing up to that devil's peak at his hairline. His eyes darted but found nothing upon which to rest his gaze.

Don't look at me, sir. I'm just Orlando's leather-clad footman.

The clock struck one note for the quarter-hour, which meant that time pressed, leaving Lizzie mere seconds to enjoy Molewood's discomfort, which she'd relate to Prudence in detail.

Poynter, playing his part as perfectly as might be expected of him, interrupted that side conversation. "Gentlemen, if we are agreed, I shall fetch our gracious hosts back to tell them we are satisfied. Viscount Orlando, will you please come with me?"

Of course, Orlando's footman had to follow. The trio found that other chamber was empty except for the stack of signed agreements to participate in the Albion-Byzantium Company.

"Parting is sweet sorrow, my love," Rowland said.

"But I want—"

"You can only return to that room as a footman." He kissed her forehead. "And you don't want to miss a moment. Go back with Poynter."

"Come, Lizzie," Poynter said. "You'll have the best seat for viewing the play you authored."

Back in the meeting room, a pestiferous clock warned that they had scarcely minutes to conclude the gambol. Poynter carried the signed agreements back from the other room. He held them aloft.

"Gentlemen, the Venetians have gone. That room is empty."

Men stood up swiftly. Chairs crashed to the floor. Sir Bythorn rushed to the door, as if to see for himself. The room was empty, not even Orlando was there. The hatchet-faced customs man let out a screech, a high-pitched wail.

Molewood didn't seem to notice that he gripped the sleeve of Prudence's solicitor. He still held it when he struck his breast in surprise.

Isn't he happy to have lost his reaver of a Robin Hood?

Poynter said, "Whatever is happening, I suggest each man claim his signed paper. Mr. Molewood, please return every man's draft on his bank."

Thus began the concerto's second part, played with gusto.

Molewood only then realized he had hold of Mr. Kidwelly. He released the solicitor and moved about the room to distribute the cheque packets to each man, verifying the name written on its wrapper. He was acquainted with all these men, so each knew they were receiving the correct packet. When he stopped near the door, holding out Orlando's packet, but not finding the viscount. While he looked around, Lizzie snatched a button from the skirt of Molewood's coat, wanting a trophy, like a country huntsman.

Brass, not gold. Yet I enjoy the threads hanging from your coat.

Molewood didn't open his packet, being too busy looking over his shoulder at Solicitor Kidwelly. He missed seeing each investor open his own packet to find a blank piece of paper.

Sir Bythorn cried out, "Rotten larceny!" Then every one of the investors was shouting.

I've now heard every expletive that men might make in English.

That noise brought Molewood to look down and open the three packets still in his possession. First, the one from Miss Mott. It contained a blank sheet.

Then, Orlando's. Another blank sheet.

Then his own. A banker's draft wafted to the floor.

Perry had warned Molewood about this. Except Perry said Molewood's participation in the theft wouldn't be discovered while the investors were present.

Molewood turned ghostly white. Then the blood rushed back to his face so rapidly, and the man's eyes bulged so, that Lizzie feared an apoplexy.

If I'd planned it, before he met Mr. Kidwelly, Molewood would find Prudence's funds lost and still be worrying about the captives on Primrose Hill. Still, all glory to Perry's neat trick.

Poynter cried, "What is the meaning of this, Molewood?"

Before Molewood could find his voice, the clock struck the hour. A heavy banging struck the door.

"Open in the name of the king!"

—

"We have a warrant to seize members of a syndicate called Hawkins' Heirs," the redcoats' leader said.

Oh good, scare everyone! Wait, Valentine Starbuck. How?

She smothered her surprise, but most men were so startled that they gripped each other's arms, their faces startled, and voices a chorus of dismay.

Poynter stepped forward. "This must be a mistake. I am Poynter, Lord Hawksmoor. This is a meeting of investors in the Albion-Byzantium Company, which is not a secret syndicate. I for one have never invested in the syndicate you named."

"And I came on a different matter," Mr. Kidwelly said. "I'm a solicitor, not a participant here."

Poynter said, "If you intend to arrest anyone, it should be the merchants called Le Casa Mercantile del Fratelli Gratiano. They have defrauded us."

The men in the room shuffled while calling out support for that notion. The Earl of Gomfrey dug his long, skinny finger into Molewood's waistcoat and said, "Wolfric Molewood is part of the fraud."

Molewood thrust away the earl's finger, his elbow smacking Sir Bythorn, who seemed to want to huddle close to his brother.

Captain Starbuck said, "The warrant cites Mr. Wolfric Molewood and Sir Bythorn Chudrakes, who fostered insurance and customs fraud for that syndicate. Are they here?"

Molewood and Sir Bythorn couldn't avoid being pushed forward. The redcoats searched them, finding letters and papers. Sir Bythorn carried a heavy purse with what must be thirty guineas.

> *I find these brothers' despair as amusing as the best Twelfth Night mummers.*

Molewood stood like a trapped animal, his eyes darker than night, hooded like a buzzard. His winged brows rose as far as his devilish widow's peak, and that pointed beard seemed to show twin trails of smoke streaming from the fire raging inside.

"Do you know who I am?" Sir Bythorn demanded.

"We do," Captain Starbuck said. "It appears from this," he rattled the purse and waved the papers from Chudrakes' pocket, "that you have betrayed your office and accepted bribes."

His shovel-square jaw jutted with each word he spoke while Sir Bythorn kept trying to explain in that creepy, high-pitched voice. His knife-blade nose turned red with rage. Lizzie had been hoping for pure fear.

I can hardly wait to describe this scene for Ned.

Starbuck gestured for his men to take charge of the two, then waved for them to depart. "If that's all we find today, I hope the magistrate and the king will be satisfied until we learn more."

With that, Starbuck followed his men and their captives, leaving only the noise and bustle of the men left behind, all rushing to get to the door. Lizzie looked to Poynter, but he hadn't yet recognized her and remained focused on the meeting room door.

That's disappointing. The duke agreed to take all the investors as a sort of tribute to the king.

The door banged open again to admit a latecomer.

—

After the king's men left with Molewood and Sir Bythorn, Rowland stepped into the meeting room and held up his hand for attention. He wore what must be a brand-new suit that Lizzie hadn't seen in his closet before. Made of a shiny, floral-patterned brocade, it was pure black, including the lining and dozens of cloth-covered buttons, and cut to a narrower form than the other men. Also, he wore no wig; his chestnut hair was tied back with a leather thong, one of the fetters from that house on Primrose Hill.

Lizzie had never seen him so well dressed.

Or perhaps it's only the glow from our day's success.

Poynter raised his voice. "Gentlemen, this is the Earl of Marborne. He's my friend and an honorable man. Please give him your attention."

Rowland spoke softly, so that his audience had to hush each other to hear. "Those arrests occurred because the king tasked the Duke of Bagsham with identifying the investors in the Marquess of Withersea's secret syndicate. The duke came to me when it was proved that the *Skylark* transgressed on the Royal

African monopoly." Rowland paused, since several men were busy whispering to each other.

Poynter said, "But did not the king give you the *Skylark* as a reward for revealing Withersea as a traitor who helped fund Monmouth's invasion?"

Anyone who is surprised has to be a pudding-headed fellow.

Rowland took a paper from the cuff of his coat, shaking it with a modest flourish.

"I will reveal to you gentlemen that I hold the Marquess of Withersea's original list of the Hawkins' Heirs syndicate."

That simple statement swept the room as if a door had been opened to a storm. Lizzie couldn't conceive of when she had admired him more, and not just because he was about to conquer the enemies of the *Skylark's* passengers.

"However," he held up a hand for silence, "upon my honor, I have no inclination to destroy your lives."

Indeed. I resolved to take only their money. I have that now.

"Will we suffer only extortion then?" Lord Didlington asked. "You'll extract payments for our protection?"

"I'd like to beg off extortion," the foolish Mr. Cokayne said. "I lost more than I can afford today."

"Nay," Rowland said. "I will not give your name to the king, merely because you participated in a scheme that crossed the Royal African Company's monopoly."

A collective sigh passed through the room. Lizzie, however, held her breath, because she still wanted more from these men. Rowland seemed about to satisfy that wish.

"I won't give to the king any man's name who will meet one condition," Rowland said.

"Then you do intend extortion." Lord Didlington huffed and crossed his arms as if offended.

As if you have a right to be affronted, you swingebeest.

"Call it whatever you wish." Rowland sounded his most affable self. "I know that each of you bought indentures for servants who came to England on the *Skylark*. Send those servants to St Martin-in-the-Fields tomorrow night when the church bells ring five o'clock. Ensure they have their indenture papers in hand and provide them with warm cloaks or blankets."

Lizzie let out the breath she'd held, careful not to move or attract attention.

Lambkin! You've done that for which I had only half a plan.

"That's all?" Mr. Cokayne asked. "You want nothing more than some poorly trained black servants?"

"And then the king won't hear our names?" The Earl of Gomfrey seemed thoughtful, perhaps even peaceful.

Rowland said, "I promise that the king will hear your name in relation to African trade only if you join a new scheme."

"We'd none of us do that." Mr. Cokayne barked a laugh.

"I thought not," Rowland said. "My own lawyer will insist before a magistrate that any man who asserts a claim against the insurance for the *Skylark* must give his name, not hide behind a secret syndicate."

Rowland used too many words making his assertion.

Poynter said, "I believe I'll go home now, since I never invested in the *Skylark's* voyage, nor made any insurance claim. I need of a dram or two of brandy to recover from my losses to the false Venetians."

—

"It's a mawkish ending to a long play," Lizzie said. "The disappointing drama where the last remaining actors describe the real excitement, which concluded off-stage."

In a carriage across the street from Jericho House, she waited with Rowland when red-coated militiamen entered the mansion with a warrant.

Rowland said, "Perry thinks you gave Molewood too much of your attention and didn't allow sufficient opportunity to observe Sir Bythorn facing the results of his transgressions."

She sighed. "Mayhap. But my only regret is that Mr. Molewood does not yet know that Perry's reavers picked over both of his houses and rescued Ishmael."

"Ishmael and I shared a few words on our journey to Primrose Hill," Rowland said. "Do you want me to again describe Ishmael's joy when he met Tia Angelina?"

"If they choose to come to Revelstone House when the weather allows, I hope to travel with them. Aurora and Felicity promised to make them comfortable at Chalgrove House until then." Lizzie glanced out the carriage window again. "I thought I saw the door open. But I suppose the king's militia isn't done inside yet."

"Did Perry's mercenaries leave anything for the militia to find?" Rowland tugged her gently away from the window and held her close, even though they'd celebrated their reunion on the carriage ride from the Primrose Hill inn to Mercers' Hall. He slipped two fingers under the wool scarf he'd wrapped around her when they entered the carriage. He stroked the hollow at Lizzie's throat.

She said, "The mercenaries were instructed to leave only African artifacts, together with all the evidence Tom gathered to show how Molewood perpetrated his many cheats."

"Including, I hope, Molewood's knowledge that Diggory Crackbone is the rightful inheritor of the Molewood fortune." Rowland kissed her fingertips, though Lizzie wore his gloves.

"Aye, though Diggory's greatest joy seemed to be in meeting his grandmother." She seized Rowland's hand to kiss his bare fingers, which were cool. Without having been under her neck wrap, those fingers would likely be icy.

"I suppose," Rowland said, "this scene feels mawkish because we cannot witness Molewood seeing his empty house. Shall we go to Sir Bythorn's residence now? The king's men should finish there soon."

"No," she said. "I obtained sufficient joy in seeing his face at the moment of capture."

"Then the next stop for the evening is Hawksmoor's house. He invited our cousins and friends to supper."

"How kind of him. Can we please stop at your house first, Rollo? I can't bear wearing breeches a moment longer."

The carriage driver had complained twice about having to walk his horse to stave off cold while idling by the square in Bloomsbury. He was happy to hitch his horse again and deliver them to Xanthus House.

With the carriage in motion, Rowland used his kerchief to wipe away what remained of Lizzie's makeup and untied the leather fetter to let her hair loose. Then he kissed her, the way they liked to kiss while riding in a carriage in the dark.

44
All's Well

— NED —

TUESDAY NIGHT

IN THE FOYER OF Lord Hawksmoor's narrow house, the butler relieved Ned and Perry of their cloaks.

"Most guests have arrived, gentlemen. We still await Miss Foxe and the Earl of Marborne."

The butler led them up to the dining hall, which held a long, narrow table with scarce space behind each chair for servants to pass as they brought hot punch to the guests.

Lord Hawksmoor greeted them in the dining hall. "I'm so very happy to have you here."

Michael, Felicity, and Winwood Oakes sat along one side of the table. Ned took a place at the end on the other side. Perry sat beside him, with Tom at his other hand.

Ned faced a fresco of an English countryside. Ah, it was the Hawksmoor estates. Truly, Hawksmoor should have asked for Ned's help, since he could have done a much better job. Landscapes came as easily to Ned as tying his shoe. Or hanging his coat on a hook. Or feeding the barn cats. Ned would be spending all of supper seeking ways to improve that landscape.

"We're also happy to be here," Tom said, "though surprised. How did you come to be involved in Lizzie's gambol?"

"I could ask the same of each of you," Hawksmoor said. "But isn't it simple? If Miss Foxe asks, we say yes."

Perry spoke a deeper truth. "Especially after what happened in Bristol." That silenced everyone while they remembered what had spawned the day's work.

Tom stood to offer a toast. "We're none of us arrested. No one took a hurt—except the actors by the Thames. And Lizzie can't get us out of bed tomorrow to do it all again."

Ned nodded, sipped his hot punch, and focused on the unfortunate cow in the fresco's middle foreground.

Perry settled a hand on Ned's knee, but even that didn't shake loose the distraction caused by a cow-filled landscape which was utterly inappropriate in such a narrow room.

After Tom's toast, one servant refilled their cups and another pair set plates before of them: artfully arranged smoked ox tongue, with a small dish of pickled eel in white wine. The butler said, "A tidbit to tide you until dinner."

Hawksmoor excused himself and stepped out of the room.

Once the earl and his servants were gone, Ned asked, "When did the Earl of Hawksmoor come to be involved in Lizzie's gambol? I am still as surprised as a fox that caught a hound."

"We'll have to ask Lizzie." Tom took a bite of pickled eel. "But Poynter is an old friend and an excellent host. I was far more surprised to see Rollo this afternoon. How did he return from Bristol so quickly?"

Noise of a commotion rose from below stairs. Tom, of course, had the gumption to open the door, so they heard Hawksmoor greet Lizzie and Rowland. When the dining hall door opened, Rowland came in first, followed by Hawksmoor.

Lizzie entered, swishing her silk skirts. Her gown, in bright Merry Widow yellow, glowed in the candlelight. Her eyes glistened. This time, it was with joy, unlike the night in Bristol when she'd wept on Ned's shoulder.

Everyone stood as if a single beast to applaud at her entry.

She dipped her head. Her curls shook as she tried to deny their applause. "No, I should congratulate all of you. It is you who are the heroes of the day."

"It's about time you arrived," Tom said. "We were forced to down two rounds of punch while waiting."

Felicity Oakes said, "It's jolly to have another woman join us, Miss Foxe. I've had to play the ingénue in this cast."

"Welcome." Lord Hawksmoor gestured to the two empty chairs by the head of the table.

However, Lizzie jutted her little finger at Tom, who then moved to sit beside Michael, so that Lizzie could sit by Rowland.

"The hot punch is most welcome." Lizzie cradled the cup. "I've had four carriage rides today and rode a mile on horseback. I've been Prudence Mott and Viscount Orlando's footman, all amid people I consider to be my enemies. You must imagine how happy I am to be in a warm room with my true friends."

"Lizzie," Rowland had his arm around her shoulder, "I hope that cup tastes of your grand success."

Hawksmoor said, "I assume you are all starved for nourishment. We'll begin supper now."

—

One servant passed down the table to remove the plates of eel and ox tongue. A second servant poured glasses of pale wine. A third servant placed new plates of chicken fricassee, which Ned decided should be called excellent. The finely chopped chicken had been formed into small meatballs, seasoned with mace and nutmeg, and drowned in white wine. The passing servants temporarily blocked sight of the fresco, except for the wretched fluffy clouds. Cambridgeshire never had clouds like that, if such even existed in nature.

Rowland, with his impeccable manners, swallowed his first few bites and wiped his lips. "I've privately saluted Lizzie for her genius and determination, but I congratulate you all on your success." He tipped his wine glass in salute. "It comes down to following a good plan."

"If only that had happened," Ned said, still perturbed by all the changes made over the past four days. "Lizzie kept adding complications. It's been chaos ever since our Friday night in gaol."

"Wait!" Rowland set his wine glass down so hard, it sloshed over the brim and onto the table. "You were in gaol?"

Tom said, "It's why the gambol was today, not last Friday."

"I'll tell you more, lambkin," Lizzie soothed, "but later. The rest of us already know about that pandemonium."

Rowland was still shaking his head when Felicity said, "It wasn't truly chaos until we lost all the hired actors last night. After the ice broke and sent them tumbling into the Thames, we had to scramble this morning to find new actors."

"What?" Lizzie gasped. "I didn't know."

Michael said, "We learned about it after you'd gone to Primrose Hill. Felicity was the hero of the moment, getting new people ready to play their roles."

"Ned stepped into his role like a gallant knight." Perry moved his hand to Ned's thigh. "He wore a red beard, which didn't really suit him."

Lizzie shook her head. "Ned wasn't supposed to be where anyone might recognize him."

"Desperate times demanded changes," Ned said. "Why do you think Winwood was there?"

"I didn't see Winwood at Mercers' Hall," Lizzie said.

"He played Viscount Orlando while you were at Primrose Hill. He dropped the bribery note for Molewood to find."

"But only a little later," Winwood said, "the other Orlando arrived. So, I left to see what I could do for the actors who fell in the river. I'll have to return tomorrow to make sure no infection or fever has advanced."

Tom said, "You played your part well, my friend."

"Who was the second Orlando?" Lizzie asked.

"It was Rollo," Tom said. "He played the part as if it were written for him."

Ned said, "When Lizzie arrived later in the afternoon, that's when the real chaos began."

"Mayhap, all that chaos was a good thing," Perry said, "not to be complained of."

Ned said, "I don't yet understand how we managed to succeed amid chaotic changes to the plan."

"The infamous plan," Rowland said, "which I never knew."

"It was a simple plan," Lizzie said. "Invite the *Skylark* investors to join in another opportunity. Take their money. Then embarrass them, so they can't pursue the false merchants."

Tom said, "Today's deviations began as soon as Lizzie got out of bed."

"It was you, Tom, who advised I stay away from the gambol," Lizzie said. "So, I went to Primrose Hill with Diggory Crackbone. I wanted to see Mr. Molewood's face when he learned that Diggory was alive, and to allow the false Miss Mott to say goodbye forever amid Molewood's anguish when the militia came."

"When you announced that deviation at breakfast," Perry said, "I felt that you deserved also to see Molewood and Sir Bythorn when they lost their illicit wealth."

"I appreciate your additions, Perry," Lizzie said. "I like how your reaver dismayed Molewood and then made him to suffer as the accused thief. I wish I'd thought of that in the initial plan."

"Parts of the gambol remain mysterious to me," Michael Oakes said, "I don't think I know much, other than printing the investor prospectus and saying my lines at the proper time."

"For my part," Hawksmoor said, "I will never admit outside this room to more than losing my investment. I won't ever confess that I lost nothing."

Tom said, "It was a pleasant day, though, as the restoration came to completion. Molewood was the largest investor in the original syndicate and in the insurance schemes. Years ago, Sir Bythorn began investing more than he could afford, so began soliciting bribes. It was so pleasant, introducing them to justice."

Rowland asked, "How did you get a warrant to send the militia to Chudrakes' house?"

Perry said, "I found his private list of customs bribes, which Tom took to his friend the magistrate."

And that's how you were able to call out Valentine Starbuck and his redcoats?"

"That's how Valentine Starbuck and his militia became involved," Tom said. "The warrant came from Sir Oliver Boxworth, who also helped release Ned and Lizzie from gaol."

"Gaol." Rowland swished his wine again, as if numb with troubling thoughts. "I still want to know."

"Later." Lizzie folded her hand over his.

There was a quiet knock on the door. Hawksmoor motioned for his servants to enter.

—

The servants passed through again, taking away the fricassee plates and setting fresh plates with roasted pike beside a cabbage pie and stewed potatoes. It was a great deal of food for being called supper, but Ned had supped on nothing since the morning's disturbed breakfast. The butler circled the table, pouring more wine, again relieving Ned of the painful image of a badly wrought Cambridgeshire country scene. That sheep in the far distance needed to be sent to perdition along with the ridiculously fat cow.

"Now about the chaos," Hawksmoor said. "Miss Foxe asked me to invest and to suggest Molewood to be our banker. I don't understand how that man managed to steal everyone's money."

Perry patted Ned's shoulder. "I played reaver at Primrose Hill and convinced Molewood under fear for his mother and ladylove to serve as thief of the bankers' cheques. However, Molewood was cheated out of playing rescuing hero to his captured women, because my dear friend Ned managed the switch."

Ned, in the middle of tasting the cabbage pie, had to swallow before he could answer. "Under the original plan, I wasn't to be in the room with the investors. However, the actor who was to play the guard at the door fell in the Thames ice."

Perry said, "Yet, Ned did perform his original job, to walk the streets of London with two knights of the post while visiting six different bankers to redeem the investors' cheques."

Ned said, "It wasn't easy work, because a bag of guineas weighs more than a pocketful of bankers' drafts, although I only went around the corner from one banker to another banker and paid the guineas into our accounts. The trick was to remember the order of banks to visit to redeem cheques and then accounts to name for deposits."

Lizzie said, "I'm sorry you had to do that in rain and sleet."

"Oh, I was hot with fear," Ned said, "and excessively warm in my mercenary's leather. Like cooked bacon in a roll. I borrowed a bankers' messenger to send Molewood's note to Sir Bythorn."

"Stop!" Hawksmoor said. "Sir Bythorn was at Mercers' Hall earlier. I saw him in the other room. That's when he sought a bribe from the Venetian merchants."

"That was..." Tom began, then looked over at Rowland. "That was a thin, older volunteer recruited at the last minute, to replace an actor who fell when the Thames ice broke."

Rowland sat back, folding his arms. "You suborned Lazarus. You bribed my butler."

"No, of course I did not," Tom said. "He volunteered. He wasn't paid like the other actors."

"I wish," Ned said, still remembering his afternoon perambulation around London, "I'd been one of Perry's reavers at Molewood's country house, which was the original plan. I felt as if I stood too close to a bonfire, having to be at the meeting room for all those hours. And that beard itched like nettles."

Perry said, "Miss Foxe, tell the others how things at Primrose Hill progressed."

She said, "I gained entry to Molewood's house there, using a forged love letter—thank you, Ned. His mother sent a message, begging Mr. Molewood to come there. I intended to stay until the king's men appeared with a warrant, so I could witness Molewood's dismay and his arrest. From that point, I had no control over what happened."

Perry said, "I did as Miss Foxe asked and hired a scoundrel called Nathaniel Merryboy to recruit mercenaries, though he calls his crew knights of the post. One crew raided Molewood's London house, to carry away art that Ned desired, and to leave papers Tom and I found that proved Molewood's illicit ways. Another crew went to Sir Bythorn's house, to deposit papers that prove the man has abused his office as a customs official."

Lizzie said, "That was our plan. I thought the plan was for your mercenaries to free Tia Angelina and to carry away any stolen goods Mr. Molewood might have stored there. I didn't expect you to take Mr. Molewood away with you, Perry. And I never expected to see Rollo."

"Mayhap, Rollo surprised me too," Perry said. "Yet it proved fortuitous when he appeared after everyone else had left Xanthus House this morning. We hatched the notion of abducting Molewood and forcing him to commit Ned's planned theft—"

"Not fair to say!" Tom cried. "Ned should always be known as innocent."

Perry said, "Mayhap, Ned's innocent days are over. Let us say that the notion came into my heart as a bit of a lark, to entice

Molewood into committing a crime. Also, I wanted Miss Foxe to witness more of the man's punishment."

Lizzie said, "Thank you again for that."

Felicity said, "Those of us in fine velvet and speaking Italian never veered from the plan. We played the same script as was intended last Friday. Flawlessly, if I may say."

Michael said, "One merchant brother left the door open for Molewood to see his brother committing bribery. Then that merchant handed the letter of intent to Viscount Orlando."

Winwood said, "I was the first Orlando, who let that letter drop where Mr. Molewood might see it. And the red-bearded guard failed to persuade Molewood to give the letter back to Orlando." He raised his glass to Ned.

"The rest of us," Felicity said, "merely played well-dressed touts who couldn't speak the king's English well."

Through this recitation, Perry had been absentmindedly tapping the back of Ned's right hand. That was the hand that wanted so badly to paint over that enormous cow.

Winwood said, "Will bad things happen to the real Venetians if the angry investors ever find any of them?"

"No chance," Tom said. "Their landlord and every man who had business with them will swear the Venetians left by carriage for Dover six weeks ago."

"With genuine English passes and insurance," Rowland said. "As soon as the two ships they leased from me can leave drydock, they'll join the real Venetians in Calais."

Hawksmoor said, "That explains most of this day's various sleights of hand. When I called for the Venetians to be fetched back to the meeting room, Viscount Orlando left to fetch them, but never appeared again."

"They say," Lizzie smirked, "Orlando has left London for the Continent, vowing never to set foot in England again."

"Too bad." Rowland said. "I've always found him to be as talented and useful as any of my own cousins."

"Nay," Perry said, "he dresses like a coxcomb and walks like a Ganymede. And he's quite light-fingered for a man who claims to be a lofty lord."

"I will confess," Rowland said, "Orlando became overly fond of borrowing my boots and court suits. I hope the scoundrel returns them before leaving England."

Tom sighed. "We'll remember Orlando as a well-meaning soul carried off by the gods because of his unusual beauty."

Ned said, "The day's story must be done." He'd listened with relief as all the chaotic pieces finally fit together, like the composition of a picture he'd struggled with.

"For the last of it," Tom said, "let's confirm that we abided by all the Restoration Rules. First, *no one died.*" He began ticking off their rules.

"Did we not," Rowland said, "specifically observe one rule: *Reave when sins are ripe.*"

"Except," Tom said, "we were pursuing people for whom *sin* is too small a word."

Ned said, "Lizzie seemed to strive to turn one rule upside down: *Never trick a woman.*"

Perry said, "Miss Foxe did just what she was taught, which is to let people trick themselves."

Lizzie smiled at that. "I think Perry has shown that we need to amend one rule." She held up her wine cup to toast him. "Our rule shall be: *Call the reavers when sins are ripe.*"

Another knock at the door. "Ah," Hawksmoor said. "It must be dessert and more wine. We've finished with this day's tasks."

The sweet dish was a tart made with gooseberry preserves, accompanied by little dishes of almonds and walnuts, already out of the shell. Ned bit into a walnut, and almost bit his tongue when

Perry again settled his hand on Ned's thigh and whispered, "You have more to do tonight than to merely find our warm beds."

Rowland said, "We should now agree on the explanation to be shared with the Duke of Bagsham, since it's he who will carry our tale to the king."

Lizzie said, "That's a job for tomorrow. We are all on our last legs. Poynter, can your people call carriages for us? We'd best depart before any of us lays his head on the table and sleeps."

When Ned waited for the others to depart ahead of him, he spied what Tom's head had hidden through the whole of supper. Beside the artist's unreadable signature was a date: 1642.

Lord Hawksmoor' ancestor had commissioned that nightmare. Poynter wasn't responsible. That made Ned even happier when Perry's arm crept over his shoulder. They walked out of Poynter's house together, agreeing that they'd both been too much among others' company for that day.

Perry linked his elbow with Ned's. "We could both do with a sip of ale and a hearty song before bedtime."

45
Countess

— LIZZIE —

TUESDAY MIDNIGHT

BY THE TIME THE carriage had crossed several streets from Poynter's house, Lizzie's lips felt swollen and numb. In the tussle of accommodating each other's limbs, there came the sound of tearing silk. Rowland lost one of his buttons, which he couldn't find under the carriage's lamplight.

Rowland insisted that this wasn't the night for Lizzie to return to Chalgrove House. "You are alleged to have been ill all this time. You can't be seen to enter that house in an evening gown."

In the foyer at Xanthus House, Rowland and Lizzie refused Lazarus's offer to attend them to their bedchambers. Bowing to that refusal, Lazarus said, "I sent Jane upstairs with warming pans when I heard your carriage."

Lizzie and Rowland stood at the door of the chamber she'd used while pretending to be Orlando. Before opening her door, Lizzie said, "Besides wearing your shoes, I've been sleeping in your bed while you were in Bristol."

"But surely Lazarus and Jane—"

She placed her fingers on his chin, tipping his head to her. "The greatest lesson I learned this week," she stepped up on tiptoes, "is that I miss you when you aren't by my side. Profoundly. Wretchedly. I don't want to miss you ever again."

He wrapped his arms around her, cradling her head in one hand, holding her close to his breast. "May I be allowed to hope this is good news for me?"

"It leaves us with the need to make one more decision."

"I'm afraid to ask. What's that?"

"I promised to tell you about my Friday in gaol. Where shall we abide while I tell the tale?"

"Oh, that decision. However, I believe the remaining decision is your promise about the date when I can address you as my countess."

"I did promise."

The clock in the hall struck two o'clock before Lizzie finished her story and Rowland had told about his Bristol journey. The warming pan had lost its heat, but they found ways to keep each other warm.

"We have all of tomorrow morning to sleep," Rowland murmured. But in only a few more moments, she dozed off.

—

Alas, Lizzie wasn't allowed to enjoy the luxury of lazing away the morning with Rowland. First, Countess got into the room, probably when Peter came in to light the fire. The dog leapt to lick Rowland's face, then Rowland couldn't persuade his dog to settle down until it lay between them. Lizzie, who was more persuasive, coaxed Countess to the foot of the bed. Yet every time they dozed off, Countess wiggled between them again.

When Lazarus brought a breakfast tray, he also delivered two notes: one for Rowland and the other for Lizzie. Hers came with a messenger from Chalgrove House. Aurora had forwarded an invitation from the Duke of Bagsham to attend luncheon at one o'clock.

"I have that invitation too." Rowland held out his message. "The duke wants an accounting of yesterday's arrests."

"I must go to Chalgrove House to dress. There's nothing suitable here that I can wear."

The yellow silk from last night lay crumpled on the floor, a tear on one shoulder separating most of a sleeve.

"I'll have Lazarus fetch a carriage. You might as well stay here where it's warm until he calls."

As if to dispute Rowland's intention, Countess once again wiggled in between them.

46
As You Like It

— NED —

WEDNESDAY PREDAWN

NED FOUND WEDNESDAY MORNING to be the most interesting of the week. Perry had gotten him out of bed with a coaxing promise to show him good news. To find the news, though, meant packing their belongings and removing to new quarters above Ezra Pelletoot's locksmith shop. Perry led him up to the promised studio while Ned was still protesting.

"You mentioned this possible change, Perry, but we didn't decide on it together."

However, upstairs at Pelletoot's, the proposed studio was filled with artifacts and paintings taken from Molewood's two residences. Which meant that Ned had his own rewards out of Lizzie's gambol: that carved ivory he'd lusted after, the unfinished *Achilles at Skyros,* and possession of the forgeries that Molewood might have used against the Touchstones. Perry held out a particular treat: the original provenance for the Lely that Touchstone had sold to Molewood, along with the original and genuine Lely sketch.

In addition to calming Ned's passion around the Touchstone forgery crisis, he also now held several of his own paintings that he'd been loath to sell. For the rest of the paintings and sketches seized from Molewood, Ned had all the time in the world to consider whether to keep or dispose of them. If Lizzie decided to go to Holland in the spring, he could go along. There was world enough and time to create provenances for paintings he might consider selling.

Then that rush of pleasure was interrupted by the message from Rowland, that the Duke of Bagsham had invited them to account for yesterday's doings.

At Littlecote, the duke's mansion in St James Place, Captain Starbuck was also present. Rowland and Aurora came with Lizzie, who was dressed in Sea Water blue velvet, as was Ned. It wasn't her best color, but he felt it united them as brother and sister. Lizzie had begged Aurora to come, for the sake of a second woman at luncheon with a bevy of men.

Ned sat with the women. He whispered to Lizzie, "Perry says you and I should not talk about yesterday's doings."

"Rollo said the same to me. As if I possess no discretion."

The three at their end of the table spoke in hushed tones about whether the hard frost would return or whether England was to enjoy a drenching rain and flooding brooks until May. At the other end of the table, his grace the duke conversed with Rowland, Perry, and Captain Starbuck.

Rowland related the story they'd agreed was appropriate when explaining to the duke about recent events.

At the end of that crafty tale, the duke said, "I understand how men were beguiled by the traitor Withersea, and so invested in his African adventure. But I don't understand why Wolfric Molewood and Sir Bythorn carried out their extensive crimes. Everyone in London expects a dose of corruption when men grow rich, but why such extremes? Especially, why cheat the king over the *Skylark* cargo?"

Lizzie sat so close to Ned that he felt her tense when the duke called the people from that ship cargo.

Captain Starbuck said, "Both Molewood and Sir Bythorn—now Mr. Chudrakes—confessed to the intelligencers that the king had so offended them, they felt forced to resist the results of the king's poor decisions."

"Mayhap," Perry said, "not the best choice of confessions when accused of breaking several laws."

"We know many people are incensed by the king," the duke said. "Especially since he prorogated Parliament. How do those men believe the king offended them?"

Starbuck said, "Because he'd granted the Earl of Marborne the ships taken from the traitor, the Marquess of Withersea."

The duke shook his head. "It's the king's prerogative to deal as he desires with what's confiscated from traitors."

"Aye, your grace," Starbuck said. "Yet both men claim the other investors should have been compensated in that seizure, since they knew nothing about that African venture."

"An astounding fabrication," Rowland said. "The syndicate called itself Hawkins' Heirs. Why choose such a name if not investing in a slaver's journey to Africa?"

"Why sell people," Lizzie asked, intruding on that conversation, despite warnings, "into indentured servitude because the king has offended you?"

"Because they had the opportunity?" The duke raised his brows with the question, to which no one had a better answer.

Rowland said, "These two men are worldly enough to know such protestations cannot possibly matter."

"Indeed," the duke said. "What other evidence do you have against them?"

"We searched their houses under warrant, and so possess a large catalog of evidence." Starbuck began listing the store of documents and ledgers seized by the king's militia:

> Letters and chits proving Chudrakes and Molewood had cheated Diggory Crackbone over customs and insurance.

And that both knew him to be the living inheritor of the Molewood estate.

A ledger listing five years of bribes received for customs officials to ignore merchants' transgressions.

The list of people from the *Skylark,* with the names of households that had purchased forged indentures.

Rowland said, "To add to that, I brought from Bristol the harbormaster's testimony about the missing people from the *Skylark*. He and the militia captain have questioned all the men involved and found Chudrakes at the base of it."

Again, Ned felt Lizzie tense beside him. She put her hand on his wrist. Her pulse beat like a blacksmith's hammer. The final piece of information they'd pursued was now in hand.

"Congratulations, Marborne." The duke tipped his cup to Rowland. "You no longer need wrestle with any of the problems and rumors that rose from the *Skylark*.

A footman bent to whisper in the duke's ear.

The duke rose from the table. "Will you ladies, and you too, Mr. Wijck, please excuse us? Marborne, Frake, Starbuck, please come with me."

—

Ned, not invited to follow with the others, used the moment to plead the usual social excuse, to find the necessary.

At the duke's mansion, Ned knew the way to the ballroom, having been in the duke's mansion on several occasions. He'd prepared for this task as soon as they'd received notice to come to the duke's house. On this Wednesday at midday, the ballroom was empty. It was also dark, since the curtains were all drawn. However, Ned quickly reached his destination and produced the slim packet from inside his waistcoat. The waxed canvas had done its job, such that the oils had no time to dry.

Even in the dim light, Ned saw that he'd remembered the colors correctly, so it took only a moment to scrawl his name and change a six to an eight, since he hadn't been born in 1660. Then he was done and out the door.

Only to run into a man at the top of the stairs, just after Ned had tucked the waxed packet back into his waistcoat.

"It's Mr. Wijck, isn't it? I heard you'd come for the duke's salon this afternoon."

It was the fellow he'd met before, the one who held the trusted role of finishing and validating Lely's paintings.

"Yes. I, uh, lost my way to where people are gathering."

"Are you creating a new work for the duke?" The fellow had all the social grace that Ned lacked, and so made their passage through the mansion easy and pleasant.

"Oh, do I smell like my studio?" Ned did indeed, since he hadn't had a chance to discard that makeshift palette.

"No, I'm only curious."

"I do have a work in progress, but it is a surprise for the duke's birthday. "The notion had come to him while the actors were rehearsing their collective exculpation in that warehouse. "I intend a presentation of Shakespeare's *As You Like It,* with the Duke of Bagsham as Duke Senior in the Forest of Arden. I hope the duke won't find it too whimsical."

He'd worked out the required changes to last week's canvas. It'd take little effort to add the duke's visage and transform the daughters of Lycomedes into the Earl of Marborne's entourage.

In the salon, the duke had hung multiple paintings on every wall, from the wainscoting to the ceiling. Lizzie and Aurora sat there, together with several others.

Lizzie said, "Prudence, allow me to introduce my brother Ned, whom you know as the painter, Eduard Wijck."

Then followed several more introductions, all painters Ned had heard of, had seen their pictures in Touchstone's gallery, but had never met. Prudence Mott, having the same grace as the Lely curator, put people at ease by indicating which works on the duke's walls could be attributed to each of the men in the room.

The conversation hummed, lifting Ned's spirits above anything he'd felt while prowling in Touchstone's warehouse. And Miss Mott truly was quite knowledgeable about work in modern England—much more than they'd coached Lizzie to be when she first met Molewood.

The duke entered the salon with Rowland and Perry. Starbuck didn't reappear. The duke immediately joined in the conversation among the artists, asking questions. But Ned had to wonder, every time his grace mashed his spectacles in place, how and why the duke kept such treasures in his salon, since he was blind as a week-old kitten.

Perry sat patiently at Ned's side through that tête-à-tête, though surely his friend would rather be anywhere else in the world. The gathering ended after people invited each other to visit their studios. This had been Ned's unspoken dream, to know and be accepted among other painters in London.

After everyone said farewell and thanked their host, Ned and Perry stood on the portico together. Ned spied Aurora entering a carriage with the real Miss Mott, then noticed Lizzie and Rowland had disappeared. When Ned and Perry were the last people on the portico, one of the duke's footmen appeared.

"Mr. Eduard Wick?"

A new jolt of dread crashed through Ned. This was to be it? The feared comeuppance for his forgeries?

"Mayhap, this is the gentleman you seek." Perry pointed subtly to Ned.

"His grace's compliments." The footman bowed and handed Ned a heavy velvet pouch. "And his grace's gratitude."

The footman disappeared as silently as he'd come.

"A gift for you?" Perry's curiosity was piqued.

Ned pulled at the pouch's ribbon ties and peered inside. Perry, having no patience, took it from him, shaking part of the contents into his big hands.

"A treasure of gold? Have you sold the duke another painting? Ah, there's a note."

Ned picked the slip of paper from among the coins in Perry's hand, reading it aloud so that he also satisfied Perry:

> One-quarter now. The rest as promised at Easter, if the person with whom we are concerned remains safe.

"This must be fifty pounds!" Perry exclaimed.

"Guineas," Ned said. The subsiding fear left him numb.

Perry clapped Ned on the back. "I've a rumbling in my head that says this is about Miss Ysabel Foxe. And to earn it, you had only to spend that one night in the customs lockup. Let's spend some of your wealth now."

Perry pointed down the lane, claiming to know of a good tavern, despite this being a neighborhood of toffs. Ned hurried to follow, still shaking off the afterglow of his first London artists' salon. And the velvet pouch full of gold guineas.

At the tavern, hot ale in hand, Ned asked Perry, "What private business did the duke drag you and Rollo off to? He didn't give you more intelligencers' tasks, I hope."

"Not as such," Perry said. "The king was there, like he was when we finished the Withersea business. He thanked Rollo for finding a bit of rot in the customs house."

"Does he want Rollo—and you—to find more?" Ned fumed, shoving his mug of ale aside. "I'd like us all to be as far as we can get from the Stuarts and the muddles they create."

"While remaining in England?" Perry's smile promised a tease. "The king hinted that he wants Rollo to marry, as a favor to his daughter Mary, and to be the kind of husband who warns his wife away from dissenters and rebels."

"That makes no sense." Ned puzzled it. "Lizzie will never turn Quaker. She's too fond of nice gowns."

47
St Martin-in-the-Field

— LIZZIE —

WEDNESDAY EARLY EVENING

POYNTER WAVED WHILE GREETING Lizzie and Rowland in Portuguese. *"Olá a todos!"*

He stood out of the rain on the church portico, looking elegant in a long greatcoat. Rowland stepped out of the carriage, equally elegant in his dark, narrow suit and coat, and held out his hand for Lizzie to descend. She still wore the winter-blue velvet gown, out of place for that evening's business.

Yes, we had to hurry away from the duke's house, but these aren't the proper garments for this.

More exuberant than Lizzie had ever known him to be, Poynter embraced her as if they were long-lost cousins. He stepped back and shook Rowland's hand.

"Rollo, you will congratulate me," Poynter said, "for being as good as you at calling an army to arms. My civil militia is rallying here tonight."

"You did it!" Lizzie embraced Poynter briefly again. "I had no expectation this could be mastered until spring."

"I knocked on people's doors, but Rollo launched the *Skylark's* investors into action." He clapped Rowland on the back, the way men do.

Rowland embraced Poynter at the elbows. "I'm happy you were prepared to be Lizzie's shining knight."

"I can scarcely claim this battle as mine. Come meet your volunteer helpers." Poynter opened the church door.

Inside, a dozen men and women were setting up trestle tables in the vestibule. Lizzie had met half of these people and greeted them by name. They in turn introduced their husbands, brothers, and cousins.

"We were surprised when the Earl of Hawksmoor knocked on our doors Monday morning." It was the diminutive Mistress Alice Fell, the leader Lizzie had met among the Quakers who yearned to see slavery abolished. "He carried your note, apologizing that it wasn't possible for you to meet with us personally. And begging us to trust him."

"I am deeply grateful." Lizzie embraced her, then shook hands with the others. "I cannot express the joy I feel for what you are doing."

"We have shelter for those who want it," Mistress Fell said. "Since you first met with us, we've found safe havens for people. And we have two Portuguese translators to help tonight."

Rowland lingered behind Poynter, looking grave.

Why not be happy, heartling? How far this is from Bristol.

She said, "Are you not so happy as I am, Lord Marborne?"

Rowland didn't answer. Taking hold of Poynter's elbow, he said, "Is this safe for Lizzie? After her risks yesterday—"

"We are standing inside St Martin's," Poynter said. "The rector is right over there. This has all the marks of sanctuary."

"Rollo." Lizzie took his hand off Poynter's arm. "We won't catch an infectious disease from dissenters. And we need to help however we can."

Before the church bell tolled five o'clock, men from the *Skylark* began to enter the church. After the bell rang, four women came in among several more men. They each carried a paper, a blanket, and makeshift bags that held their belongings.

Lizzie stood under the archway and welcomed each into the church. When it seemed that all have arrived, Mistress Fell urged Lizzie to speak. Carefully choosing words in Portuguese, Lizzie heard her voice quavering. She grasped her hands in front of her, because she trembled. With joy. With fear for the responsibility she was taking for other people's lives.

I remain fearful for them. Relief barely creeps in my veins.

She began, explaining why she and Rowland had presumed to interfere in their lives. "The Earl of Marborne was given the *Skylark,* not knowing that ship had stolen you from your homes. But we have accepted our responsibility for your wellbeing."

Then she let Mistress Fell explain that new arrangements for work and home would be made for each of them. "Or you might choose to return to your former master in London."

No one chose to return to those masters.

"We have shelter for you tonight. And you can take time to choose among new work available for you."

One man asked, "Can we go home to our villages?"

This question has gnawed at my heart since the girls first asked.

Lizzie offered the sole possible answer. "We can find new safe destinations for you, but we have no way to return you to your true homes. But if anyone believes they know how to find their village, when spring comes we will pay your passage on a Royal African Company voyage."

She briefly answered questions among the three men who had notions of returning home, then addressed everyone again.

"One thing we must achieve tonight is to learn whether you have wives, husbands, or other relations who came with you on the *Skylark*. We shall do all we can to find them, so you can be together, whatever else you decide to do."

Rowland put his hand at the center of Lizzie's back, as if to support her while she spoke. She appreciated it, but she didn't need that comfort. The restoration's success had at last begun to spread warmth through her veins.

His whisper tickled her ear. "No one else in England could have done as well as you."

She whispered, "But we still have to find at least eight more people who came to England on the *Skylark*."

"Save it for another day. I am going to beg you to rest."

"I'm not the least tired."

"Aye? Well, I am. Do you have any idea what it takes out of a man to ride to Bristol and back in so few days? And then Perry forced me to go all the way to Primrose Hill and back in the rain. And now I must stand in a freezing stone church where good manners prevent me from wrapping my arms around you."

Poynter was at Lizzie's side again. "We can let our friends finish the work, to get these people into warm shelter."

Lizzie said, "Ha! A pun. Friends. That's what they call themselves. Not Quakers."

Poynter said, "How rich are you, to pay the fare for anyone who wants to return to Africa?"

"We'll use the funds the original investors contributed to this project yesterday." She checked his expression closely. "You don't have any doubt, do you, that it was a righteous restoration? Those investors didn't earn anything from the *Skylark* except illicit indentured servants. But Tom and Perry have deep knowledge of their other cheating investments."

"Oh, it's a righteous restoration," Poynter said. "Now, my carriage is waiting to take you both home."

Before departing, Lizzie thanked her dissenter friends for their work, and shook hands with each person who'd come there to find better work and better homes.

—

Lizzie and Rowland met Poynter at his carriage, but she turned back to see the people busy with the work of resettlement.

In that moment, the candlelight inside St Martin's glimmered like the light in that little church where she'd demanded sanctuary in Bristol. That image opened a memory which swept over her like harsh wind. She wavered, her head crashing against Rowland's breast. Then she cried, harder than she'd ever wept.

Rowland held her, neither urging her into the carriage nor hushing her. When she could speak, she forced a lightness into her breath that she didn't yet feel. "Now what story shall we tell about why the Earl of Marborne stood in St Martin's Lane embracing a woman who is drenching his fine wool suit with tears?"

At last Poynter called for them to come in out of the rain.

In the carriage, Rowland drew his greatcoat over her, and Poynter added a fur rug. The carriage shuddered over the roadway, now with deeper ruts from the freeze and thaw. Lizzie got her heart to beat and her lungs to draw breath again.

Get hold of yourself, woman. Just be happy!

Lizzie said, "I am so grateful, Poynter, for what you did to accomplish this night's work."

"It's too minor to be saluted," Poynter said. "I simply did as you instructed and met with the people you engaged earlier. They made plans and used the coin I gave them to seek housing and employment for people from the *Skylark*."

"But you did what I could not do, after the Duke of Bagsham warned me off meeting with dissenters."

Rowland had been quiet since entering the carriage. He said, "I should have been enlightened enough to know what you intended, Lizzie. I admit I was baffled upon hearing you'd met with Quakers. And that the king knew it."

Lizzie tapped her nose, remembering one other detail.

"Poynter, you'll be reimbursed tomorrow with funds from the *Skylark* investors. Tom is giving you access, so you can continue to disperse those funds to bring people to safe places. You will be the hero of the entire *Skylark* debacle."

Poynter said, "No, that's you, Miss Foxe."

"Nay, I don't deserve the appellation of hero." She felt exhausted to the core, as one does after so many tears. "I am committed to action, but it's far too little. The struggle against the commerce of stealing people for New World plantations will continue for decades. All of England is too eager to get rich from trade and plantations."

Poynter coughed. "You have been kind, not reprimanding me for my own holdings in the New World. I can extract myself from that business, but I shall have to travel to Barbados if I am to prevent worse situations for the people working there."

Another notion had been ticking like a clock since Lizzie first read the letter from her friend the princess.

"Come spring, I must travel to the Low Countries. I hope to convince Princess Mary to undertake a more noble course once her father is no longer governor of the Royal African Company."

"My heart beats with delight," Rowland said, "that you remain an optimist."

For that carriage ride, Rowland held one of her hands in his, nudging his way into her palm with a finger, like a promise to hold her closely, later.

Poynter departed when the carriage came to his house, bidding them to send the carriage back when they were finished. But not long after that, the carriage came to a halt.

"We cannot be home yet, Rollo."

"It further delights my heart that you call Xanthus House your home," Rowland said. "No, we have stopped on Portugal Street. Come."

—

Light spilled from the open door of a shop. Rowland quickly hopped from the carriage and reached for Lizzie's hand to help her down—but not into the mud. A carpet had been laid out. Lizzie followed Rowland into a modiste's salon. He closed the door behind them against the damp and cold.

The warm shop room smelled of beeswax and herbs, with bowls of potpourri in every corner. But the scent that overwhelmed Lizzie's sense was the smell of new cloth. The starch and gum arabic used for sizing. It was a mélange of scents that Lizzie found almost as comforting as the scents of Rowland's bed.

Four women inside the lamp-lit shop stood in a line, obviously awaiting guests. The woman by the door, Madame Orinda, bowed in greeting, smiled broadly, and offered Lizzie a tisane in a porcelain cup of ornate Chinese design.

"To warm your hands while we talk, Miss Foxe."

Lizzie accepted the fragrant tea. "I'm surprised but pleased to see you so late at night."

The owner of the shop, the tiny and bubbly Madame Orinda, had made the quite luscious gown Lizzie wore to a feast at the duke's house before Christmas. She and Lizzie shared ideas easily, and shared that their first English forebears came to this island to serve Katherine of Aragon.

"Are we ready?" Rowland asked.

Madame Orinda nodded. "Come to the primary salon."

The shop's best fitting room offered ample room for their hostess to perform her services, with a worktable and a velvet-cushioned settle for guests. A fine walnut rack on one wall held bolts of fabric. On this night, it overflowed with silks in yellow and gold hues that glimmered in the flickering candlelight.

The other three seamstresses first huddled at the door, then at a signal from their mistress, retrieved little cakes and a crystal flagon of wine, which were set on the table at Rowland's elbow.

"I conceived a notion at the duke's house," Rowland said. "Lazarus and Madame Orinda have graciously done the work to make this possible."

"Your lordship, I believe," Madame Orinda said, "we have all that's needed to begin. Your man Lazarus brought me to the warehouse to choose fabrics. He gave me these drawings. Is this the appropriate place to begin, Miss Foxe?"

Rowland had the happy, glowing appearance of a man who believed he'd served up a treat. He said, "When I met the king at the duke's house yesterday, he awarded me all the goods Chudrakes and Molewood swindled in their schemes."

Lizzie sipped the hot wine. She couldn't manage words in the face of the most beautiful silks she'd ever seen.

"The most beautiful silks," Rowland said, "proved to be the remnants of Diggory Crackbone's Levant trade. I shall return that hoard to him tomorrow. And I'll pay him for what you choose for your wedding dress, Lizzie."

The silks glowed under the candlelight, like what a dragon's pile of gold must look like. The drawings on the worktable were from the flights of imagination that Lizzie, Aurora, and Felicity had indulged on rainy November nights.

"I am…Rollo, I'm overwhelmed." Lizzie turned to Madame Orinda. "It will take too long for me to decide. I don't want to keep you and your ladies from your beds."

"We are delighted to serve," Madame Orinda said. "We'll work tonight and close the shop tomorrow."

Rowland said, "Lady Rôche advised that this work should begin now, if you intend a May celebration. And Ned wants to know the colors, so he can procure the minerals he'll need."

"Ned has plagued me with that question since Bristol."

Lizzie set her wine cup aside and rose from the settle, drawn to the bolts of fabric. It was all more than merely silk. First, she touched a fabric thickly embroidered with three colors of silk thread plus what appeared to be gold thread. Yes, that's exactly what it was. The fabric resembled the first formal gown Lizzie had made over. When Lizzie had taken it from her mother's chest, Mrs. Bell had admonished care, saying, "Lady Rose Foxe, the last countess, had it made to wear in the court of King Charles II." Lizzie had taken the gown apart, reassembled it to be what she thought then was modern, and wore it to be presented in Princess Mary's court. How old had she been then. Eleven?

The rack held at least five bolts of silk brocade with different raised patterns in golds and yellows, each too heavy for a May wedding.

I'd have given my little finger for even one such bolt to make a gown suitable for the chilly Low Countries.

Besides bolts of three very different kinds of sheer chiffon, another bolt held a sheer fabric with, Lizzie guessed, a linen warp and a silk weft.

"Faille," Madame Orinda murmured, naming the fabric.

"Of course." Lizzie touched the shiny, closely woven fabric. Her finger felt the rib, though it hardly showed in the candlelight. Mary had given her a length of faille once, in a friendly way, on Lizzie's fifteenth birthday. She'd secretly cried over it, since the gift proved that Lizzie hadn't sufficiently hidden her poverty. That night she'd privately sworn to never again feel shame over being the destitute daughter of the late Earl of Marborne.

Lizzie's finger hovered over a watered silk. She hesitated, afraid to touch it. That gold moiré had the richest appearance of any non-embroidered cloth in the racks.

"You can touch it," Madame Orinda said. "Moiré silk is beautiful but sturdy, since it's two fabrics glued together. A note attached to that bolt claims this silk was calendared in China by peasants rocking on large stones. A fanciful notion, don't you think? Makes the moiré waves even more exotic."

"Calendar?" Rowland asked, having been silent so long.

"Two lengths of fabric are fused together, then rolled smooth," Madame Orinda said.

"Too beautiful for mere mortals." Lizzie drew her hand back from the moiré, then felt fine about touching a glossy daffodil-colored fabric woven in a square pattern. It might make a glorious cloak. Lizzie rubbed the fabric between her fingers, curious. She hadn't seen a fabric like it before.

"It's called lustring," Madame Orinda. "Many consider it too common for fine gowns and so more appropriate for upholstery. But for some—"

"Some," Lizzie spoke slowly, "would be grateful for a cloak of such sturdy cloth. Mayhap, lined with wool."

She blinked but couldn't clear the image from her mind, of the men and women sent out of their indentures, carrying thread-bare blankets not much thicker than chiffon.

"I'm sorry." Lizzie turned to the modiste. "I can't do this."

Madame Orinda only tilted her head with a curious look.

A wave of concern and, alas, unhappiness passed over Rowland's face, which Lizzie found heartbreaking.

"I'm sorry, dear heart." She reached for his hand. "I appreciate what you have contrived to create here. It shows…"

What to say to make this better?

"…deep insight and dedicated care for the woman you have known for so many years."

How awkward.

"We can do this tomorrow," Rowland said, "or another day when you aren't fatigued from a long endeavor."

"No," Lizzie said. "What I meant to say is, I don't want England's most fanciful wedding dress." She turned to Madame Orinda. "I shall not waste your time. I will need new gowns when next I travel to the Low Countries. Use this." She touched one of the thick brocades. "And this and this." She touched the gold moiré and the faille. "Make each into one of the designs we used on my last three gowns. We can discuss the lace and ribbons when you invite me for a fitting. I won't need them until late spring."

She grasped Rowland's elbow. The stricken look on his face showed that he badly needed a better explanation.

"It's because of this, Rollo." She fingered the daffodil-hued lustring. "I thought for a moment of making it into a cloak, but that brought to my mind's eye the people from the *Skylark,* in their rough clothes and insufficient coats and cloaks."

He had to clear his throat to speak. "Nothing about what you have for a wedding dress will make a difference for how we endeavor to help people who've been wronged."

"I cannot persist in longing to return to Mary's court. I've intended to return wearing fine gowns from a modiste, after years of crafting my gowns from other ladies' castoffs."

"You can do that and also have a fine wedding dress. The result will be the same for people from the *Skylark*."

The tone of sad hopefulness in Rowland's voice tore at the fine tissue around her heart.

God's bones! He thinks I don't want to marry him.

Lizzie clutched his elbow more tightly, though on any other night, she'd take care to avoid creasing the super-fine wool of his sleeve. "There isn't time to make a new gown, Rollo."

Madame Orinda gasped. "Miss Foxe, we can surely—"

Lizzie held up a hand, shaking her head. "Rollo, I'll wear the gown I had at the duke's Christmas feast. The lace needs a bit of mending, and I shall have to repair the hem. But I can do that in the carriage on the way to Revelstone House. When do you think the roads will be dry enough to travel? We can journey there with Tia Angelina and Ishmael."

Rowland's face eased, then brightened.

Like when the wind ceases blowing over a pond on a sunny day.

"We should," she continued, "send a courier tomorrow, so Camilla has time to arrange the Marborne church to her liking, and so Tamsin and Mrs. Bell can plan a wedding breakfast. And Tamsin must also warn Reverend Gamlingay to prepare to read the Church of England's Marriage Service."

Rowland's smile twitched. "I wonder if that service aligns with his Nonconformist beliefs. I'm certain he was shamming it when he had to read the Order for Burial of the Dead at Uncle Absolom's interment."

"We'll also need to warn everyone in London who will think they want to be there."

"God blind me!" Rowland grinned. "That means Ned and Tom. And Perry. And Jacob Rôche won't be happy in London if we're all going to Marborne. Also his sister Aurora and Neriah Frake. And Winwood Oakes. We'll need a convoy."

It seemed simple. How quickly it's becoming complicated.

While trying to quiet her thundering heart, Lizzie thanked Madame Orinda and her seamstresses for their kindness that night. Those young women, despite the late-night hour, seemed contented to have a light comical romance staged in their parlor.

Madame Orinda sent her young page to flag a carriage, since Rowland had dismissed Poynter's when he and Lizzie arrived, expecting that they'd be all night at this.

The same page again rolled out a carpet when the carriage arrived. Rowland again led her in an imitation of stately grace along the carpet. But instead of handing her up into the carriage in his usual way, he wrapped his arms around her and swung her into the air. They both failed to land on the carpet and slipped into the mud. Lizzie heard lace tear and knew her hem dragged.

So much for winter-blue velvet. Well, it wasn't my color.

Rowland helped her inside the carriage, instructed the driver, and sat beside her, pulling a fur rug over both of them. The page had hailed a very nice carriage.

He pressed close, His breath warmed the slight chill her face had taken while they twirled outside the modiste's shop. "I'm sorry your skirts are muddy, my countess. I take all the blame for that public display."

"It's not what I'm concerned about at this moment, Rollo."

He caught the sharp tone and drew back an inch. "What have I done?"

"I couldn't ask in front of strangers. Because it's about your meeting with the king yesterday."

"Should I fear your question?"

"Did you ask the king for permission to marry? You've been hounding me on that question since summer. You've kept that romantic notion of fulfilling your grandfather's promise."

"I did not ask him."

"Because you know how much I dislike the notion?"

"In part." He was easing his arm around her, nudging her closer. "I didn't ask, because service to the king is *not* what the earl of Marborne and his countess will be doing for England from now on."

She grabbed the collar of his coat with both hands, pulling him to her with no worries for the fine wool.

"You know me well, dear heart." She felt his lips so deliciously close. "You and I cannot do the work Uncle Absolom assigned us when there isn't a fit king to serve. We must still serve England. To do that, you and I must be bound together."

She didn't just permit the ravenous kisses he pressed on her. She begged for more, until they paused, breathless.

"Then you aren't marrying me for my title and my money?" He teased. "Not just so that you'll have proper rank and nice gowns in Mary's court?"

"The title might prove useful." She ran a teasing finger down the groove below his nose, then traced his lips. "But I can reave any fortune I need, as long as I have a righteous purpose. And cooperative cousins."

"God blind me, you're just who I always thought you were." He had his fingers in her hair, undoing the pins. "So, 'Come live with me and be my love. And we will all the pleasures prove.'"

"That's Christopher Marlowe," she said. "Not your Bard."

"No matter. 'And I will make thee beds of roses.' I care not one fig about which poet's words elucidate my sighs."

48
'Tis Spring

– TAMSIN –

"'TIS SPRING AND

WEEDS ARE SHALLOW-ROOTED"

April 15, 1686, Revelstone House

My dearest Lizzie, I am commanded to allow every underaged person sign with their own love. Hence, please first read the added page with their signatures. Jacob bids me tell you to tell Rollo that no one else holds the pen when Jacob signs his name.

Now, the only change in our household is that Madame Aguila has returned to London to help care for her sister's children, Tia Angelina has taken her place as the school mistress. Indeed, you saw when you first met her how much English she's mastered. This change has been peaceful for all, except she's much stricter in the Portuguese lessons with Camilla and me. We are expected to speak coherently. She isn't, however, strict with the girls when they laugh at our failures.

Because Jacob Rôche remained behind when you departed in February, we have yet to return to our methodical ways. Mrs. Bell still praises that you brought Mrs. Frake to our kitchen and says daily that mere housekeeping is a respite, then pretends to sigh over the changes. "It's all because," she says, "Lady Marborne—Miss Foxe that was—turned our peaceful country household into a spectacle."

Jacob remains here. He broke his foot (not badly) falling from a horse. He cried hallelujah when Winwood insisted he must abide here until it heals. It was all due to Countess running after the horse Jacob was learning to ride (the gentlest in the stable). That isn't the only event that has proved the wisdom of leaving Countess at Revelstone instead of taking her with you to the Continent.

Everyone in the house enjoys Jacob's extended stay, and he's made it clear he does not like London. While Jacob had to remain off his feet, he began drawing lessons with the girls. It's the same lessons Ned tried to foist on us in our schoolroom days, but Jacob and the girls share more success than we did.

In the schoolroom (rather than while roaming the fields), the girls defer to Jacob as "Lord Rôche," though he's more of a big brother. That role seems to suit him. Ishmael and Neriah Frake (who's supposed to be Jacob's valet) get on together with Jacob in the ways like we all did. However, Mrs. Bell forbade them from letting the girls climb the big oaks. Mrs. Frake grudgingly supported that rule. I believe that since she raised five sons, Mrs. Frake is apt to be cautious. Mrs. Bell has not changed her ways since our time, though I've reminded her that none of us ever fell out of the oaks. Except Rollo, of course.

And I shall not tell Mrs. Bell that, on the first week in March with no rain, it was the girls who showed Jacob and Ishmael how to climb the trees. Do you know our armada of old planks continues to hang aloft in the yard?

Camilla is still at work with the length of silk Rowland brought her and no longer complains that you didn't give sufficient time for anyone to make proper gowns for a wedding. Her work progresses slowly. She hasn't even finished her embroidery plans, much less started on stitching up a dress. She's ambitious for that project, because she only dares take that silk out of its box when the two of us are alone with our private projects.

In all other parts of the house, chaos reigns throughout the day. I aver: Mrs. Bell only pretends to be dismayed.

I hope what I've heard is true, that flowers flourish in the Low Countries in springtime. The only sad thing about your sudden and unplanned celebration in winter was the shocking lack of flowers. Camilla did what she could, gathering silk flowers from our mothers' chests. She's regathered them now, under a glass bell that Winwood brought back from his last trip to London.

Winwood made that voyage out, despite how he hates to travel, because he needed several herbs to treat our friends that he couldn't find in Cambridge. I suspect that London will not see much of our dear doctor, now that Tom seems at last to be healthy and thriving.

I will now share news that's not mere gossip. Tom writes that the duke is privately arguing with the king for Aurora's marriage annulment. There can't be a private Act of Parliament for her divorce, since our king still insists on prorogating Parliament to suit his own perverse needs. Tom says the duke is applying the basic argument: "After all Lady Rôche has done for you." The goal is to have the Church declare the marriage never existed. That's a better solution than Tom's proposal to create a Foxe-style restoration where Withersea sells his wife in a

Southwark marketplace. No one would agree to play the part of the missing Marquess of Withersea. The only viable part of such a plan is the surety that Tom would buy her.

Yes, my sense of humor is more wicked than ever, but I hoped to make you laugh.

Whatever the duke does to disappear that disastrous marriage, there will be enough flowers when you come home for Tom and Aurora, even if it's not until harvest time. You will come home for that, won't you? It's not proper to ask what you're up to, yet whatever the duke or your favorite princess has you two doing on the Continent, I hope it's not dangerous and that you can come to England when we need you.

Poynter is visiting this afternoon. If he bears any letters from you, I'll add a postscript. Otherwise, I'll trust him to get this into a diplomatic pouch so you can read it before summer is here.

I hope you'll be free to come back to England soon! And I'm officially sending all our love.

—Tamsin, together with the entire Revelstone household

THE END

Glossary

barmbot: A foolish person.
blockish: Stupid.
booberkin: A dully heavy fellow.
c'est naze: French, colloquially. "That sucks."
chafe: Fret.
crimping fellows: Sneaking cowards.
cucking stool: Original term for what's now called a dunking stool, for punishing disorderly women or fraudulent tradesmen in Scotland, England, and the English colonies.
dandyprat: A puny fellow.
dockwalloper: A casual laborer.
domino mask: A mask that covers eyes, forehead, and cheeks, arising at about this time from various Carnival traditions.
draughts: A boardgame, called checkers in the United States.
ell: An archaic measuring unit; about six hands' breadth or forty-five inches.
faille: Shiny, closely woven silk that has slight ribs in the weft threads.
fizgig: A flirtatious young woman.
frumenty: A wheat pudding.
fluyt: Dutch sailing vessel designed to serve as a cargo ship.
"From the smoke into the smother": From a speech by Orlando in *As You Like It* by William Shakespeare.
gadding gossips: Willful, roaming women.
Ganymede: Restoration era cant for homosexual; after the myth of a Trojan youth so beautiful that Zeus carried him off to be a cupbearer on Olympus.
glavering: Flattering in a fawning way.
goatish: Lecherous.
goose-cap: A fool.
grippe: Influenza.

guinea: A coin worth twenty-one shillings (one more than a pound). Named for the West Africa region of Guinea, the source of gold for minting the coins.

gutfoundered: Starving hungry.

"Hark at he": Listen to him (West Country dialect).

he-strumpet: A male prostitute.

Hungary Water: A scent popular in the court of Elizabeth I, made of brandy, thyme, and rosemary.

hortatory names: Christian names given to infant children by fundamentalist parents in southeast England, with the intention to guide faith and good behavior. The practice fell out of fashion with the Restoration.

intelligencer: A spy or secret agent.

in the boughs: In a passion.

knight of the post: A mercenary.

lippen: Wet and dreary (West Country dialect).

loathly: Repulsive.

longues jambes: French, "long legs," that is, long johns.

Low Countries: Holland, Belgium, and Luxemburg, on the coastal lowlands in northwestern Europe, ruled at this time by William of Orange.

lunger: A person with tuberculosis.

lustring: A glossy silk cloth, often considered common; used for both upholstery and clothing.

malapert: Presumptuous, impudent person.

mifty: Out of humor.

miting: Sweetheart.

moiré: Watered silk.

nithing: A despicable person.

Peace of Westminster: Refers to the Second Peace of Westminster in February 1674, which Charles II signed to end the third Anglo-Dutch war.

picaroon: A scoundrel.

precisionists: A Restoration-era term of contempt for Puritans.

prorogation: The discontinuation of a session of Parliament without dissolving it.
pudding-headed fellow: A total idiot.
putti: The chubby naked cherubs in Renaissance paintings.
queernobbed: Shabbily dressed.
rapscallion: An unprincipled person.
reave: To raid for plunder.
reavers: An archaic word for people who seize and carry off goods. The word in Scotland for such raiders is reivers. Alas, *Firefly* added an animalistic cast to reavers who are fringe-dwellers.
rota: A rotation of duties.
scold's bridle: An iron muzzle used in Scotland, England, and the English colonies as a public humiliation for the people (most often women) whose speech was judged troublesome or riotous. Also called branks or witch's bridle.
scrivener's palsy: Writer's cramp.
Sops-in-Wine: A shade of reddish-brown that resembles dark bread soaked in wine.
stadtholder: In the era of this story, the de facto head of state in the united provinces in the Low Countries.
swingebeest: A fellow who flounces around.
the necessary: An archaic euphemism for an outhouse or lavatory.
Tom o'Bedlam: An early seventeenth century anonymous poem in the voice of a Bedlamite beggar. Also, the alias used by Edgar in Shakespeare's *King Lear.*
varlet: A rogue.
verdomme: Dutch, an expletive. Damn it!
verily: Truly.
watcher: In this context, a secret observer for the king.

Achilles at Skyros: There are many classical paintings of this story from the legends of Achilles. Ned's choice of composition is modeled on *Achilles among the Daughters of Lycomedes* by Pietro Paolini, which is now in the Getty Museum. For more about the painting and the legend, see:
https://www.getty.edu/art/collection/objects/676/

History versus Fiction: The earl and the village of Marborne are fictional. The Bagsham, Hawksmoor, and Foxe families and their titles are fictional. The merchants and customs people are fictional, though I borrowed elements of the lives of the merchant Nicholas Barbon and the writer Daniel Defoe. That research caused me to return to *Robinson Crusoe* for a rereading, having forgotten everything except Aidan Quinn's eyes in the 1988 movie. It turns out the entire book is even more racist than you remember.

Ned's Paint Colors: Many color names are from "A Primer on the Available Woad-Paste Colours of Bristol 1574." See the list at: https://dreadquill.com/wp-content/uploads/2022/02/bristol-paint-names.jpg

Perry's Songs: A drinking song, "Be Merry My Hearts, and Call for Your Quarts" is sung to the tune of the Elizabethan carol, "All Hail to the Days" (a.k.a. "Drive the Cold Winter Away"). See:
https://ebba.english.ucsb.edu/ballad/30095/xml

The text for "A True Tale of Robin Hood" is Child Ballad 154 from *The English and Scottish Popular Ballads* anthologized by Francis James Child in the nineteenth century; therefore, we cannot verify that this text would have been known by Perry Frake. However, it's among the closest versions found for Robin Hood ballads. Since Perry is a fictional character, this text must do.
See: https://sacred-texts.com/neu/eng/child/ch154.htm

Play Notes: "The Disappointment," a comedy by the Irish playwright Thomas Southerne and first performed at the Theatre Royal, Drury Lane, in 1684.

Prorogation of Parliament: James II prorogated Parliament in November 1685 until he dissolved it in July 1687. James then planned to pack Parliament, which was to convene in October 1688. This was one of several reasons Parliament sought to replace James with William and Mary.

Royal African Company of England: The originally chartered monopoly, Company of Royal Adventurers Trading into Africa, went broke in 1672 and surrendered its charter to the R.A.C. Yes, James Stuart, as Duke of York and then as King of England and Scotland, was the governor and major stockholder of the monopoly that transported enslaved people from Africa to the plantations in the West Indies.

The R.A.C. transported approximately 5,000 people a year during the era of this story. At the Glorious Revolution, the monopoly ended, with a large share of the investment transferred to William III. Parliament ended that monopoly in 1697 with the Trade with Africa Act, which then allowed many more English merchants to engage in the business of enslaving African people.

Selling Aurora in the Marketplace: If you are Hardy-averse and never read *The Mayor of Casterbridge,* divorce by private act of Parliament was prohibitively expensive. At the end of the seventeenth century, a ritual custom was invented as a means to end an unhappy marriage. The custom seems to have persisted into the early twentieth century. If you're curious, search for "wife selling English custom."

Tea: The drink treated chiefly as medicinal through most of the 17th century. Only in the 1680s (with Catherine of Braganza as queen) did tea become fashionable. The British customs around tea were established in the Georgian era, when the rate of import had quadrupled.

Venetian Merchants: These imposters are named after Shakespearean characters. The Bassanio family and its merchants, Lorenzo and Gratiano, came from *The Merchant of Venice.* The brother called Mercutio takes his name from a witty Veronese noble in *Romeo and Juliet.* My understanding is that at this time most London gentry had not memorized the plays and sonnets in the obsessive way that Rowland has.

Acknowledgments: My profound thanks to Jacyn Stewart, Susan Urban, Laurie Cropp, Curt Colbert, Carol Buckmiller, and Martin Fossum for critical reading, and to Jane Dow for editing. Special thanks to Ajax Bell for close reading.

About the Author

ANNIE PEARSON lives and writes in Seattle. In addition to the *Restoration Rules* and *Rain City* series, she also writes the *Accidental Heretics* adventure series (as E.A. Stewart). She posts about fiction and eclectic project planning at:

www.anniepearson.com.

Writing as Annie Pearson:

Chaos House

RESTORATION RULES SERIES

No One Dies

Reap Justice

Call the Reavers

RAIN CITY INCIDENTS SERIES

The Grrrl of Limberlost

Artemis in the Desert

Nine Volt Heart

The Pirate King

Writing as E.A. Stewart:

LEGENDS OF VALERÓS SERIES

Wheel and Serpent: 1

Traitor: 2

Hero: 3

ACCIDENTAL HERETICS SERIES

1: *Bone-mend and Salt*

2: *Trebuchets in the Garden*

3: *Crux Lunata*

4: *Song of Valerós*

The Mad Woman of La Catalane: A Novella

The Blue Door… and More Accidental Heretics Tales

www.jugumpress.net

From Jugum Press

HISTORICAL AND CONTEMPORARY FICTION

Nzinga, African Warrior Queen by Moses L. Howard

Nzinga is a brilliant leader during a time of violent upheaval. This fictional biography brings to life the 17th century flourishing African kingdom, now lost, where explorers' maps of West Africa call out: "Here reigned the celebrated Queen Nzinga!"

Wheel and Serpent (Legends of Valerós series) by E.A. Stewart

To earn a place as a knight, Taresa of Valerós must get a message to the king of France. But crossing the Languedoc proves treacherous: Taresa and her friends are hunted as rebels after a murder at a Templar house. Amid the chaos and cruelty of the crusade against the Cathars, Taresa sets forth to save her friends, armed with wit, loyalty, and her lover's third-best sword.

This Charming Man by Ajax Bell

A chance encounter with an intriguing older man inspires Steven Frazier with visions of a more rewarding life. A vibrant snapshot of Seattle in the early 1990s, this story captures the drama of coming into one's own as an adult.

A Summer in Peach Creek by Michele Malo

Teenaged Faith visits relatives in Peach Creek, West Virginia in 1932. When a scandalous murder occurs, Faith discovers the corrupt underbelly of Logan County. As summer progresses and peaches grow, Faith finds her moral center.

PERSONAL VOICES IN HISTORY SERIES

We Were Walimu Once and Young, edited by Brooks E. Goddard

True stories from the Teachers for East Africa and Teacher Education for East Africa experience in the 1960s.

Find more at www.jugumpress.net

www.ingramcontent.com/pod-product-compliance
Lightning Source LLC
LaVergne TN
LVHW100503110826
845146LV00002B/494

* 9 7 9 8 9 8 8 2 8 6 2 0 2 *